The Ancients

The Ancients

JOHN LARISON

VIKING

VIKING
An imprint of Penguin Random House LLC
penguinrandomhouse.com

LIBRARY OF CONGRESS CATALOGING-IN-PUBLICATION DATA
Names: Larison, John, author.
Title: The ancients / John Larison.
Description: New York : Viking, 2024.
Identifiers: LCCN 2024000563 (print) | LCCN 2024000564 (ebook) |
ISBN 9780593831168 (hardcover) | ISBN 9780593831175 (ebook)
Subjects: LCGFT: Novels.
Classification: LCC PS3612.A6484 A83 2024 (print) |
LCC PS3612.A6484 (ebook) | DDC 813/.6—dc23/eng/20240109
LC record available at https://lccn.loc.gov/2024000563
LC ebook record available at https://lccn.loc.gov/2024000564

Printed in the United States of America
1st Printing

Designed by Alexis Farabaugh

For the matrilineal ancestors of
Evelyn Argetsinger and Ruth Diamond,
and for all those who will come after

The Ancients

Back When

Once there was a boy whose parents left to get food but didn't come home. He and his sister spent the night alone around the fire, and at first light they went for the help of their adult sister who lived across the bay in an abandoned village.

To go that far they needed their father's canoe, which first had to be carried to the water where they argued over who should steer. In the end, she was older, newly thirteen while he was still nine, so she steered as he dug with a paddle that was too long for him. They reached the village in the calm of morning. Their big sister listened. She said their parents were nearby, they had to be. His sisters handled the canoe on the return, and the boy was forced to ride in the middle like a toddler. With nothing to do, he chewed his thumbnail. For the first time he wondered if they could be the last people alive.

The tide was quick when they landed and his oldest sister dragged the canoe all alone to the shelter where their father kept it. Then she wanted to hear everything again. What their father had said when he rushed home from fishing yesterday morning, the questions their mother had asked him, what she had said before leaving the house. Their big sister studied the ground at the front door. She followed tracks he couldn't see. By then a breeze was picking up. At the river, he was carried across. He thought he saw his parents' tracks on the other side but couldn't be sure. He followed his sisters all the way to the cove and watched them whisper where sea-foam flooded their ankles. The tide that night had been one of the year's highest and now it was one of the lowest.

When they returned to the house, the fire was dying. The eldest was eighteen and she knew what to do. She packed the ember tube and a satchel of salt. Then she searched for any food left in the sand-pantry even after his middle sister said there wasn't any. Outside, the breeze had become a gale. They looked at each other when he asked where their parents were.

Finally, the boy asked this question that scared him most. 'What do we do now?'

Collapse

They crossed the tidal flat ahead of the incoming, three shapes each smaller than the last—a little boy following his big sisters. Behind, their dark footsteps were lost to the creeping reflection of sky. Their world fallen silent: no birds, no boils of fish, only the unbroken water beyond this brink of land and the mud sucking at their calloused feet.

'Come on,' the eldest called with a boot kept dry in each hand, and the thin-necked boy shouted, 'I can't! I'm stuck!'

He had never tried crossing the bay at low tide. Never thought to leave home under the slanted light of dusk. None of this was right—he knew that. The gale turned the sweat on his neck to ice and there was muck to his knees and why leave home with night so near? Just yesterday his mother promised everything would be okay and now his boots were in his hands.

His middle sister returned for him. She was panting when she took him by the elbow. 'We'll cross together.' She tossed the hair from her face and he heard the clatter of shells and beads. A band of blue pigment ran ear to ear across her nose. A maiden now when only a week before she had been a clean-faced girl. She said, 'Don't make sister angry.'

'Hurry!' the oldest yelled. She was as tall as their father and her hands were rough like his and the same protruding vein divided her forehead. 'Tide's catching up. You get wet and you'll freeze!'

He followed his sisters from the mud onto dry sand, across the flank of a dune, through the crisp limbs of a dead orchard, past the drying racks once used for fish but now abandoned, and across the sandy flat that was before a black-soiled garden of maize and squash and beans, herbs and garlic, tubers and flowers. Here, where kids used to play when there were still kids. He could remember the barking dogs, the laughter, the heavy warmth of a full belly. All the singing—he had always wanted to be old enough to join the men in their singing.

'This way,' Leerit—the oldest—demanded. She was faster through the abandoned village, her steps two of his. Her feet left deep, toe-heavy tracks he would recognize anywhere.

The houses had begun falling in on themselves, the mud and its seagrass binder piled within ribs of wood used as corner posts and trusses. Twenty-four homes, each built around a central hearth, most with three wings where children and old people and dogs could sleep together under wood heat. All now disappearing into sand.

The path led to the only structure still intact. Leerit swept aside the hide curtain and ducked within. As big as their home and yet she lived here alone, his eldest sister. He knew he could never be so brave, brave enough to sleep alone.

Maren, his middle sister, pulled her hands inside her sleeves and crossed her arms. The bright beads in her hair were clacking with the wind. 'What are we doing?' she asked. 'There's a storm coming. Brother's cold.'

It was true, Kushim realized. He was cold. He sat on frigid sand and brushed the crumbles of tide from his shins and slipped on the fur-lined boots his mother had made for him. Their warmth, like hers, was immediate.

Leerit reappeared and tucked her knife into her belt and slung a satchel over her shoulder and freed her long locks from under the strap. Her neck was as thick as her jaw, her shoulders wide with muscle. She glanced toward the horizon. 'We're leaving.'

'Why?' Maren's nose was narrower, her eyes more delicate, her lashes long and curling. 'Shouldn't we wait?' She wrapped an arm about Kushim and said to their big sister, 'You're scaring him.'

Leerit turned from the angry ocean. 'I said we're leaving.'

Then even Maren stopped answering his questions. Where were their parents? Why leave home? When their parents came back and found them missing, then what? 'Please,' he begged. 'Just tell me what's happening!'

Maren grabbed him. 'Enough! Be quiet!'

Leerit was watching from atop a boulder. She used one lock to tie the rest of her hair together at the back of her head. Her hand adjusted the knife in her waistband. Sweat was streaking through her pigments. Kushim asked his adult sister, 'Maybe they went to find everyone else?'

Leerit's eyes fell to him. Her pigments needed fixing, but instead she passed a sleeve across one eye and her skin showed through. She did the same with the other eye then brought the belly of her robe up to clean the remaining pigment from her face. This was his sister become a stranger.

When she turned and kept going, what choice was there but to follow?

Leerit didn't stop again until a rushing tributary where the water was too fast to wade. She took one look and heaved her satchel across and leapt the rapid as if it were nothing. Then she called back for them from that face naked of markings. Her mouth made no sound for the roar. His sister's eyes were colorless in that dusk.

Maren wasn't thinking of him; she was studying the place she would land. Then her back foot lifted from the ground, and Kushim was left alone on that bank. His sisters were now together without him. Their mouths opening, Leerit waving, Maren's arms outstretched toward him. If he didn't jump, he would be alone.

Kushim backed up. He looked where he wanted to land and ran. The blur of the rapid was under him and he already knew he wouldn't make it.

His boots splashed into the stream and he was under, water in his ears. Skidding, his elbow colliding with flowstone, kicking but finding no ground, drowning, this is drowning—until a breath of air.

Something had caught his hood and the current swung him around into the shallows. Fingers dug into his armpits: it was Leerit dragging him through the brush, limbs cracking under her big feet.

When he finally stood, water poured from his sleeves. It had filled his boots and ears. Already his hands quivered with this cold beyond cold. A cold like burning. Not even cold was how it should be anymore.

Leerit hated him now. 'I *told* you not to get wet.'

Hail like sizzling fat. Maren flipped up her hood but too late, and pellets melted against her spine. She could do nothing to stop their trickle of cold.

Together, she and Leerit had pulled Kushim from his wet clothes and wrapped him inside the bearskin. He'd been shaking violently and talking to people not there.

It was madness to be out here now. Leerit, who was practically a woman—who would be a woman with a spouse if the village hadn't left—she was the reason they were here now. Maren asked the big sister she had always admired, 'Please just tell me why.'

An ember dropped from its tube and flames licked through tinder and Leerit's face was born new from the dark.

Maren tried to stop shivering. 'When they come back and we're gone, what then?'

Leerit added lengths of dry willow and stems of sage and blew light into the fire. Her hands somehow moved about the flames without burning. Leerit's voice was deeper this night. 'We need more wood. Dry his clothes. Get the meat and make him eat some. Wake him and make him eat. I need him strong tomorrow.'

Maren gripped her big sister's elbow and was surprised to find it wet. Of course. Soaked from when she jumped into the stream to save Kushim. 'You're freezing.'

Leerit pulled free and strode into the night, and Maren was left alone with the hail and the struggling flames and the bearskin that was rising and falling with her brother's breaths. For the first time in her life, she couldn't hear waves breaking.

Maren took a maize patty and a strip of elk jerky from Leerit's satchel and saw her own hand trembling. 'Kush. Wake up. Everything's going to be okay.'

'It hurts,' the boy mumbled.

'Wake up and eat, okay? Then you'll be warmer. Eat, then you can sleep.'

His hand appeared and she gave it meat and maize. Someone had to take care of the boy. This is what she should do. Their mother, if she was here, would soothe him with a bedtime story. Something about summer, an adventure of Opi's when he was this age, a story of bounty beside the Sea. 'Take a bite and I'll tell you something.'

5

By then the hail was turning to rain. Months without and now rain splashed up from the ground. Kushim whimpered, 'I'm so sorry.'

'What do you have to be sorry for?'

'I fell in the stream.'

'She shouldn't have asked you to jump. It was too far.'

Rain hissed against the coals. Maren added the last of the twigs, then sat cross-legged and pulled her robe over her knees. She spoke loudly over the storm. 'There once was a warm little boy who lived in a fishing village with his two sisters and parents and many friends. He was happy because he ate fat perch from the smoking racks, and in summer he feasted with other boys on berries and beans and squash. All winter his belly almost burst with meat and marrow. Theirs was a warm life of song and plentitude beside the Sea. But this little boy wanted something more.'

She waited for her brother to ask what this boy wanted. Finally, she opened the bearskin to find Kushim asleep. The jerky was in his hand, the end hardly chewed. Maren took it and closed the hide around her brother. She ripped a bite of the meat but the flavor did nothing to settle her roiling stomach. She told herself, 'This little boy, what he wanted was a puppy.'

When Leerit finally appeared from the rain, she dropped a load of wood and opened her hands to the flames. She checked that the knife was still in her belt and took up a limb of wood and broke it over her knee and added the lengths to the flame. 'Did he eat?'

Maren told her sister, 'Some. A little. He was too cold to eat.'

Leerit's hood was up and her locks dangled free at her throat and the fire reflected from the beads and charms strung through her hair. She was old enough to be someone's mother. 'I told you to make him eat.'

'I'm a maiden now. Same as you.'

Leerit broke another stick. 'You're a child. You think they went for a swim? Stayed away overnight for fun? Our parents aren't coming back.'

The last time Maren had seen her mother: humming as she stirred a pot of old elk bones reboiled to extract perhaps one more drop of broth, Ama had turned toward the sound of footsteps, but instead of Kushim returning from gathering firewood, it was Opi back too soon from fishing. He needed his wife to come with him. He was out of breath. He'd been running; he wouldn't say why. His face by then was bone held together by taut skin. Ama pushed herself up. She left without embraces because she was coming right back. She stopped in the doorway. The last thing her mother had said was 'Don't let our fire go out.'

Now the tears were streaming and Maren knew the pigment was smearing on her cheeks and Ama would be disappointed when she saw— if she saw. When Ama had first applied the maiden-paints, she had said, *Waiting inside a maiden is all of her mother's strength. Now learn to use it. Only you can teach yourself how to endure.*

Leerit knew how to endure. She had been living alone on the far side of the bay for two moons. Maren asked her sister, 'Are we trying to catch up with everyone else?'

Their aunt had led the rest of the village away. Almost three years ago, Ama's older sister had dared journey to those forbidden mountains where the Ancients dwelled in judgment and unleashed their fury in thunderous cracks of lightning. Their mother and their aunt had fought in loud voices when they thought Maren couldn't hear. Auntie said they were going because there was only a fish or three across ten nets. The elk herds had left when their meadows were smothered by sand. Elk always decided rightly and they had chosen the mountains. *We are not elk!* Ama had yelled. Auntie had said, *You won't survive another winter on this beach.* But they had. And then they had survived another.

Now Leerit said, 'We should've left with everyone else. Auntie was right.'

But how could they follow after so long? There would be no tracks left.

'I'll find their fire-rings,' Leerit said. 'The easiest path then is the easiest path now. Go to sleep. I need to think and I can't think with you staring at me.'

Maren looked at the fire. 'Ama said those mountains are no land for the living.'

'That beach?' Leerit tossed the stick in her hands and the fire exploded with sparks. '*It* is no land for the living. Not anymore.'

When the rain stopped, stars appeared overhead and any warmth left on the landscape rose away. Leerit was stiff. Her fingers wouldn't bend. Her arms were slow to respond to commands. If the fire went out overnight, she would freeze. Without her, Maren and Kushim would die. Of starvation or cold.

Maybe Opi had seen crabs riding the high tide. He came to get his wife to help because the tide was fast and the crabs were moving to deeper water. Maybe the water was already too deep, and he dove for a crab and got one in each hand but was too weak—he hadn't been eating so they could. Ama wouldn't just watch the currents draw her husband away—she would go in after him.

Maybe it had been a school of fish. Maybe he slipped off a rock and hit his head. Maybe he inhaled water. Or maybe Ama was the one needing rescue. There were a thousand ways to die.

Whatever happened, it didn't matter. They were gone, and she couldn't alone keep two children fed. Not come winter. Not without nets of fish, not without an elk or two. And here she was, still in maiden-paints, not even allowed to call herself a woman.

This was her mother's fault. For not leaving the beach when she should have. For not following her older sister over the mountains—and why? Her mother was too hardheaded, stuck in her old ways. The stories said those mountains divided the day from the forever-night, the living from the dead. Yet those same stories were full of promises about tides and fish, the movements of crabs and fowl and elk. True once, maybe.

Kushim had almost drowned. She had told him to jump a rapid that was too wide. Of course it was too wide for her brother's little legs. If he had been pulled away into the sucking crash of water downstream, if her fingers hadn't found his hood . . .

Leerit drew her knife—it could not be doubted. She turned its weight in the firelight, this blade made by her mother's hand. An elk's tibia for the handle. Burined until the groove could hold a leaf of knapped chert tied in place with sinew and seated in the glue of boiled-down hide. Light in the hand because the stone's weight was balanced by the mass of the elk's knee joint. Her mother knew knives.

Her mother had been a woman who knew knives.

The last time Leerit saw her was on the full moon after the kids were asleep. Ama had paddled across the bay to convince Leerit to come home but instead they fought. What was the last thing she had said to the woman who made her? Leerit couldn't remember. She didn't want to remember. She hadn't considered those words could be their last.

Now Leerit's hair was wet and freezing, these locks her mother had once tended. A new bead whenever a maiden mastered a womanly skill. But the beads were less for the maiden and more for the mother: *behold, elders, how capable the girl I made.* Even a year after the village left, Ama insisted on adding new beads. *Why?* Leerit had asked. *Why does a maiden need beads when there's no one left to see?* Her mother had patted her wide shoulders. *You want people to confuse you for your father? What people?* Leerit had shouted.

Now she held the knife to the root of a lock. It would be that easy. Just cut them. Toss everything away. She said to the darkness, 'Then come here and stop me.'

The high tide had eaten her parents' tracks so there was no way to know for sure. He probably swam for a crab or slipped from a rock. She probably dove to help him. Together they were swept away. But. Maybe. Something worse.

Her mother didn't believe in demons, those creatures of the stories once brought by traders and told at night to eager, terrified faces. Ama didn't trust traders, men without families. She said their stories were not lessons. *Men when left alone together will believe anything.* As the grandmothers said, *A man without a woman is a sail without a rudder.*

Once many years ago, after a trader left the village in his canoe, Leerit had asked her father if demons were real. Opi knelt. He was still so strong then. When he smiled, a vein bulged on his forehead. His hands were rough from nets and his skin smelled of woodsmoke and fish oil. The harvests were already meager, but the grandmothers said no one could read a tide like her father; if just one net came up full, it would be his. His life on sunlit water had reddened his eyes and taught him what was true. *My love—there are as many stories as there are birds and they travel just as fast. An angler learns to follow the bird who will lead him to fish.*

She couldn't know but maybe it was a demon. Following smoke, as they did in the traders' stories, come to steal people. Anymore, how was she supposed to know what was true?

Auntie knew. She always knew. Everyone listened to Auntie—except her own little sister. When Auntie told her that they should cross the forbidden mountains, Ama had said, *There is no other side of the mountains!*

Auntie smiled so calmly. She had asked her little sister, *Then tell me, where did the elk go?*

Whatever had happened to Leerit's parents—it didn't matter. This was no time for grieving. All that mattered now was finding Auntie before winter. Leerit had to be attentive, attuned, humble. She had to decide rightly, every time. From now on, Maren and Kushim were but one wrong decision from death.

Night had just begun yet, as a precaution, Leerit dragged a pair of embers from the heat and teased them into the bark tube. Leaves and twigs piled in, ash tamped down, the lid tied closed—she set the tube where it couldn't be stepped on or forgotten. No matter what, she would not let their fire go out.

Hunger

T hat first morning away from the beach, Kushim's kick stirred Maren awake. She pushed back the bearskin to see the sky lightening. Someone was looming over her. 'Get up,' Leerit said. 'There's light enough.'

'Where's Ama?' Kushim asked. 'Where's Opi?'

Their big sister had buried the fire under a heap of sand. Leerit turned and slung her satchel and said, 'I'm going to that high point for a look. Don't linger. Tie your boots. Start upstream.'

Beyond her sister stood the fangs of those forbidden gray peaks they were somehow supposed to climb.

Kushim sat on Maren's lap. He hadn't done it in years. The morning was crisp and their breath showed and ice clung where last night's rain had pooled. He pressed his head against her clavicle. 'Why did Ama leave without me?'

Maren was sure of only one thing. If her brother was to overcome those mountains, he would need to believe. To keep moving, he would need a true story.

So their parents were alive; of course they were alive. They were waiting at the end of today's travel. Forget the tracks in the sand. Their parents hadn't walked to the ocean, they had left early to get a head start. They were going to find Auntie and the village. This was good news. No more lonely winters on an empty beach!

But Kushim was a smart boy. 'The mountains are only for dead people.'

Maren took his hand. 'You trust Ama, don't you? Over those mountains, there's green grass. There's food. Kush, your friends are there waiting. But we need to hurry,' she said. 'So we can catch up. If you walk slowly, you'll have to spend another night with just your sisters. Do you want that?'

Kushim looked at the distant summits that were aglow with dawn. 'This quiet. No waves. I feel like I can't breathe.'

'I know,' Maren said. 'Here, cup your hand to your ear like this. Now can you hear the waves?'

Kushim stood from her lap, listening. With his sleeve, he wiped his snot. 'Come on,' he said. 'Let's catch up. Opi will carry me.'

They walked for four days before Leerit saw a bird. Just a shadow traversing too fast for feet—a vulture circling. Dark body and bloodred head, feathers extending from its wing tips like five fingers. In her youth, such birds had been plentiful in summer. Opi had once pointed and told her, *In this world nothing goes to waste*. Four days since she last ate— she was hungry enough now to salivate at a vulture.

On each day of climbing, Leerit had made a show of taking her share of the provisions; she held the meat or maize and watched as Maren and Kushim ate their portions; when they looked away, she returned her share to the satchel. She needed them strong. She trusted herself to endure, but they were just children.

Now the provisions were gone. No more old jerky wearing salt crystals like frost. No more brittle maize patties from the final, meager harvest. This hunger would soon reach her siblings too, just as it had reached her mother and her father before that. Not pain in the stomach. Hunger was dizziness and dread; it was memories lost to formless currents; it was vicious cramping in the legs, in the arms, behind the eyes.

Just keep walking, Leerit heard a voice say. *To walk is to find footing. To stop is to lose it.*

Soon Kushim was refusing to go on. He was complaining of his hunger, barely half a day old. He shouted at her, 'You don't even care if I starve!'

This little boy who was used to getting his way, coddled and left unprepared for life. Where was the coddling when Leerit was young? At his age, she had so much work—detangling nets, gathering firewood, chasing dogs away from the smoke racks, fetching every little thing her mother needed. Her parents gave their attention to their newest child and commanded their oldest to do every chore. This was her chore now, to tend to a pampered little boy who had never known a day of hunger.

Maren dropped her load and began to return for their brother. She was always rewarding his complaints, just like their mother. But from here, they could be seen from ridges beyond ridges all the way to the Sea.

'Don't,' she told her sister. 'Leave him. He'll keep up.'

'You can't mean that,' Maren called. 'I won't leave him behind. He's little.'

'The one thing that kid hates more than walking is being alone.'

Near dusk, Leerit stopped in a depression in the terrain and made camp where the fire would not reflect from a cliff or a solitary juniper. She didn't tease out the embers until darkness; their smoke had to go unseen. The traders always said demons follow smoke.

'Why are you constantly watching behind us?' Maren asked. Kushim looked up.

'Go fill the bladders,' Leerit told her sister before she scared the boy further.

When they were alone about the fire, her brother commenced complaining. His stomach hurt. He claimed his foot was broken. 'If you can take a step,' Leerit told him, 'it isn't broken.'

When Kushim began whimpering, she poked him with a stick. 'Stir the embers.'

He asked, 'Why don't they wait for me?'

'Tomorrow, we'll catch up.' The story Maren had told the boy, it was her one good idea. The story was keeping him moving.

'That's what you said yesterday. And the day before. I hate walking. It's so quiet here. I want to go home. I miss home. Why did Ama leave without me?'

Leerit stirred the fire. 'You will do what your sisters tell you.'

All they had this night to busy their mouths was water. Kushim kept his hands cupped to his ears. Finally he said, 'Tell me a story. Tell me about a time when you fell down and got hurt and Ama fixed you.'

Leerit looked to her sister.

'There is a story you should hear.' Maren threw her locks over a shoulder just as Ama used to before beginning. 'He was a little boy not older than you when his father asked him to stand watch over a half-skinned calf. There were bears, so he was left a billy's horn to blow if he saw trouble come over the horizon.'

'What's a billy?' Kushim asked.

Maren answered, 'Another name for a male elk.'

'No,' Leerit scoffed. 'A male *goat*. The village used to tend a herd. The goat mothers were called nannies.'

'What happened to the goats?' Kushim asked.

Leerit shrugged. 'We ate them. But back when, we kept them for milk.'

Their faces contorted with disgust. Neither of her siblings had drunk milk since being weaned of their mother's. Leerit wondered if it was better to be her, someone who once drank goat milk and whose stomach now twisted for it, or to be them, children who didn't know what they were missing.

'What happened?' Kushim asked. 'Tell me what happened to this boy.'

Maren continued, 'It was a cold day. The boy had only the billy's horn and the wind in his ears for company. How do you think he felt?'

'Lonely,' Kushim said. 'He missed his parents.'

'And probably his sisters too.'

Kushim shrugged. 'Maybe.'

'The day got darker and the boy grew sad. He wanted his parents and sisters to come. So what do you think he did?'

'He blew the horn.'

'That's right, and his father and uncles came sprinting over the hill with their bows and blades. But did they find a bear? Did they find the boy in need? No, they found him lonely. What do you think the father said?'

'Go to bed before supper.'

'Worse,' Maren said. 'Now the boy had to stay with the half-skinned calf through the night. The family was busy on other kills, and the father said maybe staying overnight would help the boy learn his lesson. Any parent would say the same. You can't blame the father for what was soon to happen.'

Leerit leaned to whisper, 'If you finish this story, he won't sleep.'

'Tell me,' Kushim said. 'I want to know what happened.'

Maren flipped up her hood against the cold. The fire was in her eyes and her breath showed like smoke. 'The boy was brave. He kept guard through the night, and in the morning his family brought him syrup and apples. They carried him on their shoulders. This boy, he had learned his lesson.'

Kushim jabbed the embers. 'That isn't what happened.'

'Sure it is,' Maren said. 'Get under the fur and I'll tell you another story.'

'But that isn't what happened!'

'Why are you so sure?' Leerit asked.

Kushim said, 'If that's what happened, it isn't a story grown-ups would tell.'

When Kushim was finally sleeping, the sisters sat together alone under the waxing moon. For the first time since leaving, they heard a call in the dark. Leerit stood. She didn't draw the knife but her hand grasped the bone hilt because something was out there.

Maren whispered, 'I can't stop thinking about what could've happened to them.'

Leerit stepped toward the darkness.

Maren said, 'Could we be . . . ? What if we are the only people left?'

'Don't talk.'

'But,' Maren said, 'we could be the last people alive. How would we know?'

From the lack of sleep, Leerit's vision was blurring; she was hearing whispers not there. She squatted and opened her hands to the fire.

Maren kept pestering. 'Are you even listening?'

'Auntie is somewhere. She will know what to do. We should've gone with her.'

'You can barely stay awake. Leerit, you need sleep. It's your turn.'

'I don't need sleep. Go to bed. Be quiet. Stop telling me what I need.'

Maren poked the fire. 'I keep having this dream. They're calling for help and I can hear them and I'm paddling but I can't find our parents among the waves. Their voices keep getting quieter.' Maren shook her head. 'I don't want to sleep.'

Back when, she and Maren used to pass nights curled together for warmth. Sometimes Leerit would wake to hear Opi putting more wood to the fire; he would step outside for a piss and return to slide under the furs beside his wife. Sometimes there was a mumble, sometimes more. Once Leerit knew what was happening under those pelts, maiden or not, she was too old to stay in her mother's house. She was old enough for a home of her own, old enough to choose a spouse—to be respected as a woman. Because of Ama, she had been forced to stand there as her future walked upriver without her.

After everyone left, they were a village of five on the edge of the earth, the Sea unfurling at dawn, waves and wind and sand, the coast empty but for them, no traders, no travelers. Seasons became years. She thought that was lonesome. With her siblings and parents in a warm house. At night, as they slept, she would lay awake grieving for those who had left, for the life that should be hers. Grief becoming rage until she could not stay one more night with this woman whose fault it was. Ama's hands gripping at her, trying even then to hold her back. *I am leaving! This time I won't let you make me stay!*

But Auntie's house across the bay was so cold, so quiet. No one was there to help tend the fire. No one to sing.

A thick pelt, falling asleep beside the warmth of another—this need for sleep in Leerit was now, here, worse than hunger.

'Lie down,' Maren said. 'I'll keep watch. I'm a maiden now.'

'You have to wake me if you hear anything.'

'Obviously.'

Leerit could barely unknot her boots, these laces cut by her mother, every stitch hers, every needle ground by her hand, every sinew loosened in her mouth and braided by her fingers. Handiwork always brought stories to her mother's lips. Her mother's lips. *Even when your hair goes gray, you will still be my little baby girl.*

Once they were standing beside the river and everything was different. The villages were still occupied. Her own grandparents had stopped eating so the children would have enough. So her grandparents were among the first to perish. By the river, after giving their bodies to the Sea, Leerit couldn't stop crying. *It's my fault! I didn't pray when I should have!* Back when Ama's voice was as soothing as the lap of a wave: *Oh, my little girl. Hear me now. What's wrong in this world is never the fault of children.*

In the morning, Leerit startled awake. She sat up, unsure of where she was.

Crawling from the bearskin, she found herself high on a slope in silence—no waves crashing, no surf rushing back, no riffling river. Her brother and sister sat cross-legged watching her. For that moment, she couldn't remember where she was or why, she didn't know where her parents were. Then it returned to her.

The coals were cool and the wood was gone. She said, 'The fire's out.'

Maren had had time to update the pigment on her face. 'I thought you'd be glad. You're always putting the fire out by first light.'

'Where's the ember tube?'

Maren's eyes widened.

'You didn't stash an ember?'

Maren grabbed the tube and shook it. 'I thought you did!'

Leerit tried not to yell. 'Without an ember, how will I start a fire tonight?'

Maren dropped to her knees. 'I'm sorry . . . I'm so sorry. I didn't think to. You didn't tell me. I didn't know!'

'You didn't know? You watched Ama do it a thousand times and you didn't know? How could you let our fire go out?'

Maren began to sob. Kushim put an arm around her. 'Don't be mean to my sister.'

'Senseless, stupid, coddled children!' Leerit's voice was outside of her control—like everything else. 'Without me, you'd already be dead.'

There was nothing for Maren to do now but follow Leerit up a series of switchbacks and wait for Kushim at each turn. Even he was climbing in silence. They would not meet her eyes. She was the reason they lost their fire. She was the reason.

The mountains were growing taller. No more brush or stunted trees—

just a world of loose rock and steep angles where a gust might knock them over and carry them out of sight. Mountains didn't look this steep from afar.

When Leerit finally stopped to rest, Maren and Kushim caught up. He broke the silence. 'Tell me what happened. The truth this time. I'm not stupid. I know when you're lying.'

This stole Maren's breath. She needed it to be true too—their parents were only a day's travel ahead. Always just a little farther. They could not be gone forever.

Kushim sat on the rocks. 'I won't have bad dreams. You can tell me what really happened to the boy guarding the calf.'

Maren couldn't speak. 'I'll tell him,' Leerit said. She put her satchel on the ground and sat on it. 'The boy's father and uncles went back to their work and left the boy overnight. In the morning, following the scent, a bear really did come over the ridge. A bruin with no cubs and no fear. Hide thick and flashing. The boy blew the horn and his family heard, but they thought he was only hungry for breakfast, hungry and lonely. They didn't believe him. What happened next cannot be blamed on the parents.'

Here Leerit waited, just as their mother had waited when she told Maren the story. Except in that telling the little boy was, in fact, a little girl.

'What happened?' Kushim asked.

'The boy watched the bear close the distance and no one came to help him and he was alone when those giant claws and teeth reached him. What do *you* think happened?'

'He ran?'

'But can a boy outrun a bear?'

Kushim shook his head. 'I don't like this story anymore.'

Leerit took his arm. 'The boy's blood ran downhill to the half-skinned calf and refilled its body, and soon the calf stood but now as the boy. He stumbled over his own skin. By then his parents had arrived, but when the boy called their names, his mother heard only the bawl of an injured animal. Through bare ribs, she could see the boy's heart beating but she didn't know it was her son's heart, did she?' Leerit waited as Kushim's eyes welled. 'The bear was scared off by spears and shouts. The calf was killed by the mother's blade. That boy, he was eaten by his own family.'

Kushim wiped his tears. 'Please, stop.'

'Kush.' Leerit put her hand behind her brother's neck and drew him close and wouldn't let him get away. 'Tell me why this terrible thing happened. Tell me.'

'Because no one came when the boy blew the horn!'

'No,' Leerit said. 'Not that. That's not why.'

Kushim gave up trying to get loose. 'I don't know, I don't want to know.'

'Why did this happen?'

'The boy . . . he died because he blew the horn when there was no bear.'

'Yes,' Leerit said. 'He didn't do as he was told.'

'Is it true?' Kushim begged. 'Was the boy really eaten by his own mother?'

'Every day little boys are eaten when they do not heed.'

'It won't happen to you,' Maren interrupted. 'We won't let it.'

Leerit held Kushim's face in both her hands. 'Listen to me. You'll heed everything I tell you. You might not know why but you will heed me. Right, Kush? Right? Tell me you understand.'

His voice was shaking. 'I won't blow a billy's horn.'

'Forget the horn! Listen to what I'm telling you!' Tears spilled from Leerit's eyes. 'You walk when I tell you to walk. You run when I tell you to run. You do as I say and you won't get eaten. I promise.'

Leerit led her siblings ever higher until they entered the underbelly of clouds where all direction was lost but for up and down.

No water, no waves, no amount of breathing could draw enough air—here in the resting place of the dead. She shouldn't have climbed this high. She shouldn't have made them leave the Sea—so many stories commanded the living not to trespass here. She had to turn back before it was too late. They had to turn back. 'Please forgive us,' she said to no one living.

Then the clouds tore open. New sun lit the mountain. The way back was lost to clouds, but now Leerit could see all the way to the ridgeline and its lowest saddle. Was this a sign? It had to be a sign.

The dead were given to the river, which returned them to the Sea, where storms lifted their spirits on winds and delivered them to mountains— *this sacred perch upon which no living foot shall trespass.*

In the saddle, the ground finally leveled. Here was the very mountain pass that had drawn her eye all those years from the beach. The old stories told of the Ancients sitting here, watching the village below, judging every action, every thought a girl had, shaking the village with quakes and flooding it with rain, or if they were pleased by the songs and offerings, then encouraging schools of fish toward the nets and herds of elk toward the shore. As a child, she could look to this mountain and feel the weight of a thousand generations of mothers, all of them somehow wiser and more powerful than her own. She had aimed her prayers toward this place where the Ancients sat guarding the boundary between Everything and Nothing. Yet now, as she stood here, the skyline was bare but for horns of rock.

Auntie must've crossed here too; it was then as now the easiest route. But what after? The view beyond was lost to clouds.

A flicker of movement overhead. Leerit squinted. It was the vulture returning. Coming to see if they were dead yet.

When Maren and Kushim arrived, Leerit told them: 'Take my satchel. Stop out of the wind. Make camp. I'll catch up.'

Maren held her sleeve. 'You want us to travel alone? On the mountain?'

Kushim asked, 'What are you going to do?'

Leerit pointed at the circling bird. 'He waits on us to die. So I'll die.'

Before her siblings were born, back when the shoreline was green and busy with families—Leerit was hoisted into the air.

Opi carried her on his shoulders as he waded the bay when she was their only child, when every house was full and babies were born fat. He would carry her anywhere she wanted to go. 'Point to the fish,' he would say. 'I'm teaching your eye. Someday we'll catch so many together. I'll take you everywhere in my canoe. And one day, when I'm old, you can paddle me. This is all a father wants. His daughter with him forever.'

Falling backward into the waves with her still on his shoulders—she yelled and laughed at once. 'Don't do it, Opi! Don't!'

'You want me to stop?'

'No. Do it again!'

Such terror, such thrill. Back when every story was true.

———

She heard it arrive in the flutter of wind, the click of talon on stone. She couldn't flinch. There was nothing but this vulture's flesh so her siblings might survive.

A tongue licked her nose. More licks, so many on her cheeks and forehead, her eyelids. This had to be snow falling.

An ember struck her brow. Not an ember—the vulture's beak. She rolled into a lunge and the great bird leapt to meet her with talons. She had him by the foot. His wings buffeted her ears. At the attack of his beak, her fingers failed and the great bird lifted into flight. He wobbled on the breeze before soaring back over her.

'A rock,' Opi said and handed her one. He'd come from nowhere and was pointing now. 'Don't rush, aim small. There's time.' She stared a hole in the vulture's eye as it wheeled past. The rock had barely left her hand when Opi said, 'Got him.'

Bird and rock met with the hollow crack of bone. It was still flapping when it collided with the ground, still flapping when she crushed its head with her foot. She lifted the creature still quivering, the weight of its death now hers to bear.

When she looked, Opi was gone. She was alone in the clouds. Loose feathers were fluttering among flakes of snow.

Maren was leading the way when the snow arrived. It looked like knapped flint falling through water.

She couldn't see farther than a throw. Dusk was here and they needed to make camp even if this was no place to camp. Just talus and steep, forbidden ground. But how would Leerit find them in so much snow?

Kushim had his hands cupped to his ears to better hear the waves. She told him, 'Everything's fine. Everything will be okay.'

'Where are Ama and Opi? You said they would be waiting for me on top.'

She could smell her brother's furs just as she could smell her own. They'd been sweating in them for too long and the skins were beginning to sour. The snow was soaking through. Her mother would mix ash and tallow and apply the mixture with the sharp edge of a rib worked over the flesh in one direction. She'd heat the skin over coals and do it all again, and soon the sour smell would leave and the hide would again repel water. That was what Ama would do.

Maren unrolled the bearskin and called for Kushim to crawl inside before he got any wetter. She used her bare hands to move the talus until she had built a knee-high windbreak to protect him. From inside the hide, Kushim looked out on the pelting snow. 'Please don't leave me.'

'Never,' she promised. 'We'll be together always.' She adjusted the hide to better block the snow from him. He needed her to be calm—he needed her. She knew then how she needed him to need her. 'Song or story?'

'You won't leave?'

'I promise, Kush. You're a boy with two big sisters. You'll never be alone.'

Maren sang into the dark, kept singing though her throat had gone raw and her brother was asleep. Singing so her sister might hear, but singing also so the Ancients would know she was good and grateful and sorry for coming here where she didn't belong.

A hand pushed her and she fell to the rocks. She ripped open the bearskin and burrowed inside, and heaved the heavy pelt over her head and held tight, her heartbeat in her ears. The air inside was still and warm, the storm faraway. It wasn't an ancient hand that had pushed her—only a gust.

He said, 'You're never surprised when we don't catch up.'

'Shh,' she told Kushim. 'Ama wants you to sleep now.'

In the morning, the wind had stilled. The last stars were fading and the snowbound mountainside was built from shades of blue. Below them in all directions extended an ocean of clouds. They were alone, perched upon this tilted island.

Kushim's breath showed. The snow crackled under his feet, and she kept her hand on his elbow. A fall here and her hungry brother would slide all the way into clouds. He knelt to drag a finger through the snow. He held it up. His hungry eyes looked full of some dream when he said, 'Like fat spread over the land.'

Leerit was not where they had left her. The dawn light was turning the snow pink and all about them the glittering extended untrampled. First her parents and now her sister. Maren pulled Kushim close. 'Everything's okay.'

He tore free. She shouted but he wouldn't stop running. He was going to slip and slide out of sight, and she was going to be left here alone.

Then she saw what he did. Below them, among boulders, the only thing devoid of snow—a patch of dark fur.

A man. Blood on his brow and more on his hand, red in the snow. A man wearing their sister's robe. Not a man. It was Leerit—but without hair.

Her locks and beads were scattered about, icebound, like severed limbs. Someone had cut them. The Ancients. As punishment for trespassing.

Their sister's chest hardly rose. 'Help me,' Maren said. 'Quick!'

Together they rolled her body into the bearskin. Then they saw what was under her. Matted feathers—the vulture still half-warm.

There was nothing to do but take turns with their sister in the bearskin, their bodies delivering heat. 'Ama will be so mad,' Kushim kept crying. 'Is she still a maiden if she doesn't have beads?'

Maren handed her brother another strip of salted bird flesh.

'Eat,' Maren said. 'This bird died for you.'

Past midday, Leerit finally opened her eyes. Maren embraced her and Leerit said her first words since they'd found her. 'Get off me.'

'Who did this to you?' Kushim asked.

Leerit's fingers touched her head. She looked to her brother with confused, unblinking eyes.

Leerit woke again in the bearskin. She knew she was awake on the mountainside. Her hand confirmed it was not a dream: she had cut off her hair. The locks had been heavy with ice and terribly cold, and she had told her mother to help, and when she didn't, Leerit took the knife and dared her. *You don't believe I will?*

Kushim was against her, sleeping. But Maren was outside, shivering alone and exposed to the wind. By then, the stars seemed close enough to touch.

There wasn't room for three inside the pelt. Maren couldn't stay out overnight.

Using her knife, Leerit cut the seam her mother had so carefully sown. She told Maren to huddle against their brother. She opened the bearskin over top of them and crawled underneath and tucked the edges under her legs. Now they were together away from the gusting. Three bodies for one warmth. It might be enough.

At dawn, they were still alive. She rose to see the only thing moving was fog, tendrils tearing over rocks. There were only two directions: back the way they'd come or along the spine of this mountain. Everything else fell away into gray nothing.

The boy's feet moved quickly on the nourishment of the vulture. Near dusk, she insisted he drink from a pool of meltwater. They ate what remained and spent the night as they had the last, together, the boy between them, the hide tucked around them. All night the wind growled outside. In the dark, Kushim asked, 'Where are they? Tell the truth.'

'Waiting,' Maren said. 'You know how fast Ama and Opi walk. They are probably at the base of the mountain already. Tomorrow we'll see them.'

'Do you promise?'

Maren said, 'Walk fast and we'll see.'

All the next day Leerit led them through crunching, icebound snow. The daylight felt darker; winter was coming fast. She gave the boy the bird bones to suck and this tamed his complaints. When the fog finally blew free, the setting sun struck them and turned the snow to hot light. It felt like the first time she'd ever seen the sun.

'Look!' Maren said, laughing. She sank into the snow, still laughing. The sound of laughter did not make sense, not on the mountain. 'Look! Can't you see it?'

Below them, far below, the clouds were parting. Leerit saw now too: where the snow ended, greenish slopes glowed.

'What is it?' Kushim begged.

'Grass!' Maren shouted.

Leerit told them, 'Auntie was right.'

Kushim's voice was tentative, unsure. He was a boy who knew green hillsides only from stories. He asked, 'Is it beautiful?'

'Yes.' Maren was gripping him. She was crying. 'It is so beautiful.'

They might have dropped directly down an expanse of shale to the grass, but Leerit chose a route with safer footing. So they were still on the mountain when dusk turned the world to charcoal. The boy couldn't go farther. They would have to spend another night on rock. But now they knew that grass waited below them, and in it, they might find food.

Kushim was sitting against a crag when he said, 'You don't look for their tracks. You're never surprised when we don't catch up. Always you tell me tomorrow.'

Leerit knelt. She put her hand on Kushim's cheek.

'Where are they?' he asked with tears in his eyes because he was a smart boy.

'Kush,' Leerit began.

'Please,' Maren uttered. 'Not here. Not now. He's not ready.'

'Our parents,' Leerit said. 'They died. The Sea took them.'

'You don't know that!' Maren shouted. 'You don't know!'

'Kush,' Leerit said. 'You're old enough. You climbed that mountain. You made it this far. You're strong enough to know the truth.'

Sitting on the rocks, the boy was panting as if still climbing. 'No. No. No.'

Leerit took his hands in hers. 'They are dead but not gone. They're here watching over you. Wherever you go, forever. Ama and Opi are always protecting you.'

He was huffing. He was a boy trying to break free and run.

She held him. 'Kushim. Stop. You're okay. I promise. Everything will be okay.'

'But they can't be dead!'

'Kushim? What but death would keep Ama from her son?'

He collapsed into her. His sobs prevented his breathing. There was snot pouring from his nose, and she just wanted her baby brother to breathe. He shouted, 'I didn't get the firewood! She asked me to get firewood!'

'That doesn't matter now,' Leerit told him.

'But I didn't do it, I didn't get the wood! It's my fault she left!'

'Kush, listen.' Leerit was holding her brother upright. He was limp in her arms. 'Hear me. Hear what is true. Nothing wrong in this world is ever the fault of children.'

After, the days felt more like dreams than his dreams did. Kushim waded through expanses of grass—impossible green in all directions. Only at night in his dreams was there sand.

They might be dead but Leerit was right—he could still feel them. Ama's songs were always in his ear. Opi came to him in motion, in the way his feet moved about rocks, the way he'd hang an idle hand from his belt while looking in the distance. But Kushim didn't have his father like he had his mother. Opi was always in his canoe, paddling out to put down his nets, the water swallowing his blade strokes.

So Kushim walked with the fishhook in his hand, carved from bone by Opi and given to him by Leerit after she told him the truth. Opi was dead but the grooves he left were still here, the very motions that ground bone into hook, the little ridges meant to seat sinew fishing line. Sometimes, when overcome, Kushim put the hook in his mouth. This was his father drawing him nearer.

'Look!' Leerit called one afternoon. She was pointing at something. Maren got there first. A black circle—the scar of an old campfire.

The rocks were charred and old coals still gleamed in the sun and green sprigs of grass poked through black ash. 'See?' Leerit said. 'I told you. Auntie and the village followed this same creek. They had to. Every step we're closer!'

In the grass were ground squirrels running for their holes. Among wind-sculpted trees were little birds leaping from limbs. It was like journeying through a story of back when. He wished Opi was here to teach him every name.

That night the moon rose full and an owl hooted. He had never heard an owl but his sisters named it for him. Kushim watched Leerit work a bow she had cut from willow and strung with jute. She worked this bow about a stick. With each stroke, the stick spun against a chunk of sun-baked wood. He had smelled it twice already, smoke. Soon she'd have a coal, then they'd have a fire, and they could roast this hare she had stoned with a straight throw from her sling. His big sister would always take care of him. He asked, 'If it isn't my fault, whose fault is it?'

Leerit didn't stop working the bow.

'They weren't old. They were too young to die. It must be someone's fault.'

Maren told him to rest. If he did, she would tell him a happy story. But he didn't want a happy story. He didn't want to rest. He wanted to know what was true. 'Tell me!'

An ember began to glow and Leerit put a pinch of tinder against it. She laid twigs and shavings over the flames and they leapt higher, and she passed a hand across her brow to clear the sweat. Kushim was shivering but Leerit was flushed from the long effort to start this fire. She told him, 'Always stash an ember at the first chance.'

Still his big sister didn't rest. She peeled the skin from the hare and used her knife to open the belly and pull loose the entrails. She took the skewer and ran it through and set the meat over the forked limbs leveled on either side. Kushim watched as a new gloss appeared on the flesh and oils began to drop and hiss. He asked his sister, 'Is every animal a mother or father?'

Leerit shrugged. 'Or a child. Or a brother or sister. But some animals don't really have family. Not like we do. Fish never know their kin.'

'Do hares have family?'

'Yes,' she said. 'They live in dens, like our houses only underground. They keep a pantry. They stash food in it during times of plenty to eat during times of hardship. Hares can survive any winter.'

'Do hares live with their mothers and fathers?'

'Until they become a mother or father themselves.'

'Oh.'

'But we have to eat,' Maren told him. 'We're lucky to eat. Remember that.'

'The truest gift,' Leerit said. 'This creature gave its flesh so you might live.'

'But,' he asked, 'is it cruel to kill a hare who might be someone's mother?'

For a long moment, his sisters were silent.

'Yes,' Leerit finally told him. 'It is cruel. But that doesn't make it wrong.'

Each day the valley grew wider and greener and the daylight was sooner to fade to dusk. He could feel it, winter was coming. Leerit said they had to hurry if they were going to find Auntie.

Then one afternoon she stopped. Leerit pointed at the grass. She wanted Kushim to see. 'You know it's elk because they only eat the fresh tops. Elk are picky eaters.' She parted the grass to reveal a divot as long and wide as her own hand—a hoofprint.

'It's so big!' he said, and Maren shushed him.

He followed Leerit who followed the elk through a willow thicket. She stopped to point out the scrapings on the limbs where a stag had rubbed his antlers. When Kushim emerged from the willow to overlook a meadow, Leerit stopped him with a hand held back. She gestured for them to get down. Maren knelt and pulled him down with her. He wanted to see, but he didn't want to be the reason the elk ran away.

Yet Leerit rose from the grass. She walked nearer. It wasn't an elk she saw.

It was a straight line. Black and thick, it came out of the mountain like giant trees felled and connected end to end. Half covered in dirt and half held aloft, disappearing and reappearing, part of the earth—but not. It was black but also brownish red, too high to climb over, at least two Leerits tall. This thing without words to hold it; this thing no story described, an impossible thing growing from the landscape. Was it alive?

He rushed past his sisters. Maren called but he kept running until he stood beside it. He put his hand on the flank. Warmed by the sun. His palm wore black dust like some strange pigment. It was true, nameless but undeniable. Not alive but not of this place. Beside it, even Leerit looked small. She was then testing the black pigment on her tongue.

Kushim pointed. He had to show his sisters what they didn't see: small shapes carved into the side. Well ordered, clearly placed by a human hand—yet senseless.

> **NO TRESPASSING**
> PROPERTY OF
> PETROLEUM INNOVATION, FAIRBANKS
> A LIMITED LIABILITY CORPORATION

III

Dehumanization

Wind chop lapped against the boat's side. When the hull sliced a wave, seawater hissed across the open bow where she sat, her wrists bound by a coarse rope—Lilah among three others inside this wooden cage.

Her children would think she had abandoned them. She kept seeing it: her babies alone in an empty village, realizing they were alone—left alone.

'Please,' Lilah muttered now through wooden bars toward the shore-line. Because her own mother would be listening from the mountain, she was always listening. 'Please, Ama. Watch over my babies until I return.'

She had left Tamar on the sand, sprawled with his eyes open to the sky. As the boat pulled away from shore, she had prayed the children would not find their father like that, may the tide draw him away, this holiest end for a fisherman, the one Tamar would want: for his person to nourish the fish that would one day nourish his son and daughters.

He had fetched her from the house because a trader was on the horizon.

When the boat was near enough to see the shape of its sail—not the common triangle but a foreign square, not tan but white—Tamar paused. Fishing had taught him to trust his intuition. He had said, *Please, take the children and wait for me in the canyon.*

What was her answer, her exact words? *Traders are rude but not dangerous.* She needed to see the bachelor's goods for herself. The family couldn't afford Tamar making a desperate bargain. He had never been good at bargaining, even in the plentiful times. He was a man who cared too much about being liked to strike a good deal.

Then Tamar was dying and she was being pulled by the hair.

They had come with gifts of dried meat, this cruelest trick. They had grabbed her. Tamar fought with his bare hands. They gored him between his ribs. He was gasping her name. Their lives together, their babies, their home—when he had reached for her this last time, she wasn't there to hold him.

Not traders, not strangers, not people but two-legged beasts. Not people because people would not do such a thing. These could not be people.

One stood tall, hand on the rudder, eyeing their course through oversize goatlike eyes. The fat one with a furry face, the one who had gored Tamar—it dozed now against planks, its bloated belly shifting with each wave. The sail was full; their boat was fast.

This couldn't be happening. Because she was good, and Tamar was good, and Leerit and the children were good and helpful. It couldn't be real because they lived as they should. Offered every prayer in its season, sang every hymn to the Ancients, took nothing in excess. Such cruelty couldn't be happening, not to them.

And yet it was, undeniably, happening.

While daylight persisted, Lilah fought the cage built to keep her from

37

standing. Her struggles changed nothing. The bars would not break for her. She sat to fight the coarse rope about her wrists. Her flesh gave before the fibers did.

Exhausted in the dark, she considered the point of living. Why endure even one day longer without them? Just deliver her to the mountaintop; let her join her mother and her husband; she could watch over her children best from the afterlife. To reach them now, she needed the rope to cut deeper and free a vein.

By dawn, blood was dripping from her elbows but she was still alive.

In that new light, she saw the others in the cage with her. She had never been alone, only blind with suffering. There was a little girl and her big sister and a young man of another family. Left-Coasters by the markings on their faces. Staring at this grown woman who had been trying to hurt herself. This most shameful act. Because if a mother gave up, what hope was there for children?

Lilah saw the drought in their thin bones, the small sores gone unhealed, the empty look in their eyes. Children who had known only dunes and empty nets. The maiden was maybe seventeen. Smaller and frailer than Leerit. Her pigments were worn away, leaving a blue hue. Her little sister's hair was matted and contained twigs and debris.

The young man was built of hard corners of bone. One eye was swollen shut. His right fist was purple: he had fought the beasts too.

Tamar was dead. And not just him. So many people were watching her now from the mountain, her mother and grandmother, all the mothers who had ever persisted. From their perch, they wanted Lilah to help these young people, to be the woman they needed. *Endure, or how else will the children learn how?*

Lilah's own voice no longer sounded familiar. 'Who are these . . . animals?'

The maiden answered. 'They are demons.'

The young man said, 'If he comes closer, I'll strangle him.' Lilah turned to see one of their captors coiling rope.

The maiden said, 'They'll only kill you. Like they did her husband.'

Lilah sat straighter. She asked for their names. It was what a mother should do.

'Where do demons live?' Kenta, the youngest, wanted to know. Her gaze remained aimed at the floor. She was hiding her eyes from Lilah.

Rageer, the rough young man whose ribs could be counted through his flesh, answered. 'What matters is *why* they took us.'

The maiden's lips were cracked and dried blood had become a scab at the corner of her mouth. Her name was Koneet. She must have noticed Lilah watching her little sister. She said, 'She can't see. She caught the blinding illness.' Lilah knew the ailment but only among the elderly who refused to eat. Once the vision was lost, there was no bringing it back.

'I *can* see,' Kenta said. 'You don't believe but it's true.'

Koneet waved her fingers before her sister's face and the girl made no reaction.

'Let us pray,' Lilah said, because what else?

'Yes,' Koneet scoffed. 'That's what we need. More prayers from old women.'

Lilah caught herself. Left-Coasters were known for their rudeness. She couldn't blame this maiden. She had no doubt learned from her own mother, who learned from her grandmother. Children shouldn't be blamed. Lilah said, 'I'm only thirty-eight.'

In the silence that ensued, Kenta's little bound hands extended across the gap between them. Lilah took them. Kenta said, 'Will you pray for Ama? I don't want her to be sad.'

———

They had been on a sandspit looking for food when a bank of fog overtook them. From the vapor appeared this boat. The children ran but had nowhere to go. Rageer had fought but was no match for so many. Koneet came willingly rather than let her sister be taken alone. All their mother knew was that her daughters had vanished into fog.

Lilah told these children what was true. 'The Ancients have prepared you. Inside each of us is the strength of ten thousand survivors. We have endured worse.'

The hull creaked and Lilah turned to see one of their captors pawing at his groin. The purple penis was not unlike a man's as it swelled and peeled; soon urine was spraying over the side of the boat.

The awful knife that had killed Tamar was tucked at the beast's side. It wasn't knapped from glossy rock but was instead as orange as the ocean before thunder. Not oval-shaped but instead curved like an eighth moon. To see it was to hear Tamar gasping, to be dragged away as he begged for her. She was shaking again.

This creature came to the cage and opened the latch. He reached inside. Why he wanted Lilah she couldn't know. For the children's sake, she went without protest.

She could hardly hear for the pulsing in her ears. She only stood as high as his chest; he loomed over her. Even this beast's eyes were too big, with too much white. He reeked like a paddock. The curved knife that had killed Tamar was within reach. The sight of this knife—it stilled the shaking.

When he turned, Lilah grabbed for it. Her fingers almost had the blade when the beast seized her hair and bent her backward.

All she could do was stare, her eyes wide. She bared her teeth and hissed—this language understood even by dogs.

With his other hand, he did what a beast would not. He reached for his swelling member. He wanted to use it on her.

His grip on her hair was so tight, she couldn't break loose. She did the only thing she could. Lilah raised her bound hands from herself and with three fingers smeared across his eyes her menstrual blood.

She had braced for claws and teeth. But he had rushed to lean over the edge, and the whole boat leaned with him and the wind left the sail. He washed her blood from his face as if it were boiling oil.

The boat was too far from shore for swimming. Kenta was crying. 'What's happening? Where did she go?'

For the child's sake, Lilah put herself back in the cage. She closed the door. Now the bars felt somehow like protection.

Koneet was staring. 'You call them beasts but only a demon would try that.'

'Try what?' the little sister asked.

'Demons aren't real,' Lilah said. 'They belong to false stories.'

Koneet scoffed. 'Yet you believe animals can sail?'

Almost at once, the wind began to howl. The sisters had to huddle for warmth and Lilah put herself between the little girl and the gusts. The boat was moving faster. A storm was building. They needed to find the shelter of a cove.

Darkness arrived and still they sailed. Their captors lit a lantern. They started their fire with a stick dragged over wood; from nothing came the flash of flame.

For the little girl, Lilah began to sing the song that told of the birth of the world. It was this she sang to Kushim each night before bed. For children, there was no lullaby more comforting. It was what a mother should do.

In the beginning and forever, there was water. But the Sea grew lonely by Herself and sent into the sky two balls of light. The sun lifted Her waters, the moon pulled Her currents—but both were forever out of reach. So the Sea created fish-of-fin and fish-of-shell to swim through her. She gave Her children the gifts of kelp and aquatic grass. Yet Her creations remained silent, and the Sea was lonely.

In Her sadness, She drew herself down, which revealed land and mountain, and against them She made music. All day and night Her waves sang: I am that I am. But there returned no answer.

So She gathered Herself and sent upon the land a terrific wave, and in its retreat, She left forests and shrubs that dripped, and in those showers were birds with feathers and wings too wet for catching wind, and on the forest's edge where grass would soon grow lay furred creatures now slimy and contorting in mud, and nearest Her, on sand, She left woman and her man curled together and slick with tidal fluid.

The trees and shrubs knew how to grow toward the sun, and the birds were born knowing how to jump into flight, and the furred creatures were birthed knowing already which foods to eat—but woman and her man were born without fur or feather, without claws for digging or talons for spearing; woman and her man were left with only nimble hands and curious eyes; they knew nothing of how to live in this world their Mother had created. We are the only creature born not knowing our story.

The well-fed took pity on us. From Bear we learned what to eat and in which season. From Elk we learned to talk and later how to live as a herd, then as herds together sharing one shoreline. Because of them, we learned to prosper.

In return for these gifts, woman and her man gave their extra to Bear; for Elk they let their fires burn last year's grass and so brought forth greener fields. Generation after generation, this is how we prove our gratitude. For without these creatures, we would not have survived long enough to sing this story.

At dusk, all the creatures of wind and land gathered to call toward their Mother the Sea. Here was the reason She had made us. In return for these songs that only our mouths and beaks could make, She pledged to keep Her waves small, to send fish into each river, rains to every seed; for as long as Her children sang at dusk, the Sea pledged to lift the sun back into the sky each morning and the moon each night.

For a thousand generations, our children were born fatter and grew taller than their parents, and our villages swelled until they filled whole valleys, then the hillsides too. For as long as we sang, She blessed us with ever more talents. She taught us to harvest seeds and plant them nearer home. She taught us to pull water from the ground and spill it over dry crops. She taught us to catch the sun's light and save it for the dark of winter. Even to fly like birds. Upon these bounties, we became Giants upon the land.

But as we prospered, our generations forgot Bear and Elk. The time came when we no longer gifted our extra; we did not burn the brittle brush. We forgot how to share, even among ourselves. Some had plenty, ever more, while others had ever less. While old men grew fat, children starved. Rather than sing thanks to our Mother the Sea, we sang to ourselves and of our own creations. Rather than pray, we complained.

Even a loving mother grows weary of entitled children. First, She kept back her clouds and our gardens withered. Still we would not sing to Her. Next, She hid the sun and moon behind a sky of brown ash, and yet we refused to fall to our knees. Finally, She drew back her waters from her shorelines until children saw reefs like hills and fish flopping on limp kelp. Now we prayed, we begged Her, but She was done listening. Our Mother sent upon the innocent and guilty alike the weight of Her waters.

The few to survive the Great Wave were born new. No fur or feather, no claw or talon. Children without elders—they knew not their own story. Once more Bear and Elk took pity. From them, the survivors learned what to eat and in which season, how to speak, how to live as herds sharing one shoreline. Again, the creatures gave what they had, and for them, the survivors gave what they could.

We had to learn all over again how to collect seeds and plant them nearer home. How to draw water from a stream and bring it to thirsty crops. How to turn rock into blade and wood into bow. The Ancients learned the forgotten skills and vowed to never again allow their children to forget.

Two hundred and thirty-one generations since and you are ever the child of survivors, born of swimmers who reached high ground, born of Giants and those before, the guilty and the innocent. Remember the Sea who made you, remember the Giants and the Ancients who came after, remember the fate that befalls the village that thanks only itself. We remember our story because our mothers sing.

But Lilah had ensured that her family lived in gratitude for the Sea's gifts. She insisted her children sing every prayer in its proper season, live every day as she had been taught—as she should—and yet her husband was dead and her children left abandoned. Why had the Sea chosen to bring such suffering upon *her* family? What had she done to deserve this?

Was it because she let her daughter move across the bay? Or because she resisted letting her daughter move? Should she have followed her own big sister who trespassed over the mountains?

No, she knew why.

Lilah had warned Tamar not to kill the bear. She reminded him of a lesson taught to her village long before: bears, when honored and safekept, offered the people their protection. And yet this one bear kept coming to raid the family's smoke racks. No prayers or offerings could convince him away. He arrived at night, anytime there was a decent harvest of fish, which was already a rare event. Tamar reminded her that in the village of his birth, only three days' journey down the coast, bears were hunted and eaten, and the people absorbed their curiosity and strength; he had traded up and down the coast and only in this village where her lineage extended were bears protected. Tamar claimed he didn't want to kill the bear; he wished he didn't have to. But if it didn't stop eating the catch, her babies wouldn't have enough come winter. If he did kill this bear, they could feast on his gifts. More fat than they could consume.

In the end, she had consented. All blame rests always with the mother.

On the next full moon, Tamar laid out with his bow while fillets dripped juices on smoking coals. Three arrows were in the bear's chest before he realized a man was killing him. The bear roared and every child in every house across the bay woke sweating. The roar echoed back from the mountains. It was still echoing after the bruin himself had exhaled his last.

By dawn, word was spreading. Old women sucked at their teeth. Lilah's friends turned from her approach. Even her own sister raised her chin in judgment. *How could you let your husband do such a disgusting and profane thing?*

No one would help with the butchering; they would not touch the meat no matter how hungry. Tamar preserved all he could before the flesh began to sour. Over the rotten portions, he sang for the bear's forgiveness, then he used this flesh as bait for crabs that hardly came.

The tallow Lilah was able to render burned for months in her lanterns. When she offered pours to neighbors living in the dark, they refused the gift. While the children of other mothers shivered at night, her own kept warm wrapped within the thick pelt. She saw how rich were the gifts of the bear. In thanks, she sang and Tamar wore the middle claws around his neck, as men of his natal village did to honor a bear's sacrifice.

After the killing, it was true: the fishermen's nets contained fewer fish. Fewer elk came to the shore that winter. By spring, strange inexplicable sicknesses were sweeping through the village. An old man died when snot filled his chest and the remedies failed. The old women said it was the vengeful bear who moved now in spirit to bring hardship. Lilah was not invited into any circle. Even her own sister turned a cheek.

Lilah told Tamar that he had to beg for the bear's forgiveness. When she insisted he give the bow and the knives he had used to the Sea, he consented. On an outgoing tide, she poured the rest of the tallow into the waves. But Tamar stopped her from dragging the bear's pelt into the bay. *Bear was proud of his coat*, he said. *What will he think if we toss it away?*

That autumn the elk stopped coming and her own sister, the village's midwife, proposed leaving to cross the mountains. *Without elk, without fish in our nets, without bear to show us how—what choice do we have?*

The hypocrisy of a big sister! She would defy the sacred teachings to trespass upon the mountains and yet protest the death of one troublesome bear? Before a council, Lilah said too much. She regretted what she said to her sister.

When the villagers walked away from the Sea, Lilah stood watching.

She stayed watching, but her big sister never looked back. The last old women disappeared into the canyon. Leerit was there too as the village left. Her eldest daughter sank to her knees and sobbed. Then Lilah understood what it meant to be alone.

Now, somewhere in the black distance, she heard the rumbling of the Sea breaking over a reef. The hull flexed and groaned. Then a rogue wave burst across the bow and a thick wall of water splashed down. Lilah wrapped herself around Kenta and thought of the bearskin and its warmth. Let her children be warm together. Let them again be sharing one home. Let their fire be blazing and their pot full.

Their captors barked, and the sail was dropped. When the fabric lost the wind, the boat dragged to a stop—Lilah had to grip the cage to keep from being tossed.

The boat wobbled up the next swell, turned broadside, and dropped stern first through the darkness into the wave's trough. Seawater flooded over the edge. With oars, the creatures righted the boat and rode the next wave high into the air. In the cage, they hovered for a moment before being pressed hard into the floor. Now seawater was swirling about their legs. Kenta clung to Lilah. She begged, 'Please don't let us sink.'

Tamar would've taken shelter on land to pray. The creatures who killed him, these creatures who moved not unlike men—they oared on without a measure of respect for what was mightier than they were. This, the trait that forever separates animals from people: people know when to humble themselves and pray.

Onward through the night, the Sea sent only higher swells. The children heaved. Morning revealed dark cliffs of water and land lost to clouds.

But in the new day, her prayers began to work. By the day's middle, the white chop was smoothed. Each of the waves was smaller than the last. 'Notice,' she told Kenta. 'The Sea has answered your prayers.'

'Or She simply grew weary of making waves,' Koneet said.

Near dusk, their captors shipped the oars. They raised the sail. They collapsed about the stern and the boat lurched forward into even speed, drawn on by that square sail. These beasts who drank from a jug of water and shared it around like fishermen would. Water spilled from their mouths. It ran through their chin fur. Water.

Lilah took a chance; the children needed her to. With gestures and drawn-out words, she tried: 'They need to drink. Give them water. Do as I say.'

A beast looked, then looked away. The fat one grunted, and another rose and brought her the jug. It was passed through the cage door with one finger—not unlike Tamar passing her a vat of salt down from the rafters.

She gestured to her mouth. 'Something to eat. For the children.'

'You scare them,' Kenta said as she ate from a piece of dry meat.

Rageer drank, and when he put down the jug, he said, 'She marked that one with her blood and a storm rose out of nowhere. Maybe they ought to fear her.'

Days without number, always sailing up the coast with the sun at their stern. The jugs of water ran dry. Their captors didn't drink. Like goats, they could endure on nothing.

Lilah marked time by studying the shoreline. Memorizing every point of land, each sliver of reef, the beaches and coves and river mouths. For the journey home—because there would be a journey home. On those shores, she couldn't help seeing them, impossibly, her children, running over rocks and sand, running to catch up.

The sisters slept day and night. From Kenta's and Koneet's faces, she could see a vision of their mother. She could feel her out there somewhere, on some faraway beach—another woman who knew what it was to hope against all sense for your children to appear on the horizon.

One afternoon Lilah saw Koneet stir. They were the only two awake inside the cage. The maiden looked at her, then looked off at the water. Lilah again tried making conversation but the maiden responded with only grunted answers. Finally, Lilah said, 'Left Coast, Right. We are more the same than we are different.'

Koneet said, 'But the judgment in your voice. You can't hide it. Right-Coasters always think they know better.'

'No judgment.' Lilah tried touching the maiden's hand. 'Let's do what we can, let's pray.'

Koneet withdrew her hand. 'Show me the prayer that ever worked.'

Leerit too had been consumed with doubt. These poor maidens who'd known only drought and hardship when every story promised bounty. Who could blame them for distrusting—and for resenting those who sang of the bountiful life? So Lilah began as if she were speaking to her own daughter. 'A maiden should—'

'*Should!*' Koneet laughed. 'The Right-Coast woman's favorite word!'

Something was different about Koneet. She seemed older than Leerit, yet not in years. Traces of blue pigment were still clinging to Koneet's eyebrows, and yet she spoke with an authority earned by suffering and loss. 'You were someone's mother, weren't you?'

Koneet stared at the distant horizon. She commenced scratching. Her knees were already pocked with scabs.

'You don't have to tell me.'

For a long time the boat beat against the swells. Koneet's voice came as a surprise. 'It was only a dream,' she said. 'She was hungry but I didn't have food. I kept digging, checking every trap. When I woke, my baby was cold. She was . . . so cold.'

Lilah waited for Koneet to say more. She didn't. 'Your daughter is warm now. On the mountain, she has every grandmother to hold her.'

Koneet's eyes pinched shut. 'Ama returned the blue pigments. *A maiden has an easier time*, she said. *Easier time.* Pray if you want, but the Sea doesn't care about me.'

Lilah could feel those wiser generations watching from their perch. She could feel Koneet's mother on some beach, watching the horizon. She was speaking for their ears too. 'To endure is a choice a woman makes every day. Choose gratitude for what you have. Because I promise'—Lilah gestured toward little sleeping Kenta—'in this life, there is always more that can be taken.'

'I don't know if I care anymore,' Koneet said. 'I'm so tired. Sometimes I think I should join my daughter on the mountain now. I could do it. I know how.'

'Don't say that. You don't mean it. Think of your little sister.'

'I could take her too. You were trying. Look at your wrists. Don't pretend you're better.'

Lilah's wrists were scabbed and oozing. She pulled down her sleeves.

'What's the point?' Koneet said. 'Why give these demons the satisfaction?'

Lilah gathered what felt like the truest words. 'Remember the Ancients who survived the Great Wave sent over the innocent and guilty alike. When the Giants were drowned, there was nothing left. The survivors knew only loss. What if they had given up? What if the Ancients had quit trying? Your daughter would not be waiting for you on the mountain. Your sister would not be sleeping here now. Two hundred and thirty-one generations. Koneet. You forget how long is the future. You forget all those who will be counting on you.'

One day the boat turned toward a small cove tucked beneath a towering headland. Walls of rock rose over them, chilling the air and confusing the gusts. They were close enough to swim now. But even if Lilah got the girls loose, even if they made it to shore—they would have no escape from this beach for the dark cliffs hemming them in.

Their captors oared through a gap. Waves burst against rock. The boat rose with swells before stalling over sand. She heard splattering and saw a cascade of fresh water.

'Birds,' Kenta said. Her eyes stared at the floor of the cage but she was right. Overhead, perched on rocks, were two kinds of seabird. The air was rich with the smell of droppings.

Koneet said, 'I've never seen so many.'

It wasn't many, nothing compared to the nearshore rocks during Lilah's youth, but here were birds when she hadn't seen them in years. This boat had sailed past countless headlands to somehow find its way back in time.

The youngest of their captors waded with a jug in each hand up the beach toward the waterfall. There was no denying the humanity of his gait. He leaned to hold the jugs under the stream, then corked them and returned. Under the burden of their weight, he grunted. He wiped the sweat from his brow with a forearm like any fisherman.

Rageer was watching his every free move. He said to Koneet, 'You call them demons because you're afraid to say what's true.'

Kenta's little face turned toward his voice.

Koneet took her sister's hand. 'Rageer, don't.'

'Just answer me this,' he said. 'Why do men bother fishing?'

Kenta was the one to break the silence. 'Because their families need to eat.'

There were old stories told by the desert nomads when they still came to the beaches in winter to trade. The desert tribes used to wander for weeks to reach the shore. They wouldn't eat a fish, not one bite. They came so far to trade their precious goats for strings of common shells. These strange people with markings cut in the skin about their eyes wore shell beads from their ears and noses. Lilah's mother said that the desert tribes had forgotten the Great Wave. They had forgotten the Giants. They claimed to have been born not of Sea but of sand. Lilah was just a girl then, and the confused and confusing foreigners scared her. Maybe twenty-five winters had passed since she last saw a nomad, and yet she could still remember their stories.

They had performed them in dance. The most terrifying concerned a tribe who attacked like a thunderstorm, wicked, dangerous—this was a tribe of men without women who stalked about stealing children because they couldn't make their own. The desert word for this wicked tribe was *Barbarian*.

Her own mother never believed; she said the world hadn't room enough for such a tribe. *If barbarians were real*, Ama had told her frightened daughter one night, *our grandmothers would have given us songs of warning.*

The nights went on and on, and the daylight became precious and short. Now, when the sun set, their captors put fur over the cage. For the cold, they huddled together.

One day Rageer's voice startled Lilah awake. He was gripping the cage. 'There!'

On the horizon was another craft like this one, it too under a square sail. Navigating around a long arm of land reaching into the water.

When their boat passed near the same cliff, Lilah saw the tide line wearing green kelp. She could see tiny crabs scurrying. High above, yellow shrubs grew on the mountain. Plenty to sustain goats.

Their boat rounded the point and entered a placid inlet of dark water. A family of mergansers startled, their feet kicking divots on the surface until their wings lifted them into flight. The water boiled with a spooked school of fish. Lilah was again a hungry child, her mother gathering a handful of sprats from a net and putting them still kicking in her daughter's hand. *Eat your fill, my darling. The Sea gifts all we need.*

Then the sun emerged from under ashen clouds. Dark cliffs became scarlet and purple, silver and black. Every droplet of mist was an ember hovering in the air. Kenta turned her blind eyes toward the sudden warmth.

'What are they doing?' Rageer asked.

At the stern, their captors were bowed toward the sun—they were humbling themselves, growling in unison.

Koneet said, 'Demons pray too.'

At dusk, they were looking up at countless flames. A hundred flickering fires, and as many structures built into the dark slope. Too many to be a village, too much for any story. This thing, this place, this time beyond past or future. 'What is it?' Koneet gasped. Lilah hadn't breath enough to respond.

At the waterline were countless boats like this one, all tied to floating planks. Creatures—from here they seemed to be walking on water.

Loads on their shoulders. Beams suspended between them. So many legs walking.

At the edge of land stood a boat taller than any tree she ever heard described. It was enormous enough to fit five villages, ten—a boat towering like a small mountain. The ribs were still bare, the masts naked, the boards and planks freshly cut and unoiled. She could see all the way through. It was like the ribs of some huge animal after the meat has been cut free. Creatures were dangling by ropes, others scaling ladders. The air reverberated with the pounding of mallets over the voices of workers in song. Voices that belonged, undeniably, to men.

'Tell me what you see?' Kenta begged.

Rageer said, 'It's the end.'

When their boat glided to rest against planks, a long rod came through the cage bars and struck Koneet's shoulder. Rageer grabbed at it and fought.

He was dragged from the cage by the cord binding his ankles. A crowd worked together to restrain him. Not paws but hands. It was a knee pressed against his back. Rageer stopped fighting when a mallet struck his temple.

They heaved him like meat from the bottom of the boat onto the planks then into a wheelbarrow. The hard wheel thumped over the gaps as they stole Rageer away.

Lilah pulled the children against her. But then the hands wanted her. She came willingly rather than be struck with that mallet. Koneet and Kenta next. After so long in the cage, walking now was like the first time: led across the planks then onto dry ground that seemed to be heaving on waves. Up a hill. Toward a wall built of rock. When she fell, she was lifted back to her feet, her hands and knees covered in putrescent mud.

Dogs flashed across bands of light, tongues dangling, dogs running free while she and the girls were leashed together. When she tried to pause, the rope ripped her forward.

A door creaking open. Another like their captors bound her elbows then the elbows of the sisters, affixing each of them to a post in the ground. Lilah fought the braid. She hit her head against the post until her ears rang. No matter how hard, it didn't matter. In a hundred seasons of fighting, she could not get free.

More empty posts threw long shadows, each rubbed smooth by countless struggles. Here the mud reeked of urine. It was thatched with hair and beads. She hissed. She barked. What else could she do?

An orange knife rose before her face. It entered at her collar and slid against her skin. Cutting off the hides she had spent winters scraping and softening and patching, the leather hissing as it opened. The cold was instant. She bit at the knife as it came for her scalp. Locks she had been growing her whole life sliced free by the handful. Her beads and honor, shells her mother had carved for Lilah as a maiden, her whole history—now in the mud at her feet. Was her mother watching? Her mother had to be watching. 'Please,' she begged.

Kenta sobbed. 'Koneet, where are you?'

The one holding the knife laughed, and for that moment he used the blade to animate some part of a story he was telling the others. He tossed the knife onto a table and lifted a bucket of fizzing water and doused Lilah. In that cold, she knew. They were fish when the nets were full, delivered to a line of men working to clean and ready fillets, men who paid no attention to the kicks and flops of those fish still gasping.

Then the braid was loosed from her elbows and she fell forward. She pushed herself up from the mud and gathered the girls. Naked and shivering.

He was pointing the knife at a pile of furs. 'It's called *wool*,' he said perfectly. This enormous man with short-cut hair. 'There are sizes for your daughters too. Go on. You'll need it.'

To hear words from this mouth—she could only manage, 'What are you?'

But he was laughing at something another had said. Men shouting and laughing over one another. Men like men anywhere, making the best of mindless labor.

Lilah was quick to dress, then helped the girls into the scratchy fur. It had no skin to lie soft against them, but *wool* was warm—she felt at once how warm.

Kenta reached and Lilah lifted the girl onto her hip as if she were three years old, not ten. 'I won't let go.' He would have to cut her arms to divide them now.

He opened a door and pointed. 'Go on. You're done. Get.'

Kenta asked what Lilah was afraid to. 'Are you going to eat us?'

The man laughed as he shut the door behind them.

Now they were inside a circular pen—like those their village once used to contain goats. So many bodies, all standing in identical gray wool, faces staring back, bald and blank of history. Animals in their paddock.

IV

A More Natural Life

A platter of pastries was waiting at the end of the dormitory corridor. Flaky dough, fruits sliced into half-moons, their sugars turned to glaze in the oven. He wasn't hungry, not after reading his mother's summons, but Cyrus took one anyway, on force of habit.

The pastry was still uneaten when he joined his driver in the open carriage. From here, he could see the bow of the enormous boat under construction in the harbor and hear the pounding of hammers. Cyrus broke the pastry into small pieces as the horses came to speed and the wind lifted his cape. Crows were begging. He tossed what he had, bit by bit, and watched as the dark birds began to swoop from rooftop perches. It was their luck, he decided, to live such a simple life.

'A stop first,' Cyrus called to his driver.

'Very well, sir.'

Cyrus carried the polished juniper box he had just bought through a bead curtain into the firelit bedroom. His father lay on the bed. Hair soaked in sweat, pale, shivering.

He was under the finest long-fiber wool ever produced. The commodity that had made his family's reputation and built this commanding estate of rock and straight-grained wood where a man's boots echoed. Wool had given his parents lives free from struggle; even now, two servants waited on his father's every need.

One held the juniper box while another poured scalding water over Cyrus's hands. She offered him a sprig of sage that he touched to a candle. This smoke Cyrus pulled over his face. A bowl of dark blood was offered next. 'A smear below each eye,' the servant reminded him. She added, 'Sir—the Master has been asking for you.'

His father's forehead bore the deathly seal, a circle with a line through it: the Sun, and a patriarch's path home. Painted there this morning by the priest who had readied him for what would come next. The sight constricted Cyrus's throat. He could no longer deny what was happening.

His father awoke from his tortured sleep and looked at the juniper box with eyes gone dull. These were not his father's eyes.

Cyrus lifted the lid. Three exquisite bronze balls waited inside. Inlaid with depictions of the Emperor and the Sun. The finest bowlers Cyrus's new, diminished allowance could buy. 'For the next time we play a round,' he said.

'Leave us,' his father uttered, and the servants backed through the curtain.

'I'm sorry for not coming sooner.' When Cyrus should have been praying for his father's recovery or accepting the man's invitations to play a round, he was instead accelerating his studies, staying up nights, a hundred scrolls in three languages opened upon his desk. As if he might work hard enough to stave off this end. 'Let me open the shutters for you.' Of course he had theoretically known this day would come, yet somehow he had also assumed he would always have a father.

'Not the shutters,' the patriarch said. 'Add a log. Dying is cold work.'

Cyrus was grateful for a task. He hefted a piece of wood and dropped it to the flame and sparks crackled up through the chimney. His thumb smarted and he looked to see a drop of blood and a splinter in his flesh. For weeks, he had been chewing his fingernails and now they were of no use. 'There must be some remedy you haven't tried.'

His father closed his eyes. 'No cure is coming for me.'

'Don't say that!' Cyrus was startled by his own desperation. He was dizzy; he was going to vomit or faint or cry. 'You can't give up.'

The hand rose. His father touched him. His fingers were shockingly cold. With manicured nails, he withdrew the splinter.

'Thank you.'

'Pull back the wool,' his father said. 'Do that for me.'

Under the wool was a shrunken body. Black feathers lined the bedding and stuck to so much sweat. The tumors were visible on his bare abdomen like stones under threadbare fabric. The priest had written prayers on the sternum to please the Sun. Next to his thigh was a satchel.

'Take it.'

Cyrus lifted the damp pouch. He opened it to see plastic coins but also something else. A scroll of fibrous parchment that was of the highest grade and sealed with the Imperial Stamp. A summons from the palace.

His father moved a finger: he meant for Cyrus to read aloud.

Cyrus unfurled the parchment. The script wasn't scholarly or financial; such curvature and precision were godly. He read that his father had been invited to join the Emperor. For an audience of one. On a date set for next spring. Cyrus read it again just to be sure.

'After the shearing,' his father said. 'This honor will be yours. Process the year's wool. Deliver our tribute. Humble yourself before our Emperor, praise be upon him.'

'Let praise be upon him,' Cyrus repeated mindlessly.

His father explained. The Emperor demanded the family deliver a fifth more than was given the previous year. 'Not a bundle less.'

Last year's tribute—Cyrus remembered his father telling him as they had watched a performance at the theater—was an eighth more than the year prior, and he'd barely been able to cut enough wool. To process so much, his father had needed to procure a new facility and hire the manpower to run it. At the theater that night, they didn't know why his father had lost his appetite, his vigor; the first tumor hadn't yet been detected by the family physician. 'A *fifth* more? But you already give so much!'

'No bounty shall go to waste.'

Cyrus asked the obvious question. 'Are there enough sheep in the world?'

His father cringed at some pain. 'You should know better. The number of sheep isn't the issue. Sheep make themselves when they have the graze. My shepherds. They know where the last meadows hide. Give the Emperor what he asks no matter what you must do. Cyrus, do you understand? He shall reward you.'

Cyrus nearly cried. 'What else could this family possibly need?'

His father didn't blink. 'Boarding passes. He promised three. If I deliver.'

The ark's bare timbers were visible from Cyrus's window in the dormitory. At night, when he couldn't sleep and his eyes hurt from deciphering ancient scrolls, he often sat at his window and watched the construction of their city's eventual escape in the distant torchlight.

At meal time, the ark was all his fellow scholars could discuss. A thousand years' worth of scrolls in the archives, and he and his colleagues talked only of what would come next. Why they must abandon the city and soon. The drought, the diminished harvests, the escalating violence. In hushed tones, they argued over the particular details of the collapse. Civilization's next generation of philosophers and historians, and they all competed to be the man who somehow predicted the direst, most violent end.

He reminded his father that every citizen was promised a boarding pass. 'As the Emperor proclaims, "All my goodly people shall join me on my green shores."'

'Yes,' his father said. '"All my goodly people."'

Now, for the first time, Cyrus heard the slipperiness of the phrase.

His father conjured a glob of red phlegm and spit in a rag. 'When the ark sets sail . . . when the Emperor is upon it . . . do not be naive . . . no one left behind will be at more risk than a family like ours.'

'But how could *we* be left behind? As you say, civilization is cut from wool.'

His father stared. 'You take it for granted; you always have. What we do? It can be done by any man with a mind for numbers. You think there aren't families better positioned than ours? Families with purer legacies, stouter leverage? Cyrus, all it takes for a family to fall is rumor. We both know you invite plenty of rumors.'

Cyrus turned toward the fire.

Even before last year's costly expansion, their family had employed more than two hundred laborers scattered across the habitable lands. Shepherds, packers, drivers, washers, brushers, weavers, managers, guards— and that wasn't counting the indentured labor, a number twice as large. To extract a fifth more than his father had in his prime—it simply wasn't possible. 'I am a scholar. I don't know anything about wool.'

His father cringed. 'I only wish I had been the influence you need.'

'I continue to disappoint you. Forgive me, Father.'

'I don't blame you, Cyrus. I blame myself.' His father's eyes became wet. 'Remember the Highlands? Everything was perfect then. If only I had known.'

His father coughed, but when Cyrus offered a cup of water to wash the blood from his lips, his father waved it off. 'Please. Just choose a girl. Do that for me. Do it now. Without an heir . . . every struggle . . . every sacrifice . . . my whole life . . . the lives of all our fathers who came before and delivered us to this moment . . . Cyrus, why can't you appreciate all that you are throwing away?'

Cyrus washed his face before returning to daylight. He needed these moments alone to right what had toppled within him. This is what seeing his father did; here is why he stayed away. After being near the man, even when he was healthy, Cyrus always felt half-destroyed.

The money in the satchel was for his mother, to buy her a distraction. Not just a puppy or a kitten or another crow for the aviary. His father had asked him to see his mother to the auction yard and make sure she had a new servant. A child, ideally, a project to keep her busy in her grief.

The Lady was waiting for him in the carriage because there wasn't a moment to waste. Her proud nose and upright posture, her enduring youth—a most unlikely match to his old, balding, rotund father. She was adorned in an elegant long-fiber robe, and the breeze lifted its silky tassels into luxurious undulations. Across her brow was a tiara studded with the rarest blue and red plastics, each bead catching the light, perfect round objects in a world of edges; if these gems were pulled from their settings, they would be impossibly light in the hand, like vapor. *Beholding a sight as elegant as she*, his father once said of his much younger wife, *who could believe in death?*

Now his mother said, 'We have to hurry. I can't be gone long. I shouldn't go now; I wouldn't if he didn't insist. He is trying to distract me.'

No gem could obscure her sleepless nights. These weeks had aged her like years. He saw the darkness below her eyes, the weariness in how she held her shoulders—stooped under the weight of her impending grief and the uncertainty the death of a patriarch would usher. She said, 'He's getting better. You don't notice because you haven't been here. Why didn't you come? I sent so many letters.'

'Mother, you know that I am no comfort to him.'

'Don't do that.' Her chin rose. 'Don't turn this into another opportunity to pity yourself. I have been here every day and he's getting better. He called for the priest this morning but you'll see. Tomorrow he'll wake stronger, and the day after that he'll walk again. He'll be back in meetings by the end of the month. If you only knew how humble his starting point—' Her fingers rushed to her lips.

To see his mother shaking, it made his father's death feel certain. He wanted to be far away from her. He said, 'It'll be okay. You won't be alone. I promise, I'll take care of everything.'

'How can you,' she said, 'when you haven't even tried to become a man?'

The market was crowded and people reached for him. Full, half, and quarter lambs dangled in the shade of board roofs. Chickens pecked at the blood dripping from those already slaughtered. When a dog rushed, birds clucked and scurried. Eggs were stacked into pyramids built to catch a passerby's gaze. Cabbage raw, cabbage fermenting in clay vessels. Stacks of root vegetables and squash, dried braids of garlic, bulbs of onion, clusters of parsnip and carrot. Corn was being ground by great stone wheels and cornmeal patties were frying over wood heat. Laboring women shouted offers at him. Here was the last of summer's bounty, what little bounty was left.

Police were using their clubs to keep the hungry out of the way. Cyrus felt for them. Elderly workers in tattered robes who had seen their livelihoods collapse with the latest closure of foundry or fiber mill. Agrarians from the countryside, distillers who could no longer afford the price of corn, woodcutters who had run out of trees, children naked and barefoot. Cyrus thought of the satchel in his pocket. Heavy as it was, it could buy meals for all of these lowborn citizens ruined by the ceaseless drought. And yet no amount of money could deliver what was needed most: rain.

His mother insisted on stopping. She gestured at a bag carried by her driver. His armor clanged as he opened the leather and withdrew small rounds of cheese, each neatly wrapped. The crowd surged, the police pushed, and the driver underhanded rounds toward the outstretched arms of children.

Cyrus flinched at the bellow of an imperial horn. About him, children were taking their knees. Police humbled themselves. Cyrus did as everyone else and supplicated.

Above, on the flank of the mountain, at the end of a distant zigzagging road, loomed the palace's pure white walls, which were set apart and above. Its spires and balconies were visible from anywhere in the city, this the first and last architecture to behold the Sun each day. Now crows lifted from its walls, their calls carrying this far.

The city was fortified by the mountains themselves, rims and crags chosen by the Sun to protect His favored people from invasion and assault. From here, Cyrus could smell the salted water and rotting sea greens of the port. A quarter day's walk up the valley and he would be smelling the noxious vapors of freshly minted coins and the manure from those stables of horses that pulled so many carts; he would see vast pens of hogs who devoured the city's waste, as well as the aqueducts that delivered their rich feces to fields that grew the Emperor's crops. Another half day to reach the border wall and its legions of armed soldiers with bronze spears pointed out, as they always had been—yet now defending against what? Who was left outside the last city?

The crowd sighed as one creature when the Emperor himself emerged onto his balcony, his singular robe of silk-wool glittering even from this distance. The hungry masses began to chant for his eternal life. Across the city, their voices rose in unison for the one who communed with the Sun on their behalf. *Praise be upon you.*

This music foretold a significant announcement. A war or miracle. Cyrus felt his mouth go dry. Was the Emperor now, somehow, about to save his father?

Beside the Emperor appeared a wife, her towering crown of plastic aglow in the afternoon light. The city went mute. Even the crows knew not to caw.

The Emperor lifted from his wife's arms some small thing. He held it in both hands—the unmistakable cradling of a newborn child.

The crowds rose up and their voices formed a single roar of relief: the Emperor has a son, the Emperor has an heir!

Horns erupted and drums began to pound. Across the city, a spontaneous celebration came beating to life. Two police officers embraced. Even Cyrus's mother forgot herself and seized the body of her driver.

It had been three years since the Emperor began sending scouts in every direction with a single edict: *do not turn back until you find green land.* Countless platoons had disappeared across the desert, ships across the sea. Out of dozens, only one party had returned—a boat of starving sailors who had found green shores across roiling waters.

For centuries, dunes had been overtaking pastures, swallowing cities just as easily as villages, driving those lesser peoples who lived on the fringes of the Empire toward the only green remaining. Even a generation ago, men like his father could not imagine a time when indentured labor would be in short supply. But now the dunes were blowing into this valley too, and the migrating hordes were no more. Even ships now struggled to find booty, so any arrival of new indentures was certain to spark a frenzy among buyers.

His mother's carriage arrived to the auction yard too late. The traders were already drinking to the birth of the new heir. The whole city was celebrating as his father lay alone and dying. Cyrus followed his mother up the stairs to the viewing box that overlooked the corral.

Below them remained only stooped, sun-beaten heathens. Invalids and old women who couldn't bother swatting the flies landing about their eyes. All the able-bodied had been bought at auction. Here were the leftovers. Godless holdouts who had somehow managed to survive this long on some beach. Dim and vacuous, the poor things were impervious even to the currents of their own history. He wondered what life would feel like if you never saw a written word. How could it feel at all like . . . life?

The driver acted as his mother's agent. 'You're peddling fish-eaters. These'll succumb to fever before Solstice.'

The toothless trader shouted in his inebriation. 'Not these! Strong and clean, these! The best of the last! Who knows if we'll ever get more.'

The driver leaned to hear his mother's whisper. Then he pointed. She had selected a female with curved posture and gray stubble about her head. The healthiest of those remaining. When the trader whistled, a man crossed the yard with a leash.

Cyrus might've negotiated with the drunkard; he might've struck a bargain, but he couldn't bring himself to care. He counted out the man's starting price.

The streets had become a carnival that his father would never see. Cyrus told his mother he would walk, citing the lack of room in the carriage now that it contained the primitive, who was still shackled for her own good. But the truth was he was afraid to return, afraid to see his father like that, afraid to see his mother beside him. Most of all, he didn't want to be there when his father died.

'Are you sure?' the driver asked. Jernod was a strong man, tall and thick through the shoulders, hair graying above his ears. He wore a bronze helmet with a stout brim. He had been driving the patriarch for decades and had more than once drawn his blade in the family's defense.

Jernod bowed deeper than etiquette demanded, and for longer. His master would soon be dead, then the son would be the one to decide whom to fire, whom to keep. Everything outside of the archives was, in the end, a transaction.

'Where are you going this time?' his mother called from her perch. 'Don't say another lecture.'

He told her, 'I won't stay long.' And before he could see her judgment, Cyrus stepped into the mouth of the crowd.

Cyrus parted dancers and drunks. He weaved around untouchable women who begged him to let them perform favors, past the toothless with their hands outstretched, past children who stopped their spinning to watch his robe pass by, until he had left the coarse music of the marine district. He saw squadrons of police laughing. A blacksmith was one of the few still working, sweating over a fire as he pounded glowing bronze. Cyrus walked under aqueducts and past barracks and bakeries. He watched a pack of feral dogs go single file through the crack in a fence.

In a quieter neighborhood, he came across an old man in rags proclaiming from atop a testament stone. About its base were carvings of the Emperor with his hand outstretched toward that reaching arm-beam of the Sun. The unemployed sat on benches to listen to this telling of the beginning. Across the city were countless such testament stones, which were today no doubt encircled by men eager to preach upon them. After a testament, the faithful gained access to the nearest imperial hostel and were assured safety and a good meal. The man atop this stone recited with a voice of uncommon grace.

Forever and always there was the Sun. He turned current to vapor and lifted mountains from the tide. He pulled grass from rock and shrub from grass and tree from shrub. He grew man then, and next He grew each animal in his turn, first the animals of the wild before those animals of the paddock; these He gave in blessing-gift to His five sons, whom He entrusted to tend His garden and make fullest use of every bounty. And the Father-of-Fathers then populated the fields with crows that He marked black and promised a tenth of every harvest eaten on the vine for keeping pests at bay. To His sons, He made His holiest pledge: 'Use every bounty I pull forth, let no gift of mine go to waste, populate my earth, and you alone will live in knowledge that your lineage shall carry far and forever.'

It was a comfort to hear the familiar, what could never change.

The Sun sent each of His sons to wander his own path. For eighty generations, they traversed new lands. Every history originates in their journeys. Their lessons would become ours to learn.

The oldest soon forgot his father. One day he decided he would not listen to any voice except his own. So the Sun burned His eldest and His grandchildren with fires that swept down from the hills. Their fields went from flush green to sudden ash. The few to survive were sentenced to live as primitives upon the land, blind even to their own blunders.

The second brother grew fat on endless harvests until he was so large that he could not be bothered to rise with the Dawn. Rather than toil, he chose to let the fields lay fallow. He taught his male heirs to rest. But the Sun sees everything and forgives nothing. In punishment, He sent dunes to smother the second brother's crops and left him with only goats to follow forever from oasis to oasis. His heirs would never again know rest.

The third brother became thirsty. He prayed for rain but didn't wait for his prayers to be answered. He chose to abandon his fields midseason and lead his children toward water with the Sun at their back. Upon their arrival to the ocean, rather than thank the Father-of-Fathers, the third brother chose to thank the tide. In furious retribution, the Sun sent a ball of flame crashing into the horizon, and a wave built like a mountain coming for the brother and his generations. He had no escape. The third brother and his hundred sons were crushed under the weight of the tide they had trusted above the Sun.

Among His gifts, the fourth brother and his people prospered. They were taught the talent of melting ore into metal, and new lands opened for him and his plows, and he grew rich in his generations.

He ate thick horse steaks four meals a day and marrow from cracked femurs. Always he toiled as he should, never letting a field lay fallow. Yet one night, the fourth brother forgot to burn the offering of a femur overlaid with belly fat as his father had taught him. The fourth brother, in simple error, consumed this holy offering for himself. For three days, the Sun sent across the horizon shafts of lightning. Bolts struck the fields once so fertile and cracked them open. The whole earth quaked beneath the Sun's fury, and those homes the fourth brother and his sons sheltered in collapsed upon them.

To see such devastation, the fifth brother supplicated himself and his generations. After toiling from Dawn to Dusk so no field or pasture would lay fallow, he turned his face toward his Father and begged mercy. He burned each offering in its proper season. He burned an extra offering on Solstice. Thusly, he became the favorite, and the Sun rewarded him by pouring forth height so the fifth brother might stand nearer His heat, and the Sun gifted him and his generations with well-oiled skin to shine in His brightest rays. For the fifth brother alone, the Sun gave His greatest gift, a valley so wide and green that his generations could expand toward eternity. To this favorite, the Sun repeated His promise: 'Use every bounty I pull forth, let no gift of mine go to waste, populate my earth, and you alone will live in knowledge that your lineage shall carry far and forever.'

Dangling from ropes about the testament stone were the bodies of blasphemers and thieves. The longest hanging had already been picked to bone by crows.

Cyrus realized that his fellow citizens were sneaking glances at him: a man of rank among their benches. These were the illiterate masses who on a cold day might raid the archives for kindling. The poorer classes could not be expected to decipher the intricacies of the first story, its promises and edicts, significance and context, or even the role it continued to play in shaping their daily lives. Most had no idea it had been twice translated from the original; they could not fathom the nuances lost and magnified by these retellings. Yet every one of them seated here could feel the story's truth.

Today, even Cyrus felt moved. With a newborn heir, the Sun had blessed the Empire with another generation of leadership after leaving them so long in doubt. Eleven summers had passed since the Emperor began marrying. Cyrus's father would die—they all would, inevitably, die—but civilization would carry on. There was comfort to be found in the long view.

Then, a different man ascended the testament stone, shirtless and maybe a decade older than Cyrus. He began in the tone of humble tribute. He said he was a crop worker who had lost his employment. But here his tone changed.

This man shouted, 'Why must so many of us suffer? Why does the corn fail to grow? Why are the fields dry? If the Emperor is really the son of the fifth and favorite brother, tell me this: Why doesn't the Sun send him rain?'

The crowd booed. Someone threw a rock at the man atop the testament stone. He ran from those police coming to round him up.

To reach the lecture, Cyrus still had to cross what was left of the retail district, once the most vibrant part of the city. He wasted no time.

Above each door was the curved, eye-catching script from an era not so long ago when every citizen had work and coins to spend, when sellers still competed for buyers. In his youth, merchants paid artisans to design the most appealing storefronts. Now the paint was peeling and doors were left ajar. There was little left to sell, fewer still with coins enough to pay. Even a learned man had to wonder: What had they done to deserve such decline?

But nobody in this part of the city seemed concerned, not today. The Emperor's men were opening kegs of liquor. Cyrus walked past a laboring man kissing a maid. Past a boy and his father wearing common wool. The father, teetering, threw aside his cup and boosted his son onto his shoulders. To see this boy clinging to his father's strong back, Cyrus had to balance himself against a torch post.

It was Dusk when he arrived to the amphitheater and joined his peers in green robes who had come direct from the archives for the event. They sat on benches under the glow of burning torches. Their talk was of the history soon to be discussed, a scroll from the late period that involved society's transition from copper technologies to bronze eight centuries before. Cyrus had studied the text numerous times.

The Sun deposited in this valley a limitless vein of copper, but He left His tin seventy days' ride to the east in a valley controlled by a wayward cousin of the Emperor. After the cousin gifted the palace a set of tin chalices, the Emperor commanded that the tin and copper be melted and combined to demonstrate the unification of the two great cities. The resulting bronze was undeniably superior: malleable yet enduring enough to hold an edge. Within a generation, bronze had sparked vast trade lines between this valley and that one on the outer fringe of the habitable lands. It became a glorious period of collaboration and commerce; no bounty was allowed to go to waste. The Empire's foundries were soon producing limitless quantities of blades and shields, shovels and hoes. Carriages gained speed for the hard metal now rimming their wheels. But four centuries later, when a prince of that city rich with tin threatened to violate a generational contract, it was the Emperor who sent the better equipped army.

Why bargain for what you can seize? On innumerable horses grown stout on limitless Highland grass, the Emperor's soldiers and their bronze first tamed the distant city, then, valley by valley, the entirety of the habitable lands. The wealth accrued had no precedent.

Now, to make his point, a junior scholar lifted a handful of sand; it was the same sand that had overtaken the outermost fortifications and outposts, eventually swallowing the tin and thus the trade lines; it was now blowing across this very amphitheater. Because of sand, no new bronze had been forged in generations; any new metal now was simply the old melted and repurposed. How to explain the creeping presence of sand? The junior scholar argued, 'It is the Sun's challenge to the favorite. Sand is the only enemy we have left.'

'An element cannot be an enemy,' a junior scholar rebutted.

'Sand is our encouragement,' argued a third. 'The Sun wants us to cross the ocean, to that valley even greener than this one. To sail toward the barren horizon—this will be our firmest test of faith.'

Normally, Cyrus's voice was among the most prominent in any debate. He enjoyed playing the part of the doubter. Yet tonight he sat in silence. He kept seeing those tumors under his father's skin.

On the lower seats of the amphitheater, a cluster of medical students in blue robes had gathered. One turned to glance back. Ashair. His face like a gust of summer wind.

The crowd began to hush. Onstage, the night's esteemed lecturer was walking toward the pedestal in his formal regalia.

Ashair rose from his seat and ducked through a gap in the amphitheater wall.

———

Cyrus found him waiting in the quiet torchlight of the alley. Ashair turned, and his face—that angular, handsome, lowborn face—softened with relief. In his eyes was irrepressible joy. The rarest eyes, as green as a Highland meadow, lit now by flame. His hair was short-trimmed in the style befitting a faithful middle-class man. 'How's your father?' Ashair asked. None of Cyrus's colleagues had thought to ask.

They touched hands. 'It's strange,' Cyrus admitted, because to Ashair he could admit anything, 'how all the words I might use to describe the experience are vessels that have lost their contents.'

Ashair's fingers climbed Cyrus's wrist. His voice was barely more than a whisper. 'They will refill. Only in different proportions.'

'It's almost like when he's gone . . ." Cyrus needed the next words to be right and true. 'I think I'll be relieved somehow.'

'You won't be relieved to be fatherless.'

'The difference is that your father was proud of you. Mine has spent his life wishing I were someone else.'

'Trust me.' Ashair put a dangerous hand to Cyrus's cheek. 'Your father could be a tyrant and you would still be sorry to live in this world without him.'

It was this Cyrus couldn't bear the thought of missing: the release only they could bring each other in the safety of a darkness so profound that they could see nothing of themselves.

Afterward, amid the revelatory and shameful effervescence, Cyrus recalled again that evening five years ago, the night his life changed forever, when he happened to collide with Ashair during intermission at the theater. His parents were waiting in their box, and Ashair was headed back to his common seat in the lower gallery. 'Clumsy me,' Ashair had said. In the years since, Cyrus had never noticed anything clumsy about Ashair.

Neither of them had known what to do; how could they? And yet they knew they had to meet again, and again, and that their walks together must be kept from their classmates and families as weeks became months. At first, Cyrus would have argued it was the difference in caste that required such secrecy. And yet he knew it was more. There was no word for this lightning between men. It couldn't be called love.

Now, as they walked with a proper distance between them, Ashair pulled from his pocket the rolled leaf. His fingers placed it between his lips, and he leaned his angular face toward a torch burning on a street corner. When the leaf began to smolder, he drew. It's what Cyrus wanted for himself, Ashair's grace. Not the kind of grace that came from having a well-armed driver and a silk-wool robe, but the kind that could not be stolen. He drew from the leaf as if Ashair's smoke might just deliver what he wanted.

Under the spell of the intoxicant, the world became slightly humorous and humorously slight. To test his new powers, Cyrus thought of his father as he was, riddled with tumors—*dying*. The thought was somehow like poking a numbed wound.

Voices began calling for them to stop: two police officers wearing the Emperor's metal. Turning toward them, Cyrus tried to be a man with nothing to hide.

The officers carried swords, yet it was their smirks that felt most dangerous. The taller of the two pointed at the difference in their footwear. Ashair was wearing the leather slippers of a medical student while Cyrus couldn't hide the polished boots his father had given him, too rich a pair for the common scholar. 'What are *you two* doing together at this hour?'

'Coming from a lecture,' Cyrus said. 'We're colleagues.'

The officers laughed. 'You're a terrible liar!'

'We should detain them,' said the shorter one. 'Write a report—be sure to list the family names.'

'We're only coming from a lecture,' Ashair repeated. 'Is that a crime now?'

The taller officer said to Cyrus, 'Rumors can be worse than felonies. At least for a man in boots as nice as those.'

Cyrus didn't want to waste another moment. He placed the remains of his father's satchel in the taller officer's hand. 'Can I pay our fine now?'

The officer smiled. 'I like a smart man. Maybe we'll see each other again.'

They had just turned a corner when Ashair dared say, 'There's a place.'

'Is it safe?'

'It's my old neighborhood. So, no.' Ashair smiled. 'But I'll protect you.'

They navigated a narrow alley and a web of sandy streets, and like little boys, they climbed a stone fence and leapt onto a roof.

It belonged to a solar temple, the one Ashair had attended as a child. He guided them around the hole in its ceiling. 'Careful. You'll find the altar below unwelcoming.'

Cyrus looked into that long black drop. By daylight, plates of bronze would reflect and magnify the Sun's light and deliver a focused beam upon the priest below.

Together, they walked to a railing overlooking the capital. Layers of stone and timber built by generational labor, these buildings and warehouses and homes nestled here between ridges where the river found the ocean. To behold such history and architecture, such collective effort and hard-earned symmetry, this marvelous civilization carved from the wilds by human hands partnered with the divine—he felt overwhelmed by gratitude to be playing his small part within this grand performance.

There, in the distant harbor, the bow of the ark was barely visible above the roofs. The sound of hammers on wood carried like drums. 'No doubt you used to bring girls up here.'

'Just once,' Ashair admitted. 'At my older brother's urging.'

'And how'd it go?'

'Everything fit,' Ashair said. 'And yet didn't.'

Cyrus remembered the candies he had bought for Ashair at the market that afternoon and fetched them from his pocket. Ashair savored one with his eyes shut. The middle classes could no longer justify the expense of candy. Cyrus gave him all three.

Ashair broke the silence as he so often did: by asking for a story. 'Something you found in the archives. Something that happened far away. In any place but this one.'

There was one story in particular; Cyrus had found it on a dusty bottom shelf, and he'd been reading it at night when alone, when unable to sleep—when he was up late wishing he didn't have to be alone. It was about a pair of brothers from long ago. Brothers who were so often together that they learned to dream the same dreams, the same particular, impossible dream. Together, these brothers would become a bird.

'Yes,' Ashair said. 'I like this story.'

'The brothers worked in seclusion and in secret because people they told only laughed. Each day they woke and climbed together to the top of a cliff, and there they put on their wings and jumped. Every day they fell to the ground. They smashed their legs, their arms, their heads.

They wore bruises; they broke bones. No matter how they built their wings, they couldn't fly. And yet the brothers kept climbing the cliff; they kept jumping; they kept making new wings.'

'Go on.'

'And then one day, when jumping from the cliff as they had so many mornings before, the wind caught their wings—they were lifted from the ground. Imagine: instead of falling, they flew up and away! The brothers together soared over the city like a bird. Those who once laughed now stopped to watch, mouths open in wonderment at the underside of their wings. Some said it was a trick, an illusion—no man could fly. At first, nothing doubters saw could make them believe.

'But in time everyone wanted to learn how. Crowds began to clamor at their door. The brothers could have kept their secret and remained forever the only two who knew how to fly, but they chose instead to share what they knew. In time, they taught everyone how to be a bird. Soon all people were flying anywhere they wanted to go. No one walked anymore. Everyone flew.'

Ashair smiled at the distance. 'It's a beautiful story.'

'Yes, but. Eventually, with so much flying, they forgot how to walk.'

'But they didn't need to walk,' Ashair said. 'Not when they could fly.'

Cyrus raised a finger. 'One day, their wings stopped working. The wind no longer lifted. When the brothers jumped from the cliff, they merely fell as they had before.'

'Only now they couldn't walk either,' Ashair said.

In the distance, the sound of hammers grew and diminished with subtle shifts in the direction of the breeze.

'So it's a sad story,' Ashair said.

'Beautiful and sad, I think,' Cyrus said. 'These men lived together.'

'Brothers.'

'Perhaps it is only what they told people.'

Ashair's eyes were watching something far away. 'All those broken bones . . . they must have helped each other heal.'

'It is what they could do.'

Ashair asked, 'What changed? Why did the winds cease lifting them?'

'The story offers no explanation. The power they had mastered was gone as suddenly and inexplicably as it had arrived.'

Silence grew. 'I should go,' Ashair said. 'I told her I'd be home after the lecture.'

Her, the wife. Cyrus took Ashair's hand and into it placed the imperial scroll given to him that morning by his father. If anything could keep Ashair here with him, it was this: the promise of green shores across wide waters.

The moon was just bright enough to make out the lettering. Cyrus explained about the audience, the tribute owed, his reward should he succeed—three boarding passes.

Ashair finished reading. 'Why boarding passes when everyone is welcome?'

Cyrus stared.

'Boarding passes for the best seats, you mean.' The confusion on Ashair's face became astonishment—then quickly anger. He pushed the scroll into Cyrus's sternum. '"All my goodly people." He said, "*All* my goodly people."'

'I didn't know until today. I swear.'

'It can't be. The Emperor wouldn't . . . leave his people behind? The poor and needy? What about the children? They are all also his children. Aren't they?'

'Ashair. I don't know who's invited. But there can be room. For you and me. One pass is my mother's. The other is mine. The third can be—'

'This isn't true!' Ashair was holding fistfuls of his own hair. 'If he leaves us behind, we'll be buried by sand!'

'Listen.' Cyrus stepped closer. 'We can be free. No more sneaking. We can be together. Ashair. Don't you understand? This is our best chance—it is our only chance.'

Ashair said nothing. He didn't blink. This was not the response Cyrus expected.

'On those green shores, everything will be different, everything will be better. We can start over. We could tell people we are—I don't know—brothers.'

Ashair stepped back. 'There is no such thing as starting over.'

'Don't say that. Please don't say that.'

Ashair was backing away. 'She's waiting. I made a promise. I keep my promises.'

'Don't go. Not yet.'

Ashair continued past the hole in the roof. At the edge of the temple, he stopped and looked back, still with that awful incredulous expression. 'Your people will get on the ship while mine fight it out here, over what's left. How are you not outraged?'

'You know I don't control any of that. No one cares what a scholar thinks.'

'How convenient for you.' Ashair turned to leave but his feet didn't take the step. 'Just tell me this. What happened to those brothers? To all the people who could no longer walk or fly? How does their story end?'

'That is the ending. The one we have anyway.'

'So it's a tragedy.'

'It doesn't have to be.'

'Maybe it does.'

'Please. Don't leave. Not yet.'

Then Ashair was gone. The night sky above was a cold, empty expanse; Cyrus felt as if he were falling into it, falling farther into nothing, no bottom to this descent. His body wobbled; the heel of his boot was on the edge of the hole cut in the temple roof. He was teetering above the darkness below. Cyrus stepped toward the harbor.

He lingered on the rooftop listening to his city at night. There was no rush. He had no one waiting up for him.

V

Promises Broken

They had been here five days already, beside this creek and the Impossible Thing, and his sisters wouldn't tell him why. All the way up the mountain, they never let him rest and now Kushim had nothing to do but sit. Winter was coming; the days were getting shorter; the next storm might bring snow—then what? They should be walking. His sisters had promised to find Auntie before winter. They only noticed him now if he did what they told him not to. So Kushim threw a rock at the Impossible Thing. It hummed long after impact. He liked the mysterious sound.

'I told you to stop that,' Maren said. She hardly looked up. She was driving poles into the ground with a cobble and sweat was streaming from her brow.

Kushim picked up a handful of rocks and pelted the Impossible Thing. Maren muttered, 'You're worse than useless, you know that?'

One more rock waited in his hand. Really just a pebble. He didn't throw it—more a toss. But it hit Maren on the brow and she finally dropped what she was holding and rushed at him. He turned and bolted, but she didn't even bother chasing.

Leerit had been waiting in ambush beside the same trail for four days without seeing an elk. The trail held tracks—a herd moving from a bedding area to a spring of clear water and on to a slope of deep grasses—but after so long, she had to assume something was wrong. Perhaps her scent was swirling on the wind, or the keen eyes of the lead elk had seen her from a distance and steered the herd toward another valley. If only she could ask her father what to do.

The same song was echoing as she waited. She wanted to stop hearing it, this warning elders used to sing. It was about a village founded by children. They had left home to avoid those chores assigned by their elders. They grew into adults who believed they knew best and so did not bother teaching their children the old stories. Theirs was a village known for unbreakable merriment. Dancing without prayers, copulation without ceremony, feasts without offerings. Strangers journeyed great distances to join the limitless pleasures. The Sea grew furious. She sent the test of snow and ice in summer. She sent winds to flatten gardens, then sixteen days of warm rain. The river swelled when it was always low and flooded those few crops that had survived the unseasonable weather. But the village had forgotten the Ancients' songs. No one remembered how to find food when crops are destroyed.

> *Hear this now, children: an entire village, young and old, can starve among bountiful offerings they have forgotten how to see.*

'You know this isn't going to work.' It was her father's voice. He was here now, lying on the ground, propped up on an elbow, smelling the grass he was balling between fingers. Not dead, not even hurt—his face was full again, his arms thick with muscle, like when she was a little girl. She hadn't heard his approach. Finally, she asked, 'What should I do?'

'You have the wind and cover. But you're in their line of sight. Lie down.'

She had picked this spot downwind of the trail because a cluster of trees would hide her. 'How will I throw if I'm lying down?'

He touched the end of the spear she had fashioned from the blade of her knife. He was testing its edge, the one his wife had so perfectly knapped. 'Do you doubt me?'

Leerit lay down beside him, her body among the green spruce boughs and brittle bracken fern. 'Let her pass,' he whispered with breath that was cold against her ear. 'Let her babies pass. In the gap between creatures, stand and be ready for who comes next.'

'Let who pass?' Leerit asked.

'The grandmother. She's the only one paying attention.' He nodded up the hill, and she heard it then: crack, pop, the unmistakable clack of hoof on downed wood. The herd was coming—it was happening.

When she looked back, he was gone. Her father had left her alone with all that had to be done.

Maren stepped back from the lean-to she had just finished building against the Impossible Thing. Poles angled at the perfect pitch, limbs thatched over top: strong enough to support the snow's weight if this year's dark season brought snow. There was enough room for three people, their fire, and its fuel—and a winter's worth of meat, if it came. The work had begun days ago with the peeling of bark from willow stalks, which she braided into jute. Next, she had used a halved-cobble to hack down spruce for the poles. If Ama was here, she would say how proud.

It had been Maren's idea to use the Impossible Thing as the lean-to's back wall. It wasn't rock or bone or ivory or wood. The thing hummed like a drum when her brother stoned it. When Kushim found the black hole of a torn-open end, he had crawled inside the hollow center and emerged with ash on his hands and knees. As if it once carried fire.

Stranger yet were the etchings on nearby rocks. Stick men and oblong dogs shown as if born from the Thing. Nearby were small piles of pebbles, purple and green, blue and turquoise—yet every rock in this valley was gray or white or black. Leerit said people had brought those stones from elsewhere; they came here and drew themselves. *Why?* Maren had asked. But now she knew the more important question was *who.* Who left the pebbles, who built the Impossible Thing?

They had talked it over while Kushim slept. A stream with insects crawling over rocks, elk tracks in the grass, tubers growing sweeter in the mud. Leerit said they would be betting their lives on finding Auntie ahead of winter's all-day darkness. And finding her well stocked. Maren agreed. They should lay in what they needed here, where survival was possible, and look for Auntie once the light returned. *It's what Opi would do,* Leerit had said. *It's what Ama would tell him to do,* Maren had corrected.

No one had yet told Kushim.

The sky was darkening as Leerit returned from the hunt, dry grass crackling underfoot. It was a new, holy feeling: like she was a leaf carried on a riffle, weightless.

The wind sifted the trees, and a gust heaved her onward. Tiny pieces of ice were falling, so many that they made a hissing sound as they hit the spruce and grass, like the sizzle a wave makes retreating over pebbles. She opened her hand and caught not ice but sand.

She found them by the creek. Kushim was perched over the pool on a broken end of the Impossible Thing staring down at the currents. Maren watched from the grass. Leerit sat beside her. 'I found him like this,' Maren said. 'He hasn't moved. He claims there's a fish down there.'

Leerit showed her sister the blade loosened from the spear shaft and not yet wrapped back into the knife handle her mother had made, this oval of brilliant edgework in her palm. The blood was by then flaking off. Her cheeks were unused to smiling.

Maren took it and smelled it. 'You got one!'

'We'll survive this winter, at least.'

There came a terrific splash and they looked to see their brother in the creek. He came up swimming hard for shore.

'You idiot!' Maren shouted.

Kushim stood panting, still waist-deep in the frigid stream. 'I slipped.'

Maren threw up her hands. 'And now you'll freeze!'

Leerit put a hand on her sister's shoulder. 'Don't be so hard on the boy.'

Butchering had always been a village affair, happy work, laughter and songs. When the village emptied, what little butchering they did was left to just the family. Those harried and lonely sessions over a carcass—too many tasks for too few hands. Now they would butcher alone, the three of them, and really just two who could wield a knife or heave a load. It had to be done fast to protect the meat from spoilage and scavengers.

Leerit led them to where the hind was lying in knee-high grass, her head back, her tongue out, eyes open. Not the grandmother of the herd. The matriarch and her children had passed by unaware while Leerit lay hidden. She had stood in the gap between elk and readied herself for who might come walking down the trail next. By then, she couldn't feel her hands or legs; she was tingling. She let the next hind pass by, then she drove the spear behind the last rib—just like in her father's stories. It had kicked and, with the spear protruding, run a short distance. When it stopped to look back, the hind lost her balance and sank onto her haunches before tipping downhill. Now grains of sand were clinging to the dead elk's open eye. With the blade Ama gave her, Leerit had subdued a creature five times her size.

'It smells,' Kushim said.

Maren hugged him. 'That's the smell of Ama being happy!'

Leerit put them to work. Already the legs were stiff. From his fall into the creek, Kushim was shivering, so she sent him to find a stout pole. 'Keep moving,' she told him. 'You'll be fine.'

Maren noticed the worn udders. 'What happened to the calf?'

'I couldn't leave it to suffer.'

Leerit worked the blade up the chest to the brown mane of the neck and out to each hoof, then they peeled the hide from the hindquarter one pass of the knife at a time, finally severing the naked limb at the ball joint. The weight of this meat was too much for one person alone. By then, Kushim had returned with a pole and he helped slide it under the thickest tendon. The sisters rested the wood on their shoulders and stood in unison, the hindquarter suspended between them. That's when Kushim finally noticed the calf in the nearby grass. 'You killed a baby?'

She had called the calf in at a run by mimicking the sound its mother made. It had believed her and died quickly.

'Better to have both,' Maren told their brother. 'A calf can't survive alone.'

After dark, they feasted. Juice dripped from their fingers and chins, and stained their boots crossed under them. Leerit couldn't stop seeing the calf. Opi must have known this feeling. It was everything at once: relief, pride, and so much sorrow.

The hind's tusks were resting on her thigh, shining there in the firelight as they ate the first meal. Ivory, each as long as the last bone of her thumb, pried loose from where they grew in the elk's mouth above the upper teeth. She had once asked Opi, *Why bother growing tusks if they're so small?* He said, *Elk grow them for us, for our hooks.*

She would carve the ivory during the dark of winter. It's what he would do. If there were fish in this stream, they would need hooks to catch them.

'It's a good lean-to, isn't it?' Maren said, chewing. 'You haven't mentioned it.'

With a full belly, the boy could only talk of fishing. By moonlight, Leerit led her brother to the willows and snapped off a seasoned length. Kushim watched as she roughed off the limbs and peeled the bark. She unfurled a sinew leader she had carried this far. He moved closer to study the knot she tied by firelight at the willow's tip. 'Like this,' she told him. 'Now where's the hook I gave you?'

Kushim opened his mouth—her strange little brother—and gave her the hook wet and warm. He asked, 'What will we use for bait?'

A boy from a fishing village asking which bait. Once, every kid his age boasted of his prowess with a rod and net. Boys pranced about with their latest catch held out. If his son got an impressive fish, a father would carry it to every gathering of men and beam as his boy told the story. Kushim didn't even know how pathetic he was, a nine-year-old who had never caught a fish.

From her satchel, Leerit withdrew the skin of a rabbit she had brain tanned, one of several she had been saving from her snares in the hope of making Kushim a new, warmer layer for winter. Now she ran her knife down the edge to free a thin strip half the length of a pinkie. 'Trout are picky. For bait to work, you have to use the insect the trout wants that day, that moment of the day. Better to make a trout curious. A fish doesn't have hands, so what do you think he explores with?'

'His mouth,' Kushim said. 'But how do you make a trout curious?'

'What makes a boy curious?'

Her brother looked at the Impossible Thing. 'Something he's never seen before.'

'Then we'll show him something he has never seen,' she said. 'Something that doesn't quite make sense.'

'Who made it?' He was still looking at the Impossible Thing, which loomed in the moonlight.

She didn't know. She had never heard any stories of such a thing. She told her baby brother, 'Remember what I've taught you.'

That night was their first under the lean-to. They slept three abreast atop layers of pine boughs, Kushim between them, the bearskin opened and spread over top. Leerit was too warm. 'Not bad, eh?' Maren said. 'I built a good shelter, didn't I?'

'Winter will decide.'

―――

The calf appeared. It was running through grass, trusting the sounds from her mouth. But in the dream, the calf became Kushim and it was too late, the spear was already on its way. Leerit woke believing she had killed her own brother.

To settle her breathing, she had to leave the bedding and walk. She covered ground in the dark by pacing back and forth.

'Do you feel bad for the fish you kill?' she had once asked Opi as he filleted the day's catch.

'No,' he told her. 'I feel gratitude.'

'What about when you kill a rabbit or a squirrel?'

'When I kill elk,' he said. 'I feel sorry.'

'Why elk?'

He smiled, but it wasn't a happy smile. 'Elk are surprised to die. They know what it means.'

And yet the whole village had been eager as summer turned to fall, as they awaited the return of the herds to the coastal meadows. The knapping of points, the scraping of wood for arrows and bow staves. Children watching their older cousins practice shooting. At night, when Leerit was still a little girl, the stories told were of old hunts, of daring stalks and long shots, of that time when animals still came in impossible numbers.

Her first kiss had been while hiding along an elk trail. Ozi. He was a year older. They had played together as children, then for a time they hated each other, but even before she became a maiden, she couldn't stop watching the muscles in his legs. She was the one to say she was coming hunting with him. He had been set to go with friends, but now he told them to go on ahead. They jeered but he turned from them to her. His gaze in that moment lit Leerit with some new heat. He was sixteen and she was fifteen, and they walked away from the village together.

The ancient song told them to *pattern, position, ambush, repeat*. Where an elk trail crossed a creek, they used brush to build a hiding place. The creek steadied the wind, and yet Ozi was constantly checking the breeze. He was drawing and lowering his bow. He was always looking far away. When she asked, he said, 'I'm no good at hunting. My father had six elk by the time he was my age. I still don't have one.'

On that day, Leerit didn't care about the hunting. She did as she had heard older maidens describe: took Ozi's robe in her fist and drew him to her.

No elk came, to them or anyone else, on that day or for rest of the moon. And then Auntie proposed leaving. The mothers met and decided Auntie was right. Without venison, the people wouldn't survive; they had to take a chance and cross those forbidden mountains. With no fish in the nets, they had to follow Elk.

Ama refused. She said she would never leave this beach that was their home. The last time Leerit saw him, Ozi was standing in the canyon, looking back. And then he was gone. For half a year she kept watching the canyon mouth, hoping. Eventually she stopped; he was gone and she would never see him again. Her mother was to blame.

In the morning, to silence his pestering, Leerit took Kushim fishing.

She told him to slow down. Think. Once a fish is spooked, he won't come back. 'Remember this angle.' She could see the trout holding in the current before them—the first she had seen in so long. 'You can see him, but when he looks up, he can only see sky. If you keep this angle, you can get close. But never throw a shadow on the water. To trout, a shadow means a diving bird.'

Kushim's first cast landed in a pile. The fish was alarmed—she could tell by the sudden suspension of his fins. 'Don't move,' she said. 'Don't do anything.'

The hook drifted downstream out of the pool, and after a moment, the trout's fins returned to their balancing act, his body again flexing with the currents. Opi had once told her, *Only a relaxed trout will feel curious.*

He had been so forgiving of mistakes when he taught her. Now she tried to be like him. 'Cast upstream. Let the hook sink to the fish's depth before you give it life.'

This time it landed close to where she wanted and the strip of fur twirled in the current and the fish was gone. Kushim gasped and she saw the trout next as a flash under the broken current. The willow folded with jolting life and the fish burst into the air. Soon Kushim was dragging his first onto shore.

'I did it!' her brother kept shouting. 'I got one!'

She pressed the fish against gravel. 'Quick, get a rock.'

The trout's eyes were moving between them, his mouth gasping for water. She told Kushim to hit the fish between the eyes. She said what their father once told her. 'There's no mercy in hesitation.'

'I'm sorry,' her baby brother said to the trout. Then he delivered a blow that sent quaking through its body. The eyes stopped moving and stared off. The mouth went still and hung open. At once, all the vibrant colors faded to gray.

She stood, but Kushim didn't. He was still on his knees. Her brother said again to his catch, 'I'm sorry that I killed you.'

These words from his mouth made her angry, she didn't know why. 'We don't apologize. Everything dies, that's how living works.'

'What should I say to the fish?' he asked. 'I have to say something.'

'Prove your thanks by making holy use of his gift.'

Maren used a stick to tease an ember into the bark tube in case the fire went out while they were away hauling meat.

Even if her big sister didn't notice, Maren knew their mother would. She would embrace her daughter and say it was a good shelter. These tears in Maren's eyes now were because there was no one left to say how proud.

She found her siblings by the stream. Leerit was showing Kushim how to tether his trout to a limb in the water where it would stay cool and hidden from any bird. Her brother couldn't stop smiling.

When he climbed the bank, Maren took Kushim by the elbow. She smiled as he relayed a long version of the story. When he finally finished, she told him, 'Brother. I am proud of you.'

When they arrived back to camp with the day's first load of venison, Maren was wet with sweat and her breath fogged the chilled air. She rested against the structure she had built. All her weight on it. It didn't give. Leerit looked, but only said, 'This is no time to relax.'

'I want to fish,' Kushim said. 'I like fishing more. Can I? Can I fish instead?'

'No,' Maren answered when Leerit didn't. 'We need your help hauling.'

———

On the next trip, they dragged the calf whole, for the creature was small enough to move without butchering. Kushim was of no help. He pulled on a leg for a short while but then followed behind. The dragging was somehow easier without his fumbling feet.

They arrived this time to find crows pecking at the meat delivered on the first trip. Crows. To see them again was its own wonderment. Kushim threw a rock and the birds hopped into flight but went only as far as the nearest tree. Once, they were called pests.

'I can keep the crows from the meat,' Kushim said. 'I can do that while I fish.'

Leerit looked at Maren. She wiped the sweat from her brow. 'He can't much help with what's left. Two more trips whether he comes or not.'

'We shouldn't be apart,' Maren told her sister because it was true.

Leerit pointed at the flock. 'Do you have another idea?'

'I won't wander off,' Kushim said. 'I promise. I'll stay right here and keep the crows from the meat. You can trust me.'

'Let Brother be of use,' Leerit said.

Maren looked at them both. In all other matters she had deferred to Leerit, and here they were, with more to eat than they'd had in years. Kushim was already holding his fishing rod.

'Get some firewood first,' Leerit said. 'Get as much wood as you can. We have a lot of smoke to make.'

'Get wood, scare crows,' Kushim said. 'I can do that.'

'Don't go far,' Maren said. 'And no falling in the water.'

'Don't worry,' Leerit called over her shoulder as their brother and the lean-to disappeared behind them. 'The kid crossed the mountains, didn't he?' Then Leerit repeated something Maren once heard their father tell their mother: 'If you baby a boy forever, he'll never learn to be useful.'

———

Maren's legs wobbled after navigating the broken ground with the heavy hindquarter held between them. Her feet ached, her legs cramped, her shoulder was angry where she let the weight balance. They arrived to find Kushim actually helping. A pile of wood waited beside a glowing fire. The crows had given up and moved on. The boy was breaking limbs into smaller lengths. 'Is this enough wood?'

Leerit hung the meat while Maren tasked Kushim with helping her build a frame on which strips of venison could be draped. For once he didn't complain. They worked together, each of them binding limbs with jute.

'How will we carry all this meat to Auntie?' her brother asked.

Maren looked at Leerit, whose short hair was shining with sweat. This wasn't even all the meat. They had one more trip for the last of it. Finally, she told him. 'Look around, Kush. This is a winter camp.'

'But—but I don't like winter.' Kushim began to cry. 'You said we would find Auntie before winter! You said—you promised!'

Leerit was unmoved, draping cuts of meat over the trusses of the frame where smoke could bathe them. 'While we're gone for the last load, keep the fire smoking. Don't let it go out. If the meat on the bottom gets too dry, replace with it with meat from the top of the frame. You have to pay attention. Do you understand? If we don't preserve the meat, it'll rot and we'll starve.'

Kushim wiped his cheeks.

'We need it to dry evenly, slowly,' Maren told him. 'We're counting on you. Can we count on you?'

'You can't let the fire get too big,' Leerit said.

'Or too small. Do you understand how important this job is?'

Kushim sat and put his forehead against his knees.

Maren whispered to her big sister, 'Maybe he comes with us for the last load. Maybe we start smoking the meat once we're all back. Let the crows have a little.'

Leerit only said, 'Kush. I know you're disappointed, but can your sisters count on you?'

Kushim wiped his eyes. 'I caught that fish, didn't I?'

The sun was setting when Maren arrived back to camp with the last load. She was carrying the elk's shoulder over her own, the meat cool and firm against her. Leerit was somewhere behind. She had wanted to stay a moment to offer a private thanks to the elk, to the calf, to the Sea who gave so much.

Maren saw first the smoking fire, the venison steaming on the rack. She checked and found the flesh drying evenly—Kushim had rotated the pieces when he should have. But where was he now? When she called his name, her voice broke.

She found him with the rod moving in a rhythm other than the breeze's. He was trying for another fish. Her brother was fine; he was safe; he had done as he was told. The tightness in Maren's throat released. She almost laughed. Of course he was fine.

She had earned a moment of relaxation. It was true: with this shelter, with so much meat, they were going to be okay. Even if winter was long and deep with snow, they would be okay.

The breezes began to shift with evening, down the mountainside after blowing up all day, and with them arrived pleasing new smells of meadow and forest. Juniper, fungal duff, the tang of high-country sage. Darkness was coming and they would feast on trout and sizzling elk fat. Tonight, they could afford a big fire. During winter, she would wish she had paid more attention to the greenness of this place.

Kushim was fishing the pool nearest the meat pole. Already he was better at casting. Leerit had thrown a length of tripled jute over a horizontal pole and suspended the calf. Nose up, hide still on—it was there now, near her brother, turning in the breeze. If the air stayed cold, Leerit had said, it could hang for days without souring.

So much work awaited. The hides to tan, sinews to chew and braid into thread, the tough skin behind the hooves to cut free as patches for the soles of their boots. Maren would make Ama's favorite: scrap meat and half-digested greens stuffed into intestines and left to pickle. All this work so when winter's darkness arrived, they could be warm and bored and alive. To pass the endless nights, she would tell a long story, new details each time—like Ama used to when they were children.

Then came a new smell in the wind. Like rot and wet fur and urine-tainted mud. This smell, Maren knew this smell—what was this smell?

Returning to a gray day when her mother still called her *darling*. She ran after Ama and saw the hide laid open on the ground for the first time, the skin they still slept under before it was cleaned and tanned. Opi's voice, *Won't be raiding the smoke rack anymore.* It was the first bear killed by the village and the last anyone had ever seen.

Her brother was now checking his hook. She was drawing her breath to warn him when the brush shook on the bank above and a head appeared. Ears up, eyes black, hide hanging loose from the skull. A thin bear come for the calf but now seeing Kushim at the water's edge. Her brother was too busy casting to notice.

Kushim turned at the call of his sister. He followed her eyes to the hillside above him: a patch of brown in the vegetation. Whatever it was disappeared—

—only to burst from the brush in a snapping explosion of limbs and leaves, mud washed over him, as heavy as a tree, a tree fallen on him— black weight and growling and mud in his mouth, the aquatic sound of bone breaking, the whipsaw of being shaken, of being torn apart.

A bear, that's what. This, then—this had to be dying.

VI

Unholy Labors

Lilah was elbow deep in hot wash water when across that foggy surface came something like a rush of wind. She was nearly blown off her stool.

Her hands were shaking. Her belly felt as if she had swallowed a fistful of gravel. Sometimes it happened like this: a sudden, inexplicable terror for her babies.

She and the girls had been taken from the corral and put in a cart drawn by a powerful animal and driven up the hill by men who said nothing to them. This cart threaded narrow paths between cliffs built stone by stone; it rolled under bridges made of chiseled rock, under curved and glinting materials without names, this landscape where everything had been made by human hands. Yet it was somehow familiar. Here was a village that filled a valley, a village spanning even the hillsides. The boat that had stolen her from the beach had somehow delivered her back to the time of Giants.

Their tall children were walking with enormous mothers. Towering men carried oversize tools. So many people in a world she had believed to be empty.

The cart passed through a gap guarded by muscular warriors with shining blades, and a gate clanked shut behind them. When the cart stopped, little Kenta's voice shook. 'Is this where they eat us?'

Koneet answered. 'No. They won't eat us. They want us to do their work.'

Over smoking cauldrons, bald women labored, stirring and churning, lifting and wringing. Bald children carried wet flesh toward lines strung in the sun. Not flesh but wool like the robes they wore, more wool, so much wool.

In that corral, they had watched others be separated—a boy pulled from his mother, an old woman pulled from her husband. Yet here they were in this place together. Lilah knew she should utter a prayer of gratitude to still be together.

An older woman gestured for them to step down from the cart. There was fat on her upper arms, fat on her cheeks. She had markings about her eyes that Lilah remembered from childhood—this was a woman of the desert tribes! She was using the same strange yet familiar gestures and sounds. This old nomad wanted to be followed.

They entered a dark corridor. Koneet held her little sister's hand and described what they were passing. Rock walls, wooden beams, flame affixed to the wall, a heavy door, room after room lined with beds, beds built over top other beds. 'I smell cooking,' Kenta said.

The desert woman led them into the last room at the end of the corridor. It was lit by a flame that flexed with their movement. Stale air. Cold. Quiet. They were here beyond the sound of waves.

The woman put her hand to her own chest. She repeated the same sound three times. Her name. *Trinket.* When Lilah said it, Trinket corrected her pronunciation.

To again be near a woman her mother's age—Lilah felt some weight lifting from her shoulders, like she could finally draw a breath. 'Thank you,' she said. 'Bless you.' As a polite younger woman should, Lilah reached across the divide separating them and placed a supplicating hand to her elder's wrist.

Trinket's eyes narrowed and she knocked Lilah back. Then she spit a glob of phlegm. The nomad was somehow furious. What sense did this make? How rude to spit!

'You can't let her bully you!' Koneet said. 'Or she will bully us.'

Lilah wiped the spit from her cheek. She bent her brow to the older woman.

'Stand up for yourself!' Koneet shouted. 'Stand up for us!'

Lilah used a quiet voice. 'Humble yourself as I do.'

'I won't humble myself to this rude sand-eater.'

Lilah looked at Koneet. 'Don't you understand? She is the mother dog of this pack. She will keep biting until the newcomers heel.'

The muscles in Koneet's jaw flexed.

Trinket began touching Kenta's cheek. How brazen—how beyond *rude.* Kenta held her breath as old fingers probed her cheeks, her eyelids. It was too much for Koneet. She shoved Trinket aside, and roared, 'My sister is not yours to touch!'

The swing came without warning. An open hand that struck Koneet over the ear. She staggered but didn't fall. Lilah held Koneet's arm to keep her from returning the swing.

The old woman leaned. She drew a long breath of Kenta's scent. Then, senselessly and without a word, Trinket left the room.

For the first time, Lilah found herself alone with the girls. Kenta was shaking, her face wet with tears. 'I want Ama. Can we go home, please? Why can't we go home?'

Koneet was looking down the corridor. 'This is our chance. If we hurry!'

Lilah spoke in the calmest tone she could muster. 'You saw those warriors with spears. You saw how high the fence was that closed behind us. If we try to escape and are caught—they could separate you.' From their faces, she knew the thought hadn't occurred to the sisters. No, to escape they would have to learn the rules of this place, find its weaknesses, act swiftly when an opportunity arose. She told them, 'We must be patient. Think of net-setters who await the right tide.'

Koneet spit. 'I won't stay a night in this place.'

Lilah shook her. 'Listen. We don't bite; we don't bark. You will bow your head. Humbling yourself is not submission. It is the beginning of escape. We must be perfect and faithful at whatever they ask. When that woman smiles, we wag our tails. Because no one worries the friendly dog will run away.'

'My sister is not a dog,' Koneet said. 'I am no one's dog!'

'Then be water.' Lilah sang the old proverb. *The river who bends around every obstacle arrives home to the Sea.*

Inside the walls, they lived not unlike members of a village. Eating together, working together. A village but without the games, without babies crawling from mother to mother, without dogs running between feet or men telling jokes as they mend nets. A village of able-bodied women and a few children, all of them speaking the desert language, those scars about their eyes carved long ago by their nomad mothers. This village built about a single task that was never complete: washing wool.

The robes arrived in carts drawn by those same powerful animals who submitted to halters and harnesses. The women called them *horses*. Lilah was tasked with adding wool to the hot water, stirring it, working each robe over a rutted board, rinsing it, working it again, passing it to the next woman working over the next cauldron. The cleaned and dried wool was loaded into the cart last emptied, which was drawn through the open gates by the same remarkable horses, where it disappeared within the many canyons built by Giants.

Koneet joined the other young women cutting firewood. Lengths of wood arrived in carts. These strong young women worked orange saws and axes. They carried armloads of split wood and sank to their knees to stoke the fires under the cauldrons. There was never an end to the sweat on Koneet's brow.

Like a village because the women sang as they worked. Their songs were foreign to Lilah's ear, but they were built of familiar notes and upon familiar structures of climbing and falling, patterns repeated, patterns overturned. Like a village because the songs were used to mark the time, certain songs to start the day, other songs in the day's middle, still others as daylight faded. Little Kenta never missed a note; she sang these words she didn't understand. Kenta was allowed to stay by Lilah's side. The child helped by stirring the hot water and soaking robes. Lilah wouldn't leave her alone even to piss.

The other children were younger than Kenta. They glanced and gossiped about the girl who saw nothing. They made no effort to welcome the newcomer.

Like a village except darkness did not mean the end of labor. Torches were lit. Fire hung from walls. Flames to throw light, but instead of lounging or dancing, the women of this village continued their work.

In just a few days, Lilah's hands had already turned coarse and stiff. Unhappy hands, unhappy when in the water, unhappy when left to dry. Her back was sore from stooping into the cauldron; her shoulders ached from endlessly working the wool. But her hands—they were pale and wrinkled and itching. They were the hands of a stranger.

A village, except a man told them what to do. When he spoke, even Trinket bowed. Sometimes he watched them work, but mostly he stayed in his house built above the yard. Not a house he lived in. He left at night. What was this man? When faced with women, even grandmothers, he demanded they show *him* respect. Where was his wife, his children? Where were his parents? She had never seen a man so proud to have nothing.

Meals. A full belly. It was a village with plenty to eat.

When a bell finally rang, the women tidied up their labors. Lilah did like the others and splashed herself clean from a cascade of cold water and helped Kenta do the same. When the bell rang again, she and the girl walked hand in hand into an enormous room where women offered steaming bowls. Heavy bowls. Hot-in-their-hands bowls. She carried Kenta's while the girl followed Lilah with a finger snagged on her belt.

The air reeked of bodies, of breath; it was warm. Before sitting to eat, Lilah did what every other woman from their sleeping quarters did: she spooned a lump from her bowl into the bowl held by Trinket. They sat together on the ground apart from the rest.

The squash she recognized, though not the variety. The maize she recognized too, though she had never eaten such large white kernels. The meat and marrow were new, but only as new as meat can be. It was dark, tender, and each night she reminded Kenta to chew the pieces with care and never try to swallow too much.

There were unknown ingredients too. Roots as tart as any she had tasted. Tender brown morsels that could be some kind of legume. Spices Lilah's tongue didn't expect.

Every night brought a feast but also an intolerable burden. To eat when she knew her children had none.

Were they now living together in her house or across the bay in Leerit's? Did they think she had drowned and her body swept away? Or that she chose . . . to leave them? They would have followed her tracks to the water. They might have found their poor dead father. What could they think?

At night, with a full belly, she often dreamt of carrying a cauldron of this stew. Delivering it in the dark, across the beach, waves washing up over her ankles. Sometimes, in this dream, her children came running. Sometimes they did not.

They had been in this strange village for seven nights when Koneet dared refuse. It was prayer time. At night, before bed, Trinket and the other women in their quarters sank to their knees and put their brows against little piles of sand collected from the yard. They chanted a desert song. But on the seventh night, Koneet said, 'I won't pray to sand!'

Trinket barked. The other women glared at Lilah. She knew she should do something. 'Think of their words as empty satchels. Fill them with your thanks. Tonight, you ate. The Sea provided. For your sister's sake, humble yourself.'

Koneet crossed her arms. 'I won't do one more thing they tell me. I refuse.'

Trinket rose from her knees. She crossed the room and took hold of Koneet's ear and drove her face to the cobbles. But when she stopped holding her, Koneet rose back up and glared.

Trinket seized her by the back of the neck and pressed her cheek against the cobbles. Yet again Koneet rose just as soon as the hand released her. The other women in the room murmured.

Lilah said, 'Forgive her. She is young. She will pray now.' But of course Trinket couldn't understand the words and Koneet continued to refuse.

Then Trinket took little Kenta by the armpit and lifted her to her feet. 'Auntie?'

'It's okay. I'm here.' The girl was led across the room.

To Trinket's bed. Where she was made to kneel. Trinket whispered in her ear. There was a tenderness in her handling of little Kenta. She was the only child in their sleeping quarters.

Trinket returned to Koneet, but this time she walked past. She took each blanket from her bed. These she delivered to Kenta. For refusing to pray, Koneet would have to shiver through the cold night. She would no longer share her bed with her own sister.

When Trinket began to pray, all the women prayed. Then they climbed into their beds. Lilah told Kenta, who was shaking, 'It's okay. We're here with you. Always.'

Trinket pulled the blankets up over Kenta's body. The little girl laid there unmoving, her eyes wide open as Trinket passed her fingers from Kenta's cheek over her ear, as if the girl had long hair, as if it hadn't been shaved. Against the stillness of the room, Trinket began humming a tender melody. In the desert or on the beach or in a room built of stone, this was a lullaby.

VII

Yoked

Fatherless. *Fatherless.* Every day of this autumn, he was learning what the word meant.

Cyrus slid his father's helmet over his head and his ears smarted against the cold bronze. Here within the carriage that had always belonged to the patriarch but now belonged to him. No longer greeted as a scholar—now even deans would bow their heads.

'Allow me, sir.' Jernod opened the carriage door and offered a gloved hand.

The helmet's plumage caught the wind. This bronze was cast in the imperial foundry and bore the crest; wherever Cyrus arrived, he did so under the Emperor's metal.

Across the street was a solar temple. Disheveled, lowborn men sat on its steps with their dice stilled by the sight of him. The temple door was open, the altar illuminated by the divine heat of the Sun.

His father as he had last seen him: laid out in their own temple, that deathly stare toward the timeless above. The priest stood behind the altar in his ceremony of feathers, looking up into bronze plating shaped to focus divine intent, blindness his evidence of devotion and the source of his wisdom. His father had already faded to something inert. Ash or seasoned wood. The world no longer had a father in it for him. No man to point the way or push against. No one to appease. Or blame.

They carried the body from the temple and set it upon a nest of kindling. Men of metal and plumage, important men, cut their own thumbs and let their blood pool upon his father's chest. At the priest's horn, crows could be heard. They lifted from the temple walls; they flew from hidden perches. Until the sky above his father was dark with swirling birds. *The crow is black because he is allowed to fly nearest the Sun.* Crows had always been the divine's chosen emissaries; crows had guided imperial scouts to countless battlefield victories, just as they would now guide his father from this earthly body back to his source within the omnipotent Sun.

When the priests stepped back, the flocks descended. Cyrus remained until his father was only bone. What the crows left was then turned to smoke upon a bed of flame.

'Sir?' Jernod said now. Cyrus realized he had been staring. The disheveled gamblers had returned to throwing their dice.

Fleece, that was his charge. He was here to speak with his manager of laundry. As he passed through the gate, the guards took a knee. The manager bowed, his leather hat held under an arm. 'The highest of honors, Master. Welcome to what is yours.'

Before him, across the square, forty cauldrons were perched over fires and primitive women stood with wet arms. Sweat glistened from bald, featureless heads. *They are thankful to have the labor,* his father once said of his indentured. *To the heathen, our employment is unfathomable charity.*

A little girl stood apart from the rest. She was near to her mother, her eyes aimed crookedly at the sky. As if she saw a crow flying so high. 'Is she blind?' Cyrus asked.

The manager nodded toward a guard. 'Shall we retreat to my office? I'm eager to hear what brings you here today. A surprise visit! Your father always sent word.'

Come spring, more wool than ever before would flow from the Highlands, and this facility would need to convert from laundering robes to washing and processing raw material. Possibly dyeing fibers too if another facility couldn't absorb those duties. These women would have to work harder and for longer. His manager would need to bring about the necessary increase in efficiency without raising costs.

Cyrus swept back his cape and followed the manager up the stone stairs. He was near the top when he heard the commotion. A guard was then pulling the blind girl from her mother's grip. The shouting was in some guttural tongue and yet who would need a translation? 'Stop this cruelty.'

The manager joined Cyrus at the railing. 'But sir. The child is lame. I intended to separate them. Your father taught me to wait; if we separate a pair too soon, the female will never learn to labor.' The manager's eyes narrowed. 'He liked to say, *Efficiency demands a strong stomach.*'

Cyrus looked at this little man who dared speak as if he knew his father. 'When I next return here,' he announced, 'I will see this child beside her mother.'

So many ancient stories told of fatherlessness. Mostly tales of revenge or hubris, sometimes both. *To lose a father is to lose a king.* 'Where to now, sir?' It was Jernod's voice asking from the pilot's perch.

They were parked outside the laundry facility. Somehow Cyrus was sitting in the carriage when he couldn't recall climbing from the ground.

'The hospital, please, Jernod.'

———

It was a series of hasty buildings erected across a vacant lot. Men in blue moved about the bloodied and sickly, past unkempt children crouching beside ill parents. Black smoke wafted and flies buzzed.

Ashair appeared in his blue medical robe. Dried blood on his hands, someone else's blood. He waved at the flies. 'What are you doing?'

Cyrus whispered, 'Let me hire you. Just for the afternoon. Can we talk?'

A crowd was forming. It must have looked strange: a healthy-enough master speaking to a poor man's doctor.

Ashair spoke for the audience's benefit. 'I'm sorry, sir. We don't treat citizens of your standing. There's another hospital on the hill. You'll be more comfortable there.'

Patients were watching but so were a pair of senior doctors in their colorful regalia. An old woman had her hands clasped toward Cyrus as she chanted for the Emperor's long life.

Ashair said loudly as he bowed, 'I wish you well, Master.' When he rose, his eyes lingered before turning away.

Jernod was at his elbow. 'We must move, sir.' It was a statement, not a question. 'These days, one should not trust a crowd.'

Their rattling wheels carried them high above the city, the horses bucking their heads as they ascended the steep grade toward his father's estate. *His* estate.

Efficiency demands a strong stomach. His father wasn't cruel. He was the type to stop his carriage to help an old commoner in need of a supporting elbow. Yet perhaps running an industry—which lifted the lives and fortunes of so many—required learning to see not people but contributions to a greater good.

The gate opened and a bell was rung and servants hurried to their places to greet him.

Cyrus's boots clacked as he navigated the cobbles of the hallway, this sound that to his ear still portended the arrival of his father. Behind the aviary's double doors, he heard the crows. He took off his helmet before entering so they might remember his face.

His favorite juvenile dove, pulled up and away, swooped down again, this time nearer. The bird still wasn't sure. Was it the scholar who came so often to feed them or the patriarch who came only to pray?

As a child, after endless hours of tutoring, after his teachers had gone home and Cyrus was alone but for servants—his father being away with wool, always busy with wool, just as his mother was eternally occupied with her charities—he had come here to the aviary, where he could never be alone.

Now a master's jewelry jingled as he held up a chip of fried corn. The crow circled before deciding to trust. He took the offering gracefully in flight and landed on a high branch—just as he always did, the feathers of his back pressed against the fenced altitudes.

In the sitting room, Cyrus set the helmet on a table and turned the bronze until the feathers displayed their plumage toward the door. A servant entered to tend the fire. It was the old heathen his mother had adopted the day his father died. She stared dumbly when he asked, 'Are you happier here?'

'My master and son,' his mother announced from the doorway. She was wearing an elegant robe of mourning. Her hair had been put up in a rush; he knew because strands were loose, and the Lady never went anywhere with a strand loose. 'Sir,' she said, with a most dignified bow of submission.

'Please don't,' he said.

'I do not bow to my son.' She was still on her knees. 'I bow to the master of this estate. I bow to my Emperor's emissary. Nothing could make a mother prouder than bowing to her son.'

For the first time since the funeral, they sat together. Her eyes had sunk into her face, dark circles below them. He found himself nervous and unsure of how to act before her. She broke the silence. 'The master's suite. It has been made yours. As it should be.'

'Where will you sleep?'

'In quarters befitting my title.'

'Widow.'

'Oh,' she said. 'How I loathe the word. I am not nearly old enough.'

The silence returned. He had summoned her but now he couldn't seem to begin.

'Speaking of wives,' she said in a buoyant tone. 'I have some names. You'll like this. To dinner I am inviting—'

'I can't think of marriage now. I must think of fleece. Only fleece. Until we're onboard the ark.'

She brushed this aside. 'I'll handle everything. Just pick a girl and eat dinner. What kind of man would refuse the company of a beautiful woman?' The question hung between them.

The door opened and the manservant arrived with their drinks. He used tongs to add petals and stems to the bottoms of cups. He tipped the vessel and steaming water poured forth. A bronze lid was lifted to reveal morsels of sweetened marrow, congealed and formed into decorative half-moons. The manservant bowed and retreated to the background. When Cyrus nodded at him, he left the room. The door closed.

'Listen,' he began. 'I'm confused. Where is father's money? In the ledgers, all I see are debts and liens. The new facility he acquired last year, all the extra wool he delivered. He lessened my allowance to save for them. But where are the profits?'

She didn't answer. She was looking out the window.

'Please pay attention, Mother. This is serious. Without those profits, I won't be able to pay what we owe. Lenders can then seize control of the facilities. Without facilities, we could lose our license for wool production, and the Emperor might decide to take back this very estate, your home. Do you understand what I'm saying? Is this too complicated for you?'

The widow blew steam from her cup. She sipped. She set her tea back on its bronze saucer. 'There haven't been any profits.'

'Of course there are profits. Don't be foolish. Look at how you live.'

She didn't blink. 'There is a man who has agreed to help. I spent the last months trying to convince your father to speak to General Rah, and so save you this embarrassment. In the end, I had to speak to him myself.'

General Rah. Of course Cyrus knew the name. In addition to commanding the Emperor's army, General Rah held the imperial license for plastic mining. The richest man in the empire outside of the Royal Family.

She explained. 'I chose my moment carefully. Your father was bedridden and General Rah couldn't say no to a Lady soon to become a widow. He promised enough to pay off the lienholders and fund your outlays until shearing. You need only go to him. That was his condition, that you come to him yourself. He recognized your name.'

She frowned. 'Don't be angry with me, Cyrus. I would've come to you with this—had you been home.'

A Lady interfering with matters of business? This was bound to go poorly. 'What are the conditions? Do you even know what we'll owe? Did you think to ask?'

'Don't underestimate me, Cyrus. You think your father ran this industry alone? Rah's conditions hardly matter, do they? Without his funding, we won't last until shearing. Besides, the general has vaults within his vaults. He and your father bowled together, you know. He's a very important man to call a friend. He recognized your name.'

'If they were so close, why didn't Father ask General Rah himself?'

'This is not the first time your father's pride disadvantaged his family.'

In a softer voice, she said, 'Cyrus. Won't you at least consider the names? These girls are beautiful. They're young. Their fathers have money. These are girls who can become whatever their husband needs them to be.'

VIII

Strangers

When Leerit heard the screaming, she shrugged the last load of meat to the ground and sprinted down the trail they'd worn to camp.

A demon stood on two legs pushing a tree. Maren was near its top and the whole length was swaying back and forth. The demon had finally come. It was here to take her sister next. The thick head swung and looked at Leerit.

That face. She could see the whites of its eyes where the hide drooped. About its middle, the pelt sagged in rolls. Nipples worn. Not a demon—a bear. Opi had said bears were no more, but here was a bear.

The ancient stories were in her ear; she did as they told—took up fire and roared.

The flame hissed as she swung the burning stick between them. The bear abandoned the tree and dropped heavily onto all fours. It was right then deciding who would win the fight. Leerit charged.

It spun and bolted; it pushed a wall of water across the stream. On the far bank, the animal looked back, huffing, rivulets running through its fur. Leerit threw the flame, and the bear wheeled and smashed away through the forest like a boulder tumbling uphill.

Near her boots: matted grass, torn soil, plumes of bright blood—it was a kill site.

Now that fury was in her feet. She wouldn't stop no matter how hard Kushim struggled. Following the elk trail downstream, dodging limbs and stepping over fallen logs. At tributaries, Maren leapt between rocks, but Leerit simply splashed through.

How could this have happened? Kushim had done nothing wrong— he had listened and heeded. How could she have let this happen?

Kushim was on her back, supported by a tumpline, as he had been since they splinted his mangled leg and slowed the bleeding from the savage wounds to his arm and head. Broken ribs that didn't rise when he breathed—and that head wound. A tear from the bridge of his nose up and over at an angle. When she had first knelt beside his body, a fillet of scalp was hanging over his ear—she could see the white of his skull and the mud clinging to it. She sank to her knees and begged her father to tell her what to do. She begged her mother, her grandmother—she called for the Ancients. But there was only the sound of the stream splashing downhill.

She insisted they leave before even stashing an ember. There wasn't time for anything but finding Auntie. Auntie would help. Auntie always helped. They had to go. The bear would come back. The only thing she knew to do was cover ground.

The next day, they were still going. He had quit protesting. His blood was sticky against Leerit's back.

Pain from carrying him pulsed across her shoulders and down her arms; the sides of her knees burned; blisters smarted like bee stings. There was nothing else she knew to do. She pushed on. She used her body to break a path through the brush. When a rock rolled under her, they both fell heavily onto cobbles. Her face hit first. When she stood, there was blood in her mouth and a piece of tooth. She spit, righted her load, and kept on.

All day and into the next, she carried him. At some point, the brush died out. There wasn't a tree. They were descending along a rush of water. Near sunset, the hillsides became a rock-filled canyon. 'I can't keep walking,' Maren said. 'I can't! Leerit, please!'

She didn't stop. She would carry him however far; she would make herself into meat for her baby brother. Everything was her fault.

From the dark of some night, Opi finally spoke to her: *Don't take another step.*

There was only a sliver moon and she could hardly see, yet her vision was spinning, the ground under her turning; she couldn't remember how many days or nights she had been walking. But now she saw what he did. The end of land. She had walked to the edge of the earth. There was nowhere left to take her brother. 'What should I do?'

There was nothing more from him. He was not beside her. She was one step from rushing water. She had walked all this way to arrive back here, to their river. This was the place she used to wash clothes. Somehow her feet had delivered her home to a time before sand. Auntie was here. Ama was here. Everyone would still be here, together. But where?

It was Maren calling her name. Maren pointing.

Across the river, in moonlight, light shapes were moving. Shapes that bawled as they climbed the slope away from the water, away from them. The sharp clatter of hooves on rock. Somewhere a dog began barking. A strange, unfamiliar bark.

In the gray of dawn, a white speck appeared over the hilltop. Shoulders, legs—someone was following their dog. A person! A stranger. An old man, quick on his feet, white hair puffing out from the bottom of a strange hat. He used a stick taller than he was for balance. A person.

Though the distance was far, Maren called, 'Our brother is hurt! Help us!'

At her voice, the stranger stopped. He turned and retreated; he disappeared into the terrain, first his legs, then his torso, finally the white ball of his head, as if sucked down by the land. The dog went with him. Maren's voice had scared them. They must have looked like spirits come from the dead.

By then, Kushim was flaccid and gray and cold in her arms. His breathing was shallow. Every breath felt like it could be his last, like he might forget to inhale.

'What do we do now?' Maren cried.

Leerit didn't know. She had never known. She was just eighteen years old—how could this be on her?

Maren said, 'There's nowhere to go. This river is too deep to wade.'

The stranger returned, this time followed by an old woman.

Their dog swam across the riffle. He had thick black-and-white fur, and he swam halfway with his nose held high—like any dog, he wanted their scent. The old man shouted and the dog turned back. When he emerged from the water, he shook then ran straight to the man and licked his hand.

The woman was pointing. She was gesturing upstream. Pointing a finger and calling out in words that made no sense. Maren said, 'Do you think there is a ford?'

They waded where the woman directed them. The water rose to Leerit's waist. A wide river, more water than she had ever heard described. Suspended across her arms, Kushim was limp but for his splinted leg. Her brother's mouth hung open.

The stranger wore a thick hat over her ears. She had deep-set eyes, and her skin was a fabric of wrinkles. A toothless smile. There, on a boulder halfway between them, she had left something. Maren lifted a piece, smelled it, took a bite. She put a nibble to her brother's mouth. The lips didn't move.

The old woman waved; she wanted them to follow. Leerit didn't know what else to do.

Up the slope, they came to a round tent erected against a shelf of rock that offered protection from the wind. About the edges of this camp were fat birds with large breasts and small wings. They scratched and pecked the ground and scurried off ahead of the dog. Leerit hadn't seen a chicken since they ate their last hen years before.

When the old woman spoke, her barren bottom gum showed. Her words sounded like the swooshing of a brush over wood.

Maren said, 'I think she wants you to bring him inside.'

They sat in the warmth of this strange, smoky place with Kushim laid out before them. He was shivering on a pelt of short fur. The tent was made from the same fur, pelts stitched together. The fur worn by the white animals they had seen moving as a herd. The old couple had some-how built their life from these nameless creatures.

Instead of a hearth and a proper chimney, a primitive fire was built on the ground in the center of the room. Above was a hole in the ceiling, and the smoke rose toward it. The air reeked of creosote, and most of the fire's heat vanished out the hole. There was no reason to build a fire in this messy way. Over the heat hung a pot. Inside, the water was cracking and fizzling. The old woman stirred.

Kushim was so pale, he had gone dry. One hand was a fist.

The old woman's mouth made clicking sounds as she worked. Pouring the boiled water into a wooden bowl. Stirring as she added something white, white with flecks of red and black—some kind of salt?

The woman wanted Kushim. Maren said, 'Let her. Maybe she can fix him.'

The woman lifted his tooth-torn arm and slid the bowl underneath and lowered the ragged flesh into the water. Using the currents created by her hand, she cleaned his bite wound. Kushim grumbled but did not open his eyes. 'It's okay.' Maren was caressing his cheek. 'She's helping you.'

After a long time, the old woman lifted his cleansed arm from the water and snapped her chin at the man, who was watching from the entryway. He crossed the space and took the bowl and disappeared outside. When he returned, he was carrying the same bowl, now empty.

The old woman poured new hot water and stirred in more medicine and repeated the process, this time backing Kushim's head into the bowl until his bloody scalp was submerged. The hair came free first and waved in the waters. Kushim's eyelids fluttered.

The old woman took a fist of his hair. She looked at Maren. What she said made no sense. When she pulled back the tattered fillet of scalp, Kushim's unbroken arm jumped.

———

The stitching left a pattern from the bridge of his nose up across where hair should be growing. The old woman used sinew thread—but rather than a bone needle, she used one made from the same material as her cooking pot. Orange, hard. When the woman drew this needle up, the wound closed. Kushim did not react. His sleep was too deep.

Afterward, the old woman was slow to stand. Maren took her bony elbow and helped her to her feet. The white-haired man was grunting from the doorway. When Leerit looked, he smiled to be seen. He gestured. These grunts were for her.

The woman offered Leerit a clay vessel. 'It's a chore,' Maren said. 'I think you're being asked to help.'

She had to be dreaming, following an old man through rocks to the top of a bluff. Who were these people? What river valley was this? It was all she could do to take another step. She had promised Kushim she would protect him and now she was covered in his blood, and who was this old man she was trusting?

The dog moved closer, near enough to smell her but not near enough that she might pet him. Her hands were stained, her robe, her pant legs. She saw now how much blood her brother had lost.

The old man stopped on a crest of land to behold the white animals with thick fur. A herd that showed no alarm at the sight of people. The old man pointed and made the same sound repeatedly. '*Mysheep.*'

'Mysheep,' Leerit finally said.

He smiled. '*MYsheep.*'

He removed a curl of rope and moved down the hill toward the animals.

A mother lifted her head and bawled, and the whole herd called back and began to move off. Not spooked, just moving away. With skill, the old man tossed the rope and its loop landed around the neck of a young male. He didn't yank but merely drew the rope in, one slow length at a time. The old man was singing and his voice seemed to calm the creature.

He led it out of sight of its herd and produced a strange, shiny blade. With no ceremony, he drew the edge along its neck. He pointed the knife at the vessel in Leerit's hand. Which he then held to the pulsing flow. He was still singing as the creature's eyes became vague. Soon the blood slowed and the man pulled away the vessel as *mysheep* tipped headfirst into the ground and began to kick violently now that it was too late.

Together they dragged the carcass back to camp. The blood was for Kushim to drink. Leerit understood the importance of drinking blood when a person had lost so much of their own. Maren took the vessel at the doorway. 'She has bound his broken bones.'

'His eyes, did they open?'

'Not yet.'

The man whistled; he was pointing at the carcass. Their chore had only begun.

She helped him break the animals into parts, but not as Opi would. First, they hung it by the hind feet from a tripod of poles, and the man showed great skill in peeling the skin off as a sleeve—not as a flat pelt. He cut this animal as she would never think to.

He wanted her to use his bright blade, which slid easily through meat and tendon. It was heavy in the hand. She used it to free each muscle, one by one. A good tool.

He took back his knife and sliced strips from the liver and offered her the honor of the first piece. She slurped its warmth. She took another piece when the old man offered, and another, and another. He kept offering her slices. She was burping liver but didn't dare refuse because it was rude to turn down a gift. Finally, the old man laughed, and she understood: he would keep offering until she declined.

There was a well-used fire ring and the stranger built up the fire and placed over the coals a femur. This he overlaid with thick cuts of belly fat. It made no sense. He sang as he watched the rich food flare and turn to smoke.

Then he rubbed a cut of meat with salt and pushed a limb through the center. This he set carefully over the heat, now taking care not to let it burn.

When he stood, he wiped his hands and said something she couldn't understand. A large vat was set against the cliff wall, and he turned its lid and took a cup from a lip of rock and reached his full arm down into this container.

His eyes were gray and his face weather-beaten, but he wore a boy's grin when he offered her the cup. A gift. As white as milk but too clear for milk. The smell was something like the pulpy fluid in an elk's stomach. She didn't want to be rude.

The drink was heat sliding down her throat. She thought it poison, but then he downed a much larger portion for himself. He wanted her to have more. So she did. Her fingers were changing; they were becoming tingly and numb, as if they were deciding to become their own fingers, no longer part of her body.

The dog sat between them beside the fire. The man was talking now, at the dog, at the sky. Explaining things. His hands gestured not unlike the hands of old men in the village. She believed it was her exhaustion that had started the clouds spinning.

Twice more he returned to the vat to refill the cup. One side of the meat had blackened over the coals before either of them noticed. The old man only turned the roast and laughed. He had more meat in this herd than he could ever consume.

He tried to teach her a game. He rolled a white river rock, and they took turns tossing pebbles at it. The winner got to drink the juice. By then, she was seeing two or three river rocks where there was only one. The drink was clearly poison. But, somehow, she couldn't make herself care. When he offered, she drank more.

The old man was naming things. She mimicked his sounds. He laughed to hear her try, which made her laugh. '*Mutt.*' '*Yurt.*' '*Liquor.*' '*MYwoman.*'

Who was coming. At the sight of the old woman, Mutt leapt to his feet and tucked his tail and trotted a safe distance away.

Mywoman took the cup from the old man's hand. She held it between them and pointed at the burned meat. He swiped at the cup, but she simply lifted it higher and the man missed. He looked so foolish, Leerit couldn't help but laugh.

When the old man saw Leerit laughing, he said something that was in any language a curse on his wife. Mywoman retreated to the shelter, but she left with the cup. After that, the strange man was in no mood for games.

Leerit doubled and spewed milky liver across dark rocks.

The old woman was muttering and angry when she returned inside. Maren slid closer to Kushim. The woman returned her remedies to their places and took up a brush of feathers and swept the dust and ash off her things. Then her nose wrinkled with some smell.

She took Maren's wrist and lifted her to standing. Not rough but not tender either. She smelled Maren's shoulder and made a sour face. They used to bathe each day at home, twice in the warm season. But she hadn't bathed since leaving. Her robe was sour. Maren felt her face flush. 'Usually I am clean,' she said. 'I swear.'

The woman led Maren outside by the wrist. She pointed toward the river. Offered what could only be soap. The mushy oval smelled of tallow and ash.

Leerit was wobbling near the fire. 'His name is Chun!' she called in a voice much too loud. 'You have to hear him try my name!'

Maren came near to steady her big sister. 'What happened to you?'

'We played games!'

Maren pulled Leerit from the old man, from their fire, from whatever had changed her. Leerit didn't protest being led. Maren told her big sister, '*You* never play games.'

Leerit stumbled and laughed. 'It's like this is the only place I've ever been!'

At the river, her big sister splashed into the shallows with no concern for the clothes she was still wearing. 'Swim with me! Come on! All the way to the ocean!'

'Leerit, stop. You're scaring me. What's wrong with you?'

Leerit seemed glad to be floating away.

IX

Resistance

A t the shortening daylight, Lilah knew her birth sign had passed. It was the final moon before solstice and she was now a thirty-nine-year-old woman.

She could remember when her mother was thirty-nine. Fish still rolled beyond the surf; the rivers were filled with spawning, every net busy. Fish bellies smoked and delivered. Seared loin, tallow-fried maize, pickles, eggs, dancing, fat on your thighs. Once, that was thirty-nine.

Her task was to wash the wool in its filthiest form, sweat stains and worse, the robes and pants and hats of those who labored. In their pockets, she found flecks of dry leaves and crumbles of dirt, pebbles and rocks; one day she found a withered apple and watched as Kenta ate through its core. This morning, in a pocket, she found a shell. The spiraling cavern of a sea snail, faded to white by years on land. No one noticed as she slipped it into her sleeve.

Overhead, the wind roared inland. She knew the Sea must be white chop and thundering swells. Beach sand that had accumulated all summer was now being swept away on the tide. Not even the most daring fishermen would launch their canoes in this season. It was time for repairing nets, for staying put, for eating what you had stashed. *Be the water who rests in a pool, and soon you will rush again.*

The warriors called *guards* patrolled the walls, which stood too high and smooth to scale. Be the friendly dog, she had told the girls, be the river who bends and so always arrives home to her Sea. Yet Lilah herself was done bending. Her babies needed their mother. They had to know she was trying.

Her hands in the hot water, her face in the steam—she traveled backward from this confinement to the ocean. Recalling every turn, each in order, delivering herself and the sisters to those boats tied to planks. Setting sail in her mind, remembering every detail about how the men handled the rigging, steered that strange boat. Conjuring each headland and cove, the reef where waves broke in midocean, the waterfall where they refilled their jugs. This story she told herself ten times a day, twenty. At night, she traversed the sands of their beach holding a pot heavy with stew. *I am trying.*

Some robes wore dark bloodstains. There were pants with mud-caked knees. Wood chips stuck among fibers of wool. Sand that no amount of washing or beating could remove. Ingrained smoke that turned her stomach when it met the cauldron's heat. In that steam, she was breathing the sweat of strangers. Who would never think of her. While somewhere her own babies could be giving up. Because, by now, they had to assume their mother was never coming home.

The woodcutters had already finished bucking and splitting their day's load when another delivery of logs arrived. It hadn't happened like this before. Every other day there had been just one delivery of logs. This time, Koneet refused.

In the light of flames, the sweat on her skin and hair gave off steam. Koneet remained sitting while the other woodcutters pleaded with her in their desert sounds. 'Do you see my hands?' Koneet showed them. 'They're bleeding!'

A guard approached with his blade. Trinket rushed on fast feet and put herself between him and Koneet. She bowed to the guard. She spoke without pause. Whatever she said seemed to settle this man. He sheathed his blade.

Trinket tried to pull Koneet to standing. Yet the maiden remained sitting with her arms crossed. Trinket raised her voice. She slapped Koneet.

'What's happening?' Kenta asked. 'Is sister okay?'

Trinket retreated. She bent to the fire under a cauldron and took up a piece of wood with a glowing red end. When she returned, she put this smoking wood before Koneet's face. A final warning. By now, everyone was watching.

Koneet wouldn't even uncross her arms. Always a Left-Coast woman.

Trinket touched the red ember to her ear. Koneet screeched and came to her feet.

Kenta called to her sister, 'Please! Don't get hurt!'

The one called *manager* watched from above. The guards watched the gate. Trinket was always somewhere watching. In this village, there were so many eyes.

By now, Lilah understood the most dangerous eyes belonged to the manager. Most afternoons, he sent a guard to fetch a woman. He preferred a certain woman, a woodcutter, similar in age to Koneet but with softer edges, with eyes that didn't know how to refuse. This woman had no choice but to climb the stairs and enter the manager's open door.

For those endless moments, their work slowed. Every woman over her cauldron watched that door. Trinket paced. Through steam and smoke, a village of women waited for any sign.

It happened most every day, and yet Trinket did nothing to stop this man. She stood by as he took a girl up the stairs. What kind of woman would let a man do such a thing?

One afternoon, a guard rushed across the yard. He shoved an elderly woman who had been stirring. She fell to the ground. To see it, Lilah gasped.

This woman was the last of her generation. Bent in the shape of her labors, she could no longer lift sopping wool from the cauldron without Trinket's help. The guard forced this elder to her knees in the middle of the yard. He pointed a finger as if she were a mischievous dog.

Another guard dumped her cauldron, and the boiling water and dark wool spilled steaming over the cobbles. By then, the manager was descending his stairs.

Kenta asked about the commotion as she always did. 'Auntie?'

The manager lifted a piece of this ruined wool. Smelled it. The old woman had let the water get too hot and the wool had felted. She didn't look up at the men with blades who loomed over her. Her ancient hands were clasped and shaking.

The manager began a pronouncement, this man who had nothing and yet thought himself worth listening to.

'Auntie? Is Koneet okay?'

'Koneet is okay. Shush now.'

A guard began thumbing the edge of his long blade. As the manager climbed his stairs, the guard stepped within range. He readied his feet. He touched his edge to the back of the old woman's neck. She was singing; she didn't stop singing.

'No more,' Koneet said that night during supper. Only Kenta could eat, for she hadn't witnessed what they had. 'Tomorrow it could be us. I would rather die at Sea.'

By then, the corridor was lit by torches and cold air gusted down the passageway. The manager had left in his carriage; the night guards would be sitting in their wool robes and hats at the gate, warming their hands over the single remaining fire. Trinket and the other women were washing and shitting ahead of the nightly prayer. Here, now—it was the rare moment when no one was watching. Lilah could almost hear Kushim crying out for her in the night, her boy waking to learn again his nightmare was real. 'Yes,' she said.

The room where they ate dinner had two doors, the one they used to enter and another that was always shut. But she knew that behind this door food was made; the cookstove's heat could be felt through the door's wood. Somehow ingredients were entering from outside the gates, but she never saw them come through the main gate. There had to be another way inside, another way out. Lilah pushed, she shoved, but the door was clearly latched from the other side.

'Try this,' Koneet said. She offered the spoon from her bowl. It was made from the same material as their cauldrons and the guard's blades. *Bronze.*

Lilah slid the butt end of the utensil into the crack of the door. She slipped the bronze up until it met resistance. She bumped the spoon upward, once, twice, three times, and felt the latch give. The door swung with a creak.

Oven-warm air overtook them. They could see everything in the flickering illumination of torchlight. The stewpot. Wooden bowls. A lingering ember shining through a crack in the cookstove. Tomorrow, a few women and children would come to this room to cook the evening's meal, but now the room was empty.

Lilah crossed to another door. But instead of opening to the outside, this one revealed steps leading underground. 'I smell meat,' Kenta said.

Koneet went first with a torch for light. They descended into a long room with sacks and barrels, boxes and vessels. Strings of dried herbs, endless braids of onions, piles of squash, dark hindquarters on cure— food enough for seventy women for a season, more than Lilah ever imagined in one place at one time. To see it, Koneet laughed.

At the far end of the room were a set of wide doors. They hurried. Lilah freed the latch and shoved but the wood didn't budge. It was locked also from the outside. This time the spoon didn't work. In desperation, Koneet drove her shoulder into the door. She tried kicking. 'Help me! I can't do this alone!'

Lilah took hold of her arm. 'Someone will hear. You have to stop.'

'If we bring this home,' Koneet said. 'We can feed the village.'

It was true, Lilah realized. With so much food, she could put fat on the bones of her babies. She could give her son a double chin. All she had to do was get this food to a boat.

Koneet kept driving her shoulder into the immovable door. She would break herself before she stopped trying.

A creak from the kitchen. Lilah lifted the torchlight. At the far end of the room stood Trinket.

They were led into the sleeping quarters. Made to kneel. After hearing Trinket's sounds, the women sucked their teeth. Lilah needn't understand the language to feel shame. She understood. In a village, the actions of one were a risk to all. She was thirty-nine but felt fourteen again.

Trinket led Kenta across the room to her own bed. Protecting the child from whatever punishment was coming.

The guards were not summoned. Instead, Trinket pinched between knuckles the flesh of Lilah's upper arm, and twisted. It was a fierce pain, worse than a burn. She did the same to Koneet, who gasped but did not struggle.

And so it commenced. Every woman in the room took a turn hurting them. Not eagerly. Nor from anger. They did so with pity in their eyes. Which made the pain worse. This cruelty to protect them all.

X

Escape

In death, his father remained a stranger, his life's most impenetrable mystery, this man who made him yet could spare no time for him.

Except for one week, maybe ten days, when they went together to the Highlands. Cyrus was just nine years old then. On the ride, his father named each mountain. They slept in the same tent; they ate lamb kabobs cooked over a campfire. He told adventures from a time when wild creatures still roamed the countryside. For a week or ten days, his father was a man who held his son's hand—who whispered. He promised, *Together, we'll check on the flocks every year.* Yet they never went again.

The road to General Rah's estate was brushed clean of sand, and the carriage hardly rattled for the exquisitely smooth cobbles. A bronze gate with the Rah crest swung open before them and closed promptly behind. Soldiers were standing in the courtyard, on the stone wall, everywhere with bows and long gleaming swords. 'Jernod. Should I be employing more guards?'

'Perhaps, sir.'

The morning's news, conveyed over breakfast by his manservant, was enough to sour a stomach. In the fields on the edge of the city, a farmworker's revolt. In the alleys near the city's center, a police officer stoned to death. The acts of irredeemable men, the kind who would cut off their own foot just to have something to throw at you.

Jernod had driven Cyrus and his father into the Highlands all those years before. He was a man of grit and metal, scars and armor. He seemed the same age then as now, a grown man younger than Cyrus's father. They were waiting for General Rah's manservant to fetch them from the courtyard. 'Jernod, can I ask a question?'

'Sir, I serve at your pleasure.'

Given the hours they spent together, perhaps no one alive had known his father better than his driver. 'I wonder if he ever spoke of me, my father.'

'Often, sir. You were his greatest pride.' On Jernod's face was not a performative smile but the genuine warmth of a man reminiscing. 'If only you could have seen him the day you were born.'

'Before you came to work for my father, what were you? I'm only curious.'

'Sir, I was a sergeant in the Fifth Regiment of the Imperial Scouts. I fought against the primitives during the Final Uprising. The Master heard of my service and offered me a lifetime of employment.'

'The Final Uprising?' Cyrus had been obsessed with the war and its battles as a boy. Three tribes of heathens had united in an attempt to drive the Emperor's army into the sea. They might have succeeded if the Sun hadn't sent a three-month heat wave to dry up every lesser water source. The heathens boiled within their sandy hideouts. Jernod didn't seem old enough to have participated in such a momentous turn of history.

'Sir, I was born to serve the Empire. My father gave his life in battle and my mother performed faithfully as a domestic for forty-eight years. Service is our blood.'

'Do you still think of him?'

'Sir. I talk to my father every day.'

A mystery in part because what did they ever have in common? His father was a man drawn to figures, every effort balanced exclusively against its most immediate returns. In the evening, when his father read beside the fire, in his hands were lists, numbers. *Old stories can't help this family*, he said when Cyrus first expressed interest in scholarship.

General Rah's manservant led Cyrus into the great room, which was empty. Up here, high above the city, sunlight spilled through windows. On the walls, golden sculptures of bygone beasts sat perched on hard-wood shelves: lions, stags, mountain rams, long-legged antelope. General Rah had taste. It was what his father had always wanted: to be the kind of man who possessed art, water features, a bowling green. By comparison, their estate across the valley was a drab imitation.

Here actual battlefield spears were crossed on the wall, complete with bloodstains gone brown. There was a stone knife still seated in its bone handle. Beside it was a copper sword and four patinaed daggers. The history of civilization written in its weapons.

General Rah called from the threshold. He wasn't wearing the uniform Cyrus expected but instead a cloak and tunic of rich fibers. Taller than his father, decidedly more handsome. Straight bangs and greased gray hair to his shoulders, a lean and athletic build even now in his sixties. 'Join us outside,' Rah said brightly. Then, with a hand on Cyrus's shoulder, 'I apologize. My prior has run late.'

They crossed a veranda where a dozen of General Rah's chubby wives lounged in chairs eating meat cut from a hindquarter on a rotisserie. An offering of femur overlaid with fat was sending its black smoke toward the Sun. Not many could afford additional wives; the taxes went up precipitously after the first. In stride, General Rah hopped to his bowling green, and the gems about his neck and ears clinked.

In the distance, the ocean extended blue and forever. A soldier was patrolling the grass, two swords crossed on his back, two knives in his belt, bulbous muscles overlaid by tattoos. The breeze stirred his wavy hair. 'A stunning vista,' Cyrus said.

General Rah took aim and rolled a bronze ball toward the hole cut in his turf.

The man gaming with him wore a tailored beard made more dignified by its graying chin. The type of man to whom Cyrus would've had to bow not long before, the governor of drama, the man who ran the theater. Cyrus knew in a half-thought why he was here: to solicit contributions, the same reason he used to visit Cyrus's father. The governor said, 'I fear I require many rolls to the general's few.'

General Rah offered Cyrus a bronze ball. 'You can't know how dreadfully I miss your father. A rare competitor he was.'

Cyrus sent the ball and they watched it bend across the grass and past the hole. The soldier had to skip to avoid being struck. His father had once told him, *The bowl follows the eye.* Now Cyrus told the truth. 'My father was routinely disappointed by his son's game.'

'I understand you are a man of letters like myself,' the governor said, this a blatant segue to his real pitch. 'As General Rah and I were just discussing, the arts are ever more crucial in times of uncertainty. Not only for the continued support of the children I safekeep but also for taming the public's alarm; only an inspired entertainment can lift the common man from his worries. I wonder how you, Master Cyrus, would like to see the next performance play out. I am especially interested to hear your insights.'

General Rah offered the governor an envelope, which he tucked into his breast pocket without a glance. Their game was not yet over but their meeting was. The governor smiled broadly. 'I best leave you two important men to your parlay. Praised be our Sun.'

'Praised be the Emperor,' they both responded in unison. 'And may health continue to bless the heir,' General Rah added.

'How are you faring?' he asked once they were alone. Rah was tall enough to look Cyrus in the eye. His own father had been looking up since Cyrus turned fifteen. Rah asked, 'Your father's men, the managers—have they been helpful with the transition? When is the marriage?' He squeezed Cyrus's bicep with startling force. 'You know I married late as well. Let me assure you that married life doesn't have to be as desiccated as our fathers made it appear.' He gestured toward his wives. 'Perhaps you would like to try one on?'

Cyrus offered the conspiratorial grin he knew he should. 'Can I have them all at once?'

'Ha!' General Rah put in his palm a heavy bowler. 'Let us talk and game, game and talk.'

'I want to thank you,' Cyrus began. 'The support you've offered my family is immensely generous. Though I fear my mother wasn't clear on the details of our terms.'

General Rah lined up a throw but didn't send it. 'Your father's financial troubles, they're partially the result of his . . . well, he was gullible, wasn't he? Never a skeptical investor. Too quick to trust, to believe, to bet on any old scheme so long as the dolt pitching was wellborn. I'm not being rude; it's perfectly admirable that he climbed as high as he did, given his humble origins.' Rah sent the bowler and it bent with the terrain to fall heavily into the cup.

Cyrus felt an unfamiliar sensation: the urge to defend his father. 'He was not the type of man to let an opportunity go to waste.'

'These days,' Rah continued, 'no man can escape the economic headwinds buffeting the Empire. With the drought, they've become gales. The corn harvests are half what they were. The rye, the quinoa, the barley—name a crop and it is down. With the building of the ark, even lumber is in short supply. This winter'—Rah gestured toward the collectives and shanties below with a dismissive flick of the wrist—'even the middle classes will be left cold. Go on, roll.'

Cyrus watched his own ball bend and miss the cup. 'All true, and yet I am tasked with meeting a steep new quota.'

'Cyrus. You're too young to be cynical.' Rah came nearer. 'Your father was proud of you. I was glad to learn you were pursuing scholarship. Do you know that I too fancy myself a reader? Not a serious learned man like yourself but an enthusiast. I maintain my own collection. Would you like to see?'

The general's 'collection' surely consisted of a few dozen scrolls copied hastily by an enterprising hand, aged centuries by an afternoon left in sunlight, and sold with hearty testaments to authenticity. There was always a robust market for counterfeits. 'I would savor the opportunity, sir.'

'If only we could live a thousand years. From what I hear, Cyrus, you are a highly decorated scholar.'

'Were, sir. I am a master now.'

'Yes, well, freshly. The deans tell me that you were their standout, on your way to becoming the first of your generation to make senior scholar. A pity your father left us so soon. I would have liked to follow your career.'

This startled him. Cyrus had never heard anyone outside the archives speak of the deans or of being interested in a scholar's promotions. 'Did the deans really say that?'

'Cyrus, understand there remain very few masters who are still turning true profits. You may think otherwise; it may look otherwise. But most every man in your position is sustaining himself on credit against future earnings.'

'Future earnings?'

'We can't have austerity now,' Rah continued. 'We must buoy ourselves through what will be a tough winter. Imagine if tomorrow prominent men like you and me halved our staffs? Or worse, opened the gates to our indentured?' The general moved a finger and a muscle-bound soldier bent to fetch the balls. 'I would be fine, as I command the faith of the army, but you—you wouldn't last a quarter-moon.'

On huge feet, the soldier crossed the distance and dropped one heavy bowler square in Cyrus's palm. With him came a gust of musky underarm. Cyrus refused to let himself look at the muscles. 'Sir, I am hoping to clarify our terms of repayment.'

With a firm hand to the back, General Rah turned Cyrus toward the ocean. 'Honestly. What do terms matter between friends?'

'Friends, sir?'

'Old friends,' Rah assured him. 'A father's friends become his son's. Loyalty transcends generation. Does it not?'

Amid gusting winds, they walked toward the next green, which sloped down and away. 'Across that senseless water,' the general said, 'everything will be better. We won't be bound by old mistakes. Next time we'll grow the whole affair from only the most loyal elements. Cull the irredeemable once and for all. No bounty shall go to waste. On those shores, men like us will prosper as never before—so long as we stay united. Don't you agree?'

'Yes sir.'

General Rah seized Cyrus's hand in both of his own. 'Promise me. No more cynicism. Cynicism from men like us could rot the very timbers that float the Empire. Our task now is to maintain the tack. If only for a bit longer.'

That night, as usual, Cyrus couldn't sleep.

He started by going through his father's ledgers for the hundredth time if only to measure what qualified as the typical rate on a loan between *friends*. He was surprised to find a pattern within the numbers: as the years passed and his father took on additional debts, the cost of those debts diminished rather than grew. Cyrus had never been the type to find sense in numbers, but he couldn't well imagine a story in which the stakes of the conflict *decreased* as the pages turned.

Whenever he hadn't been able to sleep in the dormitory, he returned to the archives to read scrolls by lantern light. But at home in the estate, he had access only to those stories distributed by the Emperor; they were printed on common parchment for bulk circulation among the literate classes. So Cyrus stoked a fire against autumn's chill and pulled a wool blanket over his lap and settled in to read all that he had.

In one way or another, every scroll involved the green shore awaiting them across the water. He reread the well-known account of those brave sailors sent with a command to turn back only once they found greener land. The details of their voyage were riveting. Those who survived the journey described finding green meadows with chest-high graze, snow-capped mountains, groves of wild fruit trees extending beyond sight. What they saw inspired enchanting turns of phrase: 'Gentle fingers pressing streams of sweet juice from any fruit.' 'Bubbling brooks charged with their own native effervescence.' 'Here waits the gift of a landscape whose soil has not been dented by the human foot.'

Yet, on this night, even mediocre poetry could not put him to sleep.

He woke his manservant, who woke Jernod, who dutifully readied the horses and carriage. By torchlight, they crossed the sleeping city and found the campus well lit. The guards at the archives' gate recognized him despite his new garments; a few laughs and coins, and they let him enter even though he technically no longer had access. He knew the scholarly interests of the clerk on duty and took the time to ask a few meaningful questions. Then, finally, Cyrus was left alone in the familiar stacks. They smelled like dust and parchment. He was home. He pulled a well-known scroll and sat at his usual table lit by lantern light. As soon as he began reading, he yawned.

Once two kingdoms stood on either side of a body of water. Treaties bound their generations in uneasy harmony. Yet petty disagreements swelled like rising tides between them, and soon they forgot their loyalties.

The clashes began on minor islands, conflicts that killed the strongest warriors by the thousands. Yet each king had more sons to send to their deaths, and their war became perennial. Each new battle was cause for new revenge. Until no one remembered who first raised his sword.

The Sun was not pleased to see such senseless bloodletting. At last, He intervened to end what men would not.

He picked the king who wasted the least and sent the richest offerings on black smoke. Upon the other kingdom, He sent a drop of light falling from the heavens as a minor stone. No one who saw it coming would fear something so small. But when this stone struck, it bloomed into an orb of solar heat capable of melting mountains. An entire island became ash, every citizen a plume of vapor. At Dawn, the Sun sent another, and He would have sent a thousand over a thousand days to end what kings had started.

Cyrus woke upon the parchment. All day, he was too tired to think clearly. He returned home from a series of mind-numbing meetings to find his mother waiting for him. She was holding a list of names. 'How long would you have me wait to make an invitation?'

'Sir.' It was the manservant. He was bowing from a doorway. 'May I have a word?'

'Go on,' Cyrus said with relief. 'Speak freely.'

'It's the prince and heir. Sir. It pains me to convey this news.'

His mother covered her mouth. Cyrus stood at attention. 'Yes, what is it?'

'Sir, we—' The servant's voice faltered. 'We have received word. The newborn prince has perished.'

For two days after the announcement, his mother remained in her quarters. He spent long hours alone in the aviary. It was like beginning their mourning all over.

On the third day, he and his mother agreed they should eat together. Father always wanted the family to eat together. They arrived to find their seats placed at either end of the long table. His mother asked the manservant to move her closer.

When they were alone together at the head of the table, she began to cry. Her husband was gone and never coming back; the prince was dead;

142

the sand kept coming on every wind. She apologized for the show of emotion but then didn't stop crying.

Once he had assumed he would grow to become a senior scholar and his father would finally say how proud he was; the rains would return and the crops would thrive as they were meant to; the sand would finally be pushed back, and he and Ashair would become grizzled old men attending the theater together, too old to draw scrutiny. Now his mother asked the question that scared him most: 'What if the Sun has turned against us? What if we have somehow offended Him?'

Cyrus knew what his father would say. 'These are matters for men. Leave your worry to me.'

The princely funeral was unlike any other. Sorrowful horns called out from every corner of the capital. As citizens chanted, crows circled in silent witness—before spiraling to feast. The Emperor's infant son had lived only thirty-seven days.

'Why?' people cried from testament stones. 'What if there is no heir?' 'Why does the Sun allow such suffering?' Even the priests struggled to answer. Like everyone else, they had known the prince to be protected by solar hands.

At the appointed hour, Cyrus knelt before the estate's central fireplace. The air over the city had become dark and caustic. He offered plastic gems to the flames and watched them melt, as he should, these offerings to be carried on black smoke toward a most remote god. 'Forgive us,' he prayed. 'Forgive me. I will be better.'

Then finally Dawn came on the appointed day. He and Ashair were to meet; at last, nothing could keep them apart.

Yet an urgent last meeting with a harried manager made Cyrus late to the rendezvous, and Ashair was no longer waiting. Cyrus gave Jernod directions to Ashair's neighborhood. His driver didn't ask how he knew the way to this doctor's house.

When the lowborn saw Cyrus coming, they stared. Some even forgot to bow. Since the prince's death, the city seemed colder, less populated.

He left the carriage and walked alone to a row of identical wooden doors. One belonged to Ashair but which? Each shanty looked the same.

The old woman who answered gasped at the sight of him. With both hands held open, he tried to reassure her, but in his helmet and cape she saw only the tax collector.

'Ashair!' he shouted. 'The doctor. Which door is his?'

Three apartments farther down the row. He was about to knock when this door was pulled open under his hand. But not by Ashair—by the wife.

Lean with sharp features, her hair was righteously decorated and her eyes bottomless. She stared with zero deference for him. She said, 'He's not here.'

He knew her name. Of course he did. They had met before, at the theater, when she was on Ashair's arm. But in this moment, he couldn't remember what the wife was called.

Her eyes narrowed. 'You and my husband have been good friends.'

'We have,' he said. 'We are. Professionally speaking.'

She didn't blink. 'You've been friends long enough, don't you think?'

He tried smiling. 'I don't understand.'

'Has he told you our good news?'

'Ma'am?'

'Ma'am?' She almost spit. 'Don't pretend to treat me with respect now. I'm pregnant. Of course he hasn't told you.'

'Such wonderful news,' Cyrus managed to say despite sudden dizziness.

'So.' She looked boldly into his eyes. 'This is it. My husband doesn't need any more lectures. He certainly doesn't need his superior assigning him to some senseless mission in the Highlands.'

It had been a smart ploy, Cyrus thought, a promised contribution to the medical school if Ashair was assigned as the attaché to an eleven-day, imperially endorsed expedition. He had delivered the news to Ashair himself outside the hospital. If Ashair had looked perturbed to learn they would be alone together in the Highlands, it was only because he would never allow himself such uncontested pleasure.

'Now that Ashair is going to be a father,' the wife continued, 'this boyhood game of yours will end. Yes?'

She began to shut her door. Cyrus stopped its swing with his hand. But then he couldn't think of what to say. He took off his helmet. Was this between him and Ashair a *boyhood game*?

'My Ashair is a good man,' she said. 'He cares about people. He cares about me. I beg you. Please, just go away and let my husband be a good man.'

How could it be a game when the consequences were so real?

At the age of fourteen, his father had taken Cyrus to see a master accused of hiring fornication with a male. A frail, stooped man was kneeling before the prominent testament stone outside the theater, where a towering bronze sculpture of the Emperor atop a crag threw shade over the crowd gathered to watch. First the helmet, then the armor about his chest and back, the decorative wrist cuffs, then even the imperial wool underlayers—until this master was reduced to a naked man whose shriveled penis cowered inside his body.

'Will he be hanged?' Cyrus asked his father.

'Worse,' his father said with a hand gripping the back of Cyrus's neck. He would not let his son look away. 'This man will live a long life stripped of everything. His wife, his home, his every possession and friend. To eat, he will have to offer himself for indenture. Do not feel sorry for him. This is the consequence when one wastes the bounty of Sun-given seed in the dry cavity of a man.'

The hospital was bustling and Ashair was nowhere to be found. If Cyrus was annoyed, it was because precious daylight was going to waste.

'Let me go on your behalf, sir,' Jernod said. They had their carriage but also two more loaded with provisions and tents and muscle-bound men. The Highlands were notoriously unpredictable, and winter wasn't far off.

'No, I'll go,' Cyrus said. He refused to become one of those masters who was afraid to walk among the people. His heels smacked the cobbles.

Once inside the hospital, he had to cover his nose against the odor of filthy bodies. On every patch of ground were the poverty-stricken. Medical students rushed about. One student hurried now to bow. 'Master, are you ill? There's a better hospital. Shall I summon transport?'

Ashair was crossing the room. He was stooped under the weight of his medical kit and another satchel full of clothing. Here, with everyone watching, all Cyrus could think to say was 'You kept me waiting.'

Ashair bowed. 'Master, forgive me.'

Their caravan advanced up the streets, wheels chattering, and Ashair refrained from showing even the slightest hint of eagerness. They held their positions on either flank as two dignified men of varying caste should.

Soon they entered the industrial corridor where the resources of the Highlands met the workforce that would transform them. Lumberyards, granges, seed mills, smelters, meat poles, butchers, blacksmiths. Cyrus pointed to the facility that handled the dyeing of his fleece. He gestured toward another that laundered the city's wool, the very facility his father had acquired just last year. They were two of the best-kept buildings in the district, with high fences and freshly painted walls.

He had visited most of his managers during the past weeks to prepare them for what was to come, the push for every efficiency. He was now making the multiday journey to the encampment of the flock manager. In a normal year, this man would rotate the sheep and their shepherds about the stubby lowland fields along the river. By Equinox, those grounds would be mud, not a blade of grass left, and the animals would be thin. Cyrus had learned that the shortage of graze during this crucial winter period most affected the end weight of his wool. If he was to deliver a fifth more than last year, his shepherds would have to find more grass— and for that to happen, their manager would need to be properly motivated. Cyrus told Ashair, 'This journey is absolutely crucial to the future of the Empire.'

The carriage pushed through clouds of gritty smoke, which swirled in their wake. Jernod called warnings to those who busied the road with their journeys. Not the indentured but free men, many of whom were born to the indentured and rose up out of facilities like those Cyrus owned. These families lived in a collective or a hut by the river; they could make their own choices; their children might become merchants or soldiers or police. As it had been for countless generations.

A woman was carrying a loaf of bread as if it were a baby. A wide-shouldered man held a chicken by its hind legs in one hand and a knife in the other. But most people were turning to beg at the sound of the carriage's bronze-rimmed wheels. A hundred hungry faces. He made the mistake of meeting the eyes of an old woman. Her face looked like a skull draped in wet parchment.

Ashair's own grandparents had once been laborers, his great-grandparents indentured. Somewhere far back on his father's side, a few of Cyrus's own relatives had labored. Those generations rose from the lowly rungs when rising was still a forgone conclusion, the inevitable result of a lifetime of dignified effort. When the timber was endless, when corn was limited only by how many acres were planted, when the trade lines were maintained even in winter. Now he called to Ashair, 'You'll love the Highlands. There's no equal to natural beauty.'

They were to stay the first night where he and his father had, at a ranch that once tamed wild horses. By tomorrow midday, their carriage would be thundering across the unbroken expanse of empty lands where sheep and shepherds roamed as they had for centuries.

And yet with so much to look forward to and the Sun orange upon his skin, Ashair insisted on maintaining a terribly dour mood. They had never had such a chance: to spend full days together uninterrupted. The carriage was bucking with the pocked road. Cyrus pressed the edge of his smallest finger against Ashair's knuckle where it rested on the hand-rail. Flesh to flesh. Ashair finally looked at him: eyes full of mist and want and shame.

'You ought to know,' Cyrus said. 'I saw your wife.'

'Did you? Today you saw her?'

'Congratulations.'

'I was going to tell you.'

'When?'

'You know what this means,' Ashair said. They were moving faster now; they were leaving it all behind. 'We've known each other a long time.'

'Don't say *but*.'

'But . . .' Ashair lifted his chin toward the future. A tear left his eye and was pulled by the wind toward his ear. 'Everything must end.'

'Not this. Not yet. This doesn't have to.'

'Yes, you rich, stupid man. It does.'

XI

Drawn Apart

When no one was looking, Leerit drank greedily from the old man's stash. Chun found her on the ground unable to stand. He dragged her things outside the yurt; he moved his vat of merciful poison inside, and neither he nor his wife would let Leerit enter. What he barked at her must have meant *you should be ashamed.*

One night sleeping outdoors became eight, became nine, and Kushim only grew sicker.

Leerit slept curled in the bearskin beside an outdoor fire. By then, Mutt had decided to trust her. In the dark after the old couple was asleep, Mutt would come near and follow his tail in two tight circles and sink to the ground, his muzzle on his own paws, his flank against her. They slept like dogs together.

But he knew which allegiance mattered. At the first sounds of waking inside the yurt, Mutt would leave her and return to his place outside the doorway. If Chun was within sight, Mutt maintained his distance.

———

By day, she walked the river. It was bigger than any she'd ever heard described, but it was also only a fraction of itself, a thread within the massive floodplain, cobbled beaches and dry channels. She gathered arm-loads of driftwood that had washed to high ground and been cured by the summer sun. This wood she stacked on Chun's pile, each day grow-ing his stash, because he didn't have enough to last the winter. How peculiar that the man didn't stash wood for winter; what was wrong with these people? Each morning, she gathered eggs from the chickens for the old woman. These contributions were how she asked for forgive-ness. Winter was coming and her brother couldn't be moved and she wouldn't survive months of sleeping outside in the cold and dark.

Sheep bawled whenever they saw Leerit coming. From a distance, they looked like a swarm of insects. Close up, they were shaggy and ill at ease. The herd ventured farther each day from the camp, leaving hooved ground and scat in their wake. They had eaten the summer's grass to nothing. What remained was brown and brittle. She remembered the shrubs on the coast before the mothers decided to slaughter the last goats. *They will perish either way*, the mothers said to convince the men. *We should eat them while the bones still carry meat.*

Maren spent most of her day in the yurt with Lenka, the old woman, tending to Kushim. Whenever Maren emerged to toss wash water or urine, to fetch drinking water or gather wood from the stack Leerit had built, Maren talked of Kushim. The quaking caused by the fever, the swelling along his brow. He still hadn't uttered a word. Their brother who never stopped talking.

'There's pus,' Maren said. 'She bathes his head but there's always more pus. He's shriveling. Each morning there's less of him. I don't know what to do. I just sit there promising him everything will be okay. A hundred promises I don't know how to keep.'

On day ten, tiny flecks of snow blew sideways with the wind. There was no denying winter. Daylight was precious.

Leerit spent that dark morning piling rocks near the fire; she built herself a lee from the wind. Snow was already piling against it. The old man kept inside. Even the sheep remained bedded at the base of a nearby cliff.

To pass the time, Leerit picked ticks from Mutt's skin. The engorged insects hissed in the fire. It was already dusk when for no reason Mutt leapt from his place beside her and trotted into the wind. She thought he was going to growl but instead he whined. The stub of his tail began to wag.

Leerit stood too and stared into the gusts. She could only see a throw's distance. But then she heard it, a tinkle, rhythmic, like an instrument. A point of light, a man born of the storm. He carried a torch and was leading animals on a rope. The sound came from something tied to the neck of the lead creature. By then, Mutt was jumping in circles.

Goats. The man was leading six nannies burdened with satchels strapped to either side of their bodies from a wooden frame. The rope was affixed only to the lead animal, the mother. The others chose to follow on their own accord.

The man gave Mutt a treat, and Mutt rolled to let him rub his belly. Perhaps the man sensed her watching. His eyes searched for her in the darkness.

Chun called then from the doorway, and the man hollered back. She couldn't understand their words, but she knew Chun was happy to welcome his visitor.

——

He was a trader who had brought more of the worry-killing drink. In exchange, Chun gave sheep pelts, three of them. They talked this deal over inside the yurt, the trader testing the softness of the leather between his fingers, tugging the wool to make sure it was still seated tightly to the skin. Leerit watched secretly through a gap in the yurt, she and Mutt both. Mutt was whining.

When the trader lifted his robe, a puppy tumbled out, and Mutt barked. Maren held the puppy to her face. It was licking her madly. Maren giggled like a little girl on some beach.

The old couple began to argue before their guests. Finally, Chun swatted at the air and stood as if standing were unfair work. He crossed the room and dug under something to retrieve a last pelt he had kept hidden. The trader turned the skin in his hands, pulled at the wool. He patted the puppy on the head. Maren was too busy laughing to notice the trade.

Mutt helped the trader round up his goats. In firelight, he nodded at the knife in Leerit's belt, and said simply, 'We make deal?'

She had to look at him, at his glossy eyes, the flame reflected in them. She thought her ears were playing tricks.

The trader said, 'Not worth much but look at my things. Offer me.'

'You can talk.'

He smirked. 'No good the trader who don't talk.'

She took the goat's halter in her fist so this man couldn't leave. 'Where are others like me?'

'You people, ivory people, you want my salt.'

She gripped his jacket. 'Where?'

He came with her pull, offering no resistance. 'Give me knife. I tell you where.'

It was the knife Ama had made. She would never trade it.

'Trade or not, I don't care,' the man said. 'I go. Winter is near.'

She pulled the ivory from her pocket, two elk tusks she had planned to carve. 'For these, you tell me where.'

After the trader left, Maren tried putting a spoonful of broth to her brother's lips. The stitching that ran from the top of his nose up into his scalp had sunken within the swelling and left taut little valleys in his skin. Pink syrup dripped from the wound down the slope of his brow. The smell of him was foul. His lips hardly parted, but when she gave him the broth, his throat remembered how to swallow.

The day before, Lenka had built a new splint to hold the leg still, two poles on either side of the shin, leather cord wrapping it tightly. His skin over the broken bone was still purple and black and yellow. This shin was three times the width of the other. The bones had broken when the bear stepped on the leg, when the bear was biting at his arm or clawing at his head. In the wounds, she saw the bear on top of her brother—felt it again in her chest as it happened. She had seen this disaster coming. She could have prevented it.

When he gasped from his fever dream, she lifted the puppy and set him in the crook of her brother's arm. He didn't seem to notice. 'I named him Friend,' she said. 'Wake up and meet him. Kush. There's a puppy for you. Please, wake up. It's time to wake up. Kushim?'

The puppy leapt back to the ground. He wanted the broth.

Lenka was knitting and Chun was dozing with the empty cup parked on his belly. The robe Ama had made Maren was in the corner. It felt like betrayal, to shed the robe her mother had made and wear something sewn by another. But wool was warmer, and her robe was sour, and Ama wanted her children warm, didn't she?

The fire bent. Lenka looked and Maren turned to see her sister standing at the threshold. She stood in the gusting wind, the flap held open, snow sneaking past. Her sister's eyes were lit up by a most startling expression—a smile.

The bearskin was rolled and slung over her shoulder. Her knife was parked in the front of her belt where she kept it while covering ground. In this firelight, her sister glowed. 'They're upstream!'

'Who?'

'I'm leaving. You stay with him. Auntie and I will be back for you soon. Don't worry. Auntie will know the cure he needs.'

XII

Confluence

E ndless walking over sand, endlessly carrying of this vat of stew, which is going cold, scum forming over top, portions lapping over the edges until the vat is empty, dropping to her knees to scoop handfuls of broth-soaked sand, to put it all back. Still walking over dunes and down to houses half-buried, more walking, always walking.

Of course they don't come when you call. Why would they come? No matter how far you walk, you will not see your children.

A hundred years of walking, a thousand—then Lilah was aware of her body. Shaking, she was shaking. Here. Wet. This that is called a fever.

Where are my babies?

Trinket was sitting on a chair beside the bed. She looked at her own bunk on the far wall. Lilah could hardly see that far for the blurring of her vision. There, two shapes. Maren and Kushim together. Sick together.

Feed them. Please. They need to eat. Where is Leerit?

Trinket blew on Lilah's forehead. From her mouth came the voice of Lilah's mother on the mountaintop: 'Now let me watch over your babies.'

In the Highlands, the storm passed in time for Cyrus to see the ancient aqueduct on the far side of the river. The carriages were moving fast, and he barely had time to point out the strange black hole to Ashair, as his father had once to him. 'It looks like that hillside has an eye—what is that?' Ashair asked.

The metal was bent and yawning, torn open by some prehistoric sloughing of rock and debris. Whatever pieces had slid down into the river were now long gone. The black hole invited exploration, as any cave begs a man to light a torch. He had never climbed that high, but this aqueduct had become Cyrus's first scholarly obsession. Clearly forged by the Sun—for no earthly furnace could melt its metal—the aqueduct had, unquestionably, been bestowed to inspire the favored people to move water from a high-country spring to their growing population. What other explanation squared with reality?

Some scholars claimed that between its forging and its discovery the aqueduct had become a site of prehistoric pilgrimage for primitives who mistook it for a portal to their dead. Heathens would walk great distances for the chance to commune with those they had lost. Supposedly, green and blue pebbles could still be found piled in those places where they once stood to call down the shaft. Other scholars had traced these strange pebbles to the foot of a single mountain range sixty-five days' journey toward the zenith.

Of course a middle-class man like Ashair couldn't be expected to know as much. Cyrus expected questions about the moment of discovery, or the construction of their own aqueducts, or even the rituals of primitives; Ashair surprised him when he asked, 'The Sun gave a metal the Emperor has failed to melt?'

Cyrus voiced the obvious. 'The Sun didn't intend for the aqueduct to melt. He intended it to last. To teach us how to move water.'

Ashair raised an eyebrow. 'Now you claim to know the Sun's intentions? Have you ever considered that the Emperor might simply have failed?'

Cyrus managed to say, 'Cynicism is dangerous.'

Ashair stared. 'Dangerous to whom?'

They had passed agricultural fields where the indentured toiled with shovels and hoes, and managers watched from horseback. They had passed the entrance to one of Rah's plastic mines and saw laborers wheeling barrows from the earth and adding their loads to huge mounds that glistened with fragments. Powerful men shoveled this rubble into the flow of a sluice that carried the resulting slurry into a pond where still more indentured men corralled the floating plastics with brooms as they waded in what must have been icy water. A well-guarded facility on the city's outskirts would process the raw ore while others waited to mint coins and cut gems.

Ashair had never seen these industries in person, and yet he did not marvel at their size or organization or resilience. He saw only injuries—men working despite pain. He kept asking to stop, to help those in need. But there wasn't time. 'We are serving the greater good.' Their caravan had to reach the shepherds' camp before the snows arrived. 'Don't blame me,' Cyrus said. 'Blame the season.'

Now they were riding along a line of indentured men marching with roughhewn logs over their shoulders. Some were limping under the weight;

many were bleeding. Ashair wanted to stop. 'Faster,' Cyrus called to Jernod. The primitive faces became an endless blur.

At the rear of the convoy, Cyrus was surprised to see not a manager on horseback but the bronze armor of a fellow master's carriage. An arm appeared: the master waving them down. To not stop would be egregious, the stuff of gossip. Cyrus gave Jernod the command.

Without a word, Ashair hurried off toward the indentured, his medical kit slung from a shoulder. At the foreman's whistle, the laborers dropped their logs and immediately sat upon them.

Everywhere Cyrus looked, the mountains were cloaked in fog. The ground was packed brown and dusty. This master was wearing a thick robe, scarves, and a hood. Sand was stuck in the fibers. These cruel winds had turned his eyes to glass.

A fire was started and a wool carpet spread, and Cyrus reclined on an elbow. The guards had established a perimeter between them and the indentured, and for the first time all day, Cyrus could finally relax. In the distance, he saw a crowd gathering, countless men waiting their turn to speak to the doctor.

The master's people attended to the refinements. A lithe boy poured heated water over a collection of dried petals, and the air between them bloomed with the aromatics of summer. Cyrus held the cup in both hands to absorb its heat.

The master corrected Cyrus; he was two decades older and wielded his age in conversation. This lumber was *obviously* not destined for household heating. 'Only exclusive materials. My wood shall soon float our civilization across the ocean.'

The logs were long and straight with severed ends that glowed yellow. The tang of sap swirled with the wind. 'The ark requires such quantities?'

The master chuckled. 'What is an ark if not a forest rendered into planks? Better fast in our boat than rotting on some useless slope.'

The master was here only because his longtime manager—upon hearing about the new quota—had quit, a setback that forced the well-born man into the cold to oversee the last weeks of harvest himself. He pointed his beverage at the terrain. 'I will be glad to never see these drab slopes again.'

Cyrus knew the feeling. Nothing in the Highlands looked as he remembered it. Rather than wildflowers, minor spines of sand waited in the lees behind rocks.

'I cut this forest twenty years ago,' the master said with a flick of his limp hand. 'It was a tinderbox awaiting a spark. Farther up the valley, you'll see stands we didn't cut in time. Enough lumber to build ten arks burned to ash. Catastrophic waste.'

Their caravan proceeded into the dark on faith in the good sense of horses. Jernod stopped the animals only when they reached the lee of a cliff that blocked the wind. A fire was started and the guards began erecting tents in the light thrown and reflected back. For the first time, Cyrus wished he had sent a man in his stead. He could be home now, in the aviary, warm and reading. What was the point of enduring such hardship when Ashair insisted on suffering?

Cyrus found him washing beside the river. 'You wish I hadn't brought you.'

Ashair answered without looking. 'What does it matter what I wish?'

'To me it matters.'

Ashair came to his feet like a man ready to pounce. 'Do you feel nothing for them?'

'Who?'

'The timber fellers! The plastic miners! The crop workers! You don't even see them, do you? They're people, Cyrus. They're sons, brothers,

fathers. They have families. Or they had families—until they were stolen away.'

'*Stolen* is a strong word. Once maybe. Now the indentured come
willingly. Our employment is to them unfathomable charity. We alone
ensure they are well-fed.'

'You didn't just say *charity*.'

'You should see how much I spend on food. They're rewarded hand-
somely. Their children are rewarded, their children's children, because now
they don't have to live out in the wilds. It's our contract. Everyone has a
part to play and everyone benefits; nothing goes to waste. Honestly. You
are who you are because of indenture. Tell me, would you prefer your
kin had never found their way into the embrace of the Empire?'

'I hate that phrase,' Ashair said. '*Embrace of the Empire*. You can't really
believe that a man is better off working in a mine?'

'Better than starving. Besides, it is his children who will truly benefit. A man will do anything to help his children.'

Ashair laughed. 'One of those timber fellers said he hasn't been allowed a day off in three years. More, more, more, always more. Masters
name a day of rest *waste*. Constant harvest. Constantly using up men . . .'
Ashair's hand was now a fist.

'Every master is under his own pressures. You couldn't understand
the pressures.'

'Oh, couldn't I? To you, we are just numbers. You column, total, and
deduct us. Masters don't farm or mine or harvest trees—you do math!'

'Not me. Ashair. I'm not some brutal profiteer. You know me. I'm a
good person.' Cyrus stepped closer and tried a softer voice. 'Look. I
know there's so much that's wrong. But we didn't come here to argue.
Haven't we always dreamt of this? Days together, no one expecting us
home? Here, now—we can just *be*. For once.'

'A body can only handle so much!' Ashair's voice was shaking. Cyrus had never seen him so beyond grace. 'A man can be too broken to heal! The land can be too broken to heal! You're breaking us. You've broken us. Stop pretending. You *are* them. You've always been. Only I was blind to it before. I wanted to believe. In that word *embrace*. That a man can be better than his circumstances. I wanted to believe . . . in you.'

If Cyrus had been holding a rock, he might have thrown it. It wasn't that he disagreed with Ashair. All he had to do was look at the barren, overgrazed ground—and he saw it. But Ashair was letting emotion blind him to fact. 'Just tell me. What would you do if you had all the power? Free the indentured? Let the industries collapse? You think that would be less cruel? Let every man fight his brother over the scraps so his children won't starve? Is that what you want? Babies going hungry?'

'Babies *are* going hungry! I see them in the hospital every day! You say *our contract*. Please. They work and work so you can bowl—they work so you can leave them behind! The men building the ark won't even be allowed on it! Only one side has ever adhered to your *contract*.'

'You don't know what you're saying. The Emperor will take the most loyal of each rank. Across the ocean, civilization will need laborers. As many as we can get. I suspect the ark will be sent back and loaded again. Perhaps a hundred times. As often as it takes. If there were more trees and more muscles, the Emperor would have built more arks. A man of your position doesn't have a clear vantage.'

Ashair spit. 'Hide. That is my advice to you, Cyrus. When these men find out they're to be left behind, their shovels will be as good as swords.'

Cyrus tried reminding himself that he didn't invent this world and he didn't need to defend it. 'What we do, what I do, working for the greater good—it requires a strong stomach. Clearly not all men can handle the burden.'

Ashair didn't rebut. He sat heavily onto the cold cobbles. In that dim light, he looked frozen, outside the passage of time, the sculpture of a surrendering man. The silence endured. Cyrus said, 'I don't want this. I didn't come all this way to fight.'

'I don't want to fight either.'

Cyrus knelt beside him. 'You don't have to stay behind. When I cut this wool, I can give you a boarding pass.'

'I'm not scared for myself,' Ashair said. 'I'm scared for my child.'

Leerit walked by moonlight, the swish of her leggings a rhythm that ordered the darkness. Frost sparkled under her, flashing embers of purple as she covered ground.

When the moon set, she couldn't see. She had to stop. If she sprained an ankle, Kushim would die. It was that simple. But sitting, unmoving in the dark—she had never been so alone. There was no sound but for the wind over ridges and the distant slur of white water, no shapes but for the contours of mountains.

She came to her feet and continued; she had to. Almost at once, a rock rolled under her and she came down hard on her elbow. She could feel blood trickling.

Covering herself in the bearskin, she said, 'Please, Opi. Help me now.'

Each night, Ashair insisted on behaving as if his wife were there supervising. Before going to bed—in his own tent—he could be heard singing a prayer for her and the baby.

Thankfully, Cyrus had brought scrolls to read by lantern light. These stories he took on loan from the archives. Unofficially, of course. They were from the inner archives, to which only senior scholars had access, but Cyrus had the advantage of a master's bribe money. The scrolls had fit nicely under a thick winter cape; no clerks or guards noticed. Of course he would return them; after the Highlands, he'd go first thing. No one appreciated these texts more than he did. Now they were the only other life in his tent with him.

Each of the texts required slow, deliberate translation. They were meant to be sung, and in their lines, he could feel the ancient rhythms of men not so different from himself. Pleased by concision and bright imagery, parallelisms and narrative elegance. Those distant storytellers were likely fed a plentiful dinner in exchange for entertaining their hosts, and their tales passed like loyalties between fathers and sons.

One told of an ancient village from a time before copper, a collection of peoples from many lands who were together overtaken by water and became one people on the retreat, chased by a green giantess who towered above the waves. She held aloft a flaming baton. The last line was best translated as *She who followed the Sun persisted.*

The most recent, told here in a middle language that shared some words with Cyrus's own and so was quickest to decode, told of the coronation of the first Emperor.

Born of the fifth brother was a virgin who heard the Sun's voice and heeded His command to walk nearer. After the exhaustion of three days travel, she lay down in brittle grass and watched the Sun move over her. She stared with no concern for her earthly vision. From an infinite sky, the Sun sent a bolt of thunderous lightning to strike the ground beside her. It sparked the grass afire; it torched the whole valley and yet did not burn her flesh; the baby she birthed nine months later emerged full grown. Here was the first Emperor, whose father is the eternal Sun.

When his lantern burned out, Cyrus lay on his back, history a tender weight upon his chest.

Ashair didn't know him at all. What Cyrus wanted, what he'd always wanted, was a simple life, rich only in truth and meaning and companionship. He wanted to live as he was, no more numbers, no more hiding. This is why he had pursued scholarship in the first place. In the archives, a man needn't bother learning his name.

The next night, he and Ashair were eating alone by their fire while Jernod and the guards laughed from their camp set apart. Somewhere on the periphery, two armed men were standing, on duty and invisible. Jernod had insisted that two of his men always be on guard against the hungry land. They took shifts throughout the night. Four eyes and ears out there somewhere. He and Ashair were left to assume the guards could overhear every word, see every gesture. So they sat on opposite sides of the fire. Like proper men.

'Is it true,' Cyrus tried. 'You almost didn't come to the theater that night?'

Ashair's mother had been ill and he couldn't leave her, but she insisted her son use the ticket he had saved money to purchase. Her words to him that night had troubled Ashair ever since. *My poor boy who can only rest in someone else's story.*

'Had you not come,' Cyrus asked now in nearly a whisper, 'do you think we would still be here now?' It was a simple query. Had they not met that night in the theater, would they have met the next day on the street or the next year in the market—or would they still now be strangers? In other words, were they destined to come together or was this between them the result of random chance?

If they were destined to meet, were they also destined to be drawn apart? If they were fated to begin, were they also fated to end? 'If this is the last,' Cyrus whispered when Ashair didn't answer, 'shouldn't we at least try?'

The fire shone back from Ashair's eyes. 'I am trying.'

'No, you're punishing yourself because you think punishment is what you deserve.'

Ashair didn't disagree.

'You realize now that you hate me,' Cyrus said. 'Maybe you always have. If I didn't exist, you could be simply a good man.'

'No matter what happens,' Ashair said. 'I will always be grateful for the theater.'

To name a thing is to render it captive wrote an early anonymous philosopher. *To name a thing is to enslave it.*

Alone in his tent, Cyrus unfurled one more scroll, this one unlike the others.

It had been delivered to Cyrus directly by a contingent of the Emperor's army—sent on the orders of General Rah himself, from his own personal archives. In his fingers, Cyrus knew immediately Rah's scroll was a counterfeit aged by sunlight. Yet the text had arrived under the guard of sixteen soldiers, in a watertight bronze sleeve with a note signed by Rah himself. All it said was *I look forward to our hearty debate.*

But what was there to debate? The story itself was disappointingly common, the world's origin, the very poem recited endlessly from every testament stone, here in its primary language. Cyrus opened the bronze sleeve now because he was bringing a new question to the common text: If the Sun gave this valley to His favorite child, why was He now chas-

ing the same people away with endless drought? Why, if it was all fated
to end, did He ever let it begin?

The story, even in the original language, offered no answers.

If everything was given to man by the Sun, if the Sun was the origin
of every power, why would He create something that perverted His own
will? The Sun was the diviner of all destinies, the writer of all fates; the
priests' threadbare maxim was *There is no chance in creation.* For men
like his father to take issue with an element of the Sun's handiwork—
wasn't *that* the perversion?

Ancient scholars recorded the stories as they were told in their time.
It was an oral tradition then, and they were the first to anchor history
upon parchment. Therein was the primary lesson of scholarship: the
failings of words are the failings of men.

He shut his eyes and wondered what it would be like never to open
them again.

But from that darkness rose something, a single word he'd just read.

In a rush, he unfurled Rah's scroll again. He knew the last line from
memory. *Use every bounty I pull forth, let no gift of mine go to waste, populate my earth, and you alone will live in knowledge that your lineage shall
carry far and forever.* But there was something wrong with this version.
One word that wasn't right.

Not *populate my earth.* The word on the Rah's scroll could only be
translated as *repopulate.*

The congestion wouldn't clear, and Lilah could hardly stop coughing
long enough to draw breath. She tasted blood. In the torchlight of their
quarters, she could see Koneet and Kenta fighting their fever dreams.

Sleep offered no rest. She had never hurt like she hurt now, a pain like cutting beneath her sternum, as if she had inhaled shards of knapped rock. She knew she could die here. So far from her babies. They would never know what had happened or how desperately she tried to return to them. They would go on believing they had been abandoned by the woman who had made them.

Then Trinket was there with a bowl. She helped Lilah to sitting and tipped the bowl as Lilah drank the bone broth and medicinal herbs.

Trinket rolled leaves into a pinch and slipped her fingers inside Lilah's cheek. The leaves made her tongue dumb as they numbed her ragged throat. She lay back, and for the first time, she didn't feel the tickle that caused her cough.

At first light, they were already leagues farther upriver, the carriages rumbling in tandem. Even by a brilliant Dawn, none of the peaks conjured the names Cyrus's father had taught him. Each was a stranger that loomed.

Ashair was then slouched on the bench, his eyes closed, the medical kit secured between his knees. Asleep or just pretending to sleep, it was impossible to know.

Repopulate. What could explain such an error in the story called *Creation*? How could a forger overlook such a mistake? Who was that incompetent?

Jernod called, 'Sir, look!' The carriage was then cresting a hill; sprawling before them were sheep. Tiny ovals of wool drinking from the river, white dots scattered across the hillside. A complex of yurts waited on the bluff across the water. Ashair stood to see their end point.

To reach the yurts, they would follow the road down a steep hillside and ford the river. But therein was the problem, the reason Jernod had reined the carriage to a stop. A drift of sand had accumulated over the road, blocking their wheels. Already a dispatch of laboring men was wading through the flocks of sheep and the river. The water came to their waists but they mustered on. Hurrying with shovels to clear the sand ahead of these imperial carriages.

When Cyrus and his father first saw the flocks years ago, the sheep were dispersed among waist-deep wildflowers. His father had told him, *You can determine your herd's health by the ratio of ewes to lambs.* When Cyrus looked now, he saw wool in varying shapes. He was the owner of all the sheep in the world, and yet he couldn't readily tell which were ewes.

Ashair took his medical kit and leapt from the carriage. Cyrus called, 'Where are you going?'

Ashair turned back to answer and caught his toe on a cobble and fell.

Before he might think better of it, Cyrus had jumped down from the carriage. He was helping Ashair to his feet, brushing sand from his shoulder. 'Are you okay?'

Ashair pulled away. He was looking back at the guards still in the carriages.

Cyrus turned to find Jernod staring.

At the sight of Kushim, Lenka chewed her knuckle. When she opened his eyelids, Maren saw her brother's pupils rolled back. He was worse, not better.

'What do we do?' Maren begged in a language no one understood.

Lenka heated the cauldron of water. Added the last pours of the same medicine. Bathed the wound across Kushim's head. As she had every other morning. Her only answer to this crisis was to double the medicine that wasn't working.

His hair was falling out in clumps. His breaths hardly moved his chest. He was so pale, and his lips were purple. The stitches sank in deep canyons of swollen skin. Pus oozed only to be washed away in the hot water. The smell of her brother was the smell of rotting meat.

When Maren looked up, Lenka's eyes were wet. Her old hand rose into the space between them, this hand made hot by her brother's dying—it was now warm on Maren's cheek.

He'd read all of the canon and much of the commentaries; he'd attended countless lectures on lesser-known texts, studied the drawings of pictographs long ago swallowed by sand; and yet he'd never once come upon a passage or image depicting men loving men.

His father had called it *a sickness born of decadence.*

Not a sickness at all, Ashair clarified once when Cyrus asked. *Medically speaking.*

For a man to love another man—his father had said to his nine-year-old son on their Highland trip—*nothing could be more unnatural.*

Finally, the carriage jolted. The road was cleared and the workers stood aside to watch a master pass. Jernod steered the horses to the river and yelled to keep the beasts moving when their instinct demanded they stop. Hooves then wheels met the current, and the river splashed across Cyrus's face.

When they were finally across, Jernod reined the animals to a stop. There was nowhere else for the carriages to go. Here the road ended. Cyrus turned to see the laborers fording the flows. Ashair was with them, his kit held up and dry. All that effort to clear the road to the

river's edge had been for him. For a master to soak himself while crossing a river—it would be unnatural.

He could've summoned the manager of his shepherds to the city, but he
hadn't.

Now Cyrus sat in the manager's chair in the manager's own yurt, his
boots propped upon the manager's desk, doing his best impression of his
father. In his hands were leaves of cheap parchment, numbers and figures
columned and totaled. To prepare for the encounter, Cyrus had studied
the books and memorized the math. He couldn't let himself be bam-
boozled. A fifth more wool would require efficiency first and foremost
from the man doing the counting. 'I see we're down in every head count.'

The manager was older than Cyrus. Heavy wrinkles emanated from
the corners of his eyes; he was better-looking for them. Short, muscular,
a hardy attractiveness—this crude counterpoint to Ashair's lanky elegance. Now on his knees in his own office.

Cyrus took his time because he could. He practically owned this
man. 'Why?'

'Sir, the totals tend to diminish from summer to winter. Lambs perish, especially in those first weeks. It's only natural.'

Cyrus raised an eyebrow. 'I expect to see the lamb counts diminish.
Perhaps a decline of a tenth or even a sixth. But what I'm talking about
here are the numbers of rams and ewes. They too have declined. During
the easy months of summer. Do you take me as a fool?'

'Sir. It's the primitives. There's a growing population in the headwaters.'

'Primitives? You expect me to believe that?'

'The drought has delivered them. They're coming great distances.
This is true.'

Cyrus set the papers back to the desk. He held his chin; it was his father's gesture. 'Your predecessor once told a similar story. "Bears" were to blame then. Bears coming from the mountains to feast on our flocks. Except we didn't see the decline in the number of slow, sickly sheep. We saw it in healthy rams—those with the thickest, most valuable pelts. We both know what happened to your predecessor.'

'I swear, sir.'

Cyrus let the silence grow. 'The shepherds take a ram, eat a good meal, trade the skin for booze. You look the other way because it's easier to blame these "primitives," just as it was once easier to blame those "bears."'

The manager didn't contradict him.

Cyrus explained why he had come so far. The Emperor was demanding a fifth more wool than last year. Cutting that much would be the responsibility of whoever was manager of his flocks. 'Frankly, I'm no longer sure you're the man for the job.'

The manager's mouth hung open. 'A fifth more? But how?'

Cyrus pointed. 'You tell me. And I will decide your future.'

The manager looked at the walls of his own yurt as if gazing into the distance. 'To cut a fifth more, I need better graze. To reach better graze, I need men. Soldiers.'

'That's not possible,' Cyrus said flatly. 'I don't control the army.' Even if he did, he had only funds enough for the outlays already in progress.

'May I?' The manager crossed the room and poured two cups of fermented sheep milk. He offered the bigger cup to Cyrus. The manager swallowed his in a gulp and poured another. 'These are no longer the valley's best winter pastures. They haven't been for decades. The grass never gets a rest. To cut an extra fifth, I need to move our strongest flocks higher up the valley. There is still virgin graze.'

'You want the Emperor's soldiers to shovel winter from the Highlands?'

'No sir. There is a place. In the headwaters. A valley at the top of this one. Very remote. Steam rises from the ground. Thermal vents, hot springs. The grass itself is so warm that no ice can smother it. All winter, the meadows keep green. I've seen it myself. It's the most remarkable sight. Nowhere in the Empire is the winter graze so deep.'

'Why aren't we on these grasses now?'

The manager looked at him. 'Master. The primitives gather in this valley.'

'What are you suggesting? You would have me start a war?'

'No one need die, sir. The heathens follow throngs of elk to that grass. The army must only run the elk from the meadows. See, the primitive's weakness is his dependence on those animals.'

Where the river forked, Leerit took the lesser path and began to climb— as the trader had described. The roar of the distant river swelled and ebbed with the shifting terrain.

Atop the next crest of land, Leerit finally overlooked the hidden valley. Clouds were rising from the grass. The trader had called it *the place where storms are born.*

She pressed on and near dusk was startled by rumbling hooves: a winter herd bolting across the meadow. The elk stopped in a tight bunch and turned nervously toward what surprised them. When the grandmother barked, they vanished into the dark timber, a thousand limbs snapping.

There at Leerit's feet, obvious in the mud of the trail, was a child's boot print.

Cyrus found Jernod with their horses in the encampment's corral, brushing them down by torchlight. He was taking this low task for himself while the men he commanded relaxed about their fire. For the first night since they left, no one had to be on guard; this camp was protected by so many dogs. Jernod sensed his approach and ceased talking to the horse. He turned toward the darkness with his hand on his hilt. A warrior's instinct.

'Does that animal understand what you say?' Cyrus asked as he scaled the corral.

'Yes sir. Not the words but the intention. A horse knows when he is appreciated.' Jernod offered the brush. 'Care to make a friend?'

Cyrus did as Jernod suggested, passing the brush in the direction the hair naturally grew. Its bristles knocked loose mud and grit and dried lather. This close, the horse smelled like dust and sweat, a pleasing odor relative to the fecal stink of sheep that swirled on every gust.

Cyrus returned the brush and watched Jernod work the tool decisively down the animal's muscular leg. 'You've been with my family a long time.'

'Indeed, sir.'

'Do you remember the trip my father and I took here when I was a boy? He taught me the names of the mountains. Only I can't remember them now. I wish I did. I wish I could remember every detail. We didn't have long enough together.'

Jernod cleared some emotion from his throat. 'Sir, he will always be watching. For your father, there was never anything else but his son.'

It was a heartfelt speech for a driver. Cyrus felt a little embarrassed to have heard it. He turned toward the peaks. In that dim moonlight, he could just make out the curvature of the mountains. He wished he could feel his father out there somewhere. 'I rarely had the sense he cared, to be honest.'

'Your father was held back by the role he had to play in this world. Sir.'

Cyrus studied his driver. His father *had been* held back. Just as Cyrus was now. Duty to the common good kept a master from being simply a man, a father, from spending as much time with his son as he might have wanted to. Jernod was one of the few who could appreciate just how heavy was a master's burden.

Now Jernod pointed the brush at the sloping omission of stars. 'Sir. That peak is known as Mount Cataract, for the water that cascades from its flank in early summer. Maybe you remember a waterfall launching from a cliff? It looks remarkably different in the warm season. I'll call out each peak's name for you on the ride back if you like.'

'Listen.' Cyrus put a hand on the horse. 'Today, when the medical attaché fell, I don't know what you think you saw.'

His driver was still.

'Because whatever you think you saw—'

'Sir. This is not necessary.' Jernod said in a quieter, nervous voice, 'I was a soldier, sir. When two men spend time together, there grows a bond. It's only natural.'

'Natural?'

'Sir, may I? Your father—to see you now, to see the man you've become—trust me when I say that he would feel only pride.'

When Ashair returned, he threw down his kit beside the fire. By then, even Jernod and his men had gone to sleep. 'Is there any dinner?'

Cyrus passed him the cold bowl of stew and break of bread he'd kept aside.

Ashair told of the infected tooth he'd pulled, the smashed finger he amputated, the prostitute's sores that were already festering. He talked of these things while he ate; they had no effect on his appetite.

'Prostitutes?'

Ashair explained what Cyrus already knew, that the shepherds came to this encampment to spend their wages. Ashair didn't know that these men were paid in company script, which could only be spent here. But there were no prostitutes listed in any formal ledger. A ploy of the manager's then. No doubt, his father had known and decided to pretend he didn't. Let a manager have his schemes, so minor in the grand view, and he will only be more invested in the shared outcome.

Ashair finished his bowl and wiped out the remains with the bread. He was in a better humor now after treating the sickly. This was the biggest difference between them: Ashair didn't feel burdened by duty; he was the type to take shelter in it. No one had had to persuade Ashair to marry.

Cyrus nodded toward the darkness. 'Even the guards are asleep.' He unbuttoned his tent and stepped inside. Ashair studied the darkness before following.

Like the first time, Ashair was the one to kiss him. Their bodies became slick with sweat and yet they made no sound. They held their hands against the other's mouth. The shared end came too soon. 'Not the last,' Cyrus begged. 'Please, not the last.'

Somewhere a dog barked, and Ashair flinched like a thief caught in torchlight. He dressed and left the tent while Cyrus still lay naked.

Rah's scroll was there. Cyrus had been staring at the wrong word earlier and hadn't returned it to the protective sleeve. A mistake. In their passion, a knee or an elbow had compressed the text; a crease now existed across the general's parchment.

Like proper men, they regained their places about the fire, but now everything was different. As if all the weight Cyrus had been holding against himself had sloughed loose, a mountain released of its burden by avalanche. Ashair smiled. 'Tell me a story?'

The barking of one dog had become the barking of several. 'Give me some leaf?'

Ashair found what he'd brought and lit the roll against the edge of the fire. He drew the smoke and passed it.

Cyrus inhaled. He felt like he could say anything. 'What if I gave your wife a boarding pass?'

Ashair's lips bent into a smirk. 'You want to take Attessa with you on the ark?'

'The three of us.'

'Together? How?'

'I already share you. We both already share you. I am willing to share you if it means we can be on that boat together.'

Ashair took the smoldering leaf. 'What of your mother? You said three boarding passes.'

The barking dogs were nearer. Above, on the hillside, sheep began bawling.

'Say I had ten passes—would you come with me then?'

Ashair's eyes became laden and reflective.

'Do you really have to think about it?'

Ashair said, 'Tell me who has seen this green shore for himself?'

'Those sailors sent as scouts. They saw it all. Trust me: their depiction is rich with the poetry of authentic experience. They were undoubtedly inspired.'

'By green land or the certainty of watery death? Why trust them? Doesn't it seem more likely that they realized their choice was to perish or lie? What would you do?'

'I've read their account; I am a scholar—or I was. You doubt me?'

'Maybe you were persuaded because you wanted to believe. Wanting to believe is dangerous.' Ashair shook his head. 'I don't think there's land out there at all. If there was, someone would've found it long ago. We'd have stories of travelers.'

'You say that as a man not wanting to believe.'

'I say that as a man who will never again trust a word spoken by the Emperor.'

It was a startling statement. Even here, so far from civilization's walls. Cyrus couldn't help but check behind him. 'There has to be land,' he said. 'It's a matter of logic. If there isn't land to hem it in, the ocean would pour off the edge of the world.'

'Tell me of the *edge of the world*. Have you seen it? Did you dangle your toes?'

Cyrus laughed. 'There has to be an edge. You said yourself, there is an end to everything.'

Voices were calling from nearby. Ashair turned toward them. He stood.

Cyrus said, 'Why did you marry her? No one was forcing you.'

Ashair looked startled. 'Cyrus. I love her.'

'You love her.'

'One can love two.'

A voice was calling from the dark: 'Doctor! Doctor!'

Ashair shouted, 'Over here!'

Someone had to say what was true. 'That's not how love works.'

'No.' The kit was now in Ashair's hands. 'That's not how love *stories* work.'

A young shepherd appeared at a run. There was sweat down his brow. He was heaving. 'There's a boy! Upriver! He's dying!'

Drums rose from the steaming darkness as if their rhythms too were born of subterranean heat. Bonfires illuminated the fog's underbelly. Voices, women calling out and men sounding back. These songs—Leerit knew these songs! Her mother! Her father! They sang them every year. It was as it always had been: the feast of the final moon before winter solstice, this harvest festival of the coast, when young men performed those dances they had been rehearsing for maidens, when grown men performed for their wives. Could it really be—she was home?

Dogs began to bark. The singing, the drums—they came to a sudden end. Dogs rushed to surround her, growling at the stranger.

'Who's there?' a woman's voice called. It was a voice with the twang of the Left Coast. 'Who's that in the dark? Announce yourself or my dogs will bite.'

'Leerit!' she called. 'Of the Right Coast! I am one of you! I am one of . . . us!'

'If this is true, then tell me: What does the Sea say in Her waves?'

The answer rose from her in pure song, her mother's voice: 'I am that I am.'

Commotion came over the village. The woman's voice sang back. 'Welcome. Welcome home. The arduous journey is over.'

Solstice

Cyrus used his father's season tickets to take his mother and some beautiful girl she wanted for a daughter-in-law to the theater. He sat where his father had sat for every show of the last twenty years, including an opening night before Equinox when word of the terminal diagnosis was spreading. That night, a round of applause sounded as tribute from the performers gathered onstage for the Master who had given so much.

Yes, his father had loved the theater, but he also loved the prominence good seats could afford him. Here lineage mattered less than simple currency. Tonight, General Rah sat not far away between two of his youngest wives.

Cyrus saw the Emperor even before the horns announced his imperial presence. Golden cape and a golden crow perched on his shoulder, this beacon of light. As one ancient scroll put it, *So near the divine, when he raises a hand, his fingers burn.*

Below, in the common middle, Ashair was among fellow medical students chanting for the Emperor's long life. They hadn't talked since delivering the dying boy to the hospital. Ashair had managed to keep him alive that long. Mangled, black-and-blue, quaking with fever—a lost cause, but one his friend couldn't abandon. That first night in the Highlands, Cyrus had held the lantern while Ashair's steady hand cut the crusty stitching from the scalp to vent geysers of pus. After they delivered the child to the hospital, Ashair had said, 'No more lectures. Don't knock on my door. Please. I beg you to forget me.'

'Spectacular!' Cyrus's date exclaimed.

Child dancers moved to beats that emanated from the dark periphery. Drumming started from a single hand and soon grew into a multilayered rumble, as if various thunderheads floating on various strata had had their pounding choreographed to please the people. Cyrus heard himself tell the girl, 'Here, we determine even the weather.'

On the other side of the city, Lilah was singing a story of perseverance to Koneet and Kenta, who were still recovering from the sickness that had struck Lilah first.

It was an old story about the time after the Great Wave drowned the innocent and guilty alike.

> Those few to survive crossed utter destruction. Farther and farther among flood-carved dunes and trunk-snapped trees. By the Sea's guidance, they arrived in summer to forests and meadows, to rivers still swelling with fish and hillsides still draped in fruits and nuts. Here the Sea's children began again—another chance to heed only the Mother-of-All.

'Auntie?' Kenta was reaching now and Lilah took her hand in both of her own. 'Is She angry at us? Is that why She flooded our gardens with sand? Why She let us be stolen?' When Lilah didn't answer, Kenta said, 'I don't understand what we did wrong.'

Maren was singing to Friend, their faces bent near the last flames of the cooking fire here in the yurt as the old couple snored—this solstice unlike any other.

She was lower in the huge valley now, where the horses had moved their tent and belongings a few days after her brother was taken. So hot that he was convulsing, his tongue bloody. The last time she had seen Kushim, he was a body; he was no longer her brother. They had taken him to help him. Lenka was sure these tall men knew how to help. What would Leerit say when she found out? What would Ama say to the daughter who let her only son be taken?

Maren now drew from her pocket all she had left. He had liked to keep the fishhook in his mouth. When he caught his first fish, he told her, *I keep wanting to run over and tell Opi.*

Now Friend licked her face. The wind was buffeting the yurt, and the shelter bucked like it could soon be peeled from the ground and flung through darkness. Friend was licking and asking for more. Friend licking. This that could save her.

Familiar words she offered the puppy: 'The Sea spoke from Her waves . . .'

'And guided Her children to this land wanting a steward.'

Leerit was hearing these words sung from two hundred and fourteen mouths, this village of coastal people gathered within the steam born of mountains. So many faces snuck glances at the bald girl who had arrived in darkness. She was beside her mother's big sister, Auntie, the woman who delivered babies from holy gates, who guided elders from here to their place on the mountaintop—their midwife. Auntie was the only one who might have saved Kushim.

Now Auntie was holding her tightly, gray locks pressed against Leerit's cheek. The people sang. 'Within every newborn is the wisdom of ten thousand survivors.' Auntie kissed each eyelid, as Ama would. She held Leerit's chin so she couldn't avert her gaze. 'Listen to me now, Niece. You stoop under all you carry, but She delivered you for a reason. Let me shoulder this burden. Let your auntie help. Remember, you are young.'

It was on this solstice night, at the ocean's edge, that a coastal man was delivering yet another load of lumber to those pounding at the massive planks that would float the ark. Countless men of countless tribes building a boat big enough to carry any village but this one.

Taken as a boy, but by now, his hands had grown coarse, his muscles thick with months of meals and labor. Lifting lumber and carrying it on his head down muddy trails and across broken ground, heaving it into piles. His every waking hour belonged to the giant who held a whip— but his muscles, these hands, they were his own.

Across the dark, he heard his mother's voice as he had heard her every solstice, as soothing as the break of waves. Now she said unto him, 'Tonight, this wood is for you.'

His fellow laborers saw and some of these dared turn their mallets and join in. The giant with the whip was not allowed the chance to beg.

They did not stop even after the contents of his skull splattered over their boots.

So many blades swarmed and killed the coastal man, they sent him to his mother. But three of those with mallets escaped. One was stout with a thickset neck and heavy eyes who spoke in the terse voice of the Left Coast. This man was still called Rageer.

XIII

This Here Now

Maren had understood that Kushim needed help, more than Lenka could provide. She had known this as she watched the tall men load him onto a cart tethered to an animal bigger even than an elk. Only she assumed she was going with him, that Lenka was going with him, Friend and Mutt and Chun too. Leerit would catch up by their tracks.

Yet when she tried to follow the tall men taking her brother, Chun grabbed her. As Kushim was taken, Chun gripped her in his arms. She was young and Chun was old and her fight outlasted his. In the end, she ran after her brother. Panting and her legs burning until no matter how fiercely she wanted to keep running she couldn't. She collapsed to the ground. She could only watch the cart grow smaller and smaller and finally disappear over a swell of land—her brother was gone.

Then a hand appeared on her shoulder. Lenka's. The old woman had followed her into the night with a torch. With her was Friend. He collided into Maren and began to lick her eyes, to bite and tug her hair. To him, her tears were only another game.

'Please,' Lenka said in this language Maren was starting to understand. 'Come.'

In the end, she rose and followed. Because who else did she have left?

Maren could feel Leerit's judgment like she could feel the weight of her broken brother across her lap. She should have kept running. A better sister would have never let him go. A better sister would have stopped the bear. She was to blame.

But the puppy was only eager and happy. She fed him, and he nipped until she chased him around the yurt. She slept with him curled in her armpit. The puppy was always licking her. In his eyes, she could do nothing wrong.

Horses. Lenka had taught her the word when the animals arrived with their handler to move the yurt. Maren had helped load the cooking pots, the vats and vessels. She helped catch the chickens and stuff them flapping into a cage. She helped. As a maiden should.

She watched as Chun and the younger man who had brought the horses pulled the poles and the yurt sank to the ground blowing air from its chimney. Chun folded and folded again, dropped to his knees and rolled the heavy hides. The young man was ready to help lift and lash the yurt tightly across a waiting horse. It was a clear day, winter, dawn's glow fading to dusk.

She believed Leerit would follow their tracks. Of course Leerit would know where they went. Leerit would find her, then she would thank Lenka, and together as sisters, they would recover their brother and deliver him to Auntie.

Yet the stars had disappeared behind clouds. As they traveled, snow tumbled from darkness. Even the horses' heavy tracks were being erased by winter.

A maiden anywhere should study the manner of women. She must teach herself to endure. Lenka said in the strange language, 'Not that, this.'

They were sitting together inside the tent as the wind screamed. Friend slept between Maren's crossed legs. She was using the knitting sticks and trying to make the same hooking motion that for Lenka came so easily.

'No, not that, *this*.'

The fire was warm until a gust of wind rushed down the hole cut in the yurt's roof. Smoke was about them and Lenka coughed and added new sticks to the flames, which grew the heat, and soon the smoke was rushing up out of the yurt again.

Chun was so often out there somewhere tending the flock. She and Lenka were left like this, warm and alone together inside.

'Yes!' Lenka said to Maren's knitting sticks. When the old woman smiled, Maren saw the darkness of missing teeth. Lenka said, 'Yes, good, better.'

Maren felt it then like warmth, the satisfaction that comes from earning respect from an elder—knowing in that moment at least she had done right.

Lenka taught her to season a roast, to pack around it seeds and ground maize, all of it placed precisely inside a special pot with a tight-fitting lid. It was the first time Maren had seen this dark pot lifted from the rafters, except for that day they packed to move. Lenka took great care to lay the shiny container into the coals, to weight the lid with a rock, to sweep new coals over top. Soon steam was rising from the edge, and Maren's mouth began to water at the aroma.

That night, Chun returned and knocked the ice from his boots, his shoulders, his mittens. He pulled off his layers and sat beside their fire. Ice from his nose hairs was melting over his lip. He smelled what was cooking and sighed.

Lenka used a special tool to lever the pot from the fire and pry loose the lid. Steam rose about them. Lenka opened her palm and Maren knew to give her the bronze knife. With the blade, the old woman cut the mutton into strips.

When they said a prayer, Maren said it too though she didn't know what it meant.

'Go on,' Lenka told her. 'You first.'

It was the only meal Maren had eaten here that required chewing. The meat was soaked with flavor but tough. Lenka pointed at her missing teeth. She said many sounds and Maren understood. 'Please help.'

As it once had been in the village by the Sea. The old people hadn't teeth enough for their favorite meals, those remembered from youth, cooked by their grandmothers. It was forever the child's job to chew for the oldest.

Maren took a piece of meat and its maize crust. The flavors were explosive and hot, and she thought of Ama who would want to try any new flavor.

She took the masticated meat from her mouth and passed it into the waiting hand of Lenka. The old woman offered half over her husband's lips. The couple shut their eyes. Different, but the same as old people anywhere: remembering.

Before solstice, she and Auntie had made the journey down valley with a string of goats to recover her brother and Maren. They planned to suspend the boy and carry him to the village where he could heal beside warm waters. But Leerit had failed to find the yurt.

The only evidence was the stack of firewood she had collected from the river and piled neatly. She had stacked that wood because someone needed to before winter's snowfall. Now she knew: the old man hadn't collected enough wood because they were leaving that place before winter. Leaving, but for where?

It had been dark and icy, and even on her knees with a bright flame, Leerit could find no sign. She simply wasn't keen enough to read what was written out on the ground.

Auntie said, 'When the sun returns, we'll find them, I promise.'

In this valley above all others, pools of water boiled from the ground. Some were too hot to touch, their smell sharp in Leerit's nose. Other pools did not have the biting smell, and their shorelines weren't yellow. Grass grew deep around these. Why? Why some and not others? Auntie didn't know. She called it the Valley of Questions.

Here they were a village of many accents and many colors of dog. The fish didn't migrate past; the elk weren't pressed by winter to a nearby shoreline. In this place, people had to move with their food. They journeyed to each new camp on trails laid over eons by feet just like theirs.

On certain grassy slopes, those who came before had built strange stone towers taller than a man, constructed of cobbles piled with unrepeatable skill, with arms held out and antlers on top. These towers dotted the landscape. Fragments of shells sparkled around the base of each.

A few shells remained in one tower's crags, and when the wind blew, these shells still whistled.

'What are they for, Auntie?'

'What is *it* for?'

Because they were not many towers across a grassy plain but one shape over the landscape, like a school of fish or a flock of birds: so many to make one. A village standing to shepherd some movement, trying to channel the wind perhaps, necking it down into a ferocious gust. Auntie told her, 'The Ancients can teach us how to endure in this place. If we humble ourselves and listen to the quietest voice.'

'How do we know it was the Ancients who were here?'

'Who else?'

Their old camps were well established. Each was tucked out of the prevailing wind; from any firepit was a vista of steaming water. Every camp had at its center stone benches that awaited the prominent few; too heavy to lift and yet the Ancients had somehow delivered these smooth rocks into the heart of every settlement. Rutted trails led to good fishing holes, to where tubers were easily dug. The widest trail from any camp led to those pools of comfortable temperature.

No matter the camp, twice each day Leerit followed Auntie into a narrow opening in the earth with no bottom. They swam in place, feet kicking over darkness. What was down there no one knew. Overhead, fog born of this water was lit by the flicker of their winter flame. In this valley, no one need die of cold.

'You never mention them,' Auntie said now, her breath a disturbance on the water. Her hair was silver and black, and tied up with jute— those locks must have been heavy for all the honor. Deep smile lines radiated from her eyes. Ivory piercings through her forehead marked her as the midwife. Now she was simply a woman advising her own sister's daughter. 'It would do you good to talk of Kushim. Let him out.'

When Leerit told Auntie what had happened, the bear coming from nowhere to attack, Auntie had sucked her teeth. 'It is as I warned my little sister. One should never insult Bear by killing him.'

Leerit remembered Ama and Auntie arguing about the killing. 'My father gave that bear every honor. This is not their fault. The bruin was eating our fish.'

Auntie's head wobbled. 'If it was a test, we failed.'

Leerit's hands had become fists. 'If tomorrow I saw the bear who hurt him—who did *that* to my brother—I would kill that bear ten times. I would bludgeon its cubs.'

'Niece. Revenge doubles the poison.'

On another morning, Auntie climbed from a hot vent of water and stood steaming in the morning's chill. 'What you should be doing is earning beads. You don't even try. A maiden should make every effort to please her mother.'

'You talk like she is alive.'

Auntie scoffed. 'My little sister argued with me every day of our lives. I am still arguing with her. You think I wouldn't know if she was perched on the mountaintop?'

Somehow it was worse to think of Ama as still alive. Because if she was, where was she? Alone on that barren coastline, abandoned by her daughters?

After returning without her siblings, Leerit had stayed in Auntie's house, in the bearskin, refusing to come out. Auntie brought her food but she didn't eat. Because she didn't deserve to eat.

Whenever she went outside, people stared; they whispered—here was the only survivor, that maiden who lost her whole family. Of course she had done *something* to bring such suffering on herself. They all had a theory. They all thought they knew her.

Every maiden snuck glances. Girls, really. They were younger, yet they wore beads. With hair so short, she was the one who had to greet them with respect. She could say the words but couldn't mean them.

Most of her old friends from the beach were mothers now. Everyone her age was now a grown-up. When they smiled at her, it was with pity in their eyes. Everyone thought they understood. They needed to believe she had brought this suffering upon herself.

What was undeniable: Kushim was gone and it was her fault. First for leaving him alone near hanging meat and again for leaving him to the whims of strangers. After all that had happened—and without the treatments known by Auntie—he couldn't still be alive. It wasn't possible for a boy to survive the attack of a bear.

If Ama was still alive, then she was sleeping alone in the remains of their house; she was by herself on a mudflat digging for clams. Leerit had heard Opi in her ear, but she hadn't heard Ama. 'She'll find us,' Auntie had said. 'You'll see. I know my sister.' But if Ama arrived here to see the daughter who abandoned her, to learn that her son had died, what could she say to her firstborn? How could she continue loving her?

Auntie was always demanding Leerit rise from the pelts. Always insisting Leerit earn beads and sing her gratitude. For here, goats had browse and children chased puppies. The streams and lakes grew fish; the marshes gave up cattail celery and nettles; the duff offered mushrooms and sorrel. They ate dried berries picked from the high country in the heat of summer, pickled cabbage cut from rich meadows. After the day's work, there was music and dancing. Like back when, children were either playing or throwing tantrums; for children, there was never anything in between.

Yet usually their stomachs ached. Here waters grew small fish who were only reliably caught in summer. In this place, the hunters struggled to ambush elk. The nightly prayer was always the same. *Please, from the mountaintop, teach us all that you know.*

Especially, where to find salt. On the coast, salt was everywhere and worthless, but here it was scarce and prized above all else. Any fish or meat smoked couldn't last long because there wasn't salt enough to stave off rot.

Why not follow the water to the ocean where salt was plentiful? Why not live within the sound of waves? Because of *Barbarian*. This name that had arrived with desert nomads come here to trade. Barbarians were not human. They swung blades instead of offering gifts; they lived in a massive hive by the Sea but turned up their noses at fish. When Leerit asked if anyone had seen this hive for themselves, Auntie said, 'Those who try do not return.'

She had seen Ozi on her first night among them. Back when, he had been her first kiss. The boy she thought she loved. But in the Valley of Questions, he was someone else's husband.

Three years of hunting rugged country had made Ozi quick over broken ground, quicker in judgment. He moved like water; he knew a knot for every need; he was patient when teaching children to shoot a bow. His face and neck and torso were layered with honor, but his smile still began in his eyes. In his face, she could see the boy he had been when they wrestled and chased dogs and snuck fillets from the smoke racks.

Here, the grandmothers said no one could read tracks better. 'That man can look at the ground and tell a long story.'

His wife was a Left-Coast maiden with many beads. Leerit was surprised that a Left-Coaster and Right-Coaster had chosen to marry. The girl's grandmother sat each evening on the prominent stones to collect offerings and settle disagreements; Auntie had said, 'Marriage united two coasts into one village.' By now, they had been married for nearly two years, yet Ozi hadn't given his wife a child. 'Such a strong man,' grandmothers whispered, 'to be no one's father.'

How friendly they had once been, and yet, here in this valley, Ozi hadn't once met her eyes. Without hair and beads, she was awful to look at.

Not all men were good. Some here preferred to sleep on the camp's outskirts. Bachelors who had never been chosen as someone's husband. Instead of living with their mothers or their grown sisters, in this valley such men lived apart. Instead of helping, they played games. No one laughed more than these men. They were like the young stags on the edges of a group of elk. If you heard loud voices, they probably belonged to the unwanted.

Auntie sucked her teeth at these men. 'Left-Coasters,' she said when no Left-Coast mothers were near enough to hear. Many of these unwanted men were from the villages on the left side of the massive headland that had divided the people for so long. 'Left-Coasters were always lazy, but never like this.'

Act this way on the beach and men would be banished from dancing, from sharing in the harvest—they would be forced to sleep in the cold. But here, men could always swim in a pool to keep warm. They couldn't be banished from the harvest because their legs were needed to haul food the long distances required by the terrain. In this valley, the village needed men more than men needed the village.

These bachelors heeded the words of one. A Left-Coaster named Vagnu who believed himself to be important. He was short and muscular, middle-aged and yet without a wife or child. His whole life he'd gone unchosen, but here, he was listened to because he had led the hunters to many kills.

When one day Auntie told the village that the time had come to move to the next camp, Vagnu dared voice his disagreement. 'We should stay here longer.'

Leerit watched Auntie. Everyone turned to see how the midwife would respond. For all her honor, here was her burden. Auntie's eyes became wide and white. Leerit's neck hair stood on end.

Mothers called from the crowd at the man, 'Do as you're told,' and in the accent of the Right Coast, 'Who made this one? Humble your son.'

Vagnu dared meet the midwife's eyes. But whatever he saw in them caused his chin to drop.

Auntie proclaimed, 'Don't dare use that word. *Should* belongs to mothers.'

Before other women, Auntie treated Leerit as if she were a common thirteen-year-old. Fetch the firewood, start the fire, bury the dog poop before the children step in it. Her punishment for cutting off her beads was to live as if she had never earned them.

One morning she returned with an armload of wood to see Auntie and the familiar Right-Coast mothers working in the firelight. They were knapping rock and weaving new underlayers, repairing torn seams, cleaning dirt from roots soon to be roasted. A child born in this valley stood picking her nose; her mother was younger than Leerit.

No one was singing because the people were hungry. There had been no elk in days. The problem, complained the hunters, was the shifting wind; in this valley, elk always had the advantage. It was not like the coast, where the breezes were steady.

A child pulled at Leerit's sleeve. 'What are you?'

'A Right-Coaster, like you.'

The child frowned. 'You look like a boy but you wear maiden-paint.'

Leerit covered her head with her hood.

Auntie turned a half-spawl of chert. With quick downward strikes, she cracked free leaves of glossy, uniform rock. 'Take it,' Auntie told Leerit. 'My niece should know how to knap. This will please your mother.'

Ozi's mother was there, threading sinew through a small ivory needle. Her face was wide and harsh, her lips thin and cracked. She used to bark orders at Leerit and the other girls playing on the beach. Now she looked old. This woman who had lost her husband years before when, in a desperate search for fish, he had taken his nets too far offshore and been overturned by a fast-moving storm.

Before these women, Leerit tried to do right. With the base of an antler, she knocked the edges from the leaf of chert, turning it and knocking again, turning and knocking. Watching Auntie and doing the same. When her blows were properly angled and delivered with enough force, the rock broke with a clap.

'Trade me,' Auntie said, giving her instead the leaf of rock she had just worked and using her own mallet to correct Leerit's mistakes. 'See how? Do like me.'

An old woman was sucking her teeth. She kept making the sound until finally someone asked what was wrong. 'That Vagnu. How would our grandmothers fix a man like that?'

'From the first rude word, they would've banished him.'

'But our grandmothers had plenty of men to spare.'

'How easy it once was.'

'On the beach, what did we ever complain about?'

'Husbands.'

'There is always plenty to complain about with husbands.'

'Daughters.'

'A maiden will always think she knows better than her mother.'

Auntie placed the roughed point on a pad of elk leather spread over her thigh and began working its edges with the tip of an antler. Each time she pressed, there was a crisp snap. She brushed the shards from the leather and somehow her fingers didn't bleed.

Leerit's fingers were bleeding, and her arrow point was lopsided and dull. Auntie's was symmetrical and sharp, thin enough to see light through. She set it on Leerit's knee and told her, 'Not like that. Like *this*.'

One day, word spread through the village that a pair of elk had given themselves. Help was needed carrying these bountiful gifts.

Leerit went with the other maidens. They whispered as they walked along the edge of a marsh. Then they all turned at once to look at her and laugh.

Even in the light of day, the stupid girls managed to lose the trail. Leerit found it again by the sight of a broken fern. Soon she had the smell of elk and followed her nose uphill into the dark thicket. She didn't signal the maidens which way.

She arrived to the kill site to find Ozi alone working the meat. When he saw her, he leapt back from his cutting. She hid her shorn head under the hood of her robe.

Quarters were hanging by tendons and giving off steam. The clean rib cages of two stags lay propped on logs. Hides were rolled and ready to be carried; inside were scrap meat and organs. The antlers towered from heads that would soon be roasted over coals. She didn't know what to say to him and he wasn't saying anything to her. They were here alone in dense forest.

When the maidens arrived, Ozi pointed his knife toward the meat and told them what parts to carry. He was a grown man, a respected woman's husband, and they heeded without complaint.

Ozi watched them move off. When they were alone again, he spoke as if they were still peers, 'I wondered if you would come.'

She watched as Ozi knelt before the prominent elders. A flock of chickens pecked the dust about him. Children ate curds from the sleeve of a stomach. Someone was strumming an instrument with strings. This strange thing that had been traded for.

An old woman sang as she punctured the skin of Ozi's neck with the point of a quill filled with pigment. She tapped the quill with a stone, tapped again. The children laughed as they ate. Small beads of blood rose from Ozi's skin, and the marking grew. Glittering pigment that would sparkle in the summer sun. The last hoofprint left by each elk he had killed.

Later that night, Auntie took Leerit by the elbow. Her grip was sharp. 'Come with me.'

They walked together from the feast into the quiet moonlight. Dogs were growling over scrap meat. Goats were arguing over the high spot among the rocks they preferred for sleeping.

Leerit tried to break the awkward silence. 'Such a warm winter.'

Auntie walked beyond the sounds of the village until Leerit could only hear the distant rush of a rapid. Auntie bent to her knees and began picking a medicinal leaf with an old name. 'These leaves help grow a baby. And they help restore the mother after the birth. What is good for the baby is good for the mother. This is how living works.'

When Leerit delivered her own handful of leaves for inspection, Auntie grabbed her by the wrist. 'Name the medicines you see growing here.'

By moonlight, Leerit counted five medicinal plants. Auntie told her to see seven. She said, 'What do you notice about the ground these healing plants choose?'

Leerit studied the terrain as best she could in the fading light. It was steep, and she could see the earth here had sloughed loose years before in a minor landslide, one likely caused by snowmelt or a ferocious thunderstorm. The soil was shallow with rocks still poking through; grass hadn't yet reestablished itself. The place was like a scab on the skin of the landscape.

Auntie said, 'Those plants that heal us are the first to grow over wounded soil. Tell me why.'

Leerit considered her response carefully. 'What's good for the baby is good for the mother is good for the land. We are not so different from the soil under us. The Sea made us all from the same parts.'

Auntie's chin rose. 'Dog, elk, comfrey, plantain, dirt, old woman—in the story the Sea is telling, we each play an equal part. But listen now, my niece. No village is at the center of the Sea's story. No maiden is more important than any other.'

Auntie tucked the satchel of herbs into her robe. 'Each midwife is in her maidenhood set apart. When I was your age, I struggled. I was not well-liked. The mothers insisted I try on men. They said I should want to. I should like a good cock. When I was your age, the mothers didn't know what to make of me. A maiden with no use for a husband. What kind of girl is that?

'Now the grandmothers will tell you: what our village needed more than another mother was a woman apart, someone wrongheaded and different—someone strange enough to wonder what might be waiting over the mountains. I know the Ancients were preparing me, just as they are now preparing you.'

Auntie's grip became painful. 'Niece. When you let yourself stare at a married man, you are placing yourself at the center of a story that does not belong to you.'

When Leerit returned into the fire's light, she tried to keep busy. But she couldn't help smelling what Ozi was cooking for his wife and her family.

Into an elk's inverted stomach, he placed tubers and wild onions and chunks of meat. He used sticks to lift hot rocks from the coals, which he placed inside the stomach. The heat caused the stomach to grow. When the stomach stopped growing, Ozi added new rocks and again rolled tight the opening.

His wife was talking with her Left-Coast friends. She didn't see her husband.

Little boys were gathered about Ozi. They were of both coasts; among children, the differences were hard to see; even their voices were a melding of accents. These boys squatted near the fire, and when Ozi opened the stomach to replace the rocks, they leaned to smell the flavors. Ozi pulled a piece of glistening meat onto a boulder and cut it with his blade. They gobbled what he offered. Whatever he said made these boys laugh.

When he finally cut the stomach, steam erupted into the cold air. The flavors were overwhelming even at a distance. Fat and meat and tubers. Fragrant mushrooms dried in summer and now soaked whole by juices.

Ozi's wife ate the meal greedily. All she said was 'Next time more salt.'

While others danced, Leerit went for a swim in the hottest pool. She stayed submerged for too long. Finally, she climbed from the water and lingered in the winter dark, dizzy for the heat and unable to hold on to any memory.

Then, from behind her, she heard a willow snap.

It was the bear again dropping heavily onto all fours: the huff it made when its paws hit the ground, the growl from its throat as it stared her down. Leerit drew her knife.

The willow shook. From limbs appeared a dark shape. It was a man.

Ozi arriving to the women's pool, not along the trail but through the willow. Why, if not because he didn't want to be seen coming? He was looking up at the sky, as if his stepping out from a bush was a normal thing. He said in a shaking voice, 'What is it really, do you think?'

He meant the green aura dancing between them and the stars. Stories told of the winter lights. They were reflections from the Ancients' fires. Everyone knew that.

Ozi said, 'But where do the Ancients get their wood? Trees don't grow on mountaintops. And anyway, why would the dead get cold?'

She worried he could hear her heart. If Auntie saw them together, she would assume Leerit had lured him here. This would be her fault.

He said, 'Some of the stories—I don't know. Maybe they were invented for children. They don't make sense. Not anymore. When we crossed, I didn't see any Ancients on the mountaintop. Did you?'

'I don't know. You shouldn't be here.'

'If you want me to go, I'll go.'

She pinched tight the top of her robe. 'Your wife will be looking for you.'

'My wife doesn't notice if I am there or not.' Ozi shrugged. 'I came to say . . . Leerit, I'm sorry. About what happened. After the Sea took my opi, yours was so kind to me. He took me fishing. I think of his lessons often. Our fathers are together now. Two fishermen among the generations. Wherever it is the Ancients dwell.'

Women's voices could be heard in the distance. 'Go on,' she told him. 'You'll get us in trouble.'

He looked boldly at her. Was there more he had come to say? She wanted him to stay and say it; she wanted him to go; she wanted everything. He disappeared into the dark.

For days, she tried not to see him as he carried loads, practiced with his bow, fetched what his wife wanted, laughed, chased children.

All day she was quick to any chore Auntie assigned. If she saw his feet coming on a trail, she told herself she was allowed to look up because not to look would be rude. Even these passing glances from Ozi pressed the breath from her. All winter they had not encountered each other on a trail, and now they seemed to always be in each other's way.

When her chores were complete, she borrowed a bow and practiced with it. She could pick a target, and while her arrow flew, there was nothing else. She became one of those maidens who is always shooting.

But alone under the pelts, her hunger for him returned. Only there did Leerit let herself imagine his weight on her, his bare chest pressed against hers, their bodies slipping as if slickened by tallow; one finger could stir this hunger to breaking.

———

On the full moon, a woman Leerit's age began her labor and Auntie stayed busy walking with her in circles about camp. All motherly eyes were on this one soon to welcome her first child. They sang the old song. *The Sea is within you, your baby has grown in Her tidepool.* On this night, the mothers forgot to be suspicious of Leerit.

She hid to see him coming up the trail from the men's pool, topless and giving off plumes of steam. Here now Ozi's chest was curvatures of muscle, crescents of shadow in the flickering light of fires. He was thickest in his legs. As he passed her in the dark, he stopped. Somehow, he knew. He turned toward where she hid, and said, 'I have a riddle for you.'

Her face became instantly hot. 'How did you know I was here?'

He said, 'I like your smell. I did on the beach too.'

She could barely meet his eyes. 'A riddle?' It meant he had been thinking of her.

'Just a blade of grass will cut me,' he said. 'But to me the grass gives way. Say my name and you make me.'

She checked over her shoulder. Children were dancing with dogs, women her age were talking beside fires, their husbands clustered and laughing. Auntie was somewhere with the laboring woman. 'I don't know,' Leerit said. 'Tell me.'

'No, you have to guess. That's what makes it a riddle.'

'I don't know.'

Fire reflected from his teeth. 'When you have the answer, maybe come find me.'

Leerit hardly slept, and in the dark of morning, she heard feet pass by. Auntie wasn't in her pelts; she was still helping the laboring woman.

Leerit looked outside and saw a man's shape disappear from the firelight with his bow. Ozi going hunting. Had he come this close because he hoped she would follow?

Leerit pulled on her thickest robe and told the dogs to stay. She tracked him across the meadow where the moonlight turned the frosted grass to silver. She stepped on the dark patches left by his boots; if someone else came following, they would find only one set of tracks.

Ozi's steps were wide; he never stumbled. Where his tracks left the grass and began traversing raw ground, she had to look for the dark crescents made by his toes pressing down. She had decided she would watch him only from a distance; she was only gathering firewood; she was here getting an early start on the day's chores—that's all.

When she lost his tracks, she took a knee to look more closely. He had spent these three years following elk through thickets and across scree fields while she had been digging in mud for one last clam. If only she could read sign like Ozi, she might have found Kushim and Maren. If she was better, they would be among the village now.

At his voice, she jumped. She hadn't seen him for the shape of the terrain, hadn't smelled him because he was downwind. It meant he had waited here, for her.

She said, 'The riddle.'

His smile could be heard in his voice. 'So what's your guess?'

'Are you . . . the wind?'

She followed Ozi up the hillside, but he was slower than she wanted him to be, so she began making her own way.

On a ledge in the terrain, they sat an arm's length apart to watch the dawn. They were well hidden. For being alone with a maiden, a married man could be banished; she could be excluded; their shame would be all anyone talked about.

He offered her goat milk from a small bladder, and as they drank, he told her that he liked this place because from here he could watch where the burned ground met the densest forests. Across the canyon, the burn was already coming back green. He was explaining how the hunters had started many fires, some in early summer and some in late, to freshen the ground and awaken out-of-season growth; elk would travel great distances for rich foods. He said every half-burned tree would one day fall and become lush new grass. Soon elderberries would be growing two-men tall. 'Elk feeds us and we feed her.'

Then he said, 'I never stopped hoping you would come over the mountains.'

'Me? Why me?'

'Why does a man dance for a woman?'

She glared at him. 'You say this now, yet you said yes to *her*.'

Ozi shook his head. 'I didn't say yes. My wife did not propose. It is different here. We didn't choose. The council told us we would have to—'

His head turned. Something across the ravine had caught his attention.

Leerit saw it too. A hind was appearing soundlessly from the forest, her breath silver in the cold light. The elk was watching, smelling, turning to check every direction. When the matriarch walked into the open, her family followed. She continued to stand guard as her children and grandchildren busied themselves with eating the new grass growing from the ash. There in the light of the rising sun, the family commenced chattering, mews and yips, every elk speaking in its own voice. Not so different from a village.

Ozi leaned. His whisper was air against her neck. 'The grandmother remembers. She has survived fifteen or twenty winters. Think of all the children and grandchildren she has seen lost to arrows and claws and deep snow. She never stops worrying. Her worry is what keeps those children alive.'

Leerit was again standing over the blood in the grass; it was a kill site, her baby brother tangled and broken in the willows where the bear had thrown him.

'I'm sorry,' Ozi said. 'You're shaking. Did I say the wrong thing?'

Her breath was coming too fast and she was overcome by a need to flee, to cover ground. 'I'm fine.'

It kept happening like this. As sudden and unexpected as when she had arrived with that load of meat to see the bear like a demon in their camp. The smell of Kushim's blood came next, the heat of his urine against her back as she carried him, how his shin hinged where there wasn't a joint when she pulled him from the willow. The sound bone makes grinding against shards of bone.

Ozi's voice drew her back from that edge. He was saying that some-day one of the elk calves would be the grandmother, that a herd was not only many individuals but also a single ceaseless creature that moved across eons.

The grandmother lifted her nose, and Leerit felt it: the breeze had swirled around to the back of her neck. The old matriarch barked, and everyone else twirled and trotted back into the safety of the thicket. The herd had disappeared at a mere whiff.

Ozi said, 'She is the child of ten thousand survivors. Think of it: this very herd wandered our beaches; it dodged the arrows sent by the Ancients—it is the same herd who walked from the waves at the origin and somehow survived the Great Wave and what came after. We have all been here longer than our years.'

———

She returned first, via a different route. In her arms was a load of fire-wood, her excuse. She went straight to Auntie who was sitting among a group of old women. Leerit said, 'I have to find my sister. I won't wait a day longer.'

Auntie looked but seemed not to hear.

'You said when there was light enough. Now there is light. I am leaving. You can't stop me.'

Still, Auntie didn't answer. Her eyes were unblinking.

This look on Auntie's face. Someone must have seen her and Ozi together. Someone had told. Auntie could see the guilt inside her. Ama too always knew the truth.

The old woman beside Auntie sucked her teeth. The others shook their heads. Leerit was deciding to run when Auntie said, 'The Ancients—they have chosen Vagnu.'

The mysterious towers built across the meadows like a village of people with their arms held out—those towers had been built to steer a running herd of elk. Vagnu said he had heard the truth spoken from the mountaintop, and who could say otherwise now?

For he and the bachelors had slaughtered the entire herd, and everyone was needed. Elk bodies lay scattered across rocks. The grandmother, still breathing, had been dispatched with a blade to her throat.

Vagnu had blood to his elbows. He beamed to tell the story. His hunters had seen the animals and spooked them toward the towers, which had turned the elk toward the valley bottom as a single mass, just as the Ancients had promised. When the elk should have scattered, when they should have climbed high, the towers turned them down and funneled them; the individuals had followed their grandmother into a canyon where, with no escape, arrows could rain down upon them.

Men were congratulating him, women and mothers too. Left Coast and Right. He raised his bloody hands proudly. 'Do not praise *me*. Praise the Ancients who told me how to feast in this place where the wind swirls!'

Auntie said, 'But you killed too many. We haven't salt enough for so much meat.'

Vagnu's chin rose. 'Only a Right-Coast woman could disparage a man for feeding her.'

Repopulate. The word would not leave his mind.

Cyrus was looking at the map of the Empire on his office wall—only a generation old and already it was a map of the past. Settlements and plastic mines listed here were now buried under sand.

At the extreme southern edge of the map were the words IMPASSABLE DUNES, a name given centuries before to the desert that was said to extend to the precipice of the world. When Cyrus was a boy, his father had told him that those dunes were not always there. *They buried fertile fields.* He had been standing in this exact spot in the office, his father beside him, looking at this map together when it was still true. Cyrus had asked, *Where does sand come from? Who made it?* His father's answer: *If you waste bounty, waste will come for you.*

Now every field was planted, every master's quota higher; there was not a fiber or grain or bite of meat going to waste. Yet the dunes were still coming.

No doubt tonight, across the city, devout men were standing atop testament stones to sing of the beginning. Three hundred generations hence, but nothing before. Not *repopulate* but *populate*. For the devout, the sand was only a reason to sing louder.

If his father were to appear beside him now, returned from his perch beside the all-knowing Sun, Cyrus would ask the man who made him, *What bounty did old men waste to bring upon their children such destruction?*

His was a city growing desperate. Winter had brought the predicted shortages of grain and maize and wood for heating, and now Cyrus couldn't drive across town without a second carriage heavy with guardsmen. The torches affixed behind their horses threw bucking shadows over the sandy streets.

Jernod had recommended the widow cease all unnecessary trips from the estate after a Lady of equal standing had been abducted for ransom. Before the monies could be paid—it was gossiped—the Lady had been spoiled by her captors. Yet his mother would not be dissuaded from moving about the city as she pleased, not by a mere probability of violent capture. 'I refuse to live in a cage,' she had told Cyrus. So he had been forced to spend more of his borrowed funds to bolster her personal defense.

The cost of every commodity had already risen above the direst predictions. Despite careful accounting, he no longer had funds enough to cover his expenses until shearing.

Already this winter Cyrus had sent two letters to Ashair asking if he and the wife had food and firewood. He was worried about them freezing, worried they might be hungry; he was willing to send whatever. 'Just tell me what you need.' Yet Ashair had sent no response. Not one word since they dropped the dying boy at the hospital. As if Cyrus were a stranger, as if *they* had never existed.

'Are you okay, sir?' It was Jernod asking. Cyrus had been pounding his fist.

The carriage was rattling now. There was business to attend to. Cyrus asked Jernod for his honest assessment. As a man who had beat back primitives during the Final Uprising, what did he think of this plan to clear one remote valley for the sake of wool?

They were rumbling up the hill now. The sky was dark and star filled, and the torchlight was fogged by horse breath. Jernod said, 'Candidly, sir?'

Cyrus assured his driver that from here forward candor should be the assumption.

'Sir, have you ever thrown a heavy rock onto a sheet of ice?'

He had not, but he liked a metaphor. His father never trusted metaphors. They lived too far from numbers.

'Sir. Can you predict what would happen if you did?'

Cyrus considered Jernod's question. 'If the rock was big enough and the ice thin enough, I suppose it would drop through—a clean break.'

They were beyond the shanties now, and Jernod stopped them beside a pond of water that had frozen over. While the horses caught their breath and a second carriage of guards watched in confusion, they walked together to the edge of the ice. Jernod went farther and carried the torch onto the ice to show that it could hold his weight. When he returned, Jernod produced one of the bronze bowlers Cyrus's father always kept in the carriage on the off chance a game presented itself.

Cyrus did as Jernod told him. He held out the ball. He let it fall. The bowler hit the ice with a smack; it did not fall through.

But the bowler had sent fissures to the far side of the pond. Jernod lifted it and gave it back to Cyrus. He put a foot on the ice and the cracking was instantaneous. He stepped with a little more weight, and a vast slab broke and tipped. Jernod was ready; only the toe of his boot dipped under. His driver said, 'Sir. It is the same with predictions of war.'

'But this wouldn't be *war*, Jernod. Only scaring off a few wild animals who already waste too much of my graze.'

Jernod looked troubled. 'Sir. I suspect the primitives won't appreciate such distinctions.'

He didn't have any other choice, not if he was to deliver a fifth more wool. This was what Cyrus told General Rah. Without soldiers and a new investment of capital, he didn't have a chance of meeting his quota. Before such a superior man, the only leverage Cyrus had was sympathy; he added, 'I come to you now on my mother's behalf. I'm sure you would agree: a widow should not be left at the mercy of irredeemable men.'

They were meeting inside the estate this time, in a rotunda where a bonfire burned beneath a bronze chimney. General Rah was wearing his formal uniform, like those he wore any evening in the theater. Rah's officers were about them, drinking and laughing, sheaths empty of swords. Music was being played by entertainers; there were dancers and jugglers. Rah's young wives hung from the necks of partisans. Cyrus had never been elbow to elbow with the red-robed political class. Here were members of the Emperor's court who oversaw every license and permit, every acquisition and merger. Each was profoundly drunk.

To hear Cyrus speak, General Rah looked displeased. He snapped a finger, and an exotic-looking wife came close. She put into Cyrus's mouth a chunk of salty meat and began to rub his neck. Rah looked sober, the only man here who did. He said, 'I will not send my soldiers on some shepherd's errand. You must be a fool to ask.'

But Cyrus could not take no for an answer. Without Rah's soldiers, he wouldn't have the graze; he wouldn't meet his quota—there would be no boarding passes. The wife began rubbing his groin. He said, 'Not a shepherd's errand, sir. This cause is for the Empire itself. Civilization is built from wool.'

General Rah smirked. 'Is civilization not built from bronze?'

'That too.'

With a finger raised, Rah sent the wife retreating. To Cyrus, he whispered, 'Come now. Be honest. We are the only men here who know the truth: civilization is built from story.'

Rah's office was oval-shaped. Sculptures as large as imperial statues stood on pedestals about the room. Another fire was burning here, and it rendered the air in the empty space uncomfortably warm; Cyrus's winter wool began to itch.

The manservant unlocked a heavy door that swung open to reveal an even larger chamber. He hurriedly lit the torches before leaving them alone inside a room with walls so thick that they could no longer hear the music and merriment of the estate.

Scrolls towered on neat stacks for the entirety of the room. As in the archives, the air smelled of seasoned parchment—such a soothing smell. Here were thousands of texts. So many that each was assigned a series of numbers, the same organizational system used within the imperial stacks. 'You must agree,' General Rah said. 'Mine is not the collection of a common enthusiast. What did you think of the scroll I had delivered?'

Cyrus hadn't yet returned it; the scroll was still creased from his and Ashair's lovemaking. He had tried steam. He had tried flattening the crease under the weight of bricks. He kept unfurling it to look again at the crease, then at that one wrong word. 'How are we sure that it is authentic?'

Rah scoffed. 'Do you believe me to be a man who would be duped by a fake?'

'No sir, of course not.'

'Yet you dare ask me if I am proud of a . . . *counterfeit?*'

'Forgive me.' Cyrus tried smiling. 'The drink. It has left me dizzy.'

With a tight grip on Cyrus's upper arm, Rah drew him toward the exit. Whatever mood had prompted him to welcome Cyrus to his archive had soured. The door clanked shut behind them, and Cyrus was again standing among statues in the office. 'My men will retrieve the scroll tomorrow.'

'Won't you allow me the honor of returning it personally, sir?'

From behind his desk, Rah withdrew a small bronze key. It wasn't the ornate key one would expect to open a door in an estate like this one. It was old and burdened by a heavy patina.

'I will not send my soldiers to protect grass,' General Rah said. 'But— I can provide funding. With what I give, you can hire mercenaries. I'll recommend the name of a commander you can trust. His fighters will solve this Highland problem for you. They are battle-tested veterans. They are brutal, and efficient. They know how to deal with primitives.'

'Thank you, sir. But I don't intend any brutality. The men only need clear the wild animals. If we do that, I'm confident the primitives will follow.'

General Rah's face revealed nothing. Into Cyrus's hand, he placed the old key. 'In return for my help, you will deliver this.'

Cyrus could make out a vague design carved into the key's side: two swords crossed over a shield. 'I'm happy to, sir. Deliver it to whom?'

General Rah glared. 'Say nothing to the man who comes. Simply put the key in his hand. Do you understand?'

'Yes sir.'

'When the sky warms tomorrow, be at the testament stone outside the theater. Bring your guards. Wear a formal robe. You are my ambassador, my emissary. Cyrus, do not let me down. I am not a man you want as your enemy.'

The mere word from Rah's lips sent a shiver up Cyrus's back.

The general crossed the room and opened the office door. He was holding it for Cyrus. Their meeting was over.

Cyrus stepped into the hallway. The office door shut behind him, and Cyrus was alone in the corridor.

The sounds of merriment were distant and unalluring. He hurried to Jernod, who was already loading chests of coins. Seeing so much money, the corroded old key suddenly felt heavy in Cyrus's hand. He asked his driver, 'Why did my father not borrow from General Rah?'

'A driver never asks,' Jernod said. 'But I can tell you this. There were few men to whom the Master was unwilling to make himself beholden.'

By now, after so long, Lilah knew some of the language but still not enough to say what she wanted. Trinket's remedies, her careful treatments—they had helped Lilah survive the coughing sickness, the girls too. The few words she knew of the desert language felt too flimsy to hold her gratitude. She caught Trinket's sleeve and placed into her hand a shell bead.

It was the shell she had found in the pocket of a dirty robe and kept safe these months in her bedding. At night, she had used a spoon's edge to carve the shell into a bead like those the desert nomads were once willing to trade for goats. Common shells made into common beads— but to the desert tribes, these things had once been worth endless winter walking.

By now, Lilah knew Trinket had been here since she was thirty-one years old. This was her thirtieth winter among the village. Next year, she would have spent more of her life inside than out. One day, Lilah heard Trinket say—with no visible emotion—'My children have grown or perished without me.'

Now Trinket held the shell to the light. From the constant smoke, her eyes seemed forever red. Wrinkles were worn into her cheeks from a lifetime of passing judgment. She was nearly the same age as Lilah's mother would be now, were she still living.

The shell depicted what Lilah imagined a desert woman wanted to see: dunes, the sun rising, people walking free. Holding it, Trinket spoke too fast for Lilah to understand.

But Kenta was beside her. The child was picking up the language much faster. 'This brings memories of her grandmother. She wants to know where you found it.'

Lilah tried to explain. 'I carved the bead to say thank you. For healing us.'

Trinket's brow pinched; she looked troubled or angry. Lilah acknowledged, 'It's a lesser tribute than you're owed.'

Trinket surprised her when she drew her near. They were standing nose to nose, brow to brow. It was the gesture of desert women—what was shared between sisters or between mothers and daughters.

Lilah's plan was simple, as any escape needed to be. Every day the gate opened to let in carts of wool or firewood. It opened again to let out whatever carts had come inside. As a precaution, whenever the gate opened, the guards drew their blades. Most days, the gate was raised or lowered without delay; there wasn't time to sneak past. But occasionally carts would approach the gate as others were readying to leave. On these days, the gate remained open long enough for quick feet to rush past. It was a weakness. The only one she had found. Lilah told the girls how they would do it. As the gate lifted, she would tip over her cauldron and spill its contents. While every man with a blade was watching Lilah, Koneet could take her sister and slip between the stacks of firewood and run out through the open gate. Lilah would sprint after them, but only after they were safely beyond the walls. She didn't want to think about what came next. Hiding from the guards who would inevitably pursue them, navigating the senseless canyons built by human hands, stealing a boat without being seen by Giants working near the water. Instead, she thought of what came after: raising the sail, passing every headland and reef, hearing the break of waves against yellow sands. Would her children come running? What would she do if they did not?

'Be ready, heed my command,' Lilah told the sisters. 'I will deliver you home.'

Hungry people had been appearing at the gate all winter, growing in number each day, their arms reaching through the bars. By now, Lilah knew enough of the language to hear that they were asking for food, for labor. They wanted inside. They would do anything for the chance.

Beggars, Trinket called them. At first, Lilah couldn't look away from their desperate eyes. But in time, she grew used to their pleading; soon she could pass a whole day and hardly notice them. She had to remind herself how wrong it was: to see one in need and feel nothing. In any coastal village, even a hungry village, beggars were welcomed and offered the best. On the coast, no one could sit by as someone suffered.

At night, her terrors were relentless: the house she and Tamar had built was now full of sand, no tracks across the shore. In these nightmares, not even her voice worked. She couldn't call her babies' names. She didn't remember them. Morning came as relief. Waking, she always said the same prayer, her first words: *Leerit, Maren, Kushim.*

Outside in the morning, Lilah prepared tinder while Koneet came from the dark with embers. Soon the fire would be crackling. It was the only work Lilah did here that was the same as she would be doing at home—starting a fire. Everything after was senseless.

One morning, as she delivered the embers, Koneet said, 'When the wool arrives, I am taking my sister. We won't wait another day.'

Lilah looked at the guards who were busy warming their hands near a fire. Overhead, the wind was already strong. 'We can't launch a boat now. The waves would swamp us.'

'I would rather drown in the Sea than spend another day as their animal.'

Kenta took hold of Lilah's robe. 'The river knows when to rush. Sister, hear the wind. Listen to Auntie.'

Lilah said, 'We will only have one chance at escape.'

Koneet was still holding the trowel that cradled the embers. A guard had taken notice of her delay. He began crossing the yard toward them.

Lilah took the trowel from Koneet's hand and bent to put the embers to the tinder. She blew the coals to flame, and when she handed Koneet back the trowel, the guard was watching. Koneet wasn't returning to her duties with the other woodcutters. She said with so much disdain, 'You've become a dog for their food.'

Lilah steadied herself. 'No one wants out of here more than I do. My children . . .' She couldn't finish the thought.

When the guard called, Koneet turned back to her labor.

Each day over the warming water, Lilah did what she could: shut her eyes to see it again, each step back to them, turning every corner and setting sail, filling jugs at the waterfall, tending the rudder. This journey back to her children was by now in her mind like a song, like a prayer; it was an oath she recited when she fell asleep and again when she woke. Lilah had made the journey so many times without leaving this place that she could no longer be sure which details were real and which had been invented.

All she had in excess was time and regret. Back when, she had yelled too often—she used to scold her perfect children. They did nothing wrong, ever. She lost her temper because on that lonely beach she was tired, hungry, terrified; her sister had left; she was a woman without a village. She used to think about the possibility all the time: if something happened to Tamar, she would be alone on the beach with three hungry mouths. Sometimes, looking at her babies, she felt like she couldn't breathe. The day Leerit packed her things to move across the bay, Lilah had pointed a finger at her oldest. 'A woman is not meant to live alone!'

But even these memories were blurring now, as if cast through steam. Little by little, she was forgetting. The details of their daily routine, the words Leerit had said before she left, what Maren and Kushim said when they learned their sister had moved across the bay. Already, she could hardly conjure the sound of their voices. One day, she knew, their faces would be gone.

Trinket had once been a thirty-nine-year-old mother consumed with escaping. What had happened to render her an old woman who no longer tried?

On the wooden frame of his bed, Kushim found scratch marks. He decided they were left by someone before him marking days. By then, Kushim had already lost track of how long he'd been in this bed. Because he couldn't always tell dream from memory. Day from night. What was hidden, kept hidden, by him, or some part of him that didn't want to know, to remember, to be consumed by.

But he knew this was a *hospital*. He was a *patient*. New words in a new place where he had no sisters, no family but this man who sat and held his hand, who taught him to make their bird sounds. *Doctor Ashair*.

A good-enough place, a stone hearth for warmth, food put in his lap—food. There were people to watch, conversations to overhear, so many people. Patients talking, healers whispering, men quarreling. He was the youngest, often the only child. He had nothing to do but listen.

An old woman was the one to bring him water. When he pooped or pissed, which he did in bed because he couldn't walk, she took the pot out from under him. She never said a word; she would not meet his eyes. But yesterday, she had left him a cluster of grass stems. Not ripped at once from a clump, not a mess of leaves and dead stalks, but a cluster of perfect green stems all the same length. She had lifted a stem and showed him how to bend it, how to connect this one to the next. She had set both into his hands and withdrawn from her robe a finished weave of grass. He understood. It was the gift of a task for his hands. Something to pass the time.

'Thank you,' he said as best he could in their sounds. She smiled sadly.

Now, again, his sisters are looking down and he is seeing in their faces his death. The bear is still on him, that's what they don't know, paws pressing him into mud. The underbelly of black fur, parting as it flexes to reveal chasms of gray fluff and white flesh. The huffing of breath, the hissing tear of skin, his skin, the cracking of bone—his bone.

Lying here. This here now. *The hospital*. But the bear is still here somehow.

JOHN LARISON

An island or a cloud. Apart from all he ever heard described. This hospital. His sisters won't know where to find him. He left no tracks they can recognize.

Watching for Doctor Ashair, to see him coming, to be seen. Alone, so alone, never this alone, his sisters had promised he wouldn't be alone.

Doctor Ashair appeared on the edge of the bed, a sweeping decoration about his neck, golden and black, red and purple—such brilliant colors. He let Kushim feel this new scarf between his fingers. When Kushim tried to make their bird calls, Doctor Ashair smiled. It was what Kushim could do, say their bird sounds, braid grass with his fingers, make this kind man smile.

Doctor Ashair pulled from his robe a small woolen pouch and patted Kushim's shoulder. What he said made no sense, but his face was easy to trust.

Doctor Ashair moved to the next bed, a man with two purple eyes. Doctor Ashair did not smile at this man. Did not leave him a woolen pouch. Serious, nodding as he listened, his chin resting on a hand propped from crossed arms.

Kushim opened the pouch. Inside were three rounded pieces of amber. Too light in his fingers to be mineral. When he licked one, he found it sweet. His whole body lunged toward it: all three pieces were on his tongue before they could get away. He had not known a taste could be so sweet.

Doctor Ashair called to him the bird sound for this wonder. 'Candy.'

He was different now, since the bear, he knew it. He was not the same boy his mother had made. Pain could not make him cry, not anymore.

Pain wasn't surprising enough or cruel enough. He cried to be alone. He cried to no longer be the boy his mother had wanted for a son.

His fingers could feel the wound, track it from the bridge of his nose up onto the crown of his head. His chest hurt with every breath because his ribs had snapped. His left arm had eight ragged tooth holes, four on bottom and four on top. These were oozing red sores now. But his leg. It was yellow and small, and when he shifted his weight, his foot didn't always move, like it wasn't sure it wanted to stay a part of him.

His sisters were there only sometimes when he listened very carefully.

Story or song?

Story. A happy story.

Then stop crying and listen. I won't start until you stop crying.

I am not the same boy.

No, you are not. You are less.

Please don't leave. You promised I would never be alone.

Once he was on the beach with other children, dove into a wave like other children, was flipped and tossed and crunched onto sand and swept back out and tossed with the next wave, mouth stuffed with saltwater and sand. It was drowning; he knew he was drowning. Leerit saved him. Pulled him to dry sand and brushed the hair from his eyes. *Now watch this*, she had said. Back into the waves she went, jumping up with each swell until the one she wanted, diving with it toward shore, kicking, her body riding its wall, Leerit disappearing inside, his big sister bursting from the wave's hollow—her hair still dry.

How, he had asked her. *How do you have no fear? How do you not drown?*

We don't fight water, she told him. *We ride it.*

221

———

The bear was on him and he woke to re-re-rediscover he was in this place called the hospital, but this time the bear was still there; it was on his bed; it was eating from his belly! He screamed for them, for Ama and Opi, for his sisters, for Doctor Ashair. Yet the bear took its time pulling intestines like snakes from his abdomen, chewing them as they writhed, teeth smacking for more, muzzle red with his blood.

He punched; he fought back, but the bear only pinned his shoulders. It shook him. From this bear's mouth came not roars—but bird songs.

Not a bear at all. It was the man with two purple eyes from the bed next to his. He was shaking him. Stirred awake by Kushim's nightmare and here to quiet him.

Torches were being lit and that's how he knew it was another day. He watched for the old woman to come to take the pot of his urine. When she did, she put her fingers to the weave he had made of grass. She smiled. She left him to go collect the pots of other patients.

Kushim watched for Doctor Ashair. His fingers stayed busy unbraiding the grass stems. Unbraiding them so he could braid them again. He withdrew each piece from the weave and straightened it and watched it curl again with the memory of being bent and broken.

Like in a dream, the old woman returned. She arrived as she had moments before to collect his pan of urine—except somehow last night's piss was still in the pan. The grass wasn't unbraided. It was still in its weave. This moment was happening twice, but how?

Like waves lifting and pulling him farther from shore. He had been here before; it tasted like stale smoke—he was being swept away. Drowning! And then: lightning struck.

———

Reborn: faces looking down at him, his mouth tasting of blood. Tongue torn, every part of his body aching like he had just climbed a mountain. Vomit spilling over his lap.

Still morning, everyone still in their places, looking, the old woman looking. A day has passed, two days, three—but everyone is still in their places. He has aged a year while they were watching.

What happened? What did I do wrong?

The people parted to let Doctor Ashair through. He took Kushim in his arms. The vomit and tears were on them both. He held him so tightly. He had no answers, but Doctor Ashair would not let go.

XIV

Atrocity

For days after the slaughter, they had lived under the chatter of birds. Because there was only so much marrow a person could slurp, only so much venison that would fit inside a belly. As Auntie had predicted, most of the herd's sacrifice spoiled before the people could make use of it. Flocks of crows had rolled across the sky like incoming waves. The problem was the lack of salt, but also the air, which had become so warm. No snow clung to the mountaintops, no frost on the trees. Never a winter like this. The village was already hungry again. No elk had been sighted. Children in summer robes held their stomachs and complained. Each day felt somehow warmer than the last. Mothers shook their heads at the sky. Their bickering became louder each hungry morning.

Some said the elk were angry that their gifts had been allowed to rot. Others argued that the elk would return as soon as people stopped talking about rot; they should be talking instead about gratitude. No one sang when everyone argued.

Auntie called the village together. She told them that the council had decided it was time to move to a new camp. They would start over in a different part of the valley.

Yet this time many dared disagree. They wanted to stay. They were tired of walking, and this camp was good. The elk would return. An argument ensued. Voices grew louder. Auntie and the other prominent women sat on their benches listening.

A few Left-Coast women together asked for the village's attention. Auntie acknowledged them and used her own voice to call the people to silence. With a gesture of the hand, she invited these women to speak. One with harsh and squinting eyes stepped forward. 'We want to talk of something different. Of the seven of you who decide, only two are of the Left Coast. We think this council should be equal.'

Auntie explained. 'Only the Ancients can call a person to the council. They send omens. This is not for the living to decide.'

'The Ancients have decided!' a man's voice dared shout. Vagnu. The women parted to let him through. 'Just this morning I heard the Ancients whispering in my ear again. They said that another Left-Coaster should sit upon this council with you. In this valley, they said, I should be the one to help decide.'

Many in the crowd laughed outright. It was such an absurd idea, welcoming a man among the prominent few. Men couldn't think for themselves; they thought whatever their mother or wife told them was true.

Yet others seemed to be considering it. A Left-Coaster called, 'In this valley where life is hard, a village needs many men. Maybe men should help decide.'

Another from the Left Coast asked, 'Who among you heard what those towers were for? The Ancients chose Vagnu. They trust him. Why shouldn't we?'

'But the council has always been made up of mothers.'

A Left-Coaster pointed at Auntie. 'She has no children but sits on a bench! Why not a man if she can sit?'

To see someone pointing a finger at the midwife, the village gasped.

'Beware of this nonsense.' It was Ozi's mother speaking. She spit to show her fury. 'The Ancients choose our midwife, and the midwife is always on the council, and you Left-Coasters must respect what I say.'

Commotion was immediate. An elder of the Right Coast asked to speak and everyone fell silent out of respect. 'For the children's sakes, let us stop arguing. Here no headland divides us. We are one together. You make complex what is simple. Yes, we should have equal members on the council. But never a man.'

'You are right that it is simple,' a Left-Coast elder responded. 'Right-Coasters always think they know best.'

Again, they were shouting. Auntie called for their attention. She clapped her hands but their voices grew louder. No one was listening.

At a deafening sound, everyone turned, even Auntie. It was Vagnu blowing through a billy's horn.

He was perched upon a boulder, balanced there on one foot. This was spectacle; he had their attention and he knew it. 'Mothers, daughters, sons,' he began as if he were important. 'These Right-Coasters have always lifted their noses at us good people. You know I am right. They won't stop today or tomorrow or in a hundred more winters. Disdain for us is in their blood. Their mothers are to blame.'

There was murmuring, but silence returned when Vagnu raised a finger.

'Wait! Listen! The Ancients are whispering to me right now!' He cupped his hand behind his ear.

'What do they say?' asked a Left-Coast voice.

'Yes, tell us!'

Vagnu smiled. 'The Ancients have spoken. They tell me, "Two coasts, not one. In this valley, we should be two villages."'

Then Vagnu pointed at Auntie. 'Take your people wherever you want. We will remain here to welcome Elk's return.'

As the village separated itself according to its oldest divisions, even the dogs looked unsure. They whined as their pack broke apart according to which family had raised which pup. Leashes had to be used to separate littermates. Children cried because their friends were leaving. In this valley, children cared nothing about which coast.

Leerit watched Ozi at his wife's side. As a husband, he had no choice but to leave his mother and remain with his wife.

The two villages had agreed to divide the provisions equally, and yet, soon after settling into the new camp, someone discovered that what little salt existed had been stolen. An old woman sucked her teeth. 'How like Left-Coasters to thieve what isn't theirs.'

Some women wanted to send their husbands back to fetch the salt, but Auntie told them no. To send the husbands would only provoke more conflict. Instead, Auntie summoned four boys who were nearly men to journey to the valley's lone salting rocks. On the coast, every rock wore salt but here only certain rocks contained salt and they had to be broken to access the minerals. It was hard work; for these boys, the journey and labor would take many days. In reward, they would be tattooed with their first markings of manhood.

'Until our sons return,' Auntie told the people, 'we will do without salt.'

For the first time, the village passed a night without the company of song.

Only three evenings later, commotion again swept through the village. Someone was hurt. A mother began wailing.

Leerit arrived to see one of the boys sent for salt now wrapped in pelts. His friends had carried him between them. From just one look, she knew he was dying. To see him, her legs quit; she sank into the grass. Another dying boy.

His friends couldn't stop crying. They told their story. Arrows had rained down on them. They had walked into an ambush and were living only because those who fired chose to hold back and not give chase.

'Vagnu shot at our sons?' Fathers were already stringing their bows.

'Not Vagnu!' the survivors called.

The wounded one's eyes were shut. He was beyond moaning, his breaths rare and gasping. Auntie didn't even attempt a remedy.

When his mother draped herself over him, the boy's eyes flickered open. This was what he had been holding on for. The boy said to the woman who had made him, 'Ama, I'm so sorry.'

Those eyes didn't close. They went gray.

Auntie pulled back the pelts to reveal the green and sour wound to the child's abdomen. The arrow was broken midshaft. She had sent this boy to his death, and now she withdrew what killed him.

Dark blood clung to the arrowhead. A point not knapped from rock. Leerit recognized the same orange material as Chun's knife, come here now to this valley where storms were born.

At the sight, people began clamoring.

Auntie silenced them. 'Listen now. You will stay calm. Gather only what is vital. Prepare to flee. Barbarian is here. He spared these boys so he could follow their tracks to us.'

Cyrus shed his helmet and cape. He set them off to the side of the road among boulders where they couldn't be found. He put on a laborer's robe, a common hat. Looking up at the winter Sun, he wondered if his father was really there, looking down, his eye among the brightest eye of all, the grower of grass, the grower of wool, the giver of fire—the source of all warmth. If it was true that upon death a man gained such a vantage, did his father now see the truth of his son?

He had delivered General Rah's key as directed. With a full entourage and a formal cape, Cyrus had rumbled to the base of the theater's testament stone only to find no one there. As he waited, he noticed two policemen chatting. These two officers who worked together each day had an ease of gesture that could belong to brothers.

Jernod had called Cyrus's attention from the police to the approach of a man in dark robes. He wore his hood up, and from that darkness came the vapor of breath. Not a word was spoken between Cyrus and the man. He simply put the old key into the dirty, calloused hand. Then it was done. The man disappeared into an alley. When Cyrus looked, the police were watching.

Why didn't Rah send a servant on this petty errand? What door did that strange key open? These questions continued to peck at Cyrus now as he walked on his own two feet through the city's most dangerous quarters. Wearing not his proper plumage and helmet but the common wool and muddy boots of one his groundskeepers. Hood up despite the unseasonable air. Hands in his pockets. On these streets, a man could be invisible.

He was walking because Jernod had refused to drive him. His hired guard, the man paid to do as he was told, dared refuse to deliver Cyrus to his destination. 'These days, in that quarter,' Jernod had said in a tone dangerously close to lecture, 'one would need a platoon.'

With rising prices, few could afford staples. Theft, looting, even murder were beginning to feel routine in the city. The victims were too often a citizen of visible means. So when Ashair's missive arrived by courier and Jernod said no, Cyrus had no choice but to slip out his gates as a common man.

It had been months since he'd seen Ashair. He had sent a third letter and required Jernod to deliver it directly. The letter invited Ashair to an upcoming lecture; it renewed Cyrus's offers to deliver food or firewood, whatever Ashair and his wife needed. And yet silence had been the only response. Civilization may be built of stories, but a city was built upon expectations of decency and respect, basic principles that underpinned all relationships. You couldn't just go around pretending your actions had no consequences.

Cyrus startled when he heard the sound of approaching boots. Everyone dressed like him was putting their backs to the wall. He did like these commoners and bowed his head as if it were a familiar gesture. A police patrol was passing. Boots stomping as one. They were not wearing the dark wool or carrying the simple clubs once familiar to police. Seemingly overnight, their detachments had grown to at least twelve men, fully armored with bronze shoulders and winged helmets, twin swords and lances, archers in their middle ranks. They looked like a small army marching into battle.

After the patrol passed, Cyrus was soon struck by a man rounding a corner. They collided hard enough that Cyrus fell backward, yet the man didn't stop or help him up or even beg forgiveness. In his hand was a hammer.

Cyrus couldn't help but demand the apology he was owed. It was a mistake to call out. His caste could not be hidden from his voice; every face on the street turned to stare. Every face but the one who owed him an apology.

The offender stopped within sight before one of the many bronze statues of the Emperor, depicted always as being twice as tall as any human. The terrible, offensive man began shouting. 'You are a liar! You will leave us behind!' He began beating the bronze knee with the hammer.

The police patrol seized the man with ease. He didn't even try to elude them. His last act was to throw the hammer into the Emperor's belly. Now Cyrus looked away. He didn't need to witness what would happen next. Pummeled and dragged to the nearest testament stone, strung up by his feet—this man would die watching crows pick bare his bones. This had been a suicide.

They met as planned at the old park near Ashair's home. Ashair said only, 'I assumed you'd come in a carriage.'

The park had not been swept, and now ankle-high dunes were forming, blown here on the ceaseless dry winter winds. Pigeons walked about open patches of ground, their heads always a step behind. When the boy hobbled toward them, a pair took flight. One of his legs was still splinted straight. At first, Cyrus didn't recognize the primitive they had rescued.

Ashair had said the boy would die before they reached the city—*his body is surrendering*—and yet here he was. Under Ashair's care, he had beaten back the infection. Now Ashair described what he had done to the boy's scalp, how he'd cut away the dead skin and nurtured new tissue to grow in its place. The scars were deep and wide and hard to look at. During the recovery, Ashair had gone from medical student to junior doctor, with this boy as his primary patient.

Now the boy was laughing at the pigeons.

Ashair was watching. 'They said it was hopeless. Help him die in peace, they said. No one was surer than the senior doctors. I knew he would die

too, but by oath, I was bound to try. I still am not sure. Did my remedies heal him or did he heal himself?'

So much had changed since they last saw each other. A cluster of gray
hairs had sprouted at the back of Ashair's neck. He was noticeably thin-
ner. Cyrus asked, 'How is she? How is the pregnancy?'

'Healthy, normal.'

'When?'

'Midsummer.'

'Is there anything I can do? I assume you received my letters. I sent
several.'

'We have what we need.'

Cyrus let his knee touch Ashair's. 'If there is anything I can do to
help . . .'

Ashair withdrew from his touch. 'There is something. The hospital
wasn't the right place anymore. The boy has been sleeping on our floor.
Learning the language. She's taken to him more than she thought she
would. But . . .' Ashair was fidgeting; he was not comfortable. 'But with
the baby coming, with me at the hospital all night—we both think it's
time. It's been months. To finish healing, he needs to rejoin his tribe.
Maybe you could arrange it?'

The boy was sitting in the sand, and the pigeons were hopping closer
to see if some morsel might be waiting in his hand. Cyrus said, 'I never
learned his name.'

'It's pronounced *Kush-eem*,' Ashair said. There was such tenderness
about his face as he watched the boy. 'Can you arrange it? I don't know
who else to ask.'

'He can barely walk.'

'The leg will bear weight soon. He told me that his parents were lost
to the ocean. They were carried away. He sings for his sisters. His songs

will pull tears from your eyes. One needn't understand the words to feel their weight.'

Cyrus admitted, 'It might be impossible to find his tribesmen currently.'

'Why? I assumed your shepherds would know where.'

'It's complicated.'

'Complicated?' Ashair's eyes narrowed. 'Do these *complications* have anything to do with your ceaseless hunger for wool?'

'Not *my* hunger,' Cyrus said.

Ashair pursed his lips. It was a face ripe with judgment.

'I can take him,' Cyrus said. 'He'll reach his clan. If that's what you want, I will make it happen.'

They sat in silence. The child had lured the pigeons near enough to pet.

'There's something else you need to know,' Ashair said. 'It has only happened twice, and not in a while. Seizures. From the fever or the blow to his head, I'm not sure. If he begins convulsing, stand back. Move anything that he might hurt himself against. Let it pass. Don't try to suppress his body. Afterward, be gentle with him. Smile. Use a calm voice. Tell him everything will be okay. He will be confused.'

'What are these . . . *seizures?*'

'Medically, it's complicated. His fever brought him halfway to the Sun, and a spirit remembers the soaring of death. Failing once, naturally it will try again to return home. But the Sun won't let him in, not until it's his time. You'll think he's dying. Then he'll wake as if from an awful dream. He'll ask what happened.'

'What should I tell him?'

'Tell him that he's safe. Tell him he'll never be alone.' Ashair stood. He was watching the march of a police patrol. 'Will you treat him kindly? Promise you won't make him one of your indentured.'

'He'll be my guest.' Cyrus dared touch Ashair's elbow. 'There's a lecture tomorrow night.'

Ashair met his gaze. There was no mist in his eyes at all. 'Goodbye, Cyrus.'

Without a carriage, it was a long walk, and they had to go the whole way together at the boy's pace. He had two crutches cut to size and kept his splinted leg out before him. Just a common man and his crippled child. No one passing even looked twice.

The mercenary leader recommended by General Rah had been confident that reaching the valley would take longer than clearing it of its primitives. Which meant that by now his sheep were on limitless graze, their wool growing thicker than ever. In a couple of months, Cyrus would cut more fleece than his father ever had. Then he would wave the boarding passes before Ashair's face and dare him to say *Goodbye, Cyrus*.

Kushim was still crying. Before leaving, Ashair had promised they would see each other again; he had gotten on his knees to embrace the child. Yet Kushim couldn't stop crying for the only man in the city he trusted.

Cyrus stopped. He opened his hand to reveal the candies he had brought but forgotten to give Ashair. The boy took all three at once, as if they might get away. He hid them in his cheek.

'Do you remember me?'

No response.

'I was there when we rescued you. We thought you would die. You probably can't understand how close you came to dying. How much do you remember?'

The boy only stared.

'Where we're going, you'll be treated kindly. Please don't cry. I'm a good person, from a good family. You can trust me. I promise that you'll have everything you want.'

'Candy?' the boy asked.

'As much as you can eat. You'll see. We are a good family.'

It was Dusk and they still hadn't reached the edge of the city, let alone turned up the hill toward the estate. Cyrus was thirsty and tired and sweaty; he would have given a chest of coins for a carriage ride. The boy, however, wasn't complaining. He kept limping along.

While waiting for Kushim to catch up, Cyrus realized it had been years since he simply stood in this part of the city; as a scholar, he had always been lost in thought, and as a master, he only rode in armored carriages. Now he had nothing to do but listen to mallets pounding on the ark and, nearer, some old woman scolding a dog.

Down a side street, his eye caught a bronze gate locked before a military carriage. There was a familiar symbol on this armory's gate: two swords crossed over a shield. The same symbol he'd seen on the old key given him to deliver by General Rah.

It didn't make sense. Rah had ordered a heavily armed contingent to Cyrus's estate to deliver a common scroll—yet he had sent Cyrus alone to deliver access to the armory? The man to whom he had given the key didn't look like a soldier. Rah had told Cyrus, *You are my emissary.*

The boy took Cyrus by the sleeve. He was panting.

Cyrus couldn't expect him to climb the hill. He knelt. 'Hold on. I'll carry you.'

The servants were clustered in the foyer when he and the child finally arrived; they looked aghast to see their master walk through his own front door. He was once again wearing his master's robe and boots, the elaborate helmet stamped from the Emperor's metal. The boy was beside him, teetering on his good leg, both crutches in one hand.

Cyrus's mother ran into the room and, at the sight of her son, collapsed into Jernod. The driver caught her with ease, his large hand to the small of her back as he righted her. Cyrus had only been gone a quarter of the day.

A young woman in a regal gown glided into the foyer. Her hair was up in ornate design; she wore an elaborate tiara rich with gems. Her face was freshly powdered. Until now, Cyrus had forgotten his promise to dine with another prominent daughter, yet one more possible wife.

'We thought you'd been kidnapped!' his mother said, still out of breath. 'Where were you? You didn't tell Jernod!'

'Who was protecting you?' Jernod wanted to know.

His mother finally noticed Kushim. 'Did you go to the auction yard? By yourself?' The girl who had come for dinner was stepping back. She looked sickened by the sight of the boy.

The manservant inquired if he should prepare the indentured for a new arrival among their quarters, but Cyrus told him no, to prepare a bed on this floor. He said, 'It is the least we can do.'

Given the interest he'd seen the boy take in lowly pigeons, Cyrus thought to show him the aviary first. He shut the door so they might be alone with the crows. Kushim sat on the bench, his bad leg straight from hip to heel. The boy was looking up.

'Beautiful birds, aren't they?'

Kushim asked in his heavy accent, 'What they eat?'

'Kitchen scraps, I think.'

With a gesture of the hand, the boy asked, 'They do leave?'

'Here they are protected forever.'

Kushim looked at him. 'I sleep here?'

'No. I have a room for you.' He added, 'I wouldn't keep you in a cage.'

Kushim looked back to the birds. 'Can I? Sleep here. With them?'

Cyrus had to explain the obvious. 'For a boy to sleep in the aviary with the crows, it would be unnatural.'

Kushim left the bench to lay flat on the sand, as if proving sleep was possible. He crossed his hands behind his head and smiled as the birds swooped closer. Once, years ago, Cyrus had begged his mother to let him sleep in the aviary; she had refused. This boy had already been denied Ashair. Cyrus said, 'I guess I could have blankets sent.'

Kushim offered no reaction.

'For supper, you can eat anything. Name your favorite food. I want you to be happy here. It's important to me that you have everything you need. Do you understand?'

'Candy?'

'Yes, sure. But I mean the main course. What is your favorite meal?'

'Fish from smoke.'

'Not fish!' Even the thought was nauseating. Cyrus explained: 'No fish, no bugs, no dirt.' The boy stared. Cyrus offered, 'You'll have fried horse tongue. It's a delicacy.'

He was almost to the door when Kushim asked, 'What means this, *unnatural?*'

By darkness, they carried the dead boy between them to the other village. When Left-Coasters saw the boy's mother, they embraced her. Their grief was collective.

Both coasts gathered to confer in the dark. Barbarian had arrived. It was as the desert tribes had warned. On this side of the mountains, he always came eventually.

Some mothers said to bend as the river around every obstacle. Others wanted to rise up as the wave and crash down. Auntie listened with her arms crossed.

The council invited three prominent Left-Coast mothers to confer with them. Their discussions were brief. Auntie announced, 'As the tide slips past the paddle, we shall slip past Barbarian downstream where he won't expect, toward a certain canyon, where between waterfalls we can hide until he abandons his hunt.'

'It is what Elk would do,' a Left-Coast mother said. 'Hide in the place hunters would never want to look.'

'We should not cower from Barbarian,' Vagnu said.

Auntie walked to face him. All were watching. Auntie put her hand to his, this gesture of equals. It was startling to see; she had their attention. 'Vagnu,' she began. 'I am glad you are so strong. The people need a warrior now, someone bold to confuse Barbarian, to lead him away, to make him suffer. Your village needs someone courageous.'

Vagnu seemed to grow taller at these words. In a deft motion, he took up his bow and slung his quiver. 'For the mother of the boy who died, I will be this man.'

To the crowd, he pronounced with full chest, 'This boy was Right Coast and I am Left. But a mother's revenge is worth any man's life.'

'Thank you,' the boy's mother said. 'Thank this man.'

Vagnu pointed his stave toward his bachelors, then over everyone else. 'We will kill more together. We can teach Barbarian his mistake. Decide for yourself whose tracks you will follow. You can be the one who tells our story or you can be the one told of. If you are afraid of dying, ask yourself, Who lives longer?'

Many took up their bows. Ozi among them.

———

Drums began to pound. Carved and sculpted instruments reverberated. As a storm can be heard coming, they chanted, *The Sea's tempest is within me. I am her gale.*

Vagnu was stomping up dust. Men and women together becoming warriors. Orange and purple pigments replaced with bloodred and winter black.

Ozi was now stooped before the scolding voice of his wife who objected to his joining Vagnu. She wanted her husband to follow her. He was a married man. He was to do what his wife demanded of him.

Auntie told Leerit what she should do. Stay close, hold the hands of children, help with every chore. Auntie might as well have said, *Remain thirteen forever.* She took Leerit by the wrist. 'You're my sister's daughter. You have much to learn. I can't let go.'

But what of Maren? Tears broke from Leerit's eyes when she spoke the name.

'We will find my niece and nephew after.' Auntie held her. 'In this, each of us must sacrifice.'

Ozi's grandmother was too weak for arduous travel, the last of her generation, the only one who could remember a time when fishermen might be called lazy. What would become of this elder who couldn't run and yet couldn't be left behind?

Each in the village took a turn, Left Coast and Right, starting with the youngest. Bending to her where she sat beside the fire. Her old hands holding theirs, turning her face to accept their kisses. Ozi wept when it was his turn to kneel before her.

Cheek to cheek with her own grown daughters, she told them to smile, to be proud, not to lament. 'I am ready for my perch on the mountaintop. I want to see Ama again, hear the old stories as they were once told. Don't worry about me, I have lasted plenty long down here. I have seen enough of this place.'

Auntie knelt before her with a wooden cup, this steaming tea. The old woman drank it down and crossed her eyes and performed a loud burp; once more she succeeded in making the children laugh.

She smiled a final time at her daughters. She watched them until she could no longer keep upright.

As the village sang to her, the old woman lay back and died.

Without the Sea to welcome their bodies, the elder and the dead boy were taken together into the stream and let go. This way, their spirits could return to the Sea and so rise up on the next storm and arrive to their place on the mountaintop. Theirs would be a long journey, Auntie said, but the dead know patience. 'Soon they will see for themselves how those still living have honored their sacrifice.'

To the rumble of slowly intensifying drums, the warriors gathered to hear one last story. Vagnu took a knee as Auntie sang it, her words riding in pace with the drums.

> Long ago, the Great Wave crushed the innocent and guilty alike. Those few to survive were left to wander. This has happened before.
>
> We were not the only survivors upon those flood-sculpted dunes. There were others too, the few of their kind to survive. They came into our camp at dusk. They ignored our gifts of food

and kindness. Instead, they swung axes. This has happened before.

We could not light a fire in daylight; we could not sing a song; we could not walk the easy path for the tracks left behind. Our warriors were thinned by ambush, our children stolen as they drank from streams. Boys were killed by arrows shot through their bellies. This has happened before.

We fled through the day and night, and yet when we stopped to rest, they found us. Fleeing would never work. As the stag turns to wield his antlers at a chasing bear, we turned our spears toward their dark hearts. This has happened before.

You moved like wind over sloping ground; you took them by surprise. Our many rose up together as one. See a herd or flock or school moving as a single creature. See the wave made of countless drops snap shut its jaw. Let this happen again.

The drums stopped. Auntie let the silence prevail. Then she said quietly, 'Did each person who fought live? No. But those who fought and lived and those who fought and died—they are together the reason you are here now, kneeling before this honor.'

Forty fists punched the ground.

'Ask yourself,' Auntie said. 'What if the Ancients had cowered?'

With this in her ear, how could Leerit not beg? Auntie hardly listened before saying no. 'You will leave now with the children; you will stay with me. You will earn beads.'

'But I know I'm meant to fight! Look at the maidens younger than I am who are readying themselves! Auntie, I beg you. Let me be what you describe: at this chasing bear, let me wield my antlers!'

'As hardheaded as your mother.' Auntie seized Leerit's upper arm. 'This has happened before, but this time you will leave with me. As she should have.'

What had cost one coin at Solstice now cost five, and even his grounds-keepers were demanding he pay them more money or they would cease their labors. Cyrus had been putting off asking for more funding when a missive arrived from General Rah. He was to return the scroll. *Under the protection of my soldiers, bring it in your hand.*

Cyrus was holding the bronze sleeve in the general's office when Rah said, 'You must think my generosity is limitless.' The fire was burning and the air was so warm that sweat ran from Cyrus's brow. A fly buzzed about a platter of food on the desk. He had just now asked for more financing. He added, 'Sir, my father did not raise his son to be comfortable begging. I am here on your advice. I am merely trying to maintain the tack.'

General Rah took his hand from his chin. 'You annoy me. You avoided returning my scroll. Have you so little respect?'

'Sir. Forgive me. Please.'

Rah rang a bell and his manservant entered. The general nodded, and the servant retreated, and the door to the office closed with a clank. Whatever signal had been conveyed, Cyrus didn't know. Would he be stabbed through the heart or chests of coins laid at his feet?

Rah stood and pointed toward the archive. The door was already cracked, and from inside spilled forth light. For a second time, Cyrus followed the general inside. Rah would soon inspect the scroll and see the unforgivable crease. Cyrus had to decide: tell the general that his precious scroll was, in fact, a fake or play along that he had damaged an ancient artifact.

'How deeply have you read?' Rah asked as they walked among his stacks.

Cyrus tried to settle himself. 'Sir. In a scholar's fourth year, he is taught the oldest language. I would be happy to translate something for you.'

Rah stopped. 'Why do you insist on underestimating me? Tell me. Am I the kind of man who would invest in an archive he himself could not read?'

'No sir. Of course not. It's just . . . I didn't expect a general to have time enough to learn a dead language.'

'Hardly dead if scholars still learn it,' Rah said, and continued down a row. Cyrus followed past many scrolls dark with age. At a glance, some looked like they could be authentic. Past a towering statue of Rah himself wearing arcane armor. Rah patted its hip. 'My paternal grandfather nine generations back. I had this commissioned. Striking, yes? We shall never forget him.' Then Rah spoke the oldest language with impressive fluency. 'We forever walk in the shadow of great men.' It was a line from an obscure, noncanonical story, one that many of Cyrus's own colleagues would not have read.

Rah crossed his arms. He was looking down his nose at the bronze sleeve.

Cyrus tried to stop shaking. He placed it in the general's hands. The sleeve's top slid free. Rah withdrew the scroll. Despite all of Cyrus's efforts to smooth the crease, it was still obvious. Rah turned the scroll toward the light, ran a finger over the damage. His eyes lifted.

'Forgive me, sir,' Cyrus said, his voice quivering. 'I have kept it so long because I was seeking a remedy. I wanted to fix my mistake. I fear disappointing you.'

Rah lifted the scroll to a flame burning on the wall. Fire flashed up the parchment and Rah dropped the light between their boots. Cyrus coughed on the smoke.

From a rack, Rah lifted in both hands a long heavy tablet. It was the original, the primary artifact from which the scroll had been traced. Centuries older than any parchment. Cyrus knew in theory that such tablets must have once existed, but he'd never seen one. Rah spoke in the oldest language. 'What does it mean to you?'

Cyrus had to steady himself. 'All the men you sent. They weren't guarding the scroll itself. They were guarding . . . that one word.'

'*Repopulate*,' Rah said. His chin rose. 'I have the primary tablet, so do not try to persuade me that this word is a mistake. Tell me what it means.'

On instinct, Cyrus looked over his shoulder as if for a dean who might overhear. The wrong word had never been far from his thoughts. 'Sir. *Repopulate* means . . . the world did not begin with five brothers.' Cyrus drew a breath of resolve. 'Sir, it means that the very premise of Creation is false.'

Rah smiled as he hadn't during any of their previous meetings. Here was genuine pleasure upon the general's face. He touched Cyrus's chin with tenderness. 'I knew you were the right one.'

'The right one for what, sir?'

Rah continued down his well-lit stacks. Cyrus followed. Rah stopped before a table covered by luxurious wool. 'Now. Pledge a mighty oath to me. What I am about to show you cannot be spoken of outside these halls. Not yet. Not to your scholar friends, not to your pillow mates, not even to your driver. Do you swear this oath upon the wrath of the Sun?'

'I swear this oath upon the wrath of the Sun. Sir.'

General Rah did not blink. 'Frankly, I would be plenty concerned about the wrath of he who commands the faith of the army.'

'Yes sir.'

Rah pulled back the wool to reveal myriad incomprehensible objects. Here were patinaed shapes beside gleaming materials unknown to Cyrus—all of another world. There was nothing like them in the imperial archives, no descriptions in surviving scrolls. 'Breathe, Cyrus. I can't have you suffocating just yet.'

Rah lifted a circular object roughly the size of a man's hand. Decorative, intricate—but not jewelry. Cyrus knew the material to be gold, though he could not conjure the use for such an object. 'Tell me, what do you see?' Rah asked.

Cyrus accepted the object into his own shaking hands. It was heavier than he expected. 'Is it from the Sun Himself?'

'Not from another realm, Cyrus. From another *era*.'

The artifact displayed four quadrants delineated by straight grooves. In each quadrant was a single image. A barren plant. The same plant with leaves. The same plant now twice as tall. Then the plant when those leaves were about its foot. The meaning was clear enough. 'It's a depiction of the seasons, of summer and winter.'

'Do not ignore what you see because you have no name for it,' Rah said. 'This is a depiction of four seasons, not two.'

'But what else is there beyond summer and winter?'

'By now, my soldiers have excavated countless caves,' Rah said. He put his finger to a slab of rock too large to lift—not a pressed tablet of clay but a single face of stone. On it were chiseled shapes that looked almost familiar. 'We have found mysterious depictions like this one at many sites.'

At Rah's urging, Cyrus touched the shapes. The rock itself was of a variety he had never encountered. Gray and as smooth as a tabletop. The grooves were white and deep enough to track with a finger. The piece was huge. Four men couldn't lift it.

Rah continued, 'An image like this one awoke my passion for ancient history. I was a junior officer younger than you. We were seventy-six days to the southeast when marauding primitives eluded us in a complex of caverns. Always eager to distinguish myself, I volunteered to lead our attack. When I stepped inside those recesses, everything I thought I knew crumbled. No—that's not quite right. Not crumbled.' Rah looked off at a nearby flame. He was touching his chin. 'It was like I finally understood that my story—*our* story—is a minor detail seated within something impossibly huge. We are not gods, Cyrus; we are fleas. Do you understand?'

'I hope to, sir.'

'The image I saw in that cave looked like this. It was sprawled across the wall and towered well over my head. That particular depiction wasn't chiseled but painted. Now I know that it was quite common for them to use animal fat mixed with ochre for pigment.'

'Primitives made this?'

'No.' Rah chuckled. 'This is far older than primitives.'

Cyrus looked more carefully at the design. The lines were straight and parallel, and between them existed countless small squares. The symmetry was striking, the sense of perspective quite advanced. The shapes looked almost three-dimensional. Rah said, 'Tell me what you're seeing.'

'It almost looks like . . . palaces.'

'Very good. A hundred and three palaces in this depiction alone, each towering into the sky, all of them grander than anything ever built by civilization's best craftsmen.'

Cyrus asked, 'A hundred and three emperors?'

'What sense would that make? There is never room for more than one ruler.' Rah pointed. 'See these boxes here? I didn't know what they were for years, not until my men excavated a site on a bluff that rises from the Impassable Dunes. There, we found an especially compelling depiction: that image featured faces in the boxes. Cyrus, what you're seeing here. They are windows.'

Cyrus pointed to what seemed now to be simplistic renderings of human bodies. They were fluttering in midair like leaves. 'What are these supposed to be? Are these people flying?'

'We see those in each depiction. Maybe flying. But I think they are falling. I see a depiction of a civilization's mass suicide.'

'But who?' It was all Cyrus could utter.

Rah laughed. 'Yes, wouldn't we like to know! Who and when. And where did they go? And why?'

'The aqueduct,' Cyrus said. 'In the Highlands. The metal we can't melt.'

'Perhaps it is theirs,' Rah said. 'My soldiers have found other structures like it. They might have been common, but the only ones left seem to have been buried under prehistoric floods or landslides. Erosion can be like unrolling a scroll.'

He lifted one more object, round like a bowler but much bigger. It should have weighed too much for a man to hold and yet Rah gave it to him. Bronze but hollow. Carefully polished to remove what must have been a thick layer of patina. There were dents all around it, as if the object had rolled down countless stairs or survived the crumbling of a ceiling. Cyrus said, 'I don't understand what I'm holding.'

Rah pointed. 'This here is land. You can tell by the sharp lines that represent mountains. And these, these are waves. The ocean, Cyrus. You are holding their world.'

Cyrus had to kneel. 'But it's round . . .'

General Rah knelt beside him. His voice was soft now, fatherly. 'What's important, what I want you to consider, is the promise this object makes.

Think, Cyrus. These great people—whoever they were—they built palaces grander than our own and not just for their royalty. Imagine. To accumulate such wealth, a civilization's trade lines would have to be far more extensive than our own. Here is the world as these great travelers knew it. Tell me. What promise does their world make?'

Cyrus cleared this throat. 'If they are right, sir, then no matter from where a man sails, if he goes straight far enough . . . he will hit new land.'

'Indeed!'

'But . . .'

'But what, Cyrus?'

'I don't understand. If they had so much . . . If they knew so much . . .'

'Yes? Ask me.'

'If they had everything, why would they choose suicide?'

Rebellion

T he village left by darkness, climbing toward the tree line, where tracks would be harder to trace. Leerit tried to do as she should.

Little children were being carried by their fathers. Babies were given rawhide to suck. Dogs flashed on the edges. Even old men were carrying loads. Not a word said, not a rock rolled; to survive, the people moved like fog through darkness.

Ahead, Ozi's wife journeyed alone beside her mother. She was marching on heavy feet. Ozi had dared defy her and joined the warriors.

Leerit stopped and stepped out of line to piss. Yet she remained unseen in the dark as others passed. After the families, old people came dragging boughs to confuse the sign. Then she was alone.

How long would the village hide? Until summer, until winter? Maren couldn't wait that long.

Leerit could almost see Auntie's disapproving eyes. She told the darkness what she had told Ama the night her mother paddled across the bay to convince her eldest to come home. These words had been Leerit's last to the woman who made her: 'I can't be who you want me to be.'

Every morning, carts arrived with firewood, and Koneet and the other woodcutters unloaded the logs. After striking the cobbles, a seasoned length would hum.

But lately, Koneet had been lingering near a certain driver, smiling, leaning on her axe, and trying his language for herself. She was doing it again now, and the other woodcutters were watching. As they heaved and sawed, Koneet laughed at something the driver had told her.

Later Lilah caught Koneet by the elbow. 'What are you doing with that man?'

'He has a cart and a horse,' Koneet said at full volume, because no one knew their language. 'I am persuading him to help. A man like that could deliver food; he could take it from the pantry to a boat. And'—she smiled—'for him, the guards will open the gate.'

'You shouldn't trust these men. They believe they are smarter than their own mothers.'

Koneet scoffed. 'Of course you would have me do nothing.'

The manager took many young women up the stairs, but he had never before shown interest in Koneet. Perhaps he had seen her flirting with that driver.

The sun was setting as he came down the stairs. He walked among the cauldrons and pointed to every error. He was saying repeatedly—almost singing—'faster.' He stopped among the woodcutters who were loading dyed and spun wool. Young, strong, sweating women. He stepped past the one already growing his child and took Koneet by the elbow.

'No,' Lilah called. There was fury now in her hands. Before she could think better of it, she had left her cauldron; she was crossing the yard. Before this despicable man, she said, 'Me, not her.'

He didn't even look. He simply pushed past and led Koneet up the stairs.

Inside Lilah was a tidal rush; she would drown him, hold him under, pin him to the reef. She wanted to open his neck to bone and watch his lifeblood gush onto sand. Trinket gripped her. Guards arrived with their swords. Trinket talked fast. She kept her body between the guards and Lilah.

It was Koneet who saved her. She called down the stairs in the coastal language. 'Don't get hurt for this. This is nothing. He can't reach me.'

Then they were gone inside and Trinket was holding Lilah steady. She couldn't help Koneet or Leerit or Maren or Kushim; she couldn't get free; she wasn't enough.

Trinket didn't let go. She knew. Her words meant *You taught your daughter to survive. Now let her.*

Leerit found the warriors in full pigment, red fangs on their faces, black contours painted across their shoulders. In any thicket or deep grass, they would vanish; in battle, their markings would conjure terror. They were not men or women, Left Coast or Right. They were the same; they were not many but part of one. Leerit sat among them to be painted.

Vagnu said, 'If we do not drive Barbarian away, we will starve. Our nieces and nephews, our parents and elders will perish.' Vagnu would see the enemy from a distance and stalk closer. He said this hunt would not be easy. This prey was as fierce as Bear.

The voice that had been telling the maiden without beads to keep silent was now gone; within these pigments, Leerit was a part of them. 'We should let Barbarian come to us, where the advantage is ours. My father taught me to ambush Bear.'

Vagnu stared.

Everyone was looking now. 'Never let Bear see how small you are. If he charges, dodge him. If he flees, flank him. A bear should never be challenged head-on.'

They were silent.

'She speaks wisdom.' It was Ozi's voice from among the painted warriors.

Vagnu broke the silence. 'We will stalk Barbarian and overwhelm him.'

The warriors were a snake in the moonlit grass with Vagnu at the head, slithering toward a promontory from which they might spot Barbarian and plan their approach. Ozi was behind her, and said, 'What will you fight with?'

Leerit showed him what her mother had made.

Ozi unslung his kit to the grass. He had a quiver stuffed with arrows and a second stave lashed to the side. He handed her the unfinished bow. 'It still needs scraping,' he said. 'The top limb is too stiff. And you will have to tune the arrows until they fly straight.'

The Left-Coast man before her drew an arrow from his quiver and gave it to her. He sent word up the line of warriors and each sent back a single arrow until she had a clutch of mixed fletchings.

As they climbed, Ozi said, 'I never thought I could want to kill a person.'

Another warrior said, 'Barbarian is not people.'

———

As the sky warmed with orange, they found their prey by a thin plume of smoke rising from a fold in the terrain. The distance was great, but the grass would conceal their approach. Vagnu nodded. 'We must rush.'

They ran to keep up with him. Vagnu didn't slow until the last climb. As he neared the crest of this final ridge, the sun was rising and sweat streamed from Leerit's brow. Vagnu began to crawl. He had chosen this approach, she now understood, because the sun would be at his back and the wind in his face. He was a good hunter. Vagnu rose to his knees. Seeing nothing, he stood. *Too late*, he signaled with a hand. *Gone.*

Leerit and Ozi and the others joined him on the ridge. Below, the flat bottom was beaten down. There was a muddy trail and smoke still rising. Here on the ridge, the sun was warm on their skin. Vagnu said they would wait and watch to be sure. He said, 'If prey learns he is being hunted, he will be too alert to stalk.'

Ozi used a leaf of rock to scrape the top limb of the stave until Leerit's bow hummed a precise note when the string was plucked. He did this as she worked each arrow. Unwrapping the sinew holding the stone point and cutting the wood back or wrapping a larger point to the existing end. She tested each until the arrow's stiffness matched the bow's power and the shaft would fly straight.

When Vagnu called, Leerit was the first to take up her arrows and bow. She rushed to be among those leading the descent. If there was even one barbarian left, she did not want to miss his slaughter.

But there was nothing left. On the valley bottom, they milled like elk searching out morels. They found wet spots of urine, piles of feces still steaming. 'Horses,' Ozi said, studying the tracks. 'They will be much faster than we are.'

Vagnu called, 'We have to hurry!'

The sound was like a bird's wing. She stood there looking for this bird who dared dive at her. Not birds—arcing through the sky were arrows.

Ozi took her to the ground and a shaft hit him. The blood was already down his neck. 'Go!' he screamed.

Wind roaring over her ears, arrows ripping past, arrows skipping off the ground. Rocks, rocks that could protect her, rocks growing larger— an arrow smacked one and went crackling through the air with its fletching torn. Her legs kept on past the rocks. Arrows hissing overhead.

She turned into the first thicket, and where the bush ended, she raced through grass to crest the ridge. Her vision was too star filled to see, her breathing too loud for hearing. She took a knee and nocked an arrow. In the ground, she felt Bear coming.

Ozi appeared. He was covered in blood. The arrow had glanced from his cheek and cut his ear. He put his fingers to the meat of his face. 'Their smoke,' he said. 'They were luring us into their ambush.'

She could hear screaming. 'We have to go back. We have to help!'

Ozi gripped her wrist. 'Leerit. Elk does not return to the site of an ambush.'

She looked off toward the horror.

He said, 'When separated on a hunt, we gather where we planned our stalk.'

To traverse open grass was to be exposed. In every rock she saw a face, in every flicker the flight of an arrow. She didn't stop running.

When she heard a crow's call, she knew they weren't alone. From the grass on the hillside rose an arm.

The survivors were sweat streaked and wide-eyed and chewing their fingers. Less than a third of those who had been alive at dawn. People had seen Vagnu take an arrow. Lung and liver. He hadn't lasted five steps.

What the survivors had in common was they had fled instead of fought. 'We are cowards,' cried one now. 'They died because of us!'

Two of them had made it this far with arrows protruding. They were begging for help. Her aunt was the midwife, which made Leerit the closest thing.

A Left-Coast woman with a heavy brow and wide nose turned to show Leerit the arrow stuck in her pelvis. It had hit her as she fled and penetrated only to the depth of a finger. No matter how she turned, she couldn't see the wound for herself. The arrow had pinned her robe to her flesh.

When Leerit explained that the point was too far into the bone to extract, this woman reached and took hold of the arrow. She grunted as she snapped the shaft. She pointed the fletching at them, and said, 'Barbarian is right now reading our tracks. On horses, he'll overtake us. We need a thicket. We need terrain that can hide us. If you want to live to fight back, we must run.'

'What about the others?' a man asked.

This woman stared. 'With or without us, they are already dead.'

The survivors moved as fast as the wounded among them could through the dense brush. A stream ran through the thicket's center, which they followed downstream. Where the saplings thinned over bare rock, Ozi turned them abruptly toward the water. They entered the current and walked back upstream, climbing so far, until the water narrowed to nothing. When they finally broke from the streambed, they were looking upon an alpine basin. Already, daylight was dying.

———

Leerit needed to gather medicine while she could still see. Ozi followed her to where avalanches had in previous winters stripped the mountain-side bare.

She muddled leaves and applied the mixture to the flesh of his cheek and ear. Ozi didn't flinch. He took her hand. 'You were right,' he said. 'We should have ambushed him.'

Maybe.

'What we need now are his tracks. Show me Barbarian moving; show me the decisions he makes as he traverses rough terrain. From his feet, I will tell you what he thinks. And then we'll know how to kill him.'

There was a wounded man her own age who wouldn't stop crying.

His injury was to the upper inner thigh; the arrow had passed through blood-rich muscles and clipped his scrotum as he ran away. What he had needed was to lie back, to have his thigh and scrotum sutured, for a person to hold pressure until the bleeding stopped. He needed days of not walking. Instead, he had been running and bleeding for too long. From his color, she knew he didn't have much blood left. He gripped her hand and asked if he was dying. 'Tell me the truth, please.'

She didn't have a needle or sinew for sutures. All she had was the warmth of the bearskin. She covered his shaking body with it. 'You're not dying,' she told this man.

He was holding her hand so tightly. 'Do you promise?'

No night was ever so long as that one. They spent it under the canopy of willows where the wind was stilled. No fire, nothing but jerky. They had picked a place where they could listen for the sounds of rocks sliding along their back trail, as Elk would do.

She hadn't slept in more than a day, but even now, rest couldn't last. She was shivering in the cold. The whimpers of the wounded man would not stop.

Ozi wasn't sleeping either. In that dark, she asked, 'What did you tell your wife?'

'I told her she would find a better man. A Left-Coaster more like her, someone who would give her children. One day this man would come over the mountains and she would thank me for having gone to hunt Barbarian.'

'What did she tell you?'

'She said that I am not allowed to die yet.'

Near dawn, Leerit tried to wake the wounded man. It wasn't sleep that had silenced him. She shook out the bearskin and rolled it tightly.

The creek was small but it was all they had. They put his body in the water, which wasn't enough to submerge him, then built a protection of rock that no crow could unbury. They told the dead man the truth: his journey to the Sea would be long and arduous, but water always arrives, and it would deliver him, and he would rise on the first storm and take his place among the generations. From there, he would see how they had honored his sacrifice.

Leerit was the last to leave the pale corpse.

To confuse the trail and slow the barbarians, each person climbed a different route to the barren ridge. Leerit was crossing a chute when the shale under her began to slide. She knew the sound would carry. There was nothing she could do to call back the rocks.

She found Ozi already gathered with the warriors on a pinnacle where the view was uncontested. Far below moved dark shapes: Barbarian. He had heard the rocks and was making his way toward the chute. To see him, her heart beat in her ears.

Not one but many. Ever more coming out of a fold of terrain. Sixteen, seventeen, eighteen—still more. Daylight glinted from the barbarian skin, as if they were made of light. They were so tall sitting atop those animals called horses.

'Bet a blade they turn back,' a warrior said.

'Bet they don't,' said another. 'Why stop when they can overtake us?'

Ozi pointed. 'See? Horses are powerful over grass, but they don't like these steep slopes. Here is an advantage.'

Then, in the open, the barbarians stopped to confer. Forty-two were in sight now. Their horses called to one another. They bucked their heads. Even Leerit could see the strange animals were nervous.

'Ha!' said the warrior. 'They turn back! Give me that blade.'

The man handed over his stone knife.

The woman who had climbed all this way with an arrowhead in her pelvis said, 'Now it is our turn to hurt them.'

With Vagnu gone, this oldest woman had become their rudder. Her name was Gulleet. She agreed that Barbarian must be ambushed, not stalked. She listened as Ozi suggested steep, rock-filled terrain with a nearby thicket for their own escape. She listened to every voice, even the most hesitant.

'High ground is better.'

'Arrows fly better downhill than up.'

'We must trick Barbarian into walking where every advantage is ours.'

Leerit stepped forward. 'A hungry bear will follow tracks. Let me lure him.'

'Why would Barbarian follow one person?'

Leerit said, 'He will follow if he thinks I am leading him to what he really wants.'

'Which is?'

'The village.'

There was only silence.

Ozi raised his bow. 'I will be the one to go. I know how to leave tracks that are sure to be followed. Barbarian has to be convinced. He will be wary of a trap.'

Gulleet walked a few paces then returned. She announced, 'You both will go. Our ambush will be on the far side of the valley, in the opposite direction from where our families went to hide.' She named a certain canyon with rocks and the advantage of elevation; it wasn't far from a dense thicket to which they could retreat. She took Leerit's arm. 'Give us a full day's head start. Do not fail. If they find the tracks left by our families, there will be nothing to stop the massacre.'

After the others left, they were alone, just Leerit and Ozi in the seclusion of this high-country basin. While there was still light, they separated to gather firewood. When Leerit returned to their little camp with an armload, she found Ozi kneeling before flames. He was plucking a pair of grouse. He smiled. 'They did not fly. It is a good omen.'

He had no salt so instead seasoned the meat with the juices from the birds' own organs. Leerit built the fire into a thick layer of coals. They were so far removed, there was no chance of being discovered. But she was shaking. She didn't know what to say.

His voice broke the silence. 'Should I get water?'

259

'Yes, get water.'

In his absence, she was hearing again the sound an arrow makes when it hits the hollow of a man's rib cage. Her arms suddenly ached; her back seized tight as it had after days of carrying her dying brother. Sitting here, she was out of breath. She needed to go. They should be covering ground.

When he returned, Ozi said what was true. 'This could be our last night alive.'

She saw his muscles lit with the color of living flame.

'If this is our last night,' he said. 'I don't know. It is not so bad.'

She swallowed. 'If this is the end, what should we do?'

Like a man who jumped in cold water, he drew a breath. Then he stepped closer, and his arms wrapped about her. His rising thickness pressed her navel.

She kissed him. His lips were only part of what she wanted. His coarse hands slipped under her robe and followed her bare back. Under her grip, he was all hard muscle. 'You have done this more than I have,' she gasped as if climbing a mountain. 'I have never . . .'

His voice was shaking too: 'What I have done is not *this*.'

At dawn, she expected everything to be different. But nothing had changed.

In the morning light, she refreshed his battle pigments, then he refreshed hers. She thought of Kushim, the whole little boy he was on that morning before the bear attacked him. If she had made Kushim stay with her, he would still be alive.

'Do you regret it?' Ozi asked.

Kushim had deserved the chance to grow up, to be a little boy, to be a man. What had happened was because of her.

Ozi touched her cheek. 'You want to run from me, don't you?'

'Not from you,' she said.

'Do you believe the Sea brings people together for a reason?'

Ozi's hands—she wanted them; she wanted to be lifted from here and carried away. In her ear, he whispered, 'Tell me what you want.'

'I don't want you to be the wind.'

'I can be whatever you want. Just tell me.'

She was backing away but he was coming nearer. She didn't deserve kindness or tenderness. His face was painted and fierce, the veins on his arms like ropes. If he wanted, he was large enough to kill her.

When he reached, she struck his arm. He swept her at the knee and caught her; he laid her to the ground.

Now she knew she wanted to be mauled.

Lilah lifted a robe from the heap of dirty wool and felt something hard in a pocket. The guards were watching, so she simply picked up more robes and hauled them back to her cauldron, as she should.

These were robes worn by those laboring in some field; she knew because they were crusty with mud. Sometimes robes like this contained a nut or seed, but now from this pocket she withdrew a rock.

Yet not just any rock. It was black, the size of her fist, and halved to reveal a flat, glossy surface. She had seen this kind of rock just once before when a trader had brought one to the beach. Her mother had traded four whole bundles of fish for a single round. *Obsidian*, it was called. Obsidian could make knives that were sharper than any knapped from chert.

Where does it come from, Ama?

The Sea made this long before She made us.

After supper, while Kenta and Koneet readied for bed, Lilah sat alone on the hole pretending to shit. It was the first moment she'd had to examine the obsidian.

This piece had been struck before; she could tell by the divot marking the impact point. Someone long ago had broken it and likely worked the other half into a blade or several arrowheads and forgotten this piece where they had set it on the ground. Maybe a child had called, or an animal showed itself. Now Lilah held it like that long-ago woman. How many lifetimes had it been hidden underground waiting to be found, waiting to be put in a robe and delivered here to her hand?

The Ancients had sent her obsidian for a reason.

In the distance, the sun glowed within plumes of stillborn mist rising from a thousand pools. Beyond on pale slopes shifted countless white specks—sheep moving over green grass. Ozi said, 'They've not come here before. It is why the elk prefer this valley. No one else is eating the grass.'

She led them until they met the valley floor where Ozi stopped her, and said, 'Remember. We are telling a story with our feet. You have to believe it. We are two people who are not afraid. Barbarian must see our tracks and think, *Why attack now when they will lead us to the village?* If you don't believe, you won't walk the same. A good tracker knows when feet are lying.'

'I am a woman coming from the trader with a husband to carry my things.'

'I am a man following what moves him.'

'We are not scared,' she said.

He touched her cheek. 'I am not scared.'

It was this story that led them back to the campsite the village had already abandoned.

Leerit walked in confused circles because she was a woman who didn't know. They sat to talk it through. Where had everyone gone? What should they do now?

When they decided, they took up their things and headed out straightaway. A couple walking to the rally point that everyone knew. *If something were ever to happen, meet there.* They had to believe this if their feet were to tell it true.

So they moved too fast; they took risky steps; they tripped and hoisted each other to standing. On a high spot, they didn't stop to look because they were people in too great a hurry for reflection. What mattered was catching up.

The sky was dimming again when they entered a canyon with rushing water at its base. Their feet met a trail laid over eons by people and creatures. Ahead, beyond the canyon, was a plateau where elk herds summered.

But rather than crest onto that plateau, Leerit and Ozi joined the others who had come to this agreed-upon ambush by a circuitous route. Already the warriors had built a barricade of slash-wood at the canyon's top. Whoever followed Leerit and Ozi's sign into the canyon would never leave. Soon this stream would froth with the purple blood of barbarians.

It was a fireless night after another arduous day of travel. No warrior cared who shared which pelt. In the bearskin, they slept a dreamless sleep against each other. They woke in the dark and lay curled together. His breath was in her ear. 'Do you think we'll survive?'

She reached and took hold of his firming cock. 'Unlikely.'

By dawn, they were each waiting in their separate places along the rim of the canyon. The warriors weren't just hiding from the senses of men. Any bird or squirrel who saw them could sound an alarm, as these animals often did when hunters waited for elk.

Leerit passed the lonely daylight under shifting winds and tried not to think of her brother. She kept hearing the sound of his bones, the gasping of his breaths. Without the cures, how could he have survived? His wounds were too grievous. She was to blame. In a hundred seasons, he would still be dead and she would still be to blame.

The only relief to be found was in premonitions of violence: the sound of barbarians approaching, whistling to stop them, drawing the bow until her fingers were firmly in the corner of her lip before narrowing her aim to a single barb of fur. Even to think it, her heart filled her ears. There was nothing else. Opi had taught her, *See the hit before you send the arrow.*

In the afternoon, the dirt beside her began pulsing.

As she watched, dark soil was flung into sunlight. Finally, an unfamiliar squirrel peeked out and beheld the sky. His eyes were squinted, and his whiskers kept busy in the warmth. He was less than an arm's reach away, blind and easy prey.

The squirrel went back to work. Throwing dirt from his hole. He flung something onto the duff. It was what was left, the inedible stalk. A plant from last summer eaten over the winter. On this warm afternoon, a squirrel was busy cleaning its den.

The sky turned from white to red to slate gray. Nothing moved in the canyon. Her legs hurt from sitting; she focused on her pain. To move, to cover ground, would be a relief she did not deserve. Gulleet had been absolute. *Stay hidden until I fetch you.*

The duff smelled ripe between Leerit's fingers. She was testing the smell when her hair stood on end.

A man was standing below her. He had appeared from nowhere; she hadn't heard his approach. He was on the side of the trail, reading the story she and Ozi had left in the dust. He was within arrow range. But this was no barbarian.

He hadn't a horse. He was not wearing those slabs of orange that reflected daylight. He was lean and long-legged and cloaked in a swatch of dark goat fur. Close enough that the markings on his face were plain: decorative scars radiating from his eyes.

Leerit had never before seen a desert nomad, but she had heard them described. Why was this one here, so far from the desert? Had he come looking to trade?

The nomad continued up the trail. It made no sense.

She was still trying to understand his story when a beast's nose appeared. Then its eyes. Its ears. From its mouth a strip of leather led back. Below her was a horse.

When the animal took another step, she saw the barbarian upon its back. Huge, hulking, orange. From his belt hung a knife as long as an arm. A huge dark bow was in his other hand, arrow nocked. His clothing clinked as his horse walked. He was turning to look at every corner of the canyon. The nomad was their tracker.

Barbarian was close enough she could see whiskers. He looked like a man, only much too enormous.

Then came another and another, each barbarian equally hideous, only the animals underneath varying in color.

She couldn't feel her hands. She had practiced for this moment—readying her bow, drawing to a solid anchor—but now she couldn't feel anything. They were streaming by and she had already lost count.

As one huge horse passed, he began to flatulate between steps. The animal stopped, and the long fibrous tail rose. Fistfuls of steaming feces splattered on the trail. The barbarian on its back stretched like a fisherman made sore by hauling nets.

Then the horse wheeled its head. She could feel it now, how the wind had shifted against her neck. This animal was smelling what the barbarian could not. He turned to follow the horse's gaze.

The horse jolted and the barbarian upon it pulled back his bow. From downstream came the fury of screams.

She was on her feet drawing even before she thought to. But she let the string go before it reached her cheek. The arrow skipped between the hooves of the now-running horse.

Barbarians were wheeling past. One slumped sideways and hit the ground with a clack. Another was being dragged by the ankle behind a panicked animal—against the rocks his body clattered.

She was sending every arrow as fast as she could pull the string. They broke in two across rocks. One landed in the flank of a fleeing horse that seemed not to notice.

She turned in time to see a barbarian coming along the canyon's rim. He wasn't supposed to be there and now his arrow was on the way.

She heard the blade whiz past.

As his horse turned, her eyes found the flesh of the barbarian's cheek and her arrow was in flight. It stuck not where she was looking but instead glanced off the orange protecting his shoulder.

He and the horse became two. He landed already in a run. Swinging his blade of light, mouth bloodred, face covered in thick fur—he was coming to devour her.

Her second-to-last arrow broke against his orange chest. She was alone; she was going to die. She nocked her last arrow and drew. Narrowed her vision to the gap in the armor.

By then, he was so close that the shaft barely straightened before entering at his waist. Buried to the fletching.

Around the first boulder, she hid rather than keep running because she didn't want his blade in her back. When he came past, she didn't think; she caught his foot with her stave and he went down hard. She was beating him with what she had until the bow splintered in her hands. He pushed himself to all fours and swiped for her leg. Her stone arrowhead was through him and aimed crookedly at the sky. Somehow, she had a cobble in her hand and now she used it to cave in the back of his skull.

The barbarian went down like a wet net. She kept pounding as his legs quivered and his urine spread among rocks. He was a man. She was killing a man.

But not a man. Because she could never do what she was doing to someone's brother.

She wasn't standing; she was floating. Looking down on the Leerit who couldn't stop pummeling. Do it. Hurry. He is a drop and you are the ocean.

XVI

The Secret Language of Crows

On Kushim's first morning in the aviary, he had awoken to the family's chatter, the crows together on the highest branch. A mother and father and three chicks, one young enough to still open his red mouth and be fed. He couldn't tell much about them then, couldn't yet tell the older siblings apart, didn't realize they were speaking, playing, taking comfort. But as night fell, he saw how the crows scooted closer on the same branch, sidestepping until their wings touched. Parents and their baby between them, the older siblings nearby, touching wings. He decided they were a family of two sisters and their little brother.

That first morning, the crows cawed and the door opened and a man entered with a pail of kitchen scraps, and when he left, the door latched shut.

Kushim took a morsel from the pail and covered what remained with his blanket. He intended to make friends.

Once, twice, a sister swooped to take this food from his fingers. He laughed to see it, to feel the wind from their wings against his skin. She carried the morsel by beak to a branch apart and swallowed it. The parents, meanwhile, watched with cocked heads.

Then one of the sisters surprised him by landing on the sand behind him. Kushim turned to better see this crow behaving strangely. Beak up, beak down, skip-skip, *cawcawcaw*. This dance—it seemed to be for him. He wondered what it meant.

Finally, he heard a commotion at the pail and discovered his blanket had been lifted—the parents were there robbing the kitchen scraps. They burst airborne with their chunks of meat. Had the dance been a distraction?

The birds landed together on their family branch and used beak and foot to pull meat apart. They took turns feeding the squeaking little brother. His red mouth open and their black beaks disappearing inside. Kushim couldn't look away.

Eventually, he thought to try the door but found it locked.

He had a pitcher of water and people brought him four meals a day. It was the first time in his life that he had more to eat than he wanted. He shared what was left with the crows.

He was there perhaps five days when the grandmother first came through the door. She was so tall and her clothing pure white. Even when she walked, the fur pulsed. She said her name was *Widow* but he could call her *Ma'am*.

She liked to sit on the bench talking at him. She never noticed the birds but to scold them for making too much noise.

Sometimes he understood her questions. He answered as best he could. Usually, he did not. When he was quiet, she assumed he understood. It was easier to stay quiet.

One day she came and insisted he join her outside. She walked slowly like him out into the brightness, and for a moment, he was blind under so much sky. They walked a circular pathway and she watched him use the crutches. The next day she came earlier, and this time she took the crutches and gave him a staff. He was slower, but when he reached, she took his hand. Whenever he finished a loop, she gave him candy.

She spoke endlessly, like a nervous bird. The circular path they walked was within a stone fence too high to climb. Men with bows walked along it. She promised he didn't need to be afraid; they were here to protect him. He tried asking but didn't have the words. Her sound for these men was *guardsmen*. A few days later, she saw him watching their bows and asked if he wanted to become a *guardsman*. She promised she could make this happen.

He told her he would become a fisherman. But he didn't know the word, so he told her three different ways before she understood. She looked sickened. 'No, no. We must do better by you than that.'

He started walking with her twice a day, once in the morning and once in the evening. Then three times a day, always on the same circular path, always going nowhere. She took the staff and didn't give it back. As they walked, flocks of gulls sat on the fence tops. They rode the wind across the path and down the mountainside and out of sight toward the huge village below. Once he believed he was on an island or a cloud. Now he understood. He was inside a cage that was inside a cage that was inside a still larger cage.

She told him that her husband had died and her own son was now a man, and she was alone here, so alone—though he didn't understand how she could think she was alone. Her house was a village of people.

'I was a good mother,' she told him. 'I really was.' Tears fell from her eyes when she said this. He wiped the tears from her cheeks because he didn't like to see an old woman sad. She laughed. She said, 'Kushim, how is it you always cheer me up?'

She wanted to know about his mother. He explained as best he could. How at bedtime Ama had laid beside him and kissed each eyelid. How, no matter the time of day, she always knew the song he wanted to hear. His mother was on the mountain now.

'Which mountain?' Widow asked. 'Point and I will send someone to fetch her.'

He didn't know the words, so he told her simply, 'Her mountain is too far away.'

She liked it when he sang. She often asked him to sing for her the music of his village.

One evening, a group of grandmothers dressed in white like her gathered in the huge home to listen. He stood before them on a perch. His singing made them cry. They left him piles of candy.

She wanted him to sleep that night in a room by himself but he insisted. He carried his reward back to the aviary. He shared with the sisters and they shared with their baby brother.

All the sisters did was play. Together they played.

He showed a morsel of food and a sister dove for it, but he hid the food before her beak could take it. Next, he made a clicking sound as he showed the morsel, and this time he let the bird have her reward. Soon the sisters would dive only when he clicked. This game made eating his dinner much easier.

They taught him games too. They would steal something of his, often the wool hat Ashair had given him, and they would hide it among the sand or the branches. When he found it, they would caw and flap their wings.

They brought him things. A nutshell. A coin. A utensil like those that came with his food. They dug them up from the sand and flew to him.

He began trying their language, caws from the back of his throat. At his sounds, they cocked their heads. Their responses sounded to his ear like snickers. He decided crows too must like to laugh.

One warm morning, the little brother hopped from the branch he had always lived on and fell flapping to the sand. The parents cawed and cawed and wouldn't stop. When Kushim tried to help, the parents swooped to pull at his hair.

As their son wandered the sand, the parents followed over top in the branches. They were calling out the dangers. The sisters took turns dropping to the sand to feed their brother and show him new treasures.

When darkness came, the parents couldn't sit still. Their boy was on the sand and there was nothing they could do to help him.

Their cawing became frantic when Kushim approached. They swooped to scratch him, but he lifted the warm little bird. His own leg was too weak to climb so he left their chick on the highest branch he could reach. The parents landed beside their child and sidestepped until their chick was pressed between them. That night Kushim dreamt of Opi pulling nets heavy with fish.

———

Long before the door ever opened, the crows knew, somehow, who was coming. They let out a different caw for each person. The man with the kitchen scraps, the woman with Kushim's meals, Widow.

The family took baths in a pool of water atop the sand. They landed on the edge one at a time and dipped their beaks to the water and pulled it up and over them and fluffed their feathers. Again and again. He took his baths in a different room, alone. Lowering himself into a pool of water someone had somehow warmed for him. Water so hot, it turned his scars a brighter pink.

One day the crows made an announcement and he knew Cyrus was coming. Cyrus was the only other person who answered the birds with his own rendition of their language. He came often to sit and watch them.

This time, in his arms was something bulky and wrapped in clean white cloth. He set it on the bench, and said, 'Watch this.'

He took a piece of food from his pocket and put it inside a hole in the tree, much too deep for a beak to reach. He returned and sat on the bench.

The mother was the one to leave her perch. She remembered. She went to a new limb of the tree and broke a twig with a twist of her head. With her foot and beak, she cleaned every leaf and snapped the twig to length. She swooped to the hole and, with her beak, worked her stick. Then she dropped it and took up the morsel and flew with it to her favorite perch.

'She never forgets,' Cyrus said. He was smiling. Watching the family of crows made him happy too. 'Go on,' he said. 'You should open it.'

Kushim unwrapped the gift. It was new clothing, new boots. Also something thin and flat. He thought it was a leaf but it wasn't brittle like a leaf.

'Parchment,' Cyrus called it. On it were markings that looked like bird tracks. Cyrus confused him when he pointed, and said, 'That's your name.'

Four seasons. Palaces towering into the sky. Their world shaped like a ball?

In one evening, the foundations on which rested Cyrus's years of scholarship had fractured. No longer could Cyrus find relief within the archives; now, within those imperial stacks, he saw only what was missing.

Not that he could reach the archives any longer. Jernod refused to deliver him. He said the risk was too great now that few could afford staples and police patrols were coming under routine ambush. The news delivered by the manservant was rife with stories of indentured laborers breaking loose and taking up arms. Just as Ashair had predicted. *Shovels as good as swords.*

'If not Creation, when did it all begin?' Cyrus had asked Rah that night while they were still standing before his artifacts. Rah's answer: 'Beware the man who declares that there was a beginning.'

But there had to be a beginning! A start to what was now coming to an end.

And if the world was round like some ball, wouldn't the water in the ocean simply fall away into whatever bottom existed under all of *this*? There had to be an edge to the world. Mountains to hold back the sea and keep it from pouring away.

He had so many questions, so many rebuttals waiting to be unleashed—and no one with whom he could argue. Rah had made him swear a mighty oath of silence. But even if he hadn't, questioning the facts of Creation was not an option. Scholars and masters too could be strung up by their ankles.

Possessing such artifacts was an unfathomable risk even for a man as prominent as General Rah. No one was above the Emperor's justice. His manservant had to know what was inside those archives. The laborers who had delivered the heavy artifacts. The soldiers who had completed the excavations. Rah was a man who commanded unflinching loyalty— or else he would already be dead.

Cyrus couldn't help but admire the general. The risks he had taken to preserve what was true. By devoting his best years to the imperial archives, Cyrus had been avoiding risk—while, in his search for meaning, Rah had been imperiling everything his lineage had spent generations accumulating, going back at least as far as that patriarch he had immortalized in bronze.

Without the relief of the archives, Cyrus could only sleep in fits. He spent the dark nights pacing in his quarters, a stationary candle his only source of light. His shadow grew and shrunk as he crossed the room.

Most of all, he wanted stories from that time. He wanted to know how so many people existed together. What did they eat? What was their work? Who did they love?

No one would be more interested in those lost people than Ashair. No one could better help Cyrus make sense of what their existence meant now. Even the slightest thought of Ashair was overwhelming. Like grief— but worse, because Ashair wasn't dead; he was not gone home to his place within the Sun. He was absent by choice, hidden and hiding. *Good-bye, Cyrus.*

One night, as Cyrus was sleepless and pacing, he became aware of a roar emanating from outside his walls. It sounded almost like a river churning in the distance. He threw on his cloak, took up a candle, and pushed open his chamber door.

He found several of his men already in the guard tower. When they saw him, they smacked their heels and stood at attention. Jernod was among them. With a mere nod, he sent the guards back to their posts.

Jernod wasn't wearing his armor. He was dressed in thin undergarments. He had been asleep in his cottage on the edge of the estate and had woken to the same roar Cyrus heard. They stood together now to overlook their city.

It was not the sound of a river. It was the collective roar of a mob. Smoke was rising from the city, and on its underbelly flashed flame. The Emperor's once loyal subjects were now pillaging their own streets. 'It is so warm. They can't still be angry about the lack of firewood.'

Jernod turned to look at Cyrus with something like judgment in his eyes.

'Say what you think, Jernod.'

'Sir. Some of us are just now learning the truth.'

'Which truth?'

Jernod was watching now to see Cyrus's reaction to whatever was said next. 'Not everyone is invited onboard the ark.'

Cyrus looked off into the distance. 'I would change that if I could. You know I would. But no one cares what a master thinks.'

'Some of us care what you think,' Jernod said.

The ship was there in the distance of the harbor, lit by bonfires so men might labor all night. Its flanks were sealed. The masts stood naked. Those small shapes were men dangling on ropes. 'Not everyone will be invited on the first trip,' Cyrus said. 'No boat is big enough for an entire city. But the ark will return. There will be multiple voyages. Of that, I'm sure. He will not leave his people behind.'

Jernod gripped the railing. 'Will I be with you, sir? On the first voyage?'

'Honestly,' Cyrus answered. 'I'm not sure if I will be on the first voyage. I have to meet my quota first.'

Jernod cleared some emotion from his throat.

'Go on,' Cyrus said. 'Speak freely. There is a generation of trust between us.'

'Those men you hear now.' Jernod spoke toward the city. 'They are kindling.'

'Kindling?' Cyrus hadn't been expecting a metaphor. 'What do you mean? I don't understand.'

'The attacks on police, they are well coordinated. The arrowheads pulled from heroic officers—they aren't the varied points pounded by some backroom blacksmith. Nor were they knapped from rock. The arrowheads killing our best men are each perfectly symmetrical, forged of the Emperor's own metal by his own blacksmiths.'

'You're not making sense, Jernod. Are you suggesting the Emperor is killing his own police?'

'Thousands of arrows and blades,' Jernod said. 'They were stolen from the armory. Whoever looted the Emperor's metal is now using it against him.'

The armory. The very hand that had delivered the key began to tingle. 'No metaphors now, Jernod. Tell me simply.'

'Sir. I am telling you that the enemy, whoever he is—he is within our own gates.'

Maren would remember it as a winter of fierce winds followed by an early summer lit with new grass.

When Chun stood overlooking that same green, he spoke of the harsh months to come, the aridness, the danger of grass fires. Yet another winter without good snow. 'When I was your age'—his hand was to his chest—'the grass stood to here.'

By then, the maiden-paints were long gone. Maren kept her hair up in a scarf as Lenka preferred. The old woman never said as much, but Maren sensed Lenka's preference so she kept the beads hidden even when inside, even when she was hot. Lenka's own hair was so carefully tended. Each day, she used a bronze comb to tease it out.

Anytime Maren went outside, she looked past the sheep toward the horizon of this place they were now living, the view dire and familiar— always an empty lip of land.

It was hard not to let herself be consumed by the bad that might've befallen Leerit. The death that must have found Kushim.

Once, during a windstorm so fierce that the yurt kicked against its anchors, she became sure she was the last of them alive. The old couple was sleeping and she couldn't get a clear breath. Being alone in this world without family, it was worse than starving. Somehow, Lenka woke. She came and knelt beside Maren with only the light of embers to see by. She hummed and swept the sweaty hair from Maren's face.

The lambs came soon after. Wobbly legs, dripping from their births, mothers licking. She could watch lambs play all day. There was comfort to be had among lambs.

One morning, Chun had asked for her help. A ewe was struggling to give birth; she was dying in the frosty grass. Maren held the creature while Chun reached inside to free the lamb. New life spilled over him, and when Chun rose, his hands were dripping. He marked that lamb with a nick in its ear. Then he told Maren, 'So you can watch him grow. He wouldn't be alive without your help.'

Like a family anywhere, theirs was built of routine—chores and pleasures. At night, Chun made her laugh with the puppets he put on his hands. After her morning labors, Lenka liked to play a game with pieces carved from bone. Friend was beside Maren always; even her chores were his pleasure.

Shearing wool was the hardest work. So many powerful ewes, so many bucking rams. Chun caught each in turn, and she held the creature while he worked his blades against its skin. She had to learn to adjust her grip around the blades without losing control or the sheep would escape and remain uncatchable. But to hold the strongest rams, she had to upend them and use her weight. The work went on for days. Then she had to gather all the mounds of wool. When she was done, wool was piled before the yurt like a giant heap of dirty snow.

They stood awhile beside the harvest. Chun spit. For him, it was another disappointment. 'Every year we cut less.'

'They'll say it's because we're old,' Lenka said. 'They'll take our flock and give it to someone young.'

'How is it my fault if the snows don't fall and the grass is dead by summer?'

'I didn't say it is your fault.' Lenka shrugged. 'Doesn't help though, trading so many skins for liquor.'

Eventually, carts and horses came and hauled the wool away. 'Where?'

Maren asked. Chun said, 'The City.' She remembered the name. It was the same place those men had taken her brother.

Often Maren couldn't sleep. The Ancients could see her; they had always been watching her—Ama was there watching. What would she say about this daughter of hers who had let her brother be taken and chose to stay with the people who had given him away?

She remembered the old warning about being lost in a forest. *Don't go down, first climb up. The hardest path leads to the longest view.* She had never understood the meaning until now. She would remain lost as long as she let herself walk this easy path.

In the middle of the night, Maren rose from her bed. She kept silent as she stole a satchel's worth of provisions from Lenka's supply. The couple was sleeping just an arm's reach away. She lifted Friend to stop his whining. He licked her tears.

The last thing she did was let down her locks and set the wool scarf beside the fire. Before she could change her mind, Maren slipped outside into the darkness. She began to run. Mutt knew this wasn't right and barked. The wind was gusting and she was scared and Friend began to whimper.

She tripped almost at once. To protect the puppy, she landed hard on her shoulder. Friend fled from her. Whatever this game, he didn't want to play.

Before she righted herself, there was already light from under the yurt's door. The fire was being rekindled, Chun and Lenka had stirred awake at the barking.

Maren made like she had gone for a piss. She kept the satchel full of provisions hidden in her robe. But in the morning, when she woke, she found Lenka had already unpacked the satchel.

The old woman didn't say a word. Seeing Maren awake, she gave back the scarf. That morning, there were no chores. Together they played the bone game while discussing the strangeness of the weather.

In the morning, a train of carts arrived, each loaded with raw wool.

There were mud-crested fibers that had to be washed and drawn apart and dyed and spun. Heaps were waiting to be worked, with more carts waiting to be unloaded. Every woman worked harder and for longer as the crowds of beggars at the gate grew denser, louder, more desperate.

Lilah's cauldron bubbled with mud scum and lanolin. Those cauldrons down the line were full of green, blue, and red water, and the women who stirred them were stained to the elbows.

After a day of cutting wood, Koneet still had to bundle finished wool and load it onto carts. She didn't complain. One of the women working beside her was pregnant and Koneet worked faster so this woman might rest her swollen feet. No one worked harder than Koneet.

Even Trinket was laboring now. She was one of many women sitting at wooden contraptions that spun and spun as they pushed the pedals, the wool turning to yarn between her fingers.

These were days that would not end. Lilah's shoulders, her neck, and her knees throbbed with pain. She was constantly bent over the steam, arms working with resigned violence, freeing the filth from the fibers. Because with so many deliveries, they were sure to have a chance soon. Carts entering the gate would meet carts leaving, and the gate would remain open long enough for the girls to rush through. What came after didn't matter. Lilah had to believe they would escape the guards who would chase them; she would lead the girls to water; she would succeed in stealing a boat. This had to be true. The alternative was too awful to imagine.

From her cauldron rose steam that smelled of distant wallows, a hidden world of mud and grass. Somewhere there was still grass.

She wanted to believe her children were upon it; somewhere they were feasting. But she couldn't see how. If the Sea let a place like this exist, if She let a man like the manager do whatever he wanted, if She let a little girl go blind and be kept apart from her mother forever—why would the Sea suddenly care what suffering befell Lilah's three children?

Where there had been four guards, suddenly there were twelve. Guards with lances patrolled the periphery. Guards with bows and arrows were positioned on each corner of the wall. Still the beggars shook the gate. At night, they roared.

One afternoon, Lilah looked to see a young mother holding a skeletal baby through the bars. When no one took it, she laid the baby uncrying to the cobbles. It was already stiff.

Koneet turned away; her axe broke through a massive round in one blow. She broke four rounds with her next four blows. The starved infant lay nearby.

Trinket was the one to pick it up. She reached and placed the body back outside the bars. Someone else's problem.

That night after the meal, Kenta was entertaining the younger children with a story; Koneet and Lilah were together apart from the others. Lilah said, 'I worry about you.'

Koneet wasn't eating. That afternoon in the manager's office hadn't changed her, but since seeing the dead infant, her shoulders were hunched, her head low, as if she were a woman trying to shrink herself into something smaller.

'Talk. Please say something.'

'She would be a year old. My daughter would be walking. She would have said her first words. Somewhere, she is talking. That is the real place. This is the nightmare.'

Lilah put a hand over Koneet's. 'We should sing for her.'

'No.' Koneet pushed her dinner aside. 'Please. I am done with songs.'

Then one day the crowd at the gate wouldn't let a delivery through.

Guards were sent outside to push and swing; they were struck with rocks and fists, and yet they fought until they had pushed the people far enough that a cart of firewood could pass through the gate.

But as the gate closed, the crowd rushed. Some positioned themselves under the gate; they fought to hold up the bars, and together they could. Beggars began pouring across the yard like a wave cresting the beach. The guards became men fighting a tide.

Lilah took Kenta's hand. Desperate people were dashing past in their panic for food. This was their chance. Here was what they had waited so long for. All they had to do now was run.

Koneet fought through the crowd to seize her sister. In her other hand was the axe. 'What are you waiting for?'

For months, they had been patient and now the gate was open; the guards were overwhelmed, and the three of them could simply walk to freedom. Yet Lilah's feet weren't moving. Not water—they were affixed to the ground like tree roots. Run, she needed to run. Her babies needed her to run!

Koneet's brow was pinched with fury. 'What's wrong with you?'

'Please, Auntie!' cried Kenta. 'We have to hurry!'

Koneet began pulling her sister away; they were leaving without her. By the time Lilah took a step, the gate was already closing. Because of her, they had missed this chance.

When it was over, three beggars were dead. The wounded were dragged from the grounds and left piled in the street. The gate was locked shut, and a police patrol wearing heavy bronze was outside to disperse the crowd.

'We didn't have food,' Lilah tried to explain to the sisters, to herself. 'There's no food outside these gates. On the Sea, on that long journey, we'll need food.'

Koneet's words came through teeth. 'That isn't why you cowered.'

'Please don't argue,' little Kenta begged from between them.

To see the open gate—to see all those surging, desperate beggars . . . What if she had failed to remember the way to the Sea; what if she failed to steal a boat or did steal a boat but then failed to properly sail it? If she failed, these girls would starve or drown. Here inside the gates, at least they wouldn't starve or drown. 'I made the right decision,' she told them, as she had once told Leerit. 'You're too young to understand.'

Koneet spit on Lilah's foot. 'You pretend. But I know the truth. You would rather never leave here than return home to discover your children dead.'

For all the barbarians killed, their herd only swelled in number.

Camps of them had spent the winter in the Valley of Questions, guarding sheep who ate down the elk's graze to nothing. Leerit and the warriors had fed themselves on sheep. Stalking close to send a volley of arrows before escaping into thickets ahead of horses who were so fast over grass yet afraid of deep brush.

Killing sheep, killing barbarians—for Leerit, this had become her overwhelming hunger. When she wasn't on the hunt, she chewed her fingernails to bleeding. Only when looking down on her unsuspecting prey did she know what she should do.

Then, inexplicably, the sheep were gone and the barbarians too. No final battle, no reason, no conclusion. Just gone. The surviving warriors found only empty camps and beaten-down trails, grass eaten to mud. Together, they ripped bites from mutton jerky and wondered why. Had they won or lost? How were they to tell this story?

Many wanted to track the barbarians to their hive and burn it down. 'If we don't, they will only come back and do this again.'

'No,' said a lone voice. 'It is over. This is what we fought for. Let it be over.'

As Leerit listened, she felt nauseous. Her monthly bleed was long overdue. She was still trying to believe it would start again. It had to start again.

Gulleet silenced the arguments with a hand held out. All eyes turned to her. 'Look around. Barbarian is gone. You drove him from these lands. Be proud, be humble. Thank the Sea for divining it. Thank the Ancients for teaching us how.'

The warriors looked at one another. Ozi spoke next. 'But to let even one barbarian live is to forsake our friends who spilled their lifeblood.'

Gulleet took hold of Ozi's bow. 'Your death will not honor them. They traded their blood for yours. From the mountaintop, they want you to live the life they cannot.'

Gulleet stood overlooking the long view. 'You are scared to be without battle. After what has happened, after what we have done, each of us must learn again how to endure. We must help one another learn. Our families still need us. They need us to be siblings, aunts and nieces, husbands and wives. Our families do not need warriors.'

The battle-scarred exchanged looks.

It was different for her. If Leerit returned, Auntie would know she was with child. She could not rejoin the village, not after what she had done. 'I am leaving to find Maren. She has waited too long already. As you say, she needs her big sister.'

Ozi didn't know what was growing inside her; she hadn't told him because he was married and she was afraid—afraid of Auntie, of the Ancients, of his wife and her gossip. Afraid most of all of what Ozi might say. Now his brow furrowed. 'Please don't leave.'

She couldn't look at him as she lifted the bearskin and slung it. She moved her knife to the front of her belt. Finally, she faced him. 'You're better off without me.'

XVII

The End

On the morning before his audience with the Emperor, Cyrus watched from his office window as his mother walked with Kushim. The boy's limp was profound and painful to see even after being in their care for these months.

After the mercenaries cleared the valley, the wool had grown thick. By Equinox, they had moved four flocks to where every animal could grow fat. It should've been enough. But the tribesmen had returned to gleefully butcher his sheep, and the mercenaries had been powerless to stop the killing.

He'd done everything he could and spared no expense. Now the sheep were shorn, the yarn spun, the weights tallied—and Cyrus had failed. Failed his mother. Failed his father. For his family, there would be no boarding passes.

Now, outside, Kushim was pointing to some bird. Here, in their care, the child had become almost civilized. He had learned the language; he knew how to address them with respect and how to speak with dignity to a servant. Protecting this child—it felt like the one thing Cyrus had done since his father's death that was unquestionably right.

He rang the bell on his desk and the manservant entered. Cyrus said, 'Summon the widow.'

He had twice tried to tell her that she wouldn't be on the ark.

The first time, he had asked his mother to join him for tea, which they shared before a sunlit window, but she had talked endlessly about the girl she wanted as a daughter-in-law. This one was tall and graceful and born of a lineage more prominent than their own. She had come for several dinners. She was young and innocent and pure; her name was on the lips of many suitors. So Cyrus had told his poor mother, 'Yes, fine. I'll marry the girl.' Seeing the relief in her eyes—it stole all words from him.

Last night he had tried again to tell his mother. On the ceiling above his bed, all he could see was her expression when the ark sailed without her. Rather than trouble his manservant, who had retired downstairs for the evening, Cyrus went alone down the long corridor toward his mother's bedroom. He knocked. Knocked again. There was no response from inside. He shoved open the door to see a candle burning, but the room was empty.

He went next out the front door, yet her carriage remained, parked and decoupled. The servants were asleep. Only his guardsmen were awake. He asked the men patrolling his gate if they had seen the widow. 'Sir, not since she returned this afternoon.'

He thought first of a kidnapping. But how, from inside their well-defended gates?

He had known her his whole life—and yet did he know his mother at all? Wet nurses, nannies, tutors. As a boy, he had seen her for tea and treats; as an adolescent, he had joined his parents for dinners delivered by servants. A proper Lady, she had always treated her son as if he were a guest of the estate.

He returned directly to the master's quarters and locked the door. He lay on top of the bed, his slippers still on. Even his own mother concealed herself from him.

He woke sometime later at the smoke of his burned-out lantern and in that eerie light thought of Ashair.

What he knew for certain, what could not be doubted, was simple: some men are destined to die alone.

For this chance to fail, Cyrus had taken on immense debt. General Rah had lent the family a figure that would have terrified Cyrus's father. And all without any discussion of repayment. When he was revealing the forbidden artifacts, Rah had said, *I knew you were the right one.* But for what?

Cyrus had read of revolts in lesser kingdoms, when lesser kingdoms still existed; most often those rulers were deposed by their own militaries. If the rioters were kindling, Rah was the spark. With that key, he had opened the armory to their outrage.

Yet why would Rah give weapons to commoners when he himself commanded the loyalty of the army? If it was the throne he wanted, his regiments could sack the palace in an afternoon.

What really mattered was in five weeks the ark would set sail, and she wouldn't be on it. His mother deserved to know.

Now she entered his office. Suspicion lifted her eyebrow. 'Why do you look so awful?'

He moved to the window. She came and stood an arm's length away, and said, 'Kushim is such a remarkable child. He's blossoming here. Have you heard him sing? I'm not alone in thinking he has a future as a performer. When I told him of the green shore, I'm not sure he understood the significance. Of course we will take him with us. I think we should bless him with a new name. Something civilized. Don't you think?'

'I have some difficult news,' Cyrus finally said. 'In fact, possibly the most difficult. I tried to tell you last night but you weren't in your room. Where were you?'

'I was out for a walk.' His mother's eyebrows rose. 'Well, how long must I brace myself?'

'The managers haven't come through. They've fallen short. A seventh more when we needed a fifth.' He felt the fullest weight of it then, hearing his accounting uttered.

She touched her cheek. 'What are you telling me?'

'We won't be on the ark. Not on the first trip anyway.'

She laughed as he had never heard her laugh before. 'Of course we will!'

'I understand that you're surprised but—'

'No. Cyrus. Of course we will be on the ark. You are the master of wool. The Empire needs you. Think of your fiancée!'

'I've tried everything!' He was startled to hear the frailty of his own voice. 'You don't know what I've done to cut this wool! Mother . . .' Tears were streaming down his cheeks. He was crying like some toddler. 'I knew I would bring shame to Father's name!'

To hear this, her own eyes welled. She leaned toward him. But a deep breath lifted her posture, and she regained the composure of a Lady before her son and master. She said, 'You forget yourself. A man of your privilege can never have tried everything.'

The Emperor's scouts had described the green shore as a land of lakes and grass, fruit trees and nuts, grapes and endless harvests, a land that knew no drought and no winter, where deep veins of ore waited under shallow crust. He was trying to conjure the place now, trying to see himself upon that shore, to believe he might somehow still reach it—when the manservant announced the arrival of the flock manager.

The stocky man entered in formal garments. Cyrus wasted no time on pleasantries. 'You assured me if I cleared that faraway valley.'

The man offered the expected defenses. The primitives, the arid winter, the graze that didn't grow like it used to. He said, 'Forces outside of my control. No one could have predicted.'

Arguing now would not make the bundles of wool any heavier. Cyrus stood at the window. He saw his mother again walking with Kushim. She was holding the boy's hand. When had she ever held his? 'Your severance is on the desk. Take it and leave. I hope you never sleep. After all this family did for you . . . You have brought only shame upon our name.'

The manager huffed. He said, 'Without me, what will happen to the flocks?'

'What do the flocks matter now?'

Cyrus was startled when the manager toppled his chair. 'You don't know the first thing about those animals! There are no sheep to you, just wool. No plains, just graze. No men, only numbers on a roll of parchment. *You* people did this! Across those waters, you'll only do it again. Perhaps next time men like me won't let you.'

Cyrus sent a courier with a carriage of guardsmen posthaste to the hospital. 'The boy needs you,' he wrote. 'It's urgent.' Ashair came. He was wearing his official regalia: here to check the progress of a patient. Their greeting in the lobby was painfully formal. It had been months. The hair above Ashair's ears was gray. He bowed his head. 'Master.'

In his excitement, the boy rushed and fell. Doctor and master both moved to help the child to his feet. Kushim embraced Ashair and clung to him. The child was weeping.

An audience of servants watched Ashair examine the child. He checked the healing of the scalp, the new range of motion in the broken leg. He produced a ball and asked Kushim to kick it. With the inside of his foot, with the toe, with the outside, with the heel, kick it in every direction—to help his leg recover its dexterity. 'Play is what you need now.' Ashair and the boy began passing the ball back and forth.

It was all Cyrus wanted. Something more impossible even than reaching those green shores. He wanted to be a husband, a father, to someday together teach their child something worthy. How could a family be too much to ask for?

The manservant was nearby. Guardsmen on the periphery. His mother praising Kushim as he kicked the ball. Perhaps Ashair recognized what was behind Cyrus's eyes. 'Sir, if you can spare a moment.'

'Me?'

Ashair passed him the ball. Cyrus stopped it with a polished boot.

'Pass it,' the doctor said. 'You remember how to play a game, don't you?'

Cyrus tapped the ball toward Kushim, who kicked hard with his once-mangled leg. To see the ball careening away and Ashair running after it, the child laughed.

Cyrus knew then for certain: this was as close as he and Ashair would ever come.

Ashair left with only a glance back. The last words he spoke were about the boy, requesting again that he be delivered back to his people.

Cyrus told the manservant not to disturb him. He lay on his bed and stared at the same ceiling his father had while he died. Tonight, he decided, after his audience with the Emperor, he would join his father once and for all in that place where every question has an answer. He would ask first: *Why?*

With him gone, his mother would be better off. Maybe a man like General Rah could find a grieving widow one last boarding pass.

In the end, his death would be remembered as a blessing.

Then, finally, it was time. He dressed in his formal gown. He sat with his eyes shut as servants applied the most dignified paints. They greased his hair and rubbed in fractures of pyrite to sparkle in the Sun's beams. They told him he was ready.

Cyrus went directly to the aviary because he would not fail the boy. He could do better than returning him to some wayward band of primitives. He wanted to leave Kushim with something true, something that would live on when tomorrow Cyrus was gone. Yet, before the boy, he found himself unable to conjure any knowledge worth imparting. Years of rigorous scholarship and what did he know for certain?

What he wanted was a single story to contain it all, to hold every current of history—what Kushim needed to know if he was to understand what had happened and was happening and would happen again. In this world, a boy would need a story like that, a hopeful story he could trust, to not be broken by the events of his lifetime.

Perhaps Kushim could sense his sorrow, for he began showing Cyrus the new tricks he'd taught the crows. Kept saying, 'Watch this.' This boy who had lost half his head of hair, his ability to run—his family—he was the one trying to cheer up Cyrus.

Kushim held out an arm and the now-grown chick flapped down from its branch and landed near his elbow. From his own teeth, Kushim fed the open mouth a morsel.

As a boy, Cyrus had wanted nothing more than to convince a crow to trust him thoroughly enough to perch on his shoulder. He asked, 'How did you teach him to do that?'

Kushim seemed confused. 'We taught each other.'

The carriages in the front and rear were loaded with armed men. The one in the middle, his carriage, was heavily armored with bronze. Jernod carried two swords, twin daggers, and a lance because whole sections of the city had been abandoned by overrun police. To see this caravan waiting, Cyrus felt like a man proceeding to his own execution. He was ready.

His mother arrived to see him off. She was wearing her most elegant tiara. Not a strand of hair was out of place. She said formally for the crowd of servants in attendance, 'Today you will represent this family before our Emperor. Generations have built upon their fathers' efforts to bring you this chance. You, my son and master, will make your forefathers proud.'

She turned toward the approach of the manservant, who was leading Kushim. Cyrus had told the boy about the theater and why it was the best place for him. A fat satchel had already secured the arrangement with the governor of drama. Kushim had cried at the thought of leaving the crows. Cyrus had told the child honestly, 'The theater will be the safest place for you.'

But he had not told his mother, and now she snapped her head around, and said, 'No. No, you can't take him from me.'

'You said yourself the boy has a future as a performer. Think of him for once. This isn't about you. This was never about you. This has always been about him.'

His mother looked stricken. She wavered and lost her balance.

What Cyrus couldn't miss was how, as she stumbled, she reached as if by instinct for the arm of Jernod. With a hand across her shoulders, the driver deftly steadied the Lady before regaining his dutiful expression of attention.

No one else seemed to notice. But the familiarity of their bodies, their effortlessly shared movements—the intimacy was undeniable to a man fluent in the language of clandestine love.

'Please.' She stepped nearer now, near enough to whisper in Cyrus's ear. 'I need this child. He needs me. Without us, who does he have? This has always been about his best interests. You know that.'

Before everyone, Cyrus dared touch his mother's hand. In a voice meant only for her, he spoke his last words to the woman who made him. 'You deserved better.'

Rumbling down the hill, Kushim was muttering in his native language while tears streamed from clenched eyes. These were the prayers of primitives who, Cyrus might have once said, know nothing of their own history. He knelt beside the boy but was no comfort.

They couldn't stop now, not in this part of the city. Rocks clanged against the armor. He understood why citizens hated him: here was a well-fed man when their own children were going hungry. 'Soon,' he told Kushim, 'it will all be over. I promise.'

The boy gripped Cyrus's collar. 'Please! I want to go home.'

'Trust me. This will be far superior.'

Then the boy had been left in the care of the good people of the theater; it was what was best for him. The governor of drama assured Cyrus that the players would be welcomed onboard the ark. The Emperor would not leave them behind.

It was the last thing—Cyrus's work on this earth was done. The horses passed under the Emperor's portcullis and climbed the road he had only ever seen from afar.

Jernod. Jernod who had always been there. The way Jernod touched his mother—he had done so with the grace of a man familiar with the weight and movement of her body.

The constant charity events, the much older husband, last night when she wasn't in her quarters . . . His mother was beautiful—and his father had always been a round, balding, ancient, affectionless man consumed by numbers. Of course she'd taken a lover.

But the family's *driver*? It would be fodder for unrelenting gossip. Not a crime, perhaps—yet worse. Rumors were not so easily vanquished with bribes. How long had she been inviting this shame upon their lineage?

Now, here at the end, he almost hoped he was right. Because, when her son was dead and the last of the money spent, she would need the devotion of an armed man like Jernod. Someone who could protect her from what was to come. Maybe it wasn't true. Maybe he only wanted to believe in their affair, that Jernod would continue to protect her after his salary was no longer being paid. Maybe want was all faith ever was.

The carriage leveled, the horses slowed, and the wheels rolled to a stop. Numb hands, feet that floated to the white cobbles of the palace courtyard. Seeing Jernod as if for the first time—his driver gripped him. 'Sir? Sir, are you okay?'

Under the call of crows, he walked. A final procession. To stand at the center of every story. Waiting in a silent queue of masters, he the youngest. Men with more and rarer plastic in their necklaces and earrings. Better men, married men, men who met their quotas and wasted no bounty. Some he recognized. His father would know everyone's name.

His father would have met his quota and ensured his family boarded the ark.

Relief came in the indelible form of bronze. The Emperor upon a reared-back horse, spear in hand, the glint at its tip. Upon the statue's base, words had been engraved by a previous generation: THE EMPEROR SHALL LEAD HIS FAITHFUL AS THE SUN LEADS THE LIGHT.

It was a phrase he had read so often, on statues and coins and throughout old scrolls—it was the very foundation of the social contract and the greater good. The wording had never given him a second thought. Yet now Cyrus kept turning it over: *the Sun leads the light*. For what was the Sun if not illumination? How could one be apart from the other? In this life, how could cause outpace effect?

At last, it was his turn. The wings swung open to reveal an inferno of golden light. The Sunset reflected and magnified upon the Emperor sitting atop his throne. It was a light bright enough to illuminate every truth a man had spent his life concealing. Cyrus fell blinded to his knees.

The Emperor's voice echoed from the chamber walls. Cyrus's own response was tin by comparison. These words that belonged to another man. *Forces outside my control. Nothing I could have predicted.*

The Emperor boomed: 'Stand and face me.'

Cyrus opened his eyes to the scorching heat of eternal judgment.

'You have wasted the Sun's bounty. You have wasted the gifts my mercy bestowed.'

On the Emperor's shoulder stood the golden crow, sidestepping now until his wing touched the Emperor's ear. Golden feathers, golden beak, only the eyes still black, this bird too weighed down by metal to fly.

At such proximity, Cyrus forced himself to see every fiber of the Emperor's gown as if it were the last sight he would behold in this life:

the golden plating on the thighs and shins—narrow thighs, long shins, oversize knees. Beyond the gleaming metal, the Emperor's toe curled over the edge of his sandal; it was smooshed against polished rock. His were pale fingers that clung to the throne's arm, spindly with fingernails chewed to nubs. Here was the leader of men, supposedly in his prime, and yet beside the throne, within easy reach, was a wooden cane, its end worn raw.

'Face. Me.'

Cyrus looked to the Emperor's golden mask and felt the solar heat on the backs of his eyes. Bright enough to melt him. The light and the voice were one.

'Egregious shortage. Sordid rumors. Waste of skin. No passage to green shores. Strike the family name from the histories. This lineage shall never have existed.'

XVIII

To Name What Is Now

During his first moments inside the theater, Kushim was terrified.

So many faces, every eye on him. Children his age and older. He struggled to get free—until he heard their singing.

The one called *governor* held his hand, told him where to sit, then sat beside him. The children onstage wore a hundred colors, garments to the floor and others cut above the knee, some with hoods and others with ribbons of bright fabric waving from their elbows and wrists. The governor leaned and handed him something, and said, 'When you're ready, raise this.'

As Kushim raised the flag, a hundred faces parted with song. To him, for him. That's how it felt. An entire village singing for him. Dancers leapt into view; someone swung out over the seats on a rope. They were a village of children in the forest when trees were still green and forests full of creatures. A story from back when, the time of the Ancients, when the hungry had merely to pluck a fruit from its limb. Ama had told him so many stories of this bounty.

The governor leaned nearer to say, 'Tomorrow, we will find you a place among them. Tonight, you may simply marvel at our future.'

Then he announced, 'Again from "we've arrived," but this time, players, I want you to feel the words here! Don't just *sing*. Your lost friend has been found! Sing because you have no hands. All you have to hold him is your voice.'

That evening after the rehearsal, the players laughed and pulled off their costumes and gathered in tight little groups to play games until adults in gray robes arrived with pockets of bread filled with vegetables and meat, two pockets per person, Kushim included. His stomach was full after eating just one.

The governor told them to unroll their bedding. He stepped near and put his hand to Kushim's shoulder. 'Do you still want to run from me? You're thinking about it, aren't you? I have someone for you to meet.'

Her hair was up in two buns, as tall as Leerit but smiling. Jumpa was her name. 'Kushim, can I be your friend? I'll show you everything. Come with me. It's time for sleep.' She offered her hand. 'Even I was new once. We all remember being new.' Her smile melted something inside him. 'Would you like to sleep near me? I'll keep you safe.'

She dragged her blankets. She lay down within reach. She smiled at him and promised him everything would be okay. He held his eyes open for as long as he could so as not to lose her.

He dreamt that night of a time when his sisters were in the river, tending the fish traps and bickering. He wanted to be near them but Ama said he couldn't go near the river. In the dream, he looked over his shoulder to see if Ama was watching. He so hoped she wasn't watching.

———

The next day, for the first time, he stood onstage, a part of them. Jumpa held his hand. 'Don't worry if you get the words wrong. We all got them wrong at first. I'll practice with you, okay?'

At the lifting of the flag, their voices filled the space and his rose among them. This, the first time he knew that weightless joy, his voice lifted on the wings of a hundred others, a child among a village—a member of *the chorus*.

During a break, some boys called him by his name. They wanted to know what had happened to his face, and when he told them, they asked to touch the scar. Soon he was repeating the story for others. Everyone quiet but for him. The same boys hearing it twice, their faces twisted with disgust. An older boy interrupted to say there was no such thing as bears. This boy called Kushim a *liar*. 'His heathen father beat him with a rock.'

That night, when the food was delivered, the same older boy pushed Kushim from behind and he fell hard to the floor. This boy stood over him. He bent down and took the dinner still clutched in Kushim's hand. 'Liar,' he said again. 'Bears aren't real.'

Jumpa saw Kushim sitting alone and took his hand. 'What happened?'

She marched over to the boy. She seized him by the ear and delivered him whining to Kushim. Because of Jumpa, his dinner was returned. Because of Jumpa, the boy didn't bother him again.

A few days later, she brought him and the youngest chorus members to the high rim of the theater to practice the songs. They had to climb through a vertical tunnel onto a peak where the wind rustled his hair.

Pigeons clapped their wings into flight and he leaned to watch them. Jumpa called him back from the edge. She said it wasn't safe.

The city expanded all the way to the bright Sea. For the first time, he saw the source of that pounding he'd heard for so long. Near the water, a giant construction of wood, like a cage, and on it, men were working. 'What is it?' he asked.

The children told him it was a special boat that would carry them far away.

'To where?' he asked.

Jumpa answered, 'Across those ugly waters is a beautiful garden. In that place, you can have anything you want forever.'

He took Jumpa's hand. 'You are leaving?'

'Don't worry,' she told him. 'You're going too. The Emperor loves his players.'

He dreamt every night of his sisters by the river. Dream or memory, he wasn't sure. They were bickering. He wanted to go down to see what the fuss was about. But if he went down to those currents, his mother would be angry. He kept looking over his shoulder. He was hoping not to see her.

In quiet moments, the children played hand games or tag. Others hurried off to continue playing *chess*, boards spread through the vacant benches of the theater. Because of his limp, he was too slow for tag and so watched the chess pieces and began learning the rules. He liked the rules, the straight lines across the board, the even spacing of the squares. He liked that no matter how many pieces were taken, they could all be put back.

The governor approached him. 'I want to place you up front. The audience will be enchanted by the little heathen who can sing. But you need the perfect fleece.'

He didn't know this word *heathen* but he had heard it before. The governor misunderstood his confusion. 'It's just the medicine the Empire needs now. Enemies united. Enemies starting over across the ocean. There will be a place for each of us.'

'*Enemies?*' he repeated.

The governor patted his back. 'Their word, not mine. Here, we're all family.'

Another time, he sought out the governor and waited while the man listened to an argument between actors. Finally, he sent the older boys back to the stage, turned to Kushim, and said, 'Yes? What is it? Be quick, please. I'm very busy now.'

He hadn't come with a question; he had come simply to be near this man who smiled as readily as Opi. Now Kushim pointed to what the governor was holding. Like a stick but not. 'What's this?'

The governor unrolled the stick to reveal the same leaflike material he remembered from the aviary when Cyrus gave him new clothes, and said, 'This is your name.' They called it *writing*. 'You don't know?' The governor turned in his seat. 'If sounds left tracks in dust, these are the hoofprints left by words.'

He let Kushim touch the hoofprints. Somehow, they didn't change under his finger.

'Everything you hear us sing? Those words are written on scrolls like this one.' The governor opened a case beside him to reveal a flat surface of circles—countless scrolls neatly organized. 'My job is to teach you to sing the words. To dance. To act. It all begins here, with the tracks the words long ago left behind. Do you understand?'

'Who laid the trails? Who went first?'

'Stories come to us from long ago. But they are here now, safe with us. That's what matters.'

Kushim must have looked confused.

'Do you know what this is about?' the governor asked. 'Why we work so hard to get every part of the performance perfectly right? Why the Emperor rewards us with food and this beautiful theater? Kushim, without us, his people wouldn't know the meaning of their name.'

The boring part was watching the actors deliver their lines. Over and over. Kushim stopped watching the actors. He started watching the governor. This man writing and listening, his chin in his hand, a quill between his fingers. He who decided what they did and when. This man who had followed the tracks of every story. Who picked every path. To the governor, nothing could ever happen by surprise.

That's the kind of man he wanted to be. If not a fisherman, then a governor.

He was onstage with the chorus when lightning struck.

His sisters knee-deep in the river checking fish traps. Bickering. He'll get in trouble if he goes down to them, but he wants to go down to see what they were arguing over. Ama isn't nearby. Good. Ama isn't watching him.

Waking. Now. This. Here.

Pain! Ribs, back of the head, every muscle, his belly!

Trying to sit upright but hands hold him down. There had been lightning. He remembered the lightning. He remembered looking for Ama. She wasn't watching. He remembered being glad that she wasn't watching.

Then a voice from above, familiar, speaking a language not his mother's. The words took shape. 'You're with your brothers and sisters. Kushim, can you hear me?'

They lifted him on a blanket of wool and carried him from the stage through a dark corridor into the room where the governor slept. These children lowered the blanket to the governor's bed and stared. At his command, they retreated and vanished. Jumpa remained beside Kushim, holding his hand, stroking his brow. She was saying over and over, 'I won't leave you, I promise. You're safe now.'

The governor put his palm on Kushim's forehead. 'You don't appear injured. Have you had these episodes before? You were convulsing. You had us worried! Kushim, can you hear me?'

The nausea was still roiling his stomach and his mouth tasted of that awful smoke. It seemed a year had passed since he had been singing with the chorus. Every word he might utter was still hiding from his tongue.

'It's okay,' the governor said. 'You don't know what happened. It's okay not to know.'

'It's okay,' Jumpa said. 'You're here now.'

Kushim tried to sit up but it was too much too soon.

The governor patted his cheek. He crossed the room to a wall of circles—each a scroll rolled and tucked in place. His fingers ran along them until he found the one he wanted. He returned with this scroll and sat on the edge of the bed and unfurled it. He smiled at the tracks left behind by words. 'Would you like to hear a story about a boy long ago?'

Kushim took the governor's hand. He was holding it with all the strength he had left.

'It's okay. I know. My parents died too, when I was seven. Kushim, these stories became like open arms for me. Here are brothers and sisters, mothers and fathers. They are waiting for us. There have always been brothers and sisters and mothers and fathers; there have always been little boys who are afraid of being alone. Kushim, I will teach you to read, as I was taught. Do you know why? Because one day, far into the future, there will be another little boy, just like us, who needs our help.'

Already the grass was changing from green to tan. Chun was afraid for his sheep.

Maren was outside to throw a pan of wash water, the sun hot on her face, sweat running down her cheeks, the whine of mosquitoes in her ears. She checked: the horizon was, as always, barren.

A good distance from the yurt, she threw the wash water and Friend leapt to nip at the stream as it parted the air. She set down the pan and ran, a momentary escape from the mosquitoes, Friend alongside with his tongue out. She chased him, and he turned up the hill but she was too slow, so he wheeled and rushed toward her down to the water streaming from the alpine meadow. There, in the aquatic rush of air, she felt it: eyes watching her. She waved the mosquitoes from her face. Her big sister was on the opposite bank. As if born from air.

'What? Don't recognize me?' Leerit was beaming. Her hair was now a hand long in all directions. Her arms wore new muscles, veins riding high. Dark circles lined her eyes. Yet it was Leerit!

Maren leapt the stream and tackled her. 'Are you really here?'

'Careful,' Leerit said with a hand to her belly.

'Am I dreaming? Are you really here?'

Leerit's smile was gone. 'What are you wearing? You aren't one of them.'

———

They sat together in the shade thrown by the yurt. Leerit was tossing the stick that Friend liked. Each time he returned with it, Leerit had to wrestle the wood from his jaws.

She hadn't asked about Kushim. He was the heaviness within every silence. Leerit told about the village in the valley where storms are born. She told about Auntie, their old friends. She explained how she had come looking before solstice, how she wasn't good enough to read tracks over frozen ground. She had found Maren only after trying ceaselessly from one new moon to the next. 'There are so many flocks. I kept trying. Find sheep, watch the yurt guarding them, be sure my sister isn't inside. And then today, after so long, I saw Chun and his white hair.'

Her big sister was different now in ways Maren could describe and in others she could not. Her face had filled out with food, yet her eyes seemed darker, deeper set. She kept turning to look toward the horizon— she never stopped looking. As if she expected the bear to return at any moment. This was her sister but also someone else.

Finally, she stopped throwing the stick for the dog. She said, 'When did he die?'

Maren was startled to hear the word from her sister. Maren told what had happened. But she lied and said Kushim had been taken while she was asleep. She said she hadn't known until the morning. 'He is alive. He can't be . . . not alive. He's Kushim.'

Leerit didn't look relieved. She said, 'How could you let them take our brother? You should have fought for him!'

'You don't understand! He was so sick! You were nowhere. He needed help.'

Leerit cursed. 'You know that if his body was not given to the river, he will not join the Ancients. He could be lost forever.'

At this, Maren sobbed. She couldn't speak or breathe.

Leerit did not embrace or comfort her. 'Tell me, where did they take his body?'

Friend was licking her. Maren conveyed what she could. Their brother had been taken to that place where the river meets the Sea. 'The City. It's like a village but so huge. There are special healers in this place.'

Leerit said, 'It's called The Hive.'

Friend crawled into her lap, and Maren rubbed behind his ears. 'I can speak their language. We can ask until we find the boy who was attacked by a bear. Everyone will know his story. I have thought every detail through.'

'See what is obvious!' Leerit was angry. 'Boys half-eaten by bears do not live!'

Maren shook her head. 'We have to try to find him. Kushim, he is living.'

That evening, Lenka fed them from the stash of salted meat. Maren did the work of carrying words back and forth across that river dividing Leerit from the couple.

Chun was asking what had happened upriver, these rumors he heard from the trader. When Maren translated the questions, Leerit stiffened. She spoke of the fighting as if it involved someone else. To hear the answers, Chun's mood darkened. Soon his fist was balled on his knee. The trader had talked of sheep slaughtered and left to rot, and at last Chun asked the question that mattered most to him.

'Yes, I killed sheep,' Leerit said. 'I would kill all sheep. Grass belongs to Elk.'

Maren left this answer on Leerit's side of the river. She delivered this to Chun: 'No, my sister has never stolen another man's sheep.'

Chun nodded. He rose and disappeared outside and soon returned with a cup of his fermented drink. He sat and looked at what he had. He offered Leerit the first sip.

She took it from him with both hands and drank greedily. Chun received the empty cup and laughed, because what else could he do? Maren explained to her sister, 'You were supposed to share. A guest should refuse the first offer and accept the second. Now you are expected to return his gift with a gift.'

'Give these people a gift? They traded our brother.'

'You owe them your thanks. For taking care of me.'

Leerit drew from her satchel a leather wrap. Inside was a bronze knife.

Chun held the brilliant blade in both hands. In its hilt were inlaid gems. He looked at Leerit but spoke to his wife. 'It's an officer's blade.'

Lenka answered, 'We shouldn't be caught with that. They'll say we stole it.'

Leerit asked. 'What more do they want?'

'They want to know how you got the knife,' Maren said. 'They want to know what you did to get it. They want to know what happened to you after you left here.'

Leerit stared at Maren for a long time. 'You even sit like her now.'

Maren was on her knees, like Lenka. She moved to sit cross-legged like Leerit.

Her sister spit. It was so rude to spit indoors. 'What these people did. And yet you love them.'

'He needed help. She was out of medicine. What else was I supposed to do? You left me alone!'

Leerit leapt to her feet and pointed a finger. 'This woman has made you her dog and you don't even care.' She walked from the yurt without a proper thanks for the meal.

'I'm sorry,' Maren told Lenka. 'She hates me, I guess.'

Lenka patted Maren's knee. 'Sisters fight. It's natural. I promise she still loves you just the same.'

Maren found Leerit rolling out her bedding in a cluster of rocks up the hill from the yurt. Mutt was watching, tongue in, ears forward. He stayed near the yurt while Maren approached her big sister. For the first time, Friend didn't follow.

Maren said, 'Was I supposed to refuse the robe she made me? Mine was rotting.'

Leerit drew her stone knife and set it within easy reach of her bedding.

'Was I supposed to let him die here?'

Leerit shut her eyes.

'Every day I watched the horizon for you. A hundred times a day I looked. You're angry, but you're the one who left, not me.'

Finally, Leerit spoke. 'You're right. I'm sorry.'

Maren hadn't expected an apology. Now she didn't know what to do.

Leerit's eyes were wet. 'But you can't be both. You are one of them or one of us.'

Maren said, 'We're more the same than different.'

Leerit didn't blink. 'If you saw what I saw, you would not say such a thing.'

Maren touched her sister's shoulder. 'Leerit. I am us. Please believe me.'

That night Lenka washed herself as usual, dressed, then whistled to welcome back Chun—their nightly routine. Except this night she didn't meet Maren's eye.

The old couple crawled into their lambs-wool bedding. Maren had beat it out for them before and after each move. She had completed most every chore so Lenka could knit and tell stories. About how they met, how Chun asked her to be his wife—the man asking the woman— these stories that didn't fit the beach and yet fit here. Like old people anywhere, they pulled the bedding over themselves to lock out the cold.

'Good night,' she said to them as she had on countless nights before.

This time only Chun responded. 'Dream of rain, beautiful girl.'

Maren hardly slept but then she woke to a bark. Leerit stood in the entry, Mutt behind her. A purple dawn waited beyond. 'Come. If you're coming.'

Maren's hands were shaking as she rolled the wool she had slept on all these months. Lenka knelt to help. They both began crying.

Lenka drew something from her pocket and put it in Maren's hand. A container of spice. The same spice they had rubbed into meat and cooked together inside the bronze pot, this meal the couple adored but that required Maren's teeth to chew. Without her, they wouldn't be able to eat it. She wanted Maren to keep the precious seasoning. 'For your own daughters,' she said. 'Please, take it and remember.'

Outside, Friend was sitting on his haunches, Friend who never sat obediently. He kept whining. Maren asked, but Leerit shook her head. 'Not where we're going.'

She rubbed behind Friend's ears this last time. Let him lick her face. He couldn't stop whining. Somehow he knew. She had never thought of this, how she wouldn't want to leave.

On the ridge, Maren stopped to look back. Lenka and Chun were still watching, Friend on a leash to keep him. The basin was enormous and yellow green and dotted with sheep; they were but specks at its center.

In their last moments together, Lenka had leaned on the lyrics of a song she often sang. 'Wherever the flock takes you, will you remember me?'

'I'll come back,' Maren had promised. 'Once we find him.'

But Lenka shook her head. She knew how big this valley was. 'Wherever you go, sweet child,' she said in a shaking voice. 'You'll bring to those people such beautiful good fortune.'

Lilah had worked the obsidian each night when on the shitting hole, her only moments alone. A simple cobble had been enough to crack free leaves of rock, each blow sending a precise break at the angle she directed. These scraps she might have kept as coarse cutting pieces, but each only heightened the risk of discovery, so she let them fall through her fingers into the hole. She worked with fury. She worked when she needed sleep. She wouldn't miss another opportunity. This—knapping rock—this is all she knew to do.

Eventually, she had a rough oval-shaped piece with good purchase. But to hone a cutting edge, she needed an antler point—in this place without antlers.

Finally, she thought to try a bronze stake that supported the drying line. Well after dark, she pulled it. Its point was hard but dull. While others slept, she used it to pressure-knap the edge. Delicate, precise work, just as her aunts had taught her. Then, before dawn, she slipped into the yard to return the stake before the guards noticed it missing.

As her foot pressed the stake back into its place between heavy cobbles, she heard a voice belonging to a man. He spoke in the desert language. 'What are you doing outside the dormitory?'

The finished blade was under her robe. Her hand found it. She turned to face him.

The guard brought his torch between them. The light was blinding. But then her vision returned and she saw his boyish face. His voice was deeper this time. 'I said, why are you awake?' He was one of the new guards, so young, a man in body alone—he didn't yet believe his own story.

She stepped past his torch. She put her hand to his. She said as best she could in the language, 'Should I be afraid? I heard a noise. Are beggars inside again?'

His relief was visible. He smiled. 'Don't worry, woman. You're safe. See that gate? It's closed. Go back to bed. I will protect you.'

In the morning, the manager didn't show. For the first time, there were no deliveries of wool. Even the guards kept glancing over their shoulders. This village that had longed for a day of rest now didn't know what to do with idle hands.

Eventually, Trinket called the women together around a fire and the children sank into their laps. Like any village, this one rubbed the feet of the pregnant woman. In thirty years, Trinket told them, there hadn't been a single day without labor before now.

Every conversation was muted; the women kept looking over their shoulders at the gate, at the guards. The police patrol was gone, as were most of the beggars. 'What's happening?' someone asked. Trinket was chewing the inside of her cheek.

Only Koneet labored. She split all the remaining wood. She fed their fire. When the wood was split, she stacked it. Trinket told her to sit, to rest, that she was making everyone nervous, but Koneet said in the desert tongue, 'Stacking wood is what I can do.'

By the afternoon, they were still without wool. The guards were pacing. Lilah was in the courtyard playing guessing games with Kenta when she heard a whistle from the gate. A man was there: the homely driver.

Koneet went skipping to him. She kissed his hand; she put it to her cheek. The guards did nothing to stop them. The guards were friendly with the driver who came every morning with firewood.

After the driver left, the women were begging answers. 'He was told there will be no more work, not for him,' Koneet explained. Trinket grunted. Other women swatted the air before their noses as if this news were a bad smell.

A grim silence fell over the village.

'What will happen to us?' someone asked.

They were all looking to Trinket. Trinket began to sing.

For the rest of the afternoon, they sang the same songs in the same order as any other day, and at supper they ate the same meal and in the same quantities and then they put themselves to bed to the usual desert prayers.

Lilah laid awake, turning the blade in her hand. She had to believe the Ancients had sent it for a reason. Otherwise, what? There was no reason?

Maren had followed Leerit up the mountain. Her feet were unaccustomed to hard travel, but her sister was never stronger, so the distance between them only grew as they climbed. When Maren finally reached the spine of the ridge, she was startled to find her sister sitting beside another, a man she recognized from when he was a boy on the beach. Ozi. When he saw her, he took his hand from Leerit's belly and stood. His hood was up for the alpine wind but now he took it down. He greeted Maren as a husband should greet a maiden. He was tall and thick, a coastal man rich with smiles. There was a scar on his cheek and a rip through his ear. He was marked for marriage. 'Do you remember me?'

Maren met her sister's gaze. 'You got married?'

'No,' Leerit said. 'Not me.'

She looked at her sister's belly, which Ozi had been touching. She asked her sister, 'Are you pregnant?'

Ozi answered when Leerit didn't. 'The Sea brought us together for a reason.'

All day they followed the ridge. Shale and cliffs, brutal going but free from the dangers of the trail below. Ozi told of the barbarians who glowed in the sunshine, who lusted to kill good people without cause. When he spoke of them, his voice was terse. When they had to scale some slab of rock, he led and reached back a hand to help Maren.

Below, she could see where the green grass gave way to the brown valley bottom. Already it was so dry. The river was only a meandering thread.

At a pinnacle of towering rock, Ozi went ahead to scout the safest route, and Maren was finally able to ask her sister, 'Did you tempt another woman's husband?'

'Not like you think.'

'What did Auntie say when she found out? Have you been banished?'

Leerit said, 'You don't understand how much things have changed.'

They slept that night and the next two by seeps of water, these birth-places of the river below. Under the red skies of dusk, Maren rolled out the wool Lenka had given her while Leerit shared the bearskin with Ozi. To muffle the sounds of their coupling, Maren had to sleep with her robe piled over her ear. The sister she knew would never seduce a married man.

Ama was somewhere watching. Maren said to the woman who had made them, 'Forgive her. Without you, she has had so much to carry.'

After his humiliation at the feet of the Emperor, Cyrus had asked that a bath be poured. He told the manservant that under no conditions was he to open the door. For what would be the last time, Cyrus undressed himself by torchlight.

He had been flirting with the idea for half his life. So it wasn't a fateful turn; it was the inevitable result. He had always known he would use a ceremonial blade just like in the old stories of soldiers facing imminent defeat. There was honor in knowing your moment to die.

As he lowered himself into the water, he heard cawing from the aviary: the crows were being fed. He would miss them. He would miss so much. He had never paid enough attention to the beauty that existed outside the archives, the poetry beyond the confines of language. If he could start his life over, he would live differently.

He rushed the bronze edge to his forearm. The skin flexed before it gave and blood clouded the water. Even this test cut hurt. He wished it wouldn't hurt. Somehow, he hadn't considered the pain of dying.

He knew his mother would be heartbroken. For that, he was sorry. At least she could finally transcend the shame caused by his persistent existence.

Ashair would be thunderstruck but he would understand, perhaps even feel a measure of relief. Yet Ashair would also blame himself. He would think like a doctor. The courses of action he might have taken to preserve life. Maybe he deserved to be a little tortured by regret.

The crows kept calling. Cyrus remembered Kushim among them, a chick perched on his arm—that child who had fought so hard to live. Each day mustering on with injuries too profound. Children survived only because they couldn't comprehend the end; they never considered welcoming it.

Somehow, he could hear Ashair telling him how wrong this was. 'You don't want to die.'

'Oh, really?' Cyrus said to the empty room. 'Watch this.'

He had planned for his last thought to be of Ashair on the first night they spent together; they had sat like strangers on the benches of the amphitheater to hear a lecture on primitive herbologies. Afterward, they had gone for a long walk that carried them to the ocean and back; there wasn't a pause in the debate until the Sun rose and threw their presence together into unrelenting light. But here now, at the end, Cyrus couldn't stop remembering their last kiss, six months before, in the Highlands, when Ashair was resting in the fold of Cyrus's arm. Under the wool blanket, Ashair's toe had tracked Cyrus's shin to his knee. Ashair had asked that the scroll, which had just borne witness to their lovemaking, be put back in its protective sleeve.

Those people who existed before scrolls, before Creation, one man per window and so many windows in each towering palace—thousands of men, perhaps thousands of thousands, who had once lived—they were brothers and sons. Yet they considered their fate and decided to jump.

Now Cyrus could hear Ashair saying, 'But you don't want to die because you hope to be dead. You fool. You want to die to prove you are alive.'

XIX

Inevitability

In the morning, Lilah watched the gate open and the manager arrive in his carriage as he had on any other day. Three carts of dirty robes came soon after. Only three when for months there had been eight or nine, once seventeen. The women commenced laboring but slowly this time so the work would last.

The manager came down his stairs. The women he pointed to gasped; they begged. But each was pushed through the gate. The manager's eyes looked past Lilah and selected the woman she had worked beside since the first day.

Across the yard, Koneet was struggling to bust a round of wood. Koneet who never struggled to cut wood. She hit the same piece again and again, and when her axe stuck, she had to lift both axe and wood, and come down. Twice, three times, four. The round wouldn't split and each impact echoed. The manager pointed.

Koneet was separated from her axe. There was no chance for goodbye. The guards pushed her outside onto those angry streets alone. Koneet disappeared without a glance back.

Lilah sank to the ground. She had lost another daughter.

———

Koneet was gone because Lilah had failed to act. She hadn't fled when they had the chance.

The only way Kenta could sleep was if Lilah mustered the will to tell a happy story about her big sister. So Koneet was busy catching and smoking fish. Koneet had a boat that she hid in a cove, and each day, it sat lower in the water from the weight of smoked fish. Soon, Lilah promised, the wind would carry them all home.

'What will happen then, Auntie? After we go home?'

It was almost too much to consider. 'We'll find perch flopping on the sand. Even old men will carry bellies of fat. When she sees you, your mother will come running.'

Kenta squeezed her hand. 'Maybe my eyes will work then.'

Lilah held her hand tightly. 'We'll sit together and watch fish jump.'

The next day, she looked and saw the manager coming down the stairs. He stopped to watch their labors. She failed to look away in time and his eyes found hers. It was too late; he was crossing the yard. He stopped before her cauldron.

He reached past Lilah. To caress Kenta's chin. The girl was as still as ice. These months she had been growing on the plentiful food. Now he turned her face until her eyes were aimed toward him.

Lilah would not let this happen. She was a thirty-nine-year-old woman and she knew how to get a man's attention. The right smile could render one senseless. There was a reason women didn't leave men in charge.

He grinned. He reached for the rim of Lilah's collarbone, which she had exposed to the sun. His fingers were as cold as kelp. 'Fun,' he said. 'Mother and daughter together.'

Finally, Maren followed her sister onto a peak and saw for the first time the gray-blue ocean far in the distance. She hadn't beheld the Sea since they were still three siblings together, climbing a far-off mountain. For Ozi, the divine had been hidden for more than three years.

Maren and Ozi prayed, but Leerit said nothing. Maren watched her sister who could not look away from The City at the Sea's edge. Neat textures of tan and brown. It did look like a hive. It looked also like something she had heard about in old stories, the villages built by Giants, villages that filled valleys and even hillsides—before the Sea punished them for refusing to honor Her.

Leerit righted the knife in her belt. Her voice was as harsh as the wind. 'Before we leave, we will burn it down.'

Near midday, Leerit turned down a seep that collected others and soon grew into a creek that smelled of algae. They were close now. She told Ozi to string his bow. They advanced on stalking steps. When a rock rolled, Leerit turned to glare at her clumsy little sister.

She stopped in the last thicket. Ozi put his chin on her shoulder and wrapped his arm around her belly. They were close enough to The Hive to see it was made of cliff walls, figures moving atop them like bees. These cliffs weren't cliffs at all but had been built by hand where the river wanted to flow. The water was hemmed in by banks of piled rock.

Barbarian dared claim dominion over even the river. He deserved whatever death she could bring him.

'It's bigger than I expected,' Maren said. 'But how can we find Kushim
among so many?'

Ozi answered when Leerit did not. 'The ocean is huge and yet the
fish gets caught. Your opi used to say, *Doubting is what makes a net come
up empty.*'

Now the manager sat in his chair, exposed. He was waiting on her. He
wanted her mouth. He didn't know what she had in her fist. He was calling for Kenta, who stood by the door, unseeing. He wanted the child too.
Lilah understood clearly now: she could not fix everything but she could
fix this. 'Don't worry,' she told the despicable man. 'I will take care of you.'

On the edge of The City, Maren hid her hair and beads under the scarf
Lenka had given her. She told her older sister, 'You can't walk among
these people dressed like that.'

'You will have to go first,' Ozi told Maren. 'Steal robes for us like the
one you have.'

He was right; she knew it. But her breath came faster at the thought
of entering The City alone.

He shoved her shoulder, the gesture of a big brother. 'Feeling brave?'

'No.'

'Good. Scared keeps you alert to every danger.' He said it with a grin,
this man who like her sister had fought and lived. 'I would be worried if
you weren't scared.'

Leerit caught her sleeve. 'Ama would tell you to remember. You are the daughter of ten thousand survivors. Every strength that kept them alive lives on within you. Hear their voices.'

Lilah was on her knees. She had taken the manager's cock in her hand. Her other hand held the blade. She had failed before; she would not fail now.

Because she had been delivered here. She might have died beside Tamar and yet she had been spared. She might have died of that awful winter sickness but she had been spared. Why had the Sea kept her alive if not for this? She had delivered her here, to this honor. This was the reason.

In the old language, Lilah told the girl, 'When he cries out, open the door. Go down the stairs. Be careful not to trip. Do not rush but do not stop until you are with Trinket. She will protect you. She will know what to do.'

'Auntie?'

'Do not worry about me. One day your sister will come for you, and you will sail home together. As it should be. But promise. As you sail past my village, promise me you will stop.'

'No, Auntie. Please don't leave me.'

'One day you'll understand. My life was brought here to protect yours.'

Maren chose the shadowed side of the street. She skirted between a cluster of shacks with mud walls and clay shingles. On the ground, she stepped around thin people curled in balls, sleeping. She hoped they were sleeping. Men were carrying loads. Men were bumping shoulders and yet not stopping to laugh or apologize. Long lines of men standing and waiting. Thick crowds of men in bronze armor with lances and swords. Maren knew the language; but here, from these mouths, it was all unfamiliar.

As she walked, she kept glancing backward. She had to memorize each turn of the cliffs. She would have to find her own way back. She had never had to find her own way.

Birds sat just out of reach, gulls and crows, but also fat blue birds that were new to her. They sought the shade too; white feces stained every leeward ledge. When they flew, their wings clapped. It was the only good sound The City made.

She saw women hanging wool robes. She saw wool draped over cordage, adult robes beside those of children, and though she might have grabbed two, she could picture the mother who had trusted this line for her laundry. The Ancients could not want her to steal from someone's mother.

So the sun was hot before Maren found her chance. A cart heavy with wool robes was rolling down the street, drawn by an old horse that was struggling under his harness. Alongside the cart walked a man with a helmet and a sword. She fell in behind, following the smacking of those hooves around countless corners.

Finally, the cart paused before a passageway cut into a cliff, an entrance guarded by heavy bars. Here, people were gathered, sitting and waiting, swatting at flies. They were begging for work; they wanted inside. The man with the sword was joined by more who began pushing these people. The bars lifted with a squeak. The cart began to roll. By then, she had a robe in each hand and a mess of others were falling to the ground.

The man with the sword yelled but she was already rounding a corner. He didn't bother giving chase.

She found Leerit and Ozi where she had left them. They were plucking fat blue birds. Feathers the color of seawater floated over sand.

Lilah could feel them watching from the mountain, her mother, her grandmother, the grandmothers before, back all the way to the watery beginning. They stood as they did so often, in silent judgment. Seeing Lilah now, how could they have nothing to say?

It was her children in her ear. *Ama,* they still called her. *Not this. Be the river that bends, be the river that never breaks, be the river that finds the Sea. Like you taught us.*

But this man had to die; he couldn't be allowed to go on. If she was killed, what did it matter? She would meet her children on the mountaintop. She would see Tamar again. This was the fastest way home.

She readied the blade.

'Please,' Kenta said. She was alone in the corner. 'Please, Auntie.'

She turned toward the child. Kenta had sunk to the floor. Her arms held her knees.

On her own deathbed, her mother had said, *A woman does not live for those who are already gone. She lives for those who will come next.*

Lilah wanted to believe she was meant to die. She wanted the end because it was easier than learning to persist. What would her mother say now? What was her mother saying? *The hardest path leads to the longest view.*

Kenta's voice: 'Please, Auntie, please! Don't leave me here alone!'

Lilah hid the blade deep in her robe. She took a gonad in each hand.

She told the despicable man who was now gasping and wild-eyed, 'Shush, stupid boy. I am the woman sent here to teach you what your mother forgot.'

Cyrus's mother was right: a man of his privilege could never have tried everything.

For her, he was once more rumbling toward General Rah's estate, this time locked alone in an armored crate on wheels. The carriage was being led by two carts and trailed by two more—a total of thirty-five armed guards to protect his one body. They passed between burned-out buildings and veered around columns of debris. Everywhere citizens booed them.

Crossing the city now required passing through four checkpoints, three manned by terrified police and a fourth, on the hill leading to Rah's estate, established by his eager army of bronze-clad soldiers.

When they arrived inside the safety of Rah's gates, Jernod's hand was there to help Cyrus down from the carriage. Around him, guards took up their positions. Every man here had taken an oath. They were duty bound. But how long could it hold? What was really stopping these blades from turning on the one who employed them? Was it really just coins holding this all together?

The day was too hot for bowling. The manservant delivered Cyrus into the shade of ornamental trees, where General Rah sat with his feet soaking in an invented stream. The breeze turned a wheel that pulled water from the ground and sent it flowing over tile before it spilled like music into a pool where Rah's wives swam naked.

The general was in a perplexingly good mood. He offered Cyrus a rare liquor. 'It's made from the berries of a nearly extinct tree. Forty days travel to reach the grove. Breathtaking, yes?'

It was undrinkable. In the distance, the ocean and its end loomed. 'Marvelous,' Cyrus agreed.

General Rah was bare on his top half but for a small key on a chain. Beads of sweat ran down his lean sternum. Even in his sixties, he was muscular and imposing. Rah glared now over his drink. 'Do you know what your problem is?'

'I think I do, sir.'

'Your problem is not *what* you are, Cyrus—it is that you believe *them* when they tell you what you are.'

Rah poured out the rest of his liquor and snapped his fingers toward the manservant, and said to Cyrus, 'Don't drink swill just because a man calls it rare.'

'Even if that man is a general, sir?'

Rah smirked. He commanded the manservant to fetch fruit wine from the coldest corner of his cellar. 'I'll confess something to you, because I think you sensed it when we were alone in my archives. I am not a natural scholar. I've always been a man who gets bored reading. On the battlefield, I long for the silence of a stack of scrolls. But once among the scrolls, I long for the blood and urgency of a battlefield. Is it a curse or a blessing to never be content?'

The wives were splashing one another. 'Perhaps both,' Cyrus said.

Rah glared. 'I'll spare you from boring me with whatever rote prelude you've prepared. I assume you're here for boarding passes. After spending chests of my money, you somehow still failed to meet your quota. And you think that I think I've wasted my effort on you. That I regret giving you those chests of coins.'

The general leaned closer. 'See, everything is a battle. Each side reads

the other's actions, formations, and postures for any sign. The victor in
the confrontation is the one who designs his postures to elicit the response he desires. To win, you must lure your enemy into confusing
advantage with disadvantage.'

'Then a general is also a storyteller.'

'Yes, war is its own fiction. It is fictions within fictions, and its history will be another.' Rah smiled. 'I assume you've asked yourself what I
was buying with those chests of coins.'

'With all due respect, sir—the more important question is what were
you buying when you put the armory key in my hand.'

'Ah, yes.' Rah sighed. 'Good. Tell me this story.'

Cyrus looked about them. Guards were walking along the periphery.
The manservant was returning with the wine. Rah's wives had quit their
splashing.

'I assure you,' the general said, lifting a cup from the platter. 'On
these grounds, loyalty can be assumed. Be candid now. Pretend your
future depends on it.'

Cyrus sipped his wine. 'The rioters, they are merely your kindling.
You saw their discontent, and you stoked the fire when you opened the
armory to them. I think I know why.'

General Rah's face gave away nothing. He held his wine.

'I have spent nights considering it,' Cyrus continued while suppress-
ing the quivering in his voice. 'If you merely wanted the palace for yourself, you would have seized it with your army. Assuming your soldiers
would do as you asked, and I'm confident they would. But you want more.'

Rah stared.

'Eventually, the rioters will sack the palace for you. Then you can be
the one to extinguish the fire you started. "Look, citizens," you'll pro-
claim, "I saved civilization when the Emperor could not." This is what

you want most of all: for his people to lose their faith in him. Only then will they be ready to believe in you.'

Rah drank his wine in one gulp. Cyrus became aware of the soldiers moving along the edges behind him. Jernod was all the way in the courtyard, out of sight. He had been a fool to speak so candidly. He drank down this wine that might be his last.

'In fact,' Rah finally said. 'You are the one who blew flame upon the kindling. I am merely the man who hired the police to witness the exchange. See, the story they will tell—if I call upon them to do so—is simpler than the truth: you were invited into my house. While here as my guest, you stole a very important key from me. Then you sold it for chests of coins to the leader of an insurrection. Your motive was wool. You would do anything for boarding passes.'

Cyrus remembered those police officers from the night he delivered the key. There was a familiarity between them that could have belonged to brothers. 'I am the one who will be blamed. With those coins, you bought deniability. You bought your escape.'

'Really,' Rah said while looking at his own fingernails, 'I bought leverage. Which should reassure you. For leverage used is leverage gone.'

'Leverage? What do I have that could possibly be of value to you?'

'There is that doubt I mentioned.' Rah lifted his cup, and the manservant stepped nearer to refill it. Next, he refilled Cyrus's. Rah offered a toast. 'To the Empire.'

'To the Empire,' Cyrus repeated.

'In my archive, do you remember that statue of my own great-grandfather nine generations back? He lived during the golden age when the wealth we accrued built the palace that still stands on the hill. Here is the truth.' Rah leaned nearer to tell it. 'My grandfather was this city's most prosperous, most generous, most significant . . . emperor.'

Cyrus didn't dare move. He must have misheard.

'Do not be surprised. Do you really believe that the invalid in the palace now was born closest to the Sun? *My* lineage ruled this empire for centuries before *his* usurped our throne.

'I am only alive because my greatest-grandfather's infant son was spirited away into the Highlands in the moments before the family was massacred. That infant returned a nameless indentured man, but one who knew his calling. Across the generations, we have never forgotten why we are here.'

Now when Rah spoke, spit leapt from his lips. '*We* built this empire! *He* has torn it down! The Sun wants that family gone! For proof, look no further than the sand filling our streets. He cannot save civilization. *He* is the reason it is dying!'

Rah reclined. He gulped from his wine. When he spoke again, his voice was calm. 'Across generations, my fathers under a new name clawed our way back. They served with faith and dignity, just as I have. We have never given anyone cause to doubt our motives or suspect our origins. My forefathers toiled endlessly to deliver me to this moment.' He looked at Cyrus. 'And I am the one who has delivered you.'

'Delivered me to what exactly, sir?'

'Once we're on board the ark, the fires here will fade behind us at the speed of wind. But these rumors about you, Cyrus, they will not be so easily suppressed. This is perhaps the only complication I did not anticipate. I will need the partisans to trust you. But how can they trust a man who fucks men?'

Cyrus swallowed. 'You must be confused. I am engaged. To a girl of prominent lineage.'

'We're past bluffing,' Rah said. 'We both know your engagement was cancelled when that inbred usurper erased your family's name from *his* history.'

The moment sprawled. Rah looked toward his wives who were now floating on their backs in the pool. 'Cyrus. A man like you, he ought to have rushed to take a wife, two wives, three. A man like you, he ought to have made a show of all his wives.'

Cyrus looked again at the general. As if for the first time.

Rah put two fingers to the pulse of Cyrus's wrist. 'Leverage, but also incentive. Only I can give you a chance to redeem yourself. To start over. We shall find you a wife, maybe three. These rumors will fade because men will see you beside me and be afraid to utter them. Don't you see? I alone can bring honor back to your father's name. After Solstice, two leaders will board the ark. Yet across that ocean, only one will step onto green shores. You will stand with me, Cyrus.'

'But I have never swung a sword. I've certainly never killed anyone.'

Rah snorted. 'I did not choose you for your prowess in combat!'

'Why did you choose me? What can I possibly offer you?'

'Still so much doubt! It is a mark against you. But I think you can overcome it with the right guidance. Son, you must stop trusting the eyes of men to tell you who you are. In battle, the man who reacts is the man who loses, and everything is battle.'

Rah reclined and crossed his bare feet. 'Cyrus. Your father failed to teach you to bowl; you developed no allegiances. You have no brothers, no uncles, no father; from what my sources tell me, you hardly made a friend among your peers in the archives. To use a metaphor that I know you understand, you are a sheep without a flock. Yet, according to the deans, you are a scholar of rare determination. So we are perfect for each other. After all, both of our lineages were erased by this man. Weren't they?'

'Yes sir.'

'More important, Cyrus, we both know the most vital truth: a ruler is the story he tells. An emperor is only as powerful as his people's belief in that story.'

'You want me to write the history that places you at its center.'

'You must only tell the truth. And what a truth it is!'

Cyrus looked at his own hands. They were shaking.

General Rah leaned nearer and squeezed the flesh above Cyrus's knee. The pain was sharp. 'You seem not to understand the opportunity before you. This world did not begin with that man's lineage, and it certainly does not end with him on the throne. Cyrus, I can make you higher than any dean, more powerful than any master. I can make you our civilization's great historian. Across that ocean, your accounts will be read for thousands upon thousands of years.'

The thought was like wind lifting him: *thousands upon thousands of years.*

'My greatest-grandfather understood that power does not come from domination and subordination. A ruler of people must first listen. He must let his people rest, for rest is not the same as waste. Cyrus, the Sun has delivered me here to shepherd His flock. Do you understand? I alone can see our future. I alone know that *this* is not an end but a beginning.'

'Yes sir.'

'Across those waters, every man in my empire shall live in a palace that towers halfway to the sky. In my city—here is a pledge, Cyrus—no child shall ever go hungry. My people will love me for it. Just as they loved my greatest-grandfather. And they will love you for telling them the truth. What I showed you in my archives: that was not only the past—it is also our future.'

This time, when the manservant approached, he brought with him a gleaming chest. Rah stood to meet the bronze. He used the key dangling from his neck to open the lid. From the darkness within, he withdrew a minor scroll bound by ribbon. 'How many?'

They were boarding passes. Cyrus almost said three. 'Four, sir.'

As he reached to take what was offered, General Rah seized his wrist. 'Tell me. Who is the Sun's truest enemy?'

'Sir. The Emperor is our enemy.'

The day was hot and they were the only people in The City with their hoods up.

Where they saw men wearing bronze, they turned. When they saw crowds shouting, they slipped into shadowed passages.

As they traversed the canyons, Maren spoke to any woman who would listen. She asked about the boy wounded by a bear. At her question, some looked confused; others laughed. She thought it was her accent that troubled people. But then a certain woman told her, 'Crazy girl. Bears live only in children's stories.'

She stopped mentioning the bear. She mentioned only Kushim's wounds. Surely someone would remember such a boy. Finally, a woman suggested they check the *hospital*.

But there were many hospitals. In the third one they reached, an old woman pushing a cart took Maren by the hand. She said, 'Maybe I saw your brother in winter. But if I did, that boy is gone.'

'Where?' Maren asked. The old woman told her that children with no one to claim them went to the *orphanage*. A big house for children without family.

So she set about asking for directions to the orphanage. When they arrived at a square building, they found a man sweeping the front steps. He said there was no boy inside with a scar like the one Maren described. 'I would remember a child like that.'

———

The next day, Leerit said they should bathe. It was hot and so near sol-stice that the sun hung above them. Leerit led them from the buildings and streets through brush to a secluded bend in the river. Deep, slow water: the perfect place to swim, and yet there wasn't a track anywhere in the sand. Leerit took off her wool robe, and said, 'Barbarian is afraid of water. Which means he is afraid of everything.'

Maren rinsed, then left her sister and Ozi swimming to sit on the bank in the shade of willows. Kushim was all she could see in the silver water or in the white sky. If her brother was already dead, would she know?

Ozi joined her. With the coastal breeze, the willows rustled just as they once had years ago beside the bay. The markings on his skin were sparkling. Leerit was then underwater. Maren said, 'What does your wife know?'

Ozi looked at his hands.

'People will gossip about my sister when this baby is born. She will be cast out. If you go home—back to the village in the mountains—this will be a shame told for years.'

Ozi said, 'Everyone will know that I am to blame. I will make sure of it.'

Leerit came up for air. She turned and dove, and her feet sent up a splash.

'Blame doesn't matter,' Maren said. 'Blame is past. This child will have to live in the future.'

Leerit and Ozi were napping together in the willows when Maren saw children approaching. Four girls and two boys who wore wool just as

muddy and soiled as her own. They had been laughing but now fell silent. They were clearly surprised to encounter someone else in this hidden place.

The oldest snapped her chin upward, and said, 'Who are you?' Her
sun-faded hair was tight with cruddy locks. A cord went from her waist
to the neck of a short-haired dog with a wide face and a well-fed body.

Maren approached as if she weren't afraid. She said in the language
of this place, 'We're looking for a boy with a limp and a scar from here
to here.'

The dog pulled at its cord. It barked and chomped at the air. Maren
stepped closer and reached. 'Careful,' the girl said. 'He'll bite your
hand off.'

But the stubby tail began to wag—this dog only wanted to be closer
to the girl thinking kindly of him. He stood on his hind legs and planted
his front paws on her and was grateful to have Maren rubbing his ears.
'Have you seen a boy with a scar like that?'

The girl spat. 'You aren't from here. Where did you come from?'

'Far away,' Maren admitted. 'Nowhere you would know.'

Her name was Xan and she claimed to be twenty, but Maren thought
she couldn't be older than fifteen. Xan said she knew someone they should
meet. Someone who would know how to find their brother. She promised that this person would know where Kushim was.

Leerit shook her head. 'We can't trust one of them. It could be an
ambush.'

Xan was then on a knee petting her dog's belly. His paws were up
and his tongue was dangling loose. Hers was a trusting dog. Maren told
Leerit the truth, that maybe the Sea had sent Xan to help.

Leerit spit. 'Barbarians only help themselves.'

But Ozi stood beside Maren. He spoke to Leerit, 'We can follow for a little way. We can turn back if we need to. What if this she says is true?'

'It's not,' Leerit said. 'I promise she is lying.'

To the children at her side, Xan was like the eldest sister. They heeded her every command. She led them to where the air was rich with the aroma of smoking meat.

When she pointed, three of the children slipped away. The others waited in the shade. Xan put an arm out to slow Maren. 'We have to be careful.' She nodded toward a crowd of armed men she called *police*.

They snuck through narrow passages, then walked across the open and stopped near a fire with a roast of dripping meat turning over top. They were in a line of people wearing beautiful robes and shiny ornaments. The meat was tended by two men with thick arms and wooden batons in their belts. One was adding wood to the fire while the other was cutting pieces from the roast and laying them into wrappers made of fried maize. When it was their turn, Xan said to the woman behind the partition, 'Two, please.'

The bald woman scoffed. 'You don't have money.'

'Right here,' Xan said. She reached as if fishing for something in a pocket.

From behind the woman came a great racket. It was a stack of firewood collapsing. The men tending the meat rushed toward it, as if they might keep the remainder of the stack from falling. By then, Xan had leapt the partition and taken the meat by its spit. As the woman grabbed at her, Xan extended the meat toward Maren.

A man swung his baton but he was too late. The other was then rounding the counter. He was too large to keep up, too slow through the crowd. Maren and Xan ran with the spit of meat held between them. Behind came the police and behind them a crowd of hungry people.

Xan turned into an alley. At the end was a crack in a wall just wide enough for their bodies. Ozi was nearly too big. The police in their armor collided with the wall and could only reach gloved hands through. Their shouting fell away.

Xan led the children to where the river flattened and braided before meeting the Sea. Gulls and seabirds were picking at the wrack and perch flashed in the shallows. In the sand, holes had been left where clams retracted their siphons. In no direction could they see a person or any evidence that thousands lived close by. Beside such a rich estuary, a village could keep fed forever.

Maren watched as Xan used a bronze blade to cut thick slabs of meat and gave an equal portion to all, including the dog. She told the little children to chew carefully and not to choke. Maren thanked the Sea before she ate.

Leerit and Ozi ate apart, uphill among the rocks. Maren was alone near Xan. She asked, 'If so many are hungry, why is no one here catching food?'

Xan pretended to vomit. The children laughed. Xan said, 'That's why nobody trusts you people. If given the chance, you'd eat my dog.'

The sun was descending toward the ridgeline when they entered a part of The City where sand filled the streets. Here it was too deep for carts to roll. Eerily quiet. No police. No beggars. Nowhere did Maren see mothers or children.

'Stop.' Leerit took Maren by the elbow. 'I've let you go far enough.'

Xan took Maren's other elbow. 'Tell your sister that he's just ahead. She's already come this far. She wants to meet him. I promise. He's one of you. He'll know where to find your brother. Trust me. I fed you, didn't I?'

But this time Ozi agreed with Leerit. 'This place is ideal for an ambush.'

Maren told them, 'Go, then. I'll find you later at the river.'

Leerit squeezed. 'I said we're leaving!'

Maren ripped free her arm. 'For Kushim, I am willing to take this chance.'

They could hear drumming. The beats grew louder as they walked up the sandy street.

Leerit startled when a man stepped out of an archway. Hard jaw, eyes lit by the ember he was smoking, hair back in a tail. Bulbous muscles rose across his bare chest. His gray pants had been cut at the knees and tendrils of wool dangled loose and sand clung to his shins. In his hand was a bronze blade.

'They're with me,' Xan said.

He hadn't taken his eyes from Ozi.

Xan said to this man, 'Look. I'm not stupid enough to bring trouble.'

He sighed and rapped the wood behind him, and the door unlatched. It was a passageway. Fires were burning within. Music spilled out.

They arrived into an open courtyard. So many people were dancing on bare feet. Everywhere were shining blades. Shields and lances stacked on the ground and leaning against the walls. Sleeves of arrows. More weapons than people, and there were so many people. 'Nomads,' Ozi said. 'But with barbarian weapons.'

Dogs chased one another. The hindquarter of what could only be a horse turned over a fire. Xan had to yell to be heard. She was pulling Maren's sleeve. 'There he is!'

They parted sweaty bodies to reach someone shorter than Ozi. He was barefoot and shaved bald and wearing only wool pants. In his belt was a bright blade, almost exactly like the one Leerit had given Chun. His chest and arms were made of massive muscle. His face was marked with the honor of the coast but also, more recently, with small scars around his eyes that had been cut by a precise blade—markings of the desert.

Into Xan's hand this man counted coins. Payment for delivering them. Xan pocketed her money and said, 'This is Rageer. He will help you.'

Lilah had been kicked and beaten, pushed down the stairs, and dragged outside the gate. She understood the manager's shout: 'Someone kill this dog!'

A guard put her on her knees in the street. 'Hold still,' he begged as he drew his sword. That voice—it was familiar. She turned to see the same boyish face that had found her in the courtyard the night she used a bronze stake to finish knapping the obsidian. 'Don't move!' he yelled at her. 'Please, be still!'

'You have never killed before,' she said in the desert language.

'You shouldn't have done what you did. This is your fault, not mine!'

He was young; he didn't know what to believe—he was a full sail with only the manager for a rudder. She told him, 'I am your mother. If you kill me, I will never stop whispering in your ear. My story will be the only one you hear.'

He stared at her unblinking eyes.

'That man decides your life, but does he have to live it?'

The boy looked behind him into the courtyard. He glanced up the street. By the armpit, he lifted her. 'Run. Don't let me catch you.'

The bruises on her brow and arms and knees were still swelling, but the obsidian blade remained inside her robe. Ever since, Lilah had been searching the canyons for Koneet.

In the city, she could walk anywhere. No one tried to stop her. No one cared what she did. People passed by without a glance.

Like water, she moved downhill until she found the Sea and those boats tied and waiting. Here where they had made landfall—the same place but now in a new season. Everywhere stood men with blades.

She passed a cart that was piled with bodies. Many of them elderly, all of them long dead. Stacked now like lengths of wood. The smell was potent. From their sunken cheeks, she recognized what had killed them. Hunger.

She found water being pulled from the ground and allowed to splash on the streets. She pulled back her hood to drink. Here were thin children taking their turn at the flow. She thought they were staring at the swelling on her brow until a man asked where she had been eating. Her face was fuller than most. Her body had fat. When she told him, he nodded sadly. She understood him to mean *I lost my job too.*

Lilah let the water flow over her face. She let it cool her injuries.

When she wiped her eyes, a young mother was next in line with two sons. Whatever words she said, Lilah didn't understand. Yet they stood together and laughed when those little boys began stomping up puddles.

That night she slept with her back to a wall among beggars. She had nothing under her and nothing over. She woke at every approaching footfall. In her short and frenzied dreams, she was always walking across endless dunes, now with a pot empty of stew.

She continued searching but there were too many people. She would never find Koneet in this huge place.

She thought of the boats. She could steal one; she could set sail alone. It was possible.

She found her way back to the familiar gate. She sat with her back to a wall where, like so many beggars, she could see inside. She would be patient like an angler watching a net. Because Koneet would eventually come for her sister who was still inside. These girls who needed her as she needed them.

Nothing changed but shadows and the songs being sung. When the tone switched, she knew the women were dumping the wash water and tidying the day's work. Kenta was nowhere in sight. Trinket must be keeping her safe inside.

The manager came limping down his stairs. She was glad to see him still in pain. She had left him with much to think about.

He was making the last inspection. Soon the women would eat stew, steaming bowls of grains and vegetables and chunks of meat. Kenta, at least, would have a full belly.

Lilah waited as long as she could. But eventually her hunger demanded she try to find something to eat. She thought of the river cutting through the city. She thought of fish and clams and everything good and holy.

As she began to walk, she heard a crow calling. But this crow did not sound exactly like a crow.

A hooded woman stood at the bronze gate. A familiar shape. Lilah rushed. She crossed the street. She put her hand to the shoulder. It was Koneet who turned.

She wasn't alone. The homely driver listened to the language he could not understand. When Lilah asked, Koneet gave her a biscuit of hard-tack. All they had.

There outside the gate, Koneet was like boiling water. 'We followed each guard on his walk home! We kept approaching them until we found one we could trust to help!'

Lilah looked anew at the homely driver. He had crooked shoulders and a stiff back. He was older than Koneet but younger than Lilah. His eyes twitched with nervousness when he spoke. Lilah asked in the coastal language, 'Why does he help you?'

Koneet gripped his arm. 'He wants on the boat too! He says any place is better than here. He says he loves me.'

The sorry-looking man smiled at Lilah. He didn't know the words but he knew they were talking about him.

Lilah had to sit down. For so long she had endured and yet it was Koneet who had found the way. Koneet who saw the manager freeing women and so worked dumbly, hitting the same round over and over while those beside her busted theirs in two. She made herself the member of the herd needing to be culled. And when she was outside the gate, she did what she had to. Found the driver, convinced him to help, bribed a guard. All this time Koneet had been the river's ceaseless flow, the unrelenting refusal to be stopped. When Lilah cowered, Koneet rose up.

'Tell me,' Lilah said. 'What should we do now?'

In Cyrus's office was his father's map of the Empire, hanging in the same place since he was a boy. He used to come study it, this map that perhaps bore his predilection for scholarship, hours spent tracing every contour. The river, the Highlands, the branching limbs of remote valleys. Ocean and sand and impenetrable mountains. Blue dots marking each oasis. The sites of battles, the locations of enemy surrenders. The minor, oblong shape of their city where the river met the sea. History plotted by its places. He had stood here with his father those years ago, the man's thick finger drawing the route they would take to check on the flocks. Days of travel to barely cross the map at all.

Every archive was a curation, every history a creation. All his years of reaching for the oldest, dustiest scrolls in the imperial archives—hadn't he always been hoping to find some record of men loving men? Just one kiss, one caress, one mention of a king with a man for his queen. If they existed, someone had erased them, obliterated love like theirs from the histories. It was men who named the unnatural.

On that far shore, as civilization's great historian, Cyrus could fix anything. He wouldn't do it for General Rah; he would do it for boys like him. And for those unlike him. Here was the reason he had been born at all.

———

As the servants retired, he dressed in the robe of a groundskeeper. There wasn't a moment to waste. He bribed his own guardsmen not to alert Jernod, then slipped outside the gate.

As he descended the hill with his hood up, just another laborer going home, Cyrus noticed that something was different about the evening. The air was still. Then he realized: the banging of hammers had fallen silent. The ark. He could see its gleaming planks, its crows' nests, those huge sails furled tightly along the masts. No longer distant, their salvation was imminent. With four boarding passes, he could deliver them all.

He reached Ashair's house as the couple was preparing for sleep. Ashair cracked open the door. Cyrus said, 'Please.'

For the first time, he was invited inside and the doors were locked behind. Two tiny rooms, a place to sleep and a place to sit at a table with two chairs. The pregnancy alone seemed to take up half the room. Everything clean and tidy, not a grain of sand, and yet, somehow, the apartment was even less than he'd imagined. There was a single break of bread resting on the shelf.

Cyrus could hardly contain himself as he set two boarding passes on the table between them. 'Attessa,' he said. 'One is for you.' They were cut from the thickest parchment; flakes of pyrite glittered from within the skin. The lettering was written in liquid gold, and a gold-dipped crow feather was affixed within the imperial stamp.

Attessa reached for one of the heavy passes. She looked it over, swaying on her feet, her free hand on her belly. She had insisted the men sit in the only two chairs because the baby was making her back sore.

Ashair drew a boarding pass to hold. He looked at his wife. Attessa put her hand to her husband's shoulder. She said, 'What about our families?'

Cyrus explained what should have been obvious: that across the ocean everything would be better. Their child would have enough food. With a little luck, Cyrus explained, he would have a prominent position in the government; he could use his privilege to protect them. To give their child every opportunity.

Ashair dared slide the boarding passes back across the table. It was not the reaction Cyrus had been expecting.

'Think of the sand!' Cyrus didn't want to be shouting. 'This is our only hope!'

Attessa was a schoolteacher and she wielded her authority now. 'How dare you raise your voice in my home. I am not impressed by your title.'

Ashair put his hand over Cyrus's. 'Friend.'

'Friend? The city is at war with itself. The fields, the forests, the graze—you said yourself this land is broken beyond repair. How could you elect to stay?'

Ashair looked to Attessa before continuing. 'When Kushim came into our care, he was so broken. I was sure he would die. You think I healed him. But I only gave him the chance to heal himself. That's what I've learned. A good doctor does not control; he does not manage—he facilitates. Healing was not invented by men. Healing is the way of things.'

'A body is not a landmass, or a city, or a civilization. You are abusing a metaphor!'

Attessa said, 'And yet you people are at *war* with everything.'

Ashair broke the silence. 'Why are you so sure there is green across those waters? Is it the account of those imperial scouts you believe? Tell me. Because I have read everything available to a doctor. I have listened to every priest who will console a lowborn man. What do you know that I don't? Who is it you are trusting with your future?'

'I have held something,' Cyrus began. 'An ancient map. Bronze and round and older than anything you think possible. It shows that land exists across every ocean.'

'Every ocean? There is more than one?'

'This world is bigger than you can imagine.'

'And you trust their map, why? Simply because it is old?'

'Ashair. You don't understand. It was made by people greater than we are.'

'Greater? What does that mean?'

'Their cities. They were bigger. Their trade lines more extensive. These people were incomprehensibly . . . advanced.'

Ashair shrugged. 'Okay. So we trust this ancient map that says there is land across the waves. But by now, why would that far shore be any greener than this one?'

Instead of admitting that he had no answer, Cyrus said, 'If there's not something better, what's been the reason for any of this?'

Ashair was too smart to answer. Instead, he said, 'You want to believe, and that is all you hear—your want. Cyrus. Ask yourself, as I have: Why are we afraid of sand? Don't goat herders live on sand? Haven't they for millennia?'

'Goat herders! You would have us live as primitives?'

Ashair didn't blink. 'You would put your faith in that ship and the men steering it—before changing how you live?'

'Civilization can't go backward.'

Ashair raised a finger. '*Backward. Advanced.* What are these words you toss around? Who do they belong to? What is "primitive" about Kushim?'

Cyrus pounded a fist. 'Now you play word games. But I have read every history. There is always a better place! Those who prosper rush toward opportunity!'

Attessa laughed. 'Now he is at war with my table.' It was startling to be laughed at by a woman.

This was going poorly. He needed to start over. Cyrus drew a breath, and said, 'Forgive me. Ashair, do you remember those brothers? The brothers who flew? That story I told you?'

'I remember that after they flew they forgot how to walk.'

'That's not the point of the story. The point is, they kept jumping.'

Ashair looked at Attessa's hand, which was held in his own. 'What if we choose to trust the gifts that are before us? Choose to feel grateful that we can walk rather than breaking ourselves trying to fly?'

'You mean give up?'

Ashair reached across the table to take Cyrus's hand. He was holding both of them now. 'An attempted cure can bring three new ailments. When the trusted cure fails, why do we double the dose? Intervention itself can become the problem. We always know less than we believe.'

'Be passive. Do nothing. How will doing nothing help save your child?'

'I'm not saying be passive or do nothing. I'm saying maybe we don't have to wage war against every problem. Maybe we should be skeptical of what rich men call *progress*.' Ashair smiled. 'Kushim told me something. I keep thinking about it. He said, "Don't fight water. Ride it."'

'Philosophy won't stop the valley from dying. We are being swallowed by sand. For the sake of your child, you can't just surrender.'

Ashair didn't look away. 'Cyrus. Just because we've been retreating from sand for so long doesn't mean sand is our enemy.'

'This here now—Ashair, why can't you see this is our last chance? If you don't get on the ship . . . this is . . . this will be . . . the end.'

Attessa pulled her hand free. She said to her husband, 'I told you, these people are blinded by their own reflections. It is raw privilege that allows him to call all we have left *the end.*'

———

Later, alone in his own bed, Cyrus couldn't sleep.

He rose and walked his halls on bare feet. Past his mother's quarters. He didn't knock. He didn't want to know if she was there or not.

He returned to his office. Here he poured himself a liquor and watched the maroon of Solstice Dusk become the purple of Solstice night. He poured a second drink and looked again at the map on the wall. When the third drink was gone, he felt ready to down a fourth.

In the morning, his mother found him in the aviary. He was sprawled on the sand, sick and spinning. He rose to her voice, and the young crows took flight. 'I'm unwell,' he said. 'I've made myself unwell.'

She came close. She put her hand to his elbow. In the other was a cup of water. 'Cyrus, drink this.'

'I don't want to.'

'Water is what you need,' she said.

'But it's not what I want.'

She was beautiful; she had always been beautiful. Now her eyes welled at the sight of him. 'I blame myself. It was my mistake to let my son believe that *want* could ever compare to *need*.'

Solstice

The homely driver's name was Trennan, and by the aura of solstice night, he guided his horse through the rear loading gate. The guard charged with manning this rarely used entrance began tying his own feet. Koneet used his key to open the pantry. Vats and roasts, bulbs and tubers, an endless series of sacks heavy with beans and maize. The agreement was that a third of the food was to be delivered to the guard's parents; after a minor blow to the head, he could tell the manager that thieves had scaled the wall and overwhelmed him. With such unrest in the city, who would doubt the story?

The obsidian blade was ready in Lilah's pocket as she entered the dark kitchen. Her hands tracked the rock walls; she knew where to bend to feel for each stool and bench. Then she entered the torchlit corridor, and soon the door to their quarters was creaking open under her hand.

Kenta was asleep in Trinket's bed. They were curled together. Lilah stepped nearer and her shadow left them, and at the sudden light, Trinket's eyes opened. A grandmother's good sense.

Trinket rose from the bed and tucked the covers to Kenta's neck.

With a gesture, she backed Lilah from the room into the corridor; she closed the door behind them. Lilah said she was here for Kenta. Trinket whispered, 'How did you get in?'

'I'm taking her.'

'You can't have her.'

This was not something Lilah had predicted.

Much of what Trinket said next was lost to Lilah's ear but she understood enough: Trinket believed Kenta was better off here, safe inside the gate, with food and children and a village to tend to her. To take the child was to put her at risk.

Lilah said, 'I won't leave without the girl.'

Trinket jabbed Lilah in the chest. 'To take her, you'll have to kill me.'

Rageer knew nothing of their brother; he was not interested in helping. He was thinking only of revenge.

And yet Leerit was in no hurry to leave. They had spent the night, and now Leerit and Ozi were helping Rageer hone bronze blades. All about them were desert people; Rageer was leader of those few from the coast. Leerit told Maren to make herself useful and mix pigments.

Rageer's shoulders were dark with boot prints. Thirty-two men killed by his blade. Maren wanted to know about his old village, how he had come to this place, if there were others who had come with him, but Leerit talked only of battle. She told Rageer, 'Upriver, we hunted Barbarian like the Ancients hunted Bear.'

Rageer said, 'Here we've caught Bear sleeping in his den.'

'Stab him through the heart,' Ozi said, 'before he wakes.'

Rageer's face was expressionless, his eyes haunting. 'This began long ago but we can end it, here, now, forever.'

'It is our honor and burden,' Leerit said. She looked to Ozi. 'This is why the Sea delivered us here. To burn this hive to the ground.'

A huge desert warrior in bronze plating began shouting from atop a pile of sand. Across his eye was a gash still swollen. From his helmet grew twisting horns stained with blood. Everyone turned to listen. Maren could hardly see over so many heads. Rageer began trading one sound for another.

'We have many fathers, but we are all from the one great thing that was here before man could name it; we are brothers with goat and oasis and birds too who show us where water hides, with shrub and mountain, with cliff who shades us, with sand who moves under us. But now one brother has chosen to stare himself blind at the sun. He dares bind our hands; he rapes our sisters. He works our bodies like his tool. He has named our suffering *peace*.'

The warriors roared. Hilts pounded shields.

Maren pulled her sister's elbow. 'We can't give up.'

Leerit glanced at her but then turned back to listen.

Maren pulled again. 'He's our little brother!'

It was sudden and shocking: Leerit gripped Maren's neck and shoved her back onto the sand. Maren was looking at the bright sky and the dark shape of her sister against it. Leerit growled, 'Grow up! A boy cannot survive a bear attack!'

Maren swatted the arm that held her down. 'You think you are fighting. But this is surrender.'

The obsidian was ready in her fist.

Trinket pushed Lilah a second time. 'Tell me now how you got in. Beggars will follow you. They will overwhelm us. Tell me!'

Lilah tipped her head toward the darkness. 'I will show you. Follow me.'

Lilah led her into the dark kitchen where the walls were thick and sound would not carry. Down the stairs into the dank pantry. Shelves were already empty, but others were still weighed down, a cartload stolen but still so much food remaining.

Lilah let Trinket rush past and exit the loading door and step into the solstice dawn. Koneet and Trennan were lashing down the cart. The guard was tied on the ground and bleeding.

Trinket drew a breath to call out. She was about to sound the alarm. Perhaps it was the sight of the open gate that stilled her.

Beyond the walls, shafts of orange light were cutting through mist. Purple shadows spilled across empty cobbles. Pigeons in flight were turned to sweeps of blue. For the first time in thirty years, here was a new day without a wall barring it.

Lilah pulled the loading door closed. She used the sharp edge of obsidian to wedge the entrance shut. With the blade, she locked Trinket outside.

Leerit was stomping in rhythm, her feet kicking up sand. Black and red pigment stained her short locks, red slashes ran down her arms, red canines over top black cheeks, the whites of her eyes were bulging. This was no one's sister.

Rageer wore yellow spots upon his brow and neck and back and chest, down his arms, on the backs of his hands, yellow spots on his bald head. His eyes caught Maren watching. In his stare was a darkness as empty as the gaps between stars. She had noticed it from the first glance, but now it was unmistakable. Like a tallow lamp burned out, his eyes were the black smoke that was left. Rageer was what her sister had half become.

Maren took Ozi by the hand; she pulled him from the dancing. He was no longer a coastal man rich with smiles; he was red and black and holding bronze. Maren pleaded, 'Please, stop this.'

The whites of his eyes were harsh. 'We are but the Sea's gale.'

'No.' Maren pointed at Rageer. 'You have made yourself *his* gale.'

When Cyrus woke on Solstice morning, there was already a pastry waiting. He paced as he ate it. He stared again at the boarding passes.

Out the window, a plume of smoke caught his eye. It was black and blooming, growing wider by the moment. He leaned for a clearer view. He knew this building! The imperial archives were burning.

When Lilah finally pulled the obsidian from the crack and stepped outside with Kenta, she didn't prevent Trinket from taking the child in her arms. Kenta spoke the desert language. 'We're going home! Are you coming too, *Sabi*?' This the desert name for grandmother.

All Trinket could say was 'But it isn't safe.'

Kenta's hands felt for her face, found it. Those hands explored the old woman's eyes, her tears, her brow, her chin. 'On our coast, we have so much sand to share. Sabi, please. Come with me.'

Only one man had motive for burning the Emperor's curation of history.

Cyrus sent the manservant for another pastry, and while the hall was empty, he slipped from his room into the courtyard—where he approached a common delivery driver about an early ride.

The driver helped him hide among crates. A small contingent of untrained security resumed their positions on the sides of the carriage, enough swords to dissuade a would-be thief yet not enough to suggest any value in the delivery. The note he had left for his mother said he would see her next at the theater. 'To the archives,' he told the driver. 'Hurry.'

The jostling pained him and yet there was no way to move. Almost at once a crate fell and pressed him with its corner and no one came to lift it. Cyrus made himself small. As he lay there, he knew: he had always been making himself small.

Kushim hardly slept. He wasn't alone. The children around him had spent solstice night tossing and turning. Now, from behind the stage, sounded the ceaseless preparations of the crew, props being cut and painted, mallets banging. Everything in a rush.

When the meal whistle rang—he couldn't eat. He couldn't stop picking at the scar on his forehead. His mouth was dry no matter how much water he drank.

Jumpa took his hand. Once she had been a little girl in this theater and now she was the oldest. She told Kushim, 'No matter how nervous you are, you should always eat before a performance. Sustain your strength. Come sit with me.'

Cyrus overtipped the usher and sat alone in the family seats.

By the time the meager cart had arrived, the archives were fully lost. Every fact and fiction gobbled by flame, whole millennia of history and interpretation sent up in great plumes that billowed black from the windows. The life's work of thousands of men like him turned to ash in a morning.

It was a loss too staggering to comprehend. A loss that would carry forward for countless millennia. In that distant future, so impossibly distant, no one would even be capable of comprehending what had been lost generations before their own birth—let alone who was to blame.

Cyrus had directed the driver to the theater because where else?

Now sitting above so many empty seats, he watched as the stage was set, as the performers practiced their songs—here where men determined even the weather. His hands wouldn't stop shaking. A song could never catch fire.

They were sitting together among others from the chorus. Jumpa had told him that every seat in the theater would have a person in it and all those eyes would be watching them here onstage. He could see just one person watching now, a lone silhouette perched high up.

The governor called their attention and all the children turned toward his voice. Their silence was utter.

Under his eyes were dark bags; for all the preparations, the governor was still wearing the same tunic as yesterday. But now he put on a wide smile and leapt onto a bench, spun around, and tapped a rhythm with his feet—even the dourest children laughed.

He told them, 'My players. I adore each of you. You know how much I cherish our time together. We are family, aren't we? No matter what happens tonight, no matter if you remember your lines or forget them, sing beautifully or off-key—remember: my love for you will only grow deeper.'

It seemed no time had passed, yet crowds were already starting to fill the seats below. Cyrus kept looking for Ashair.

When the usher's voice announced an arrival, Cyrus turned to see him step into the box wearing his formal blue robe and the polished pair of boots Cyrus had bought him years before. Ashair held Attessa's hand. Before her, shrouded in middling wool, was the protuberance of their child. He had invited them as he left their apartment. He couldn't let that night be their last. This between them should end where it began.

Now Cyrus asked Attessa, 'May I order you something? As an apology?'

She declined without thought. But then her hand touched her belly. She looked at him and almost smiled. 'Do they have kabobs?'

He called a double order down the stairs and joined the couple at the railing. There was such simple relief to be found in the company of others.

Ashair turned and they held each other's sidelong gaze. Like the first time. At intermission, in the lobby, all those years ago. When they were two bachelors, young enough to raise no suspicions. Just a medical student and a junior scholar. Back when hope was bountiful and easy to hold. Across the ocean, he would become a man forced to sustain himself on memories. Now Ashair asked, 'Have you decided what you'll do?'

'I don't see that I have a choice. A man like me would be ripped apart.'

Ashair did not rebut.

Attessa was watching. She said, 'My husband and I stayed up all night talking. I don't understand this between you—I'm not sure I can—but maybe I can learn to accept it. What I know for sure is that my Ashair has hardly smiled since he stopped going to lectures with you. If you get on that boat, he will only be half the man I married. I love him too much to be the reason.'

Ashair looked squarely at Cyrus now. The expression on his face was terror. There was nothing graceful about his grip on the railing. 'What if you were to stay and wear common wool? What if we were to call ourselves . . . cousins?'

The governor arrived with a fleece made especially for Kushim. It was wool, but it had been dyed to look like a bear pelt. The shape of a bear face had been sewn in, with eyes cut out, and teeth waited where teeth should be. Not teeth, Kushim realized, but carved pieces of wood. The governor positioned this fleece over him; he lined up the eyes; it was already making Kushim hot; the governor said, 'Perfect.' Kushim assumed that the governor wanted to cover his ugly scar.

'What's wrong?' the governor asked. 'Doesn't it look authentic? Your people wear pelts, don't they?'

'No one wears fur like this.'

The governor smiled. 'Here onstage, we imply truth—we are not bound to it.'

The theater reverberated with voices as citizens took their seats. General Rah was just entering his box with his many wives. He wore his most dignified armor, complete with ornate helmet. When General Rah saw Cyrus, he nodded.

At the usher's announcement, Cyrus's mother appeared in the box and shrugged off her cape to reveal a new gown. She was wearing her finest jewels, all of them. He could tell she hadn't slept any better than he had. Somehow, it felt like his fault.

But if she was surprised to see common robes in their box, she didn't show it. She greeted Attessa as if they were women on equal footing, and Attessa returned the generosity by noting the brilliance of his mother's gems, the youthfulness of her smile.

His mother's chin rose ever so slightly while greeting Ashair. She said, 'Oh yes, Kushim's doctor. I didn't realize you and my son knew each other.' Then, 'Is this who you see at those lectures?'

Cyrus turned toward the sound of boots and saw Jernod enter in full battle armor, a four-fold shield over his shoulders and bronze plates protecting his thighs. A fountain of horsetail atop his helmet gave a fearsome nod. He assumed his position by the door, lance straight and dutybound.

Cyrus withdrew the boarding passes. He gave one to his mother and the other to Jernod. He said to the man who had driven him so far, 'This assures your seat.'

Jernod had lived his duty. He had fought and survived, yet now his voice was barely audible for the emotion sweeping through him: 'I am . . . invited?'

His mother's eyes filled with tears. When Jernod looked at her face, his too became wet. At once, Jernod drew a breath and regained his attention, the lance sharp before his gaze. There hadn't been a word between them, not a touch, and yet Cyrus was sure now of the depths that existed between them. This was what he could do for her, the one thing. Give his mother the man she loved.

The Emperor's siren thrust them back to duty.

His mother took his forearm and guided him to the railing. She whispered, 'Across that ocean, we can begin again. It's what we need. A new start for you and me.'

Leerit had wanted her to wait at the river, and Maren consented. But instead of going downhill, she had followed them up barren streets. Now the warriors were silent over the sand, no words but for the flash of hands. Small teams splintered off and disappeared into shadowed alleys. Ozi and Leerit followed Rageer.

Where the sand had been swept from the streets, they saw men in red cloth, swords and blades, armor flashing in the sunlight—soldiers. Alone, each was a young man weighed down by metal. Together, they were a beast sprawled to block the way.

Maren couldn't feel her hands, couldn't steady her breath. She gripped her sister's sleeve. Leerit saw her now and roared, 'What are you doing? I told you to wait!'

Then, from the distance of two streets came the screams of battle, the clash of metal on metal. Horns sounded and the soldiers before them hurried toward that fighting to reinforce those being overrun. Here was the diversion.

Leerit seized Maren's wrist, and together they advanced.

A giant building was rising before them like a canyon wall. Rageer out front was the first to meet the police guarding it, a force so minor they turned to flee from the painted bodies swarming them. The suddenness of the bloodletting—

Leerit pulled her onward, forward. Past people who gripped at arrows in their backs, over a pool of blood borne of a severed arm. In each dying face, she saw someone's brother.

Leerit pulled with ever more violence. 'You're going to get us killed!'

From inside the building rose a familiar song. Maren couldn't place it at first, but then she remembered. Here was Lenka's daily prayer to the sun.

The chorus inched together like crows until their wings touched. To see so many faces before them, watching them—Kushim felt dizzy. The lightning could strike at any time. He didn't want to fall. Not now, not ever—but certainly not now.

'In through your nose,' Jumpa told him. 'Out through your mouth. Keep breathing or you'll have no wind when you need it.'

He adjusted the pelt on his head. He tried to remember the chick in the aviary. Everything would be okay. He was one crow among his flock.

It was all Cyrus could do to notice the performance. To not obsess in hypotheticals.

He and Ashair sat side by side. Attessa was at Ashair's other shoulder, busy with the platter of kabobs. 'There,' Ashair leaned to say. 'I bet that's him. Chorus, front row, in the pelt.'

Kushim was about the same age now as Cyrus had been the first time he had climbed the stairs to this box with his father. That performance had been about an older boy who flew through the air to help younger children in need; a shard of the Sun's light was always there to counsel him. Cyrus had understood almost nothing. He had been too mesmerized by the children flying, children together running from a man with a blade for an arm, the impact of a sword announced by the collision of cymbals. It was what he wanted: to be like those children, one of many. Afterward, his father leaned near to say, 'What did you think of the story?' Cyrus hadn't noticed a story.

Now the protagonists were building anew their civilization upon green shores. No enemy chased them, but there is always an enemy: this time one of their own.

'How inspired!' his mother whispered. She was pointing offstage. A door had swung open along the lower gallery, not far from a contingent of doctors and Ashair's typical seat. Entering there were more actors. These were decorated in primitive paints. They held impressively authentic spears. Even at a glance, it was apparent how fully they believed in their roles.

Leerit had boosted Ozi to the top of the stone wall, then her little sister because she couldn't leave Maren behind. Together they dropped from the wall, and she pulled Maren through the first open door. 'Don't you dare fall behind.'

Leerit stepped into a crowd. Children were dressed in flowing gowns, their faces painted with pigments. They were muttering, whispering, prancing, stretching, jumping. Everywhere were children. She hadn't expected children.

'What are they doing?' Ozi asked. None of the children noticed them. Everyone here wore wild paints.

'See?' Maren said. 'It's a village!'

A call sounded, and the children around them rushed through a brightly lit gap in the fabric. From beyond came a thunderous sound new to her ears. Leerit went to this gap to look for herself.

Barbarians were sitting in neat rows, children and their parents, barbarian families perched high above on ledges in the cliff walls—more faces than she'd seen in her existence, all clapping for those children now dancing before her in a beam of sunlight.

'Show me,' Ozi said, an arrow on the string. He was readying his feet for a shot. He didn't need her to point. The highest perch of all. Wearing a robe the color of the sun, a golden bird on his shoulder, just as Rageer had said. This one who was Barbarian's heart.

'It's too far for an arrow,' Ozi said. 'I need to stalk closer.'

But warriors were now streaming in. The slaughter began.

Like elk come alert to hunters among their beds, elk stampeding toward any escape. But not elk. Not barbarians. These were mothers and brothers and sisters; they were fathers standing to die first. Here was the massacre of a village.

An arrow struck the wooden railing beside Cyrus's grip. Soldiers were already evacuating General Rah from his box. Jernod seized Cyrus by the collar. 'The ark!' There wasn't time to decide; there wasn't even a chance for goodbye. The last Cyrus saw was the terror in Ashair's eyes.

Jernod peeked around the bend before committing them to the passageway. He pushed Cyrus before him and said, 'To that exit. Now.'

But heathens were streaming through. More were coming from the other direction. Their screams froze Cyrus with terror. Jernod pushed him toward the only escape—a narrow window. 'Here,' he said with impossible calm. 'I need you to jump.'

Cyrus climbed onto the sill, looked down, and stepped off. He rose from the ground to half catch his mother. Her tiara fell, and when he reached for it, she pulled him away. Jernod balanced his landing with the lance.

Around the corner, a beast met them at point-blank and swung. Teeth red with pigment, eyes so white and wide, the body covered in yellow dabs of gritty paint. Worse than any nightmare.

Jernod ducked the blade, and the butt of his lance took the primitive in the back of the knee. Before he could recover his balance, Jernod had wheeled to razor open the throat.

Here it was. More blood than he knew a body could hold. Mouth gasping, eyes fading to gray, hands reaching, wrists curling back—a man trying to float on his back. Death. It was what he had delivered to the Highlands. For the greater good.

Jernod stepped over the corpse as if it were a mound of dirt. 'The ark will not wait!'

The children were pushing in different directions. Going nowhere because everyone was fighting to go somewhere. Leerit shouted to Ozi—they had to save the children.

A voice boomed. She saw him over the mayhem, a man wearing green. He was calling to the children and they were like sheep for his voice. Caught within the flock, she and Maren and Ozi surged through the tight passageway. When a little girl fell, Ozi lifted her back to standing. When she tripped again, he carried her on his hip. In his other hand was his bow and clutch of arrows.

Finally, they emerged outside—but it was no use. They were hemmed in by a stone wall. The man in green was trying desperately to open the only hatch.

With a hand, Leerit moved the dainty man aside. She drove her shoulder into the wooden door. Ozi was there too. They struck the door in unison and yet it wouldn't budge. Their only escape was somehow stuck.

When Leerit looked, the man wearing green was pale. In his eyes, she saw herself reflected. To him, she was a demon.

Jumpa was holding Kushim's arm. She wouldn't let go. Her grip hurt. 'Are we safe?' he asked from under his fleece.

'Soon.' She held him so tightly that he could hardly breathe. 'The governor knows. He always knows.'

Somewhere Kushim heard pigeons taking flight.

The door wouldn't open so Leerit gave Ozi a boost. His fingers found the top of the wall; he pulled himself up. Once there, he reached back to take the hand of the little girl who Leerit was lifting to safety.

She reached next for Maren. But her sister was too far away, surrounded by children. Leerit boosted the nearest child, and as she did, her eye stopped on a boy wearing wool like some strange pelt.

Maren had seen him too. She was taking this boy by the arm. She pulled off the wool. A wicked scar ran across his brow. Impossible. Yet, somehow, it looked like him.

A ruthless cry sounded from where the door had been. Leerit saw two painted warriors bursting through with blades lifted. This had been their ambush. A sword went through the middle of the man in green.

Before the blade could swing again, Leerit's fist struck the desert warrior in the kidney. Not her fist—it was the knife Ama had made. He took a staggering step and swung around to look at who had done this. She was painted; she was one of them. The confusion drained from his face and his knees buckled and he sank. With his last strength, he gripped her ankle.

An arrow protruded from the other warrior's chest. She saw him gripping at Ozi's fletching as a second arrow passed through his neck and broke apart against the wall.

The man in green was on his knees. Blood was coming through his fingers too fast to stop. He was not concerned with his own dying. He was waving for the children to go on without him. He was trying to leave them with a smile.

The sky was raining ash when Lilah and Koneet turned the last corner before the harbor. Soon they would steal a boat; they would be lifting the sail. Trennan was leading the horse and cart with the provisions hidden under a pile of dirty wool, Kenta and Trinket riding together on top. People were running past. People were running both ways. To see what was before them, Koneet stopped Lilah with a hand held out.

The harbor was consumed by smoke. A hundred fires on the water, bursts of yellow through gritty plumes as whole sails ignited in a flash. The smaller crafts were burning. These boats had been set on fire. Their escape was burning up.

'What's wrong?' Kenta asked. 'Why are we stopped?'

All that remained was the giant boat. For the smoke, Lilah could only see its stern.

Koneet was the one to say, 'We need to hide this food. Now.'

Maren picked their route, first away then down through narrow alleys toward the river. Ozi carried Kushim on his back. Leerit had a little girl clinging to her front. Behind them, following a woman Leerit's age, came the tribe of children.

Where she saw men clashing, Maren turned. Where the buildings were burning, she went another way. Soon, they reached a broken wall of rock and slipped through a crack into a thicket of willow.

Beyond, the river was splattering and a breeze rustling; from here, they could hear no violence. The youngest children were the first to put their hands to the water.

Kushim took Leerit about the neck. He gripped Maren too, their three faces pressed cheek to cheek to cheek. He held so tightly. He couldn't breathe for his sobs. Their perfect little brother. 'I'm sorry! I'm sorry!'

The wound that had been a fury of red when he was dying was now healed over. He was a boy with belly fat, with fat on his cheeks. Leerit was kissing him all over.

'I am not the same!' he wailed.

'Yes, you are,' Leerit told him. She pressed his face in her hands and sobbed. 'You are our little brother.'

Below, through wafting smoke, appeared the grand structure of the ark, two stories with a third on top. Dozens of orange dots hurried about the deck preparing sails. From portholes protruded the heads of horses and goats and sheep. Soldiers were marching up a ramp. Others were using spears to hold the crowd at bay. Officers on horseback shouted orders. There, overlooking his men from the safety of the top deck, was the bright helmet of General Rah.

Cyrus turned to see the Emperor's royal carriage leave the cobbled roads, jolt hard up a wide ramp meant just for him, and disappear into the belly of the ship.

On the water burned every lesser boat, set ablaze so no one could follow.

The ocean was churning with men. They were jumping from land; they were swimming. Those who had reached the hull of the ark clung now by fingernails. Some had already become bodies. They were being climbed over, used for purchase.

When his mother stumbled, Cyrus lifted her back to standing. She kicked off her awkward boots and continued faster on bare feet.

Jernod delivered them into the madness before a narrow foot ramp. Everyone was shouting, boarding passes waving in the air. A partisan in a red robe had just been let through; his red-caped wife and their child ran up the ramp as if the land were fire. With raw force, Jernod parted the crowd, and Cyrus kept his mother gripped tightly to him.

The ark loomed over them; it obscured half the sky. He'd never been so close. He hadn't appreciated how big. The timbers were rounded, every protrusion sculpted in radiant design—the most advanced ship he had ever seen. There was an old, familiar story carved into the stern: the Emperor boldly below the Sun, the Emperor pointing the way, the Emperor wading in chest-high grass—the story everyone wanted to believe.

A soldier was shouting for Cyrus's boarding pass. His mother had already given hers, Jernod had given his, and now it was Cyrus's turn to follow them up the ramp.

But that story: a man had carved it there to be seen from here. A man who didn't know because no man knew. The Emperor was faceless, an emperor was always faceless. It didn't matter who. The next valley they fled would be that one. And someone like Cyrus would invent a story to explain why.

It wasn't sand they were fleeing; it was themselves.

'Hurry now!' Jernod shouted.

'Cyrus! What are you waiting for?' his mother begged.

The ark was pulling against its tethers. The ground under him was going nowhere. In every story, men went somewhere.

Jernod flinched as crows swooped overhead. Not bird wings but fire—burning arrows now sticking into the wood of the ark. At once, the oils used to treat the lumber flashed to flame. The fire climbed, licking at the ship.

Somehow fire made the crowd on land only more desperate to board. Soldiers could do nothing to hold back the surge. Farther inland, rioters were drawing a next volley of flame. Those citizens being left behind, here now to cut down those escaping.

There was no authority left in the shouts of officers. Soldiers were abandoning their lances to retreat faster up the ramp. Jernod gripped Cyrus by the collar, as if he might lift him from his feet.

But Cyrus took hold of the railing. He held on.

Jernod yelled for the roar, 'You have to leave him! If he loves you, he wants you on board!'

Cyrus stared at Jernod who knew the truth of him. All Cyrus could utter was 'This can't be outrun.'

By then, those firing arrows had been cut down. The flames were being extinguished by efficient lines of sailors delivering and throwing buckets of water. Already, the tethers were being cut. The ark leaned seaward.

Tears broke from his mother's eyes. She was beautiful and frozen. 'Cyrus! Don't do this! Don't give up!' As the crowd half carried her up the ramp, she reached for him. 'Have faith!'

'Mother!' Cyrus called. 'I do.'

XX

In the Beginning

Fires sparked by combat spread from shanty to shanty, rooftop to rooftop, until they reached the boundary of the city, over which embers lifted like birds to land among dry grasses and brittle shrubs, and there the fires united and were carried by new winds. For five days, flame covered ground faster than a lathered horse.

On the sixth day, fire was soon to consume a band of coastal people come over the mountains in search of green grass. They became trapped in a rugged canyon. The people understood they were soon to die. While parents wept, an old woman remembered an older story. She told her daughters to give her the ember tube. They did though they couldn't understand why. The air was by then almost too hot to breathe. The old woman walked with the smoke into the heart of the canyon. She let the ember loose and fed it dry stems. When the flames from down valley reached the people, they were already standing safe on blackened ground.

The children laughed as they drew on their friends' faces with ash. They ate roasted seeds plucked from burned soil. It was a tale they would one day tell their own great-grandchildren. How fire saved them from burning.

On the seventh day, the winds that had propelled the flames rested.

But on the eighth, the Sea roiled anew. From Her waters lifted black clouds so thick that they delivered night in summer. Lightning cracked the sky and water gushed forth. Those people hiding in the city could hear the smacking of rain as it overtook their neighborhoods. What they had prayed for was here.

For sixty days and sixty nights the wind blew. Water cut gullies through sand and carved ravines from rock; it dumped bridges and roads and swept away any who dared defy water. Never had people known such a ferocious storm.

The armies that continued to battle through fire and rain now had to flee rising currents. They climbed onto those roofs not burned, each an island amid the torrent, and there they found not just their tribe and not just their enemy but children too who knew nothing of the origins of violence. Those who insisted on revenge soon died. Some of those who chose peace perished when the island on which they sheltered was toppled into the tide. Many simply waited and starved.

We say the flood gave way to an age of survivors, a time when no mouth had use for the word *enemy*. Those who once feared Sand now longed for dry ground. Those who had trusted the Sun could not deny the power of the Sea. Those who had heeded only waves saw now how the Sun turned flood to mist, current to fertile field, barren dirt to new growth. It was an age when mothers commanded muscle-bound warriors which seeds to plant first. There wasn't time to ask, *Who is to blame?* Crops had to germinate if the children were to survive the coming darkness.

From those shared harvests were born the roots of our tribe. Not of Sand nor Sun nor Sea, but of all three. Not forged by war but bound by that which unites all creatures: hunger.

THE ANCIENTS

Together, we are the Ancients' grateful children. Hear them singing: *Every tool you need you have in excess. Do not fight water—ride it.*

Once there was a river hemmed in by the labor of men—this greatest achievement, to subdue a river. On leveled channels, he built his houses, temples, and monuments. On drained wetlands, he grew gardens too vast to tend alone. The river stayed a river.

Born from dark cracks on distant slopes, bending around every obstruction, each drop together a serpent across the valley floor, cutting silt and later mud and then downed wood before drought and winds again returned the river to carving sand. Ceaseless and never sleeping, the river stays a river.

Yet once men commanded other men to lay stones, to bolster those shores, to contain the ceaseless for simple purpose. When the river undercut his stones, he brought more. When the river flooded over top, he brought taller stones. But for these, the river only flowed faster and hit the far bank and flooded that land. More stones, man thought. I said I can subdue a river.

Some began to say the stones weren't working, that they would never work. Bags of sand would do. So many bags of sand. Shoveling and stacking. The river, it stayed a river.

Some said the stones and bags were the problem. They said to dig channels, to steal flow where it was needed—this brilliant advancement that brought water to new fields. Yet the river stayed a river.

Collapsing dikes and dams. Houses and monuments and temples swept away. Sixty days of rain to make a monster. Sixty of sunlight to make again a gentle ford.

371

Mounds of rubble littered the floodplain, a wasteland left to ripen under the summer sun—fertile ground for those who will nurture crops.

As the rains pounded, Kushim told of a place he knew built on high ground. That's how his sisters and those twice-orphaned children of the theater came to weather the deluge within the same high walls as Cyrus, Ashair, and Attessa.

They ate from the stores contained in the estate's pantry; they wore robes with no regard for color; they kept dry by the heat of a single fire. Outside, rain poured from the roof and carved a stream from the road. It was easy to believe they lived together behind a waterfall.

Each day the children divined a new story and by evening put on a show for those grown-ups worn down with their worry. Jumpa included them too. Ozi amazed the audience with trick shots loosed from his bow. Leerit, who once believed herself to have no use for laughter, became the children's reluctant jester. Attessa, swollen with pregnancy, was cast as the benevolent mother. Ashair played the doctor, sometimes hapless, sometimes miraculous. Cyrus asked always to be the bumbling antagonist. He learned he had a talent for making children laugh; he could do it with a mere expression.

Here was the lesson Cyrus would remember one day as governor of the revived theater: children, when left alone, will invent a comedy.

One day Leerit walked into the rain. Below, she saw not the city nor the flood but the slanted lines of downpour. She asked her mother high on some mountain, 'Who taught you to bear this burden? Back when we were still together—do you remember the night when Opi was telling me of a big fish that almost sank his canoe? He was using those wide gestures of his. You looked across the fire and our eyes met. We laughed at this funny man—our man. I hope you remember. Maren wasn't born; I was the only other person on your beach then. It's what every child deserves. A mother who lives only for her.

'But, Ama. I can't be that woman. I'm not strong enough. Once my brother was dead in my arms. Killed by a bear. My brother was dying and I was the reason. I can't be the reason. Please—this is too much to ask.

'Just tell me, Ama. Here is what I need to know. How is bringing a baby into this now not the same as killing him?'

When Trennan's cart and the food it carried was stolen, they had to run together through the chaos of that city coming apart. Burning buildings collapsed. Men poured their blood across dark cobbles. Kenta could see none of it. Lilah carried her while Koneet steadied Trinket, the nomad who hadn't traveled in thirty years.

It felt miraculous to arrive back to the bronze gate they knew so well, this time as beggars reaching their arms through. By then, the guards were gone, the manager disappeared. Standing in the courtyard was a village of frightened women. When they saw faces they trusted, they welcomed them.

The fires could find nothing to burn inside those walls. The wind could not topple stone. When the rains started, their waters drained through pipes laid underground until those clogged. The courtyard became a swirling eddy for the river flowing down the street and later for the tide sweeping back inland; the bronze gate meant nothing to water.

By then, the women had shuttled the provisions from the pantry up the stairs to what had once been the manager's office, set high and apart. There, the village passed ceaseless days of deluge, and when the sun finally lit upon them, Koneet was the first standing in the light. She told Lilah, 'After this, we'll find plenty of wood for our boat.'

One day, when sunlight still felt unfamiliar, Kushim and Cyrus entered the aviary. For the standing water, Cyrus carried Kushim on his shoulders and delivered him to a sturdy branch. About their ears, mosquitoes hissed to life.

The sisters were swooping. Their little brother could join in flight. He remembered and landed on Kushim's shoulder. He opened his mouth for a morsel.

The little crow flew when Kushim began climbing. The broken leg trembled under his weight. Yet he climbed past even the abandoned nest, a knife held in the grip of his teeth.

While the branches bent and bobbed and Cyrus called for him to be careful, Kushim sawed. The fibers were coarse, but soon the knife broke through and the netting began to fall open.

The sisters went first. When they called, their brother came next. Kushim lost sight of the crows against the brilliant summer sky.

He and Cyrus stayed as the parents hopped to the opening. The old birds called out, but they didn't pass through. They had lived too long inside to dare venture out.

'Does not knowing get easier?' Cyrus asked the boy weeks later when they were alone together planting the garden. He had lost her to smoke as the wind caught the sails and drew the ark from land. He could only hope his mother had reached her green shore.

To survive, Cyrus had thrown aside the Emperor's metal and stripped off his elegant robe and stood naked in those streets. Now Kushim said, 'Talk to her. Wherever your mother is, she can hear you.'

'How do you know it's true?'

Kushim shrugged. 'How do you know that it is not?'

Later, when alone, Cyrus stood in the old guard tower as he once had with Jernod. He tried speaking to the distant sea. He felt foolish. Yet he returned the next day and the day after. In time, it became his secret prayer, the tower his temple, the climbing of the stairs the day's essential ritual. When fog obscured the view, still he climbed. In the mist, he could almost see their mast.

Labor began late one night and Ashair became a frantic husband. It was Leerit who held Attessa's hand and walked with her about the corridors. They didn't share a language, and yet together they watched the Dawn shift from purple to maroon to pink. At each contraction, Attessa stopped and hung from Leerit's powerful frame.

Ashair followed. He tried to rub his wife's back. He told her what was happening within her body. He said the name given by doctors for every stage of her labor. He kept narrating until Attessa finally grabbed his lips between her fingers. 'Who do these names help?'

After Equinox, Kushim was pulling weeds in the garden when he saw three crows riding the wind. Ashair and Attessa were bent together picking pods from the vines. Cyrus sat in the damp shade of a lone tree. In his lap lay their swaddled child, whom they called Remember. He saw the crows too, their dives and spins. Cyrus asked Kushim, 'Are they playing a game?'

Kushim knew each by their call. When the little brother came near, he circled once, then twice, then swooped low and landed on his shoulder. Kushim offered every sweet pea in his pocket.

Each day after, it was the same. The crow came and landed and was happy to be fed. Soon he was bringing in his beak treasures. A seashell, a chip of bark, a useless blue coin stamped with imperial script.

This crow was on Kushim's shoulder when next he smelled the smoke and lightning struck. He woke on the ground with the taste of blood in his mouth; faces were staring down at him; the crow was circling above. He laid there sobbing to be a boy who so often had to die.

'No,' Maren told him. 'You are a boy who gets to be reborn.'

The last known salting rocks had by then been broken and used. No traders had arrived to the Valley of Questions since the Great Rain. No venison or mutton or fish would keep without salt. The steaming pools were lost under marsh, and the children complained of mosquitoes. The village decided they had no choice but to follow their river.

They walked at the pace of the slowest member. Some had fought the barbarians and some had hidden, and others had survived the grass fire to come over the mountains alive. These included a mother from the Left Coast who told a harrowing story of losing two daughters to a foggy morning.

What had burned at the start of summer was already brilliant green. Those patches of grass that hadn't burned—high enough that they still retained water when the fires were spreading—those were now yellowing in the sun. The children saw herds of elk on edges of thickets and flocks of sheep ahead of strangers with dogs. Once on a slope of chartreuse grass, they saw a black dot moving ahead of two smaller dots: a mother bear teaching her cubs.

Mounds of ancient cobble lay across the valley bottom. The dirt of whole hillsides had been carved away by water and sent to settle over exhausted grasses. In every pool and across every riffle, the midwife saw fish rising.

'What's that?' a little girl asked. She was pointing to something that climbed like a mangled snake from the landslide. Black and huge and glinting in the sun. It was an impossible thing; no names could hold it.

The midwife told the girl, 'We made that long ago when we were Giants.'

'Why?'

'We have forgotten why.'

Her young eyes reflected the sharp horizon. 'So we have been here before?'

'Yes, child, this has all happened before, and like last time, we will learn again to thrive.'

After the flood, lumber was everywhere. Homes and buildings spilled over; their pieces piled anywhere the water had eddied. It was Koneet's idea to build the boat on the bed of a salvaged cart. This way they could construct their escape inside the protection of the courtyard and, when it was ready, deliver the craft whole to the Sea's edge. Trennan said he wouldn't sleep until he found two horses strong enough to pull.

When children arrived to the gate, they were let through. When a father arrived with his surviving babies, the bars were lifted. Trinket said everyone inside should help build the boat.

They used the facility's saws to cut the lumber to length, its axes to hone the joints. They ground circular plugs to fasten the planks to the hull. Children sketched their stories onto the sides with charcoal while old women sang and weaved the sail.

One evening under cooing pigeons, Lilah stood at the railing and overlooked the courtyard. Her hair was growing back though it wasn't yet long enough to hold a bead. The work was done for the day. Kenta was teaching the youngest children a coastal song. Trinket was cooking a desert meal over open flame.

Lilah could feel them watching from the mountain, her mother, her grandmother, the grandmothers before, all the way back to the watery beginning. They stood in silent judgment. They had endured, persisted, survived—but not for her, not for this.

One day, when she met Tamar again, Lilah would put her hand in his. With his arm around her, his breath in her ear, she would tell him: every child is ancient.

Then one day in late summer, the wind changed direction. Instead of blowing inland, it blew offshore. The air was warm, the sunlight pleasing on their skin. Soon winter would descend and, with it, ferocious waves. On what might be the last bright morning, Kushim begged his sisters to take him to the beach. 'Can't we just play in the water like back when?'

Crossing the remains of the city, they saw children climbing on piles of flood debris. Mothers and fathers hanging wool robes. Dogs snapped at flies. When a bare-chested man saw them, he quit sawing wood and asked if they had anything they wanted to trade.

Kushim smelled smoke when no one else did. Familiar smoke. He began to brace himself for the flash of lightning, but then Maren smelled it too. Cyrus, who was shoulder to shoulder with Doctor Ashair, tried the coastal language. 'Someone make campfire?'

Leerit's eyes were wide. His big sister might've run if not for the giant swelling that was soon to be her first child. She cradled her belly in both hands, and said, 'Not a campfire. Someone is smoking fish!'

Rather than follow the route laid by men, they turned directly into the willows. Already the riparian was heavy with new growth. Every limb was still dressed in debris—stems of grass and air-dried kelp caught in the highest branches—yet even such torrents had failed to pull loose the roots.

When they emerged from rustling leaves, Kushim saw what he had only ever heard described.

Racks weighed down with fillets. Middens of clamshells and little girls squatting to pull more from the coals. Grown men laughing as they mended nets. Old women standing barefoot in the tide to safekeep boys his age who were diving through waves.

Maren skipped. Leerit and Ozi stood wary.

In that moment, Kushim felt something that even late in life he would be powerless to describe.

He turned from his sisters toward what had once been the harbor. A shape was coming toward him down the beach. Behind her was a cart and two horses, a crowd of people knee deep in the wash loading provisions into a boat as it bucked with each swell. Too far for faces—he knew her only by her gait.

On that leg now healed, Kushim went running.

AUTHOR'S NOTE

About 195,000 years ago, a dramatic shift in the Earth's climate turned the savanna and jungles of Africa to sand, forcing our ancestors to migrate toward a narrow band of habitable land along the coast of modern-day South Africa. Genetic analyses suggest that every human alive today is a descendent of just a few hundred people who managed to survive this harrowing epoch.

Beside saltwater, on a diet of fish and sea greens, our ancestors persisted for millennia. As the climate began to stabilize—and the savannas and jungles again crept across the continent—some of our people returned to walking, and some of these eventually left Africa all together, in time settling the entirety of Eurasia, the Americas, and countless archipelagoes in between.

Those difficult years beside the sea made us who we are. The archeological record suggests that it was during this period that we learned to live in communities larger than our immediate families and to make enduring art. The many adaptations that arose on the terminus of the African continent helped propel us around the world; they allowed us to thrive in environments where earlier human populations had struggled.

We became so successful, in fact, that we now stand at the threshold of our own terrifying climate shift, an event so profound that it can only be fully comprehended in the context of deep time. The grimmest climate models suggest that in a few millennia Africa—as well as the Americas—could again become wind-swept dunes, with habitable land existing only at extreme latitudes.

As terrifying as that prospect is, we should remember that we have been there before—and we learned to survive with less.

The Apocalypse, Doomsday, the End—these are ideas born of fiction, and yet today they creep into even educated conversations about our future (or as some will quip, the lack of one). To call these *end times* is to turn our backs on the next two hundred thousand years of human communities that, in all likelihood, will be wandering the planet we left them.

Though perhaps we are right to sense *an end*. We can't presume the current progression of technology. Any look at the full scope of human history reveals countless examples of technological regression, often in correlation to dramatic shifts in environmental conditions. Any technology may be just as fragile as the ecosystem of nature, culture, and alliance that fueled it.

Ultimately, climate change might be best understood as a new incarnation of the oldest biological problem, one facing every form of life on the planet. Deer, trout, kudzu, sapiens—we are all hardwired to exploit our surroundings until the point of collapse. Each of us in our own way moves toward opportunity, and when that opportunity runs out, we adapt or contract.

The thought experiment that is *The Ancients* was born of paintings left behind by the descendants of those few hundred survivors on the southern terminus of Africa. In Europe, in Australia, across spans of thousands of years—again and again our ancestors felt compelled to suck ochre and warm tallow into a reed, put their hand against rock, and blow. They might have done so for any number of reasons—but among them must have been a belief that one day someone or something would glimpse this humble proof of their existence. That is, they believed in the future. Can we?

ACKNOWLEDGMENTS

Profound thanks to Ellie Rose, Navah Penina, Naomi Aviva, and Reuben Reed. This book wouldn't exist without you. It wouldn't be readable without the heroics of Chris Parris-Lamb, Ellen Goodson Coughtrey, and Emily Wunderlich. Thank you, Andrea Schulz, Brian Tart, Kate Stark, Rebecca Marsh, and Mary Stone at Viking. A big shout-out to all the sales reps at Penguin Random House—thank you! A special thanks to Sylvie Rabineau and the team at WME. For their continued support: Rebecca Gardner, David Gernert, Nora Gonzalez, and Will Roberts at the Gernert Company. Thank you to all the Larisons who supported and inspired the writing: Elaine, Jim, Ted, Sarah, Maggie, and Rhone. Thanks to Mo Bloom, Isaac Bloom, and Marcia Diamond. For the arguments, insights, and inspiration: Andy Burton, J. T. Bushnell, Nickolas Butler, Betty Campbell, Thomas Christensen, Tracy Daugherty, Paul Dresman, Joy Jensen, Tim Jensen, Ted Leeson, Ray Malewitz, Z.A. Marcum, Nate Keonigsknecht, Steven Perakis, Marjorie Sandor, Keith Scribner, Sky Silga, and Dylan Tomine. Thank you to independent booksellers and librarians everywhere, especially Jack and Sandy at Grass Roots Books and Music in Corvallis. Thank you, Diana Van Vleck, for the gift that keeps on giving. And for all the recent and essential help: Tracy Danes, Jennifer Moles, Chelsea Cohen, Sara Leonard, Ivy Cheng, and Raven Ross. Finally, my sincere thanks to you for reading.